Acknowledgements
Front cover design Ken Fisher
Original painting Karen Wallis Coleman

ABOUT THE AUTHOR

Martin Spencer Coleman was born in 1952, Leicester, England. He has been a professional artist and gallery owner for over thirty years. A keen sportsman, he is an avid follower of Portsmouth Football Club. Over the years, he has written several magazine articles and been interviewed on BBC radio in connection to his artistic endeavours. His paintings are collected worldwide. He is married to a fellow artist, Karen, and has one son, Jordan. They currently live in an old Parsonage in Lincolnshire.
This is his first novel.
www.spencercolemanfineart.com
enquiries@spencercolemanfineart.com

DEDICATION:

To Karen, with much love. Thank you for your remarkable insight and dedication to this novel. You truly believed from the very beginning…

Published by Cambridge House Publishing LLP
Suite 7,
Mayden House,
Long Bennington Business Park,
Newark NG23 5DJ

ISBN 978-1-908252-13-5

FROM A DAMAGED SOUL
Raw emotions lit the night
Sharpened knives began to shine
Stretching pain in final run
First betrayal, next was none

Monster egos came to pass
Soon surrender, sane at last
Done the counting, severed past
Dance again in hot bloodbath

Weak with anger looking back
Amber rage in vengeful path
Tearing memories apart
Shades of poison in the heart

Fell asleep in Devil's nest
Woke up next to rictus flesh
Fear came and cut a sliver
Mournful tears run like a red river

Jorge Aguilar- Agon, B.Agr., AEA, AAPB, FRSA.

ACKNOWLEDGEMENTS

My eternal gratitude to all those that made the impossible become reality.
As all authors' are aware, it takes more than one person to write the
damned thing. If only it was that simple.
All errors that remain are mine. To those that persevered and knocked
it into serious shape, I say: Thank you. On record, this goes to Karen
(especially), Dr Hilary Johnson, who doesn't take prisoners, Richard
Eadie, Helen Corner, William Robinson, all those unsung people who
answered my crazy questions, to the person who started it all with that
phone call…and to those who always offered unflagging encouragement:
RJ Ellory, Vee Hempsey, Jordan and Talia, Andrew and Mathew, David
Suchet, Karen Maitland and Michael Fowler. Finally, to my parents:
They too believed. Thank you all.

ALL THE RAGE
BY
SPENCER COLEMAN

PROLOGUE

WINTER 2005, MAYFAIR, LONDON

He knew her dark secrets. The recollection of her was crystal clear and just as painful now as it had been during those years in between. The past never vanished entirely; it simply retreated into a corner of his brain. All it needed was for *something* to expose the hidden scars once again. This was one such moment. Standing alone on the street, staring, he recalled the scent of her body, her lustful kiss, her sex.

The painting hung in the gallery window as a solitary piece, measuring four feet square, encased in a gold and black baroque frame. The girl was painted lying naked upon crumpled silk sheets. He knew that looking into her emerald eyes was a dangerous game, a distraction without exit.

She was unknown to others, perhaps, but not to him; memories could be so heartbreaking. Back then, she caused such havoc. Today, though? All that remained was this: a simple female nude, staring back in his direction. The expansive scale of the canvas, however, ensured a greater power – a sensual invitation to examine with the eyes and caress with the fingers. Exposed skin and hidden flesh. Forbidden parts: who exhausted their fiery passion here? The question would haunt him to his grave. The heat of her alluring body, combined with the abandoned gaze and glistening, tumbling wet black hair, told of a sexual encounter. He knew of it so well.

His eyes focused upon an accompanying card. The gold lettering named the artist as Patrick Porter (Deceased). The portrait was titled *'A' on green silk*. It was an oil on canvas priced at £55,000. Her inner secrets did not come cheap.

He was sure that many people had stopped over recent days to view this sumptuous piece. The painting first mesmerised, and then captured those who dared to admire it. On this miserable late afternoon in November, the man in long raincoat and trilby stood firm on the pavement. Gazing intently, he was transfixed by this image of a soiled goddess. He examined every detail of her nubile proportions, recalling the dark Italian skin, the ample breasts, the slight opening of her slender legs. He imagined being part of her mystery again. Her mouth was moist and inviting; the full red painted lips quivering with youthful mischief and pained decadence.

According to his memory, the girl in the painting was between sixteen to eighteen years of age, and rather unnervingly, there was a touch of cruelty behind her demeanour. It was this that had caught his eye. He was hooked. Minutes passed. Half the hour was gone in a flash. The sky darkened, and rain gradually fell. This wouldn't deter him. He lit a cigarette and simply stared, trapped, needing to own her, possess her as he once had, and imprison her.

More disturbingly, he knew the workings of her mind. He was aware of what she was thinking and how she had first manipulated and then diminished him.

He suddenly grew restless, aware that the proprietor in the gallery had noticed his interest in the painting, and was ambling toward him. He sighed, anticipating the usual patter: an invitation to enter the premises, engage in conversation, sample a small drink together; a glass of fine burgundy perhaps...even a little negotiation. He resisted the temptation. *She* was enticement enough, and he had paid many times over for her pleasures.

He tightened the white silk scarf around his throat, adjusted his raincoat collar and disappeared as if he had never existed.

Further down the street, the man took shelter in the doorway of a shop. He was cold and impatient for a taxi. His eyes scanned the empty road. Fat chance. However, nothing could distract from the professional pride that had overwhelmed him just moments earlier, while gazing in the gallery window. There was a certain egotistical pleasure from seeing a work of art displayed so predominantly, created by the hand that held the cigarette to his mouth.

CHAPTER ONE

SPRING 2006, MAYFAIR, LONDON

The sky on this morning was clean and watery, with a lemon sun emerging above the bare branches of the trees surrounding Berkeley Square, Mayfair. Michael Strange always enjoyed this particular route through the elegant public garden, which ultimately led him to his gallery on Cork Street, situated just a few blocks further on. After parking his silver BMW 6 Series Coupe, he reminded himself that he had undertaken this walk maybe a thousand times. Usually, he moved briskly and purposeful on a journey that was at best a fifteen-minute trek. Today though, he found himself slow of pace. His eagerness to get to work had evaporated. Some days he felt good. This was not one of them. Within his current fragile existence, *everything* of any consequence was touched with despair and foreboding. Lately, he was enthralled by the absurdity of life and death in equal measure. It hadn't always been like this, but he was at his very lowest point. The words of Dylan Thomas burned into his head, *"Rage, rage against the dying of the light."* In truth, the light behind his eyes was fading fast into a kind of sightlessness. A thought crossed his mind: the blind never see the truck coming; they only hear the sound of the approach. Then it's too late. Far too fucking late.

This was his London. This was March and, despite the bright weather, Michael normally associated this month as a black hole, winter's backside. Raw and brackish, it was for him a seemingly dark procession of long hours and achingly dull vacuums. All that he knew and trusted was on the verge of going down the pan. He paused near the gallery, drew breath, and gathered his thoughts. It often went like this. Surprising mood swings. Where was this madness coming from?

Normally, he liked to arrive on the premises at nine-thirty, open the mail, consume a strong black Columbian coffee, discuss matters of the week with his secretary, Kara, then catch up with the sport pages from *The Times* and eventually settle down with the tasks in hand. It was almost a daily routine. However, of late he had developed an unwelcome habit of reflecting on the dreadful things in this world with an unhealthy morbid fascination. It was happening more and more, and it wasn't to his liking.

Take London, for instance. Just as March can be a solemn month, so too can London be a solemn city. Michael marvelled and despaired at the insidious interaction of over ten million inhabitants, ebbing and flowing like the great tidal waters of the river Thames. The city had many uneasy cultural divisions between its clash of people, a kind of tribal occupancy, almost. Strangers, after all: a complexity of egos and ambitions, survival and lust. After the atrocity of the tube suicide bombings, misguided hatred now prevailed, resulting in a mass of people who were either confused or wary of their neighbours. All that remained was a vast contradictory melting pot, a city deep in loathing, a city full of love. Perhaps even a place to hide within.

He banished such a notion, and told himself to get a grip on the week ahead. It was a Monday, his team, Chelsea, had drawn 1-1 against Arsenal at the weekend and all was apparently well with the world. He deserved a second cup of coffee.

He surveyed his kingdom. The gallery Churchill Fine Arts occupied an imposing corner site on one of London's prime locations and had been trading for twenty three-years. It began on Albemarle Street before establishing its current standing in the city specialising in contemporary figurative paintings from around the world, most notably from Russia, Cuba and Spain, as was the latest trend. The title of the gallery came from his wife's maiden name, which Michael felt was appropriately grand, durable and patriotic. It worked. The "Strange Gallery" somehow did not have the same dignified importance to it. Opening time was ten and as he glanced at his Cartier, Kara pushed the button to retract the electronic grille from the window and turned the brass "OPEN" sign to make it visible on the door.

Michael William Strange was considered to be a highly successful businessman, well regarded throughout the world of art, with a secondary interest in a modern conceptual gallery in Shoreditch, East London and an art magazine entitled *All the Rage* publicising the latest trends and promoting up-and-coming artists in the capital. His influence and knowledge were far reaching and reflected in his fortune, with homes in London, the Home Counties and Marbella in Spain. His biographical details would have him contentedly married to the same woman, Adele, for twenty-six years with one son, Toby, now living in New York, working in the money markets on

Wall Street. *Who's Who* described Michael as an international playmaker of many diverse talents.

On the face of it, he had it all. As he idly contemplated this blessed scenario he began to feel his hands become hot and wet with perspiration. He removed his horn-rimmed glasses from his face and rubbed his temples, feeling a distant migraine rumbling in his head. *He had it all.* Earlier, during his walk to work, he had given out the contented air of a man in control. Acknowledged on the streets, he waved happily to his fellow shopkeepers. He stopped to buy flowers for his secretary, knowing he was away on her birthday the next day. Little details, but they meant so much. He even shared a private joke with a traffic warden who was in the process of booking an illegally parked vehicle belonging to the proprietor of the gallery next to his. Sweet justice.

Yes, on the face of it, he really did have it all. Following his last health check, barely two weeks earlier, his doctor had stated that he was in the rudest of health. Again, just yesterday morning, on opening the mail, he discovered a premium bond win of five hundred pounds. On top of that, Kara briefly interrupted him to tell him that an invitation had arrived for a private dinner engagement at Buckingham Palace. He shrugged. It came with the territory.

Michael thanked her politely, presented the flowers ('Freesias, my favourite!' she said) and then removed himself quietly to the basement bathroom. Standing at the sink, he sprinkled cold water on to his face and then stared long and hard at his troubled features in the wall-mounted mirror. He groaned aloud. It was an unflattering reflection. He was forty-eight years of age and although everything appeared to be perfect, the truth was…he was going broke.

In fact, he was going under, going down.

His recent birthday on the 26th February had signified a low point in his life. He had spent this uneventful evening alone in his duplex apartment, without celebration. That was eight long nights ago, and since then he had remained in solitude, adrift. In most social circles this period was politely referred to as a trial separation, a time to find "space" and reflect upon life, and more importantly, his marriage. Just before his birthday, Adele had matter-of-factly announced – insisted – that their union was at an end. She wanted a divorce and a very substantial settlement; substantial enough to reflect her current social status and maintain the standards she had come to expect and…to hurt him like hell. He faced possible ruin. Just like that. It scared him shitless.

Of course, it was never "just like that". He understood the deep seated problems and the rifts that existed between them. But still, it was a massive shock to the system. If he were brutally truthful, the signs had been there for him to see. Little cracks, huge chasms, but, as with many long relationships, he was only too aware that the well of passion had dried up and, slowly, companionship and shared experience turned to something else – what was it? *Ah yes*, a partnership of compromise, then apathy, a reluctance of accountability, the death of marriage.

He recalled with a shudder how her words had dropped over the breakfast table like spilled sugar granules – they seeped everywhere, far reaching, scattered forever. Once spoken, they could not be retracted or swept away.

Adele, with cold steel in her eyes, had said, 'I need space, Michael. Put the bloody newspaper down. I want a divorce.'

Looking back, hurt by those cold calculated words, he did not fully recognise this same woman. He knew *everything* about her, but they had become insufferable strangers; impostors living under the same roof. It was a bitter pill to swallow. He did not put the newspaper down, merely ruffled the pages. Torn between anger and resignation, he remained steadfastly impassive, as only the English can do so well.

Thinking back about this absurd ability to remain in control of his emotions, his reply had been impeccable, and without hesitation: 'Yes, very well. I'll move to London.'

Clearing his head, he shook off his malaise, returned to his desk, and checked his diary. His first appointment of the day was at 11.30am with an up-and-coming artist, a "thirtysomething" self-opinionated painter called Marcus Heath. It was a routine discussion in relation to a forthcoming exhibition entitled "Confessions." Between them they decided on thirty paintings for the first autumn show of the season to be displayed on the upper gallery space, beginning 15th September. During their meeting Michael noticed he was impatient with this brash young man and in turn he detected Marcus Heath's displeasure at his pessimistic assessment of the possible outcome of the show. The work didn't excite him. He understood that the young man wanted the reassurance of knowing if the exhibition in the current economic gloom would be a success, before embarking on it. Michael's response was unenthusiastic, but he endeavoured to be a little more positive, if only to remove the gloom on Marcus's expression. Sadly, it was a losing battle. Michael had other more pressing priorities on his mind.

*

Kara began to sort through the late morning post. She discovered the usual invitations to various gallery previews, an electricity bill (red reminder), catalogue proofs, and an envelope marked 'private and confidential,' also several business flyers relating to printing requirements and gallery wholesale equipment. During an uneventful period she cleaned the kitchen crockery and worktop, typed two letters and took eight phone calls. Several of these she dealt with herself, the rest she jotted on a notepad for her boss.

As was customary, Ronald arrived just after twelve o'clock to take charge of the front gallery. This allowed Kara to go out for lunch and the gallery to remain open, especially if her boss had a lunchtime appointment as well. Continuity of business was essential. Ronald was sixty years of age, rather dapper in navy suit and red striped shirt and loud tie. He worked part-time, four days a week. His hours were twelve till four daily, except Thursday, when he visited his elderly mother. On this day his duties included changing the paintings in the windows, attending to clients, preparing a parcel for shipment to California, and then pricing and hanging four new acquisitions from an artist that had been delivered the day before. Ronald was calm, professional, possessed a sharp wit and preferred an orderly existence and a routine without incident. Each evening, his boyfriend, also called Ron, arrived promptly to accompany him home. Often they would all divert to the local watering hole, The Duke of Wessex, for happy hour. Kara enjoyed this ritual encounter – the affectionate greeting of a big hug and often a small gift from one to the other. She referred to them, quite naturally, as "The Two Ronnies."

Kara applied lipstick, pulled on a long black wool coat and gathered her notes together. She was tall and slim and dressed with an assured elegance. Aged twenty-eight, she currently lived alone after the break-up of a long-standing relationship, and had worked at The Churchill Gallery for a little over five years. She enjoyed her position in the firm and considered herself a good amateur artist as well. The best of both worlds, she smugly reminded herself.

The door to the main office was open. This allowed her to pop her head through without the need to knock.

'Back at the usual time, Michael,' she said. 'I've sorted the mail. There are three phone calls that will concern you. Sir Andrew Lloyd Webber requires confirmation regarding delivery of his painting; Lauren O'Neill needs a valuation on several works of art, oh, you'll like this – she owns a Patrick Porter! Her number is on the pad. And finally, the framing workshop requires clarification on two jobs – apparently, your writing is indecipherable! You'd make an excellent doctor.' She placed the yellow notepad on his desk, turned sharply on her fine heels and called back, 'Can I get you anything?'

She knew by Michael's vague expression that the little aside joke regarding the medical profession had passed him by.

'I'm fine for the moment, Kara. Ask Ronald to put the kettle on, Earl Grey would be perfect.'

*

Michael heard a muffled conversation in another room and assumed his tea was on the way. He studied the list from Kara. Who was Lauren O'Neill? He initially dismissed this as a request for insurance valuations, which for him often meant tiresome and underpaid work. Still, Kara did mention a Porter original. Perhaps he could persuade her to sell it? He underlined her phone number with a marker pen. He dutifully telephoned the workshop, reaffirming the framing measurements in question with his senior framer, Johannes Brouwer. They had worked together for over fifteen years. Michael felt a great loyalty to his staff. He hated failure, and the bleak mood which had descended upon him made conversation short. Careers were at stake here. If the worst came to the worst he would have no choice but to remove people from their jobs, however horrible that task would prove to be. He knew that costs would have to be cut drastically in order to survive the downturn in the economy.

Ronald entered silently with a silver tray and Earl Grey in a bone china cup and matching saucer. He cleared his throat. 'Ron sends his regards, Mr Strange. He particularly likes the Alexander Averin of the two boys bathing in the Black Sea. The picture is overpriced, of course.' He placed the tray down on the desk.

Michael was amused, and distracted, as he usually was by his conversations with his employee. 'Please reciprocate my regards to Ron when you see him. I trust he is on sparkling form. Incidentally, it's the Mediterranean, just off Antibes, and it certainly is not overpriced. Well, *maybe...*'

They laughed fondly, with Ronald voicing both their thoughts, 'Well, whatever. Actually it is the men he favours. Just typical of him, of course. Like the water in the painting, he's terribly shallow, I'm afraid, especially when it comes to fine art appreciation.' He retreated to the door, a thin smile and a raised eyebrow, delivering the punch line: 'Of course, on matters of greater importance, he can go surprisingly deep, as deep as he likes.'

*

The afternoon in the gallery moved unexpectedly fast. There was no time for any more idle chat. At one stage Ronald sold a small oil of a ballerina (Russian) for £2,500 and agreed for a larger painting to go out "on approval". Kara eventually settled the matter with the framing workshop and spent the remainder of the day updating the mailing list. Michael tried to busy himself, mainly with the contents of the next month's issue of *All the Rage*. However, his mind lacked concentration and he was angry with Adele. He knew that any impending divorce and the financial repercussions that would follow could be catastrophic. Ruinous, in fact. Pressure encased him, squeezing and suffocating like a straightjacket.

It was 4.45pm. Kara and Ronald had departed moments earlier to avoid the mounting problems with the underground "go slow". The Mayor of London, Ken Livingstone, had a lot to answer for, according to Kara. Michael began to reshuffle his briefcase and contemplate eating alone once more when the phone rang.

He slowly lifted the receiver, his voice less than enthusiastic. 'The Churchill Gallery,' he announced.

'May I speak with Michael Strange?'

'Speaking…'

'My name is Lauren O'Neill. I called earlier. No one got back to me.'

He detected a slight impatience in her tone, but it did the trick. She somehow gained his immediate attention. Her voice was husky and honey-warm, alluring even underneath the initial starchiness.

He took up the conversation. 'I do apologise, Mrs O'Neill. Your message was passed on to me: simply an oversight. I had every intention of coming back to you. I believe you require a valuation on various paintings.'

Her voice remained guarded but precise. 'My husband is an artist; possibly you may recognise his name – Julius Gray?'

'Your husband?'

'Yes. I preferred to keep my own name, and since he subsequently walked out on me, that wasn't a bad decision in hindsight. Perhaps it was an omen of things to come. Anyway, are you familiar with his work?'

'No, to be honest with you,' Michael replied, without wanting to tax his brain unduly at the end of the day. 'Should I be?'

The caller fell silent, then said, 'Julius exhibited mainly in Germany and Scotland, his Glasgow outlet was the Oberon Gallery. Unfortunately, they are now closed. The owner had a heart attack.'

Michael rubbed his chin and loosened his tie. 'What would you like me to do, Mrs O'Neill?'

'Please, I prefer Lauren. I have a problem, Mr Strange. My husband deserted me, many years ago.' She hesitated, clearing her throat. 'He is now living overseas with . . . with another woman. To simplify matters for you, we are currently contesting the value of our assets. To be perfectly blunt, I'm broke. Many of his major works are still here at the home we once shared and I believe they have a considerable financial worth. Of course, *his* advisers tell me they are worthless.'

'And you presumably want someone to verify valuation for your solicitor?'

'Precisely.'

Michael stifled a yawn. He chose his words carefully. 'Unfortunately, Lauren, I am not the man for you. I would need to be familiar with both his work and current market prices in order to provide a correct assessment. Surely there is someone else, an agent that he employed perhaps, who would be better qualified to deal with this?'

'I am willing to pay,' she interrupted, 'generously.'

Michael was struck by the immediate contradiction between being "broke" and her ability to pay generously. It did not add up, but he chose to ignore it. 'I appreciate your generosity, Lauren. However...'

'I will make it worthwhile, Mr. Strange. Please, this is important to me, I don't know who else to turn to.

Everyone I know in the art world would have an overriding loyalty to Julius. This is a very delicate matter. Will you help me?'

There was a certain childlike vulnerability to her voice. He took a deep breath and hesitated as to whether to get involved, especially after her earlier remarks. However, something indefinable drew him to her.

'Mr Strange,' she continued, 'a while ago you displayed in your window a painting by the artist Patrick Porter. It was a very fine nude.'

'Indeed we did. I understand you own one?'

She lowered her voice. 'I own twelve in total, to be exact.'

Michael lifted a hand to suppress a gasp. For the first time during their conversation his brain engaged, triggering a full alert message to start taking her seriously. He sat upright in his chair, well and truly hooked.

'All oils?' he enquired casually, trying to keep a damper on the mounting excitement in his voice.

'Yes.'

'And…*and* are you aware of the price we were asking for that piece?'

'Yes, which is the reason why I want to sell them all, Mr Strange.'

Michael cleared his throat. 'Then we both know this represents a considerable amount of money, Lauren.' He held his breath for a moment and removed his tie altogether. Beads of sweat formed on his brow.

'I did say I would make it worthwhile,' she murmured. She let a silence drop between them, which seemed to reinforce her viewpoint.

It was becoming a game of cat and mouse, in his opinion. He delayed his response, his mind a whirl of possibilities and fiscal calculations. Now he understood the contradiction. *God, she was good.*

'Why don't you call me Michael,' he said, 'and let's meet and discuss this further over a drink.'

*

Later, he began to think about the gradual disintegration in his life. He had thought of the word "ruinous" earlier in the day, and now, toying with his single malt and idly overlooking the steel coil of the River Thames below, he realised that he was swimming against the tide. And these were treacherous waters. The glass frontage to his riverside apartment afforded him a magnificent panorama of London and the dazzling lights reflected in the icy flow. In the distance he caught sight of the Houses of Parliament and the London Eye, now motionless. Beneath him, the white hulls of sleek and opulent yachts bobbed in the private moorings. From afar, the sound of a horn blasted from a huge dredger as it pushed against the swirling cold current. Michael watched all this – *his London* – and yet felt detached, a forlorn figure on the landscape.

He began to examine the motives behind his wife's demand for a divorce. In the morning post he had received a letter marked "private and confidential". It made heavy reading. The letter from her solicitor clearly marked out her territory, insisting on a financial settlement of a proposed one million pounds, the villa in Marbella and maintenance of £100,000 per year. On top of that was a secondary list of "minor demands":

the Mercedes, furniture, paintings. If she had intended to hurt him, damage him, she would undoubtedly succeed, spectacularly. Adele had petitioned for divorce citing "unreasonable behaviour." Moving across the room in order to refill his tumbler with his third whisky of the night, he caught sight of his reflection in the window glass, a grotesque apparition of the man he once was. It greatly disturbed him that he was visibly shrinking.

Beyond this, the business had suffered badly post 9/11 and since the more recent tube bombings. A decrease in tourism from overseas visitors had hit the City in dramatic fashion and as a result, business in the gallery had plummeted, suffering in particular from a lack of turnover from rich Americans. Trade had dropped by over twenty-five per cent. This was not recoverable. Even more of a concern was the unpalatable fact that his lease was up for renewal shortly, triggering a large rent increase on his prestigious premises.

It went further. The current tax demand for January 31st, his accountant informed him, was close to £150,000. He hadn't paid it. The Inland Revenue had written to his advisers with confirmation of an official investigation into his tax affairs. It was strictly "routine business" they pointed out with professional coldness. He knew what this entailed.

All in all, Michael had held his composure with remarkable aplomb. On the outside he appeared calm and collected, even untouchable, but within, his insides churned and tightened like the unforgiving grip of a python. There was simply no escape. Slowly but surely, his empire, his world, was being constricted. It was dying.

Showering and refreshing himself, he ate a light supper of grilled tuna and green salad, washed down with a glass of chilled Muscadet. However, his mood of apprehension did not vanish, unlike the wine, which began to make his mindset more bullish. He would not lie down and let Adele walk all over him. He would fight back as he had always done in the face of adversity. A calculated plan of vicious counter-attack began to formulate in his head. And then, inexplicably, he thought of Lauren O'Neill.

This was a woman who intrigued him deeply. Her voice conveyed a sexual undertone, an invitation to sin. He held a visual picture of her in his head and it enraptured him. Earlier, on the phone, they had arranged a meeting at her home for the following day. He would ascertain the collection of her husband's canvases and endeavour to produce an overall valuation, as she had asked. More importantly, it gave him an opportunity to market the twelve paintings by Patrick Porter. In this respect, he saw a way to raise a great deal of money. Handled properly, the sale would actually raise a substantial amount of capital for him. He cared little for the work of Julius Gray. Quite simply, by employing a tried and trusted camouflage technique, he might ensure a survival of sorts, and find a solution to pay off his wife. It was his only shot.

Lauren O'Neill would be a formidable woman, he concluded. He sensed that from her manner, and his feverish imagination, she was tactile, very attractive and probably dangerous. But nothing, he had to admit, actually pointed towards this. It was his fantasy. It surprised him that he cancelled his appointments so readily in order to see her. It surprised him still further to admit to a certain nervous tension building in his stomach. What was he looking for? *Idiot,* he muttered to himself.

Before retiring for the night, he phoned Kara.

'Sorry it's so late,' he told her, 'but I won't be in tomorrow.'

Kara responded by stifling a yawn, which he picked up on. 'Oh, OK,' she said. 'Can I contact you on your mobile if anything crops up?'

'Sure. Oh, by the way: Happy Birthday!'

'Yeah, right.'

'I'll make it up to you.'

'Promises…'

Michael detected a losing battle. 'I've cleared my appointments for tomorrow and left you a list of priorities on your desk. It'll be a long day for me, I feel. Appraisals: quite a lot it appears.'

'Is this to do with Mrs O'Neill?' Kara asked.

'Yes,' he answered. 'Her details are now in a file on the computer.' He hesitated, adding, 'Something big may be in the offing.'

'Oh, really' she teased, 'anything to do with a certain artist you might want to get your eager dirty hands on?'

'Kara, this is not a game,' he said, reeling from the effects of the alcohol. It surprised him to see he had consumed the whole bottle. It made him nauseous and unsteady on his feet, but he was in full flow now. He dismissed her little joke. 'I cannot stress the importance of all this. I do not intend to get my hands on *just* anything.' He stopped for a second, imagining this woman called Lauren. It consumed him. 'I intend to get my eager dirty hands on everything. The rewards are just too great to ignore, and I won't be denied. Is that understood?'

Michael halted his rant. He hated himself for this display of anger and knew that Kara would be embarrassed. Where had this suddenly come from? *Idiot.*

He waited for what seemed an eternity before she responded. His gut twisted. He imagined a knot tightening in her stomach as well, such was her feeble comment.

All she managed was a pathetic, 'Oh...'

Michael's impatience surfaced once more. He gave her no chance to react further. With one swift movement, he clicked the line dead.

CHAPTER TWO

In spite of his uncharacteristic rage last night, Kara Scott had to admit to a certain soft spot for her employer. He wasn't perfect, but at least he remembered her birthday. Michael was handsome in a craggy sort of way, his charm centred on an irresistible combination of lived-in easy looks and wonderful manners, with a roguish twist. Most appealing were his deep-etched laughter lines and silver swept-back hair, just a shade too long. He stood nearly six feet tall and carried himself well. She often found herself standing back and admiring his sharp wit and sparkling eyes as he held court during an opening night at the gallery. He always attracted women. He always had a story to tell. With a glass of champagne in one hand, dressed in an immaculate white silk shirt and navy wool summer suit, he was an impressive man, a man who stood out in a crowd. Kara had more than a soft spot for him; she was a little in love with him.

On this morning, as she paced the gallery, her thoughts were confused and more than a little troubled. She was concerned about her boss. Something was wrong, amiss, and the conversation they had last night on the phone left her feeling nervous and rattled. On the face of it, his recent behavioural change from considerate normality to downright bizarre was more than understandable, taking into account what she now knew. Two months earlier, Adele had confided in her the fragile state of the marriage and how things were "likely to go". Kara was shocked, genuinely. Never had she detected anything untoward in the relationship up to that point. They were a glamorous couple and seemed to have everything. Now, in the blink of an eye, it all appeared to be going down the pan. Kara was aware that business had been poor and the financial pressure had been building, and she was also privy to the investigation by the tax office. It was she, after all, who was asked to supply the necessary accounts. She knew the score. But this was entirely different. It hit her like a bombshell. Her own parents had divorced, so she knew all too well just how bloody messy it was going to get.

She began to resent Adele. Looking back, Kara could now recognise little things which had fragmented this marriage. Little things which at the time seemed unimportant: Adele had stopped attending exhibitions, her days working in the gallery decreased; she even went on holiday to Marbella without Michael. Then there was the blazing row she had the misfortune to interrupt one Saturday last year. It went on…Kara could so easily make a list. Why had she not seen it before?

If she had felt anger toward Adele, then it was natural to show sympathy, a kind of protection toward Michael. He was falling apart right before her eyes. It wasn't *just* that odd conversation last night, there were many other instances when he had been sharp and intolerant. She recalled his impatience with Marcus Heath. Such things were harmful to him and his reputation, and she wondered if she should say something. It hurt her to see him suffering in this manner.

Then there was the question of his wife and the damage she was capable of inflicting. Kara knew of her glamorous past. Adele Churchill was a former debutante, privately educated at Roedean and later, much to her parents' displeasure, a bit part actress before marrying Michael. She was used to the best things in life and had been considered the "it" girl of her day. She had been photographed by Parkinson and Snowdon and adorned the front cover of *The Tatler* magazine. Before Michael, she had conducted a whirlwind romance with a dashing Hollywood actor and was also implicated in a drug scandal. It was even said that she had secretly had an affair with a married senior politician in the government of the day. Intense speculation meant that her picture was on the front page of every daily tabloid for months on end. But all publicity was good publicity to Adele and it was widely known that she manipulated all those who came across her path, particularly the media. Now, Kara acknowledged with a touch of admiration, not many people could lay claim to that dubious achievement. Such was her beguiling power.

Adele controlled both her husband and their impending divorce, and Kara did not need to speculate as to the eventual winner. If proof were ever needed, Adele had instructed one Sir Benjamin Joshua Stone to act upon her affairs. He was acknowledged to be the meanest, hardest and most ruthless matrimonial lawyer in London. Even more disturbingly, Adele had seen fit to pass on this information to Kara. It came during a reluctant tête-à-tête over lunch several weeks past.

Kara's stomach turned, sickened by the memory of the cold triumph   contained in Adele's voice that day.

*

Michael dressed casually in grey trousers and navy polo neck, black suede slip-ons and a fine dog tooth check sports jacket with double vent. He examined his appearance in the mirror, pleased that he had shaved extra carefully this morning. He felt pretty good. On top of that, the weather forecast promised unseasonable sunshine and light winds. He would take the flame red TVR convertible for his trip.

Leaving behind the bustle of the traffic on the Kings Road, he zipped along Cheyne Walk, out beyond the Fulham Road and over Putney bridge towards the A3, heading south. He made excellent progress and enjoyed the soft caress of the winter sun on his face. It was refreshing to get out of London. This mood didn't last long. He cursed under his breath as he hit unexpected road works at the Surbiton underpass, but thankfully it was a minor delay. Soon he was powering the engine along the stretch of dual carriageway to his final destination, a small hamlet on the outskirts of Guildford. This was where he would meet the woman who called herself Lauren O'Neill.

*

If Kara had misgivings as to her feelings toward Michael and his current predicament, she could not deny they were strong and her unease deepened as the morning progressed. She could not reason why. Ronald arrived bright and perky, and immediately she became infuriated by his banal banter. Normally, Kara enjoyed the gossip on the street, but today it was an intolerable intrusion. Retreating to the sanctuary of the computer room, she suddenly saw the clearer picture. Within her grasp, she held the ammunition that would enable Michael to fight his battle against

Adele. As his secretary, she was privy to confidential matters, sensitive issues which she knew could prove highly embarrassing and damaging if revealed to the correct authorities. This, though, would make her position in the company untenable. Adele was also her boss, after all. She knew that what she planned was called espionage, seen as the ultimate act of betrayal. At first, the idea of this chilled her to the bone. It was crazy. Then she thawed. According to her sense of logic and fair play, it was an act worth pursuing. She had no choice. Michael needed an ally. Grasping the moment, her heart pounding, she clicked into the company computer and searched for the file which she knew would reveal the coded documents that she could decipher with expert ease.

*

The village of Old Hampton nestled snugly within the green folds of the countryside, somewhere between Guildford and Petersfield, just within the Surrey borders. It was the kind of place that you explored on a cold Sunday in search of old antique shops and a lunchtime pint in a traditional heavy wooden beamed public house. As he idled past The Royal Oak the faint smell of a roaring log fire invaded his nostrils, reinforcing this view. Michael promised himself to return soon.

He took the narrow ancient pack bridge over shallow waters and followed the river as it flowed listlessly beside the road past the timber- fronted cottages and a small knot of shops. Out beyond the squat Norman church, he glanced once more at the hastily scribbled directions which Lauren had dictated to him over the phone. A sharp left and soon he entered rich arable farmland and narrower muddy winding roads. Within seconds he spotted the red mail box which she had told him to look out for attached to a tree, slowed at the corner marked Deceptive Bends (immediately chuckling to himself recalling the title of the 10cc album) and entered through the open metal gate and down the private lane which would lead him to Laburnum Farm, his destination. He braked to a halt, checked his appearance in the interior mirror, and brushed imaginary flecks of dandruff from his shoulders. He also checked the time: 11.40am. Ten minutes late.

The long gravel drive was strewn with weeds and dead leaves. Pale yellow sunlight filtered through the naked branches of the black trees. As he approached, he spotted the old thatched house ahead; the ghostly scene made him think of an Atkinson Grimshaw painting from the 1800s. The surrounding garden was bordered by overgrown laurels. Even from a distance, he could see the signs of neglect. The windows were gloomy, the woodwork peeling. Cagily, he stepped out of the car. Silence hung in the damp air. He yearned for a similar quietness to help soothe his feeling of discord, but from somewhere a torrent of noise rushed through his head like a tidal wave, gathering an awful speed. He knew what it was: a trouble brewing. Inwardly, he was screaming at himself.

To the right of the house was a huge timber and granite tithe barn, dangerously leaning from old age but supported by massive concrete buttresses along one side. In front of the double doors was a mangle of farm implements, car bits and the remains of a fire, smouldering. Well, he pondered apprehensively, it was time to meet the Lady of the Manor.

He slowly gathered his briefcase from the passenger seat and made his way to the entrance of the house, pulling at the heavy door chime which signalled his arrival. In the same instant, he was startled by the intimidating sound of a large dog growling and scratching fiercely from the other side of the door. Unnerved, Michael took a step backward.

*

As part of her job, Kara was responsible for keeping all records relating to official purchases and sales. They were first logged on the hand-written ledgers and later transferred to the computer. Michael preferred to present a hand-written invoice and insurance valuation to his clients. This was indeed slow and laborious but he insisted on this old fashioned courtesy. Many of the paintings which came into the gallery from artists were supplied on a sale or return basis. This certainly suited the economics of running a commercial business; it provided extremely good cash flow. Other acquisitions came via the auction houses, through agents or direct purchase from the artist. Kara permitted herself a wry smile. Always, without exception, the margin of profit was greatly enhanced by these three means. The downside was the possibly of the painting taking a long time to sell: hence a larger overdraft. That was where the expertise of the gallery owner came to the fore. And Michael, she freely admitted, was certainly right to the fore. He rarely made a bad error of judgment. She shrugged: Except in the case of Adele, perhaps.

Kara knew Michael and had great admiration for his working methods. He was a successful businessman, and in the early days he and Adele had been a formidable team, her high profile image greatly enhancing the reputation of The Churchill Gallery. The halcyon days. This no one could deny. In fact, Kara's predecessor had credited Adele as the brains behind the success of their establishment. Without doubt, sex and glamour were perfect ingredients in this glorious world of attracting money and prestige. If Michael was the public face of chivalry and respectability, then his wife was the architect of greed and power. She devoured both with expert ease.

If this appeared fanciful or too far-fetched, Kara had the means and the proof to dispel the other side of the coin: That which cleverly portrayed Adele as the dutiful wife. During her initial training, Adele had insisted on teaching the basics to Kara. Get that right, she would say, and "I can then explain the complications of ready cash; and how to disperse it". Within three months, she was entrusted with this knowledge and easily understood the hidden implications: back door money. No tax to pay.

With this in mind, Kara took a deep breath and keyed in Document 2002, a file containing all transactions for that year, the year that she joined the firm. Her mind was abuzz, and so immersed in what she trying to accomplish she hadn't noticed that she was being watched until she became aware that someone was standing directly behind her, looking over her shoulder.

'Hi.'

Kara jumped out of her seat and raised her hand to her heart in the same beat. Swivelling in her chair, she gasped, 'Can I help you?' Vainly, she tried to hide her guilt by thumping the button on her computer to close down the document. At the same time she attempted to regain her composure, but the young man who blocked the doorway was an intimidating presence. She felt a trickle of sweat down her neck.

The young man stood awkwardly and then appeared embarrassed. 'Ronald sent me through,' he said. 'Sorry to scare you.'

'You didn't. It was just a shock, that's all,' Kara snapped unconvincingly. She stared at him intently, recognising a familiarity to his face. 'Do I know you?'

'I called yesterday. We met very briefly.' He extended his hand. 'Marcus. Marcus Heath. I had hoped I'd made a better impression.'

Kara dropped her guard. She was still angry but managed to take his hand. 'I'm so sorry, of course I know you. I feel such a fool.'

Marcus smiled with affection. 'No worries,' he shrugged, 'hey, if you're too busy, I can sort things with the *other* lady.'

Kara let out a burst of laughter at his cheeky reference to Ronald.

'Of course,' he added reassuringly, 'I'd feel a hell of a lot safer with you.'

'Not necessarily,' she flirted, appreciating for the first time the artist's fine good looks. 'And no, I'm not too busy.' She turned and switched off the laptop, her mind now in a swirl of confusion and foolishness.

'Looks important,' he said, pointing to the screen.

'Er, no. It can wait,' she replied, regaining her poise. Her birthday prospects were looking up. 'What can I do for you, Marcus?'

Without a backward glance, he turned and glided effortlessly toward the inner gallery, leaving her alone and still sitting. Inexplicably, she rose, ready to follow, catching the aroma of his aftershave. 'It's just that,' she heard him call over his shoulder, 'the big boss man, he asked me to bring in three original pieces for the forthcoming brochure. Apparently, the photographer needs to do a transparency of each for the publicity blurb.'

'Isn't the show in September?' she asked, following meekly.

'Yep. I thought I'd strike while the iron's hot. Boss man was a little tetchy, you could say decidedly underwhelmed with the prospect of an exhibition featuring yours truly.'

'It was a bad day, Marcus.'

'Bad day, eh?' he echoed. His smile was infectious. 'You should try this: I get a distinct put down from boss man and a right in the face come on from the other guy as I leave. How would you deal with that?' He faced her again. 'What's your name, anyway?'

'Kara,' she said, with a wide grin. With reference to the "other guy", she continued, 'Ronald is spoken for; you will be pleased to hear. Although I know he does have an unquenchable weakness for firm young flesh.'

Marcus moved closer. 'And you…?'

'I prefer older men,' she declared, adding, 'I like the sense of style that maturity brings.'

'Ah,' Marcus said, pondering the point. 'So you have a thing about boss man...'

Kara smiled, protesting: 'Now you're getting too personal!'

'An artist,' he said, with assured cockiness, 'knows no boundaries. It makes us what we are: free spirits. You cannot be offended by anything I say or do. It's what makes you so attracted towards me.'

Kara stabbed a playful finger into his chest. 'If that's so, you'll have to explain your sense of style, Marcus. It's lost on me.'

After Marcus had departed (with her private mobile number, she cursed mildly) Kara gathered his paintings together and placed them in the storage room for safety and then emailed the photographer the necessary instructions to collect when convenient. She liked Marcus but shared Michael's assessment of his work. It was overblown and vain. Just like him. Still, she concluded, if you get caught in a hurricane you are likely to get sucked in. She pondered this scenario and decided quite recklessly not to seek shelter. She would take the storm full on.

'Ronald,' she said, shouting her words to the other end of the gallery. 'You're a fine judge of men. What do you think of Marcus?'

*

The Lady of the Manor stood to one side of the door, her left leg stretched at an angle to prevent the onslaught from her overzealous guard dog. Holding him tightly on a lead, she extended her willowy hand

and engaged Michael's grip with a fragility that was almost a caress.

'I do apologise for Bruno's behaviour. I live alone,' she said, 'and he's overprotective to the point of hysteria. But he keeps me feeling safe.' Her eyes met with his. 'You must be Michael Strange.'

'I'm a little late, Lauren,' he shouted above the barking. He gesticulated with his hand. 'Lovely village. Have you lived here long?'

'Oh, fifteen years, I guess.' She forced the dog to retreat into a side room, closing the door firmly. 'That's better. Now, first priority: I insist you join me for a glass of wine.' She beckoned him in.

'Well,' he hesitated, moving gingerly into the oak-panelled hallway, 'I have to be careful, I am driving.'

She moved her seductive green eyes to meet his again. 'Please be gracious and join me. The bottle's already opened.'

He curtailed his initial discomfort and said, 'It will be a pleasure then.'

'It's a Barola, 1971. Do you approve?'

'Yes, a very fine wine,' he answered, mightily impressed.

*

They sat opposite each other, but close enough, in the conservatory and Michael at last had the chance to study her. She small-talked about the village and the house to begin with and later revealed the troubles with her husband, the errant artist. But, to be truthful, it all washed over him. He enjoyed the exceptional wine from Italy and sitting there, he could imagine himself in an old farm in Tuscany. He loved Italy in the winter, and he was suddenly reminded of a past holiday. And opposite him sat a woman of bewitching beauty; her pale white skin and tumbling red hair conjured a vision of rare intensity, a ravaged soul. Rossetti would have painted her, possessed her, and worshipped her. He was spellbound.

He drowned in the emerald pools of her eyes, and like mother of pearl, they emitted fractured light and incredible depth of colour and shading, intensifying her mystery and mood. Her skin was opaque, like fine English porcelain, her mouth large, full-lipped and expressive. She tossed her wild hair back from her face, revealing a strong sculptured profile with a long and slightly flat nose, but it was most flattering to him. In this light, he recalled the Pre-Raphaelite portrait of Vanessa Wilding, the creature of *Beauty*, and thought that this woman who sat before him was born to a different age. He could not paint her, like Waterhouse, nor possess her, as Dante with Beatrice. But from afar, he would *adore* her. For him, time seemed to stand still in that one indeterminable moment.

'Are you all right?' she asked, leaning forward in her chair.

'I'm so sorry,' he answered, slightly embarrassed. Lowering his gaze into his glass of wine, gently swirling the contents with the motion of his hand, he said, 'This Barola is rather good, but it is not conducive to concentrating the mind. I was daydreaming, I'm afraid.'

Lauren lifted the bottle from the flagstone floor, gesturing towards a refill.

'I'd better not.'

'Do you live far?' she enquired, refilling both their glasses anyway.

'Chelsea Harbour.'

'I have friends in Battersea. I travel up by train every few weeks. But mostly I try to keep out of the city. London is far too claustrophobic for me.' Lauren sipped her wine and lit a cigarette. Exhaling, she added excitedly, 'I insist you stay for lunch. It's the very least I can do for you. There is a great deal of material to look through.'

Michael declined her offer of a cigarette. He began a futile protest in respect of the first suggestion. 'I couldn't possibly...'

'Nonsense, it's a simple dish.' She laughed, confessing, 'Leftovers from last night. Just cold salmon, if that's ok? I'll add a green salad and French bread and we can wash it down with water, assuming the wine is too overpowering for you. Now, how can you resist such a temptation?'

He raised his hands in mock surrender. 'Well, in the circumstances I can hardly refuse. It sounds delightful.' Secretly, he was more than thrilled. He was intoxicated with the scent of her physical presence, which grabbed like an overwhelming sensation of...of...it was unlike anything he had ever experienced before.

Lauren rose from her chair and came to sit beside him on the wicker sofa. 'Michael, I have a tendency to be overbearing in conversation. Since you have arrived, I've talked non-stop about my troubles and told you everything about my husband and my difficult circumstances.' She edged forward and touched his arm. 'If I'm honest, I am feeling raw and vulnerable... and a little scared. Can you understand that?'

'Of course,' he muttered, relating privately to his own situation. 'It's hard coping on your own.' He was happy for her to leave her hand where it was.

'Michael, you just *being* here helps. It brings a little normality back into my life. Being lonely, being alone, facing an uncertain future…well, preparing a simple lunch for two is important to my sanity. Please understand. So thank you.'

He instinctively reached out and took her hand, marvelling at the touch of her skin. 'Lauren, I'll do all I can, within my capabilities. We'll try and unravel this mess.'

'Michael, I need to sell this house, desperately. It's too big and costly to maintain by myself.'

'Hopefully,' he answered, 'we will sort out the finances to help you survive and then move on. I will need the details of your solicitor.'

'I'll fax them to your office.' She squeezed his hand, smiled, and stood above him. 'Thank you for your support, Michael, you've been so kind and reassuring. It's rare to find that in a man these days.'

He watched as she retreated to the kitchen door. She was thin and tall, gliding with the languid grace of a gazelle. This beguiling woman, just who was she?

'Lauren,' he called out. 'Is…is Julius *likely* to be coming back to you?'

Before she vanished into the other room, she turned and fixed him with an icy stare. 'No,' she announced. 'Julius is where he wants to be. He will not be coming back, not to this house or to me.'

*

Whilst he could hear her tinkering in the kitchen, Michael wandered over to an annex at the far eastern gabled side of the house, beyond the heavily beamed drawing room. It was here, she explained, that he would find what he was looking for: the studio of Julius Gray. It was an impressive space, a double height conservatory with acres of glass, and a spiralling staircase leading to a mezzanine floor that protruded out from halfway up the outer wall. Someone had drawn the blinds on the windows, shutting out most of the light. All that remained was a gloom of abandonment.

At first sight, it was a chaotic environment in which to work. The studio was dominated by four large wooden easels, placed in a semicircle, close to each other in order for the artist to move swiftly from one to the other. This was how Julius created his masterworks, Michael guessed. Four identical sized canvases sat upon these easels, each of which appeared unfinished. The artist had literally run the same brushstroke, with the same colour paint, across each of the paintings in turn, duplicating the pattern but not the same rhythm. Julius worked fast and furious, Michael gathered, allowing for a common group of paintings with immediate but separate spontaneity. The work was vivid and colourful and hypnotic. The man had talent, just not to his taste, Michael concluded.

Looking around further and treading carefully, Michael tried to make sense of the stacks of cobwebbed canvases piled against the walls, atop the cabinets and in the drawers of the huge map chest. There were hundreds of charcoal drawings, pastel sketches, diagrams, abandoned ideas on bits of scrap paper and board and, within one open-plan side cupboard, a skyscraper of exercise books filled with his doodlings and written observations. All around was the unruly mix of paint pots, paint tubes, brushes, cleaning fluids, cameras, a home-made light-box, metal frames and unused canvases. On a cluttered desk, he discovered several dusty brochures proclaiming Julius's work in shared exhibitions, both home and abroad. As Lauren had earlier mentioned, his main source of artistic output found its way to the Oberon Gallery in Glasgow. This was true, judging by the many publications strewn across the table bearing their logo. As he sifted through, idly contemplating lunch, something began to nag him, and the more he tried to decipher his concern (foreboding?) the more this feeling receded back into his brain. Something, however, did not seem right.

He got back to the task in hand. This was a massive undertaking. It was perplexing to even consider, and one that he quickly decided he could not do, or wish to do. However, there *was* the small matter of the twelve paintings of Patrick Porter, he reminded himself. So far, they had both avoided this subject and he had decided to allow Lauren to raise the topic in the normal course of events. He did not wish to reveal his inner anxiety by showing too much eagerness on the subject. Greed was a powerful motivator. He just had to keep control of it, for now.

In the meantime, the current job was exhausting and dirty work, forcing him to stifle a cough from the grime stuck in his throat. Going through the motions was becoming tedious…and then he saw it. Moments earlier, he had removed a heavy gilt frame, standing nearly to his shoulder, which leaned against a far wall. In the gloom, his eyes alighted on the painting concealed behind it. Christ, it stopped him in his tracks. The canvas revealed a stark and somewhat crude image of a naked woman, her limbs angled grotesquely and openly, inviting the onlooker to gape at her large purple breasts and inflamed genitalia. The labia had, in fact, been painted perversely oversized, in minute detail, and effectively portrayed the woman as deformed and unashamed, wantonly baring her available charms, exposing her to ridicule. On closer inspection, the artist had depicted a red scar on the left breast of the nude figure, and further lesions on both her wrists. At first sight, Michael was repelled by the portrait and the nastiness with which the sitter was graphically shown. The pornographic image revealed the artist to be a hater of this woman, for she had been violated permanently in this depiction of ugliness. And yet, in a strange manner, he was irresistibly transfixed by this vision of an alternative take on beauty. It took his breath away because he immediately recognised that Julius had painted the portrait of his wife.

'What do you think?'

He swivelled awkwardly, caught like a thief in a shop. He released the frame as if it was contaminated. It thudded against the wall.

Michael composed himself sufficiently to hide his awkwardness. 'Well,' he gestured with a wide exaggerated arc of his arm, 'Where do I begin? It's a real mess to be frank with you.' He'd hoped that his theatrical over-the-top motion was sufficient to distract her from the clatter he had just made. The painting embarrassed him, and surely embarrassed her. Why else would it be hidden?

'Oh,' she murmured, 'I was rather hoping you would approve...'

'*Excuse me*?' He was now flustered, and hot.

'Of my dress, silly!' Lauren had an infectious laugh. 'I've changed into something I *thought* you might like. What do you think?'

Michael's face turned red. Thankfully, she was not referring to the offending canvas.

'I keep putting my foot into it, don't I?' He said lamely.

'Somewhat.'

He took this opportunity to study her with an appreciative eye.

'Stunning,' he said finally. 'Lovely…you look absolutely lovely. The dress becomes you. I'm beginning to feel that I'm on a date!'

She laughed again, tossing her head back, the black silk skirt swaying with her easy body movement. 'The salmon's ready. Can I drag you away, or is your professional curiosity above that of having a date with a girl who dresses for lunch?'

'I'm honoured,' he said, laughing. 'Lead on, I am but your humble servant.' In reality, he was still reeling from the sight of the painting, the laughter simply deflecting from this hideous shock.

Fortunately, Lauren joined in the fun and appeared to have missed his uncomfortable reaction to her creeping up behind him in the studio.

'And therefore, you must do as I command!' She responded with a mixture of gaiety and edginess in her voice.

He followed her like a lamb to the slaughter.

*

Michael washed his hands in the kitchen sink as Lauren laid the table and served the fish and side salad. This was an immensely agreeable time, he reminded himself. These moments helped to deflect from his personal trials and tribulations, by letting him think about her problems. He found himself listening to her with a patience he had never found with Adele, aware that his fixation with this woman who dressed for him and cooked for him was both appallingly pathetic and – he recalled his earlier description – dangerous. For God's sake, she could be fifteen years younger, he chastised himself brutally. Fantasy was a dark and double-edged weapon.

Over the next hour, they discussed the many implications of valuing her husband's work, and the logistics of presenting such a big task. He reminded her of his misgivings and lack of expertise, and suggested she contact one of the big galleries in Germany or Scandinavia, which had represented Julius in the past. They, he suggested, would be better equipped to deal with the financial issues. The obvious route was not to her liking, he soon realised. A frown deepened on her forehead.

'I have my reasons, Michael. I do not believe I can trust these galleries. Julius has strong contacts over there and they will be loyal to him. I need someone who is independent and I can trust *with my life*.' He noted this emphasis on these last words, but he quickly dismissed it.

'So,' she pleaded, 'will you help me?'

He thought long and hard. 'To a degree, yes,' he replied. He paused. 'To be fair and accurate, we should of course be in contact with your husband.'

'No!' She flashed her temper like an erupting volcano, burying her head into her slender hands. 'He has no say in this matter! Do you think he has rights? Tell me. I want to know. As far as I am concerned, when he left this house he left my life, for good. He betrayed me and humiliated me and...and...God will seek a terrible revenge on him.'

Michael sensed that she was beginning to reclaim her inner control, now shaking her head with a slower and more dignified purpose.

'Believe me, Michael, he will find only sufferance and madness with *her,* a hell on earth. He'll wish...' Her voice trailed away into nothingness, replaced by a soft whimper and a teardrop in her eye.

Michael was rocked momentarily by this sudden alteration in behaviour. Instinctively, he removed his handkerchief from his own pocket and helped dab her eyes.

'Can I have some more water?' she asked.

He refilled her glass. 'I know this has been hard for you. Perhaps you should see a doctor.'

'No, I can handle it most days. I don't want tranquillizers or sympathy. It bloody hurts – right here.' She thumped her chest with a clenched fist. 'I want Julius to experience the same feeling, the rejection, the apathy, the utter crushing humiliation, the brutal disregard for another human being, betrayal, the damn lies I've had to put up with, his smugness, the misplaced pity...' She permitted herself an unexpected smile, and then said, 'Yes, I think maybe I do need a doctor.'

He made a pot of tea and cleared away the unfinished meal while she rested. She sat by the window in the kitchen, looking out to the rear orchard. After a few minutes she was sufficiently composed again.

'I've been an idiot and a complete bore,' she said. 'You've been so kind to me; maybe you will be my doctor?' Before he had a chance to answer, she spoke again, 'I want to show you something. Have you still got time?'

He glanced at his watch. It was just gone three. He had largely forgotten the reason for being here. Although her outburst had disturbed him, he couldn't pull himself away. 'It's fine by me. There's nothing that can't wait.' His stomach tightened as he prepared his next line. 'Lauren, I saw the painting of you in the studio. Do you want to talk about it?'

She was unmoved. 'Rather flattering, don't you agree?'

Her voice had an air of resignation to it.

'Let me show you something, by way of explanation.' She stood. 'This way, but be prepared for what you're about to see.'

She snatched a glass of red wine from the table and led him through a maze of corridors to the rear of the house. At this point, she climbed the narrow steep stairs, with Michael in tow. The horrible odour of damp air seeped into his nostrils.

'It's OK, Michael,' she said, looking back at him. 'I'm too tired to seduce you,' she teased, taking his hand.

At the top of the galleried landing, she threw open a door and switched on the ceiling lights to a room beyond where she momentarily stood. Lauren laughed and entered, swirling her body in a mad, rhythmic dance.

He could tell she was becoming dizzy. She stopped and drank greedily from her glass of wine, recovering her balance briefly. He was certain that the alcohol had failed to dull the pain he saw behind her eyes.

She swayed unsteadily on her feet again. Searching for him, her eyes narrowed and she beckoned him with her little finger.

He followed. Once inside, his eyes blinked once, twice. Adjusting to the bright light, it took barely a second before he was immediately transfixed by the scandalous images on the walls.

It was evident to him that this was the marital bedroom, the four poster a cascade of rich red and gold drape silks. The matching sheets were half-submerged beneath oversized pillows and assorted ethnic cushions. Affixed against one wall, opposite the bed, a giant plasma TV screen overfilled the space, but it was dwarfed by the numerous large paintings which now caught the eye. Michael counted six, seven, eight nude pictures... all depicted in the same graphic style as the one in the studio downstairs. They were *all* of Lauren. More disturbingly, each and every one revelled in the exaggerated, contorted sexual parts of her body, fashioned in a manner to strip her of the last remnants of dignity and decency. *Christ!* he thought. The shock hit him hard. Each image represented the degradation of Lauren O'Neill.

'Why, why, why?' he said, spinning around the room, his eyes ablaze with fury. 'Oh, my God...Why did he hate you, to do *this* to you?'

'He didn't hate me, Michael. He found them erotic. It gave him perverse pleasure to control me, manipulate me – imprison me.'

Michael was almost speechless. Eventually, he calmed down enough to ask, '*Why* did you let him do it? *Were* you a prisoner of his?'

She gulped the last of the wine. 'No. I loved him madly. I wanted to please him, endear myself to him, and enslave myself to him.'

'This can't be right,' he whispered under his breath, shaking his head in disbelief.

'He was the only man I truly loved.'

He turned to confront her. '*Was*?'

Lauren grabbed the bedpost, momentarily regaining her poise. She attempted to remove the strap of her dress from her shoulder but the movement was clumsy and unattractive.

'Take me to bed, Mr Strange. Tonight I will be *anything* you desire. Tonight, I will be your...' Her frail voice petered out. He knew she was slipping fast into unconsciousness. He could see the hysteria in her eyes.

He quickly reached out to protect her fall...too late! Her body crumpled heavily to the floor. His first reaction was to try to revive her, but Lauren had blacked out completely.

Michael was stunned, and appalled by what had happened so very, very quickly. Minutes earlier, Lauren had seemed to be in control. *He* was in control. But this horrible room, this house, this woman were beginning to spell bad news: seriously bad news.

Coldness took hold, making him shiver. A kind of evil prevailed in every joist, every creaking floorboard, and each and every dark corner. He had to get out, now, before a shadow descended and blocked out all light. That's how he felt, entombed and chilled to the bone. As a child, this blackness and *"a world of make believe"* had scared him. Now, in this alien situation, the old feelings of fear and uncertainty came flooding back to haunt him once again. It was as if he was hypnotised, rooted to the spot: imprisoned in this God-awful room with her.

Just who was she?

A fallen angel: or the devil in disguise?

CHAPTER THREE

Michael awoke the next day, exhausted and bewildered by the weird events that had unfolded at Laburnum Farm. Given these circumstances, it was no surprise that he had uncharacteristically slept in. He wished only for a calmness to prevail. Clearing his head, he gulped water, checked the time by the wall clock, and cursed aloud. He padded to the kitchen, switched on the kettle, listened to the news headlines on Radio Five and slumped on the stool next to the breakfast table. His mind rattled with images of a half-naked woman lying unconscious at his feet. What was he getting himself into?

Reality kicked in. Phone Kara, he reminded himself urgently; but his brain was having none of it. It felt like a watermelon being smashed against a wall.

Taking two aspirin, he gradually and painfully began to recall the events of the day before. It transcended into a nightmare of sorts, one he did not care to repeat. Tarantino could not have scripted it better. But, on balance, he felt sorry for Lauren, discovering a deeply complex woman who had seen her own precious world collapse beneath her and as a result, found coping with it almost unbearable. Was that so hard to fathom?

After she had fainted at his feet, he remembered that somehow and with great difficulty he had lifted her onto the bed. In her state of half undress, it was an undignified manoeuvre. Then he checked for facial bruising and carefully supported her head to rest atop the soft pillows. He also managed to stir her awake just sufficiently so that she opened her eyes momentarily and smiled at him. It was a confused smile. However, this simple recognition gave him the confidence to leave her alone and in relative safety. In truth, he was terrified by the strange circumstances he found himself in. What would have happened if she had hit her head? Suppose she had swallowed her tongue? How could he explain his presence right here in the bedroom? What if she had died? Fuck. His mind had been in turmoil, just thinking of how his hands had been shaking and his shirt heavy with sweat. He recalled thinking *Get a grip!* He had sucked in air deeply and slowly and calmed himself adequately, in order to sort things out. Before leaving, he managed to pour a glass of water for her, placing it on the bedside table accompanied by a hastily scribbled note in his own rushed handwriting. It read:

Impossible to stay, but I'm sure that you will be OK on your own. Put the experience down to one of life's rich tapestries which we would rather forget. I've turned everything off, but I didn't dare let the dog out! Main door locked, key put back through the letterbox. Speak to you soon. Michael. P.S. In case you are wondering, no, you did not do anything to be ashamed of. Your behaviour was perfectly understandable in the circumstances. Great wine, though! I was happy to be there as a shoulder to cry on. Bruno wouldn't be so sympathetic to me. XX.

Now, in the cold hostility of the morning, he had grave doubts about her improper manner and the story she had told him. Hastily, he drank a black coffee, the first of several, and immersed himself under a very hot shower, lingering for an extra few luxuriant minutes. Damn. He had forgotten to contact his secretary.

*

During the rest of the afternoon and over an uneventful weekend, Michael received no word from Lauren. Even the fax that she promised to send detailing her solicitor's name and address failed to materialise. Although he knew how to contact her, he was reluctant to do so. On the one hand she held a certain fatal fascination for him, and she had made her intentions clear in the bedroom. It would have been difficult to resist the temptation had she not collapsed at his feet. On the other hand, he readily admitted this could so easily spiral out of control and drag him into a world that he would not be able to handle. Either Lauren was a clever and manipulative schemer *or* an innocent, damaged woman in genuine need of comfort and support. Naturally, he preferred to think of her in the latter terms. He *wanted* to be there for her, even if his reasoning was less than convincing.

Recollecting the events of their time together, he decided that the accumulation of pills and alcohol had contributed to her downfall. Clearly depressed, she had self-inflicted a heady cocktail which would have probably downed a bull elephant. It was her way of dealing with the pain and sorrow, he deduced. It was clearly the wrong way. A thumping headache would surely testify to this when she finally awoke.

But still he pondered. Although he could not put his finger on it, little things began to aggravate him and make him feel uneasy. Her anger was suppressed and raw and her temper quick to surface. She spoke of spite and vengeance and, more disturbingly, retribution. Yet she displayed outward signs of tenderness and compassion. When he analysed all of this, he pictured Lauren O'Neill as a volcano waiting to erupt.

And what of Julius Gray?

Where was he now living and with whom? Who was this mysterious seductress that he had run off with? Who had last seen him alive? Lauren had indeed spoken of him in the past tense: surely a slip of the tongue. Yet, it was evident from the set-up in the studio that the artist had left quickly. Had this Julius simply ran off with his mistress without a care or need for his work which he had carelessly left behind? Maybe, just maybe, Julius was forced to leave, forced to…to…he searched frantically for the right word…to escape. Many questions remained unanswered.

Putting all this aside, Michael tried to refocus on his failing business and failing marriage. But it was proving to be a hopeless task. Lauren was in his head, all consuming.

*

On the Monday morning, he called Kara into his office for their regular weekly meeting. They discussed the weekend events, or rather, lack of weekend events, and agreed between them that certain preferential clients needed jolting into action. Often it would be a case of following up several prospective customers' requirements and gently trying to coax them to part with their hard-earned money. Something had to happen and fast. Business was grim. All the retailers throughout the West End were bemoaning the lack of trade. It was bleak for everyone, the hotels, restaurants and the theatre. Two leading shows had already announced their immediate closure. With the continual threat of terrorist attacks in the city, London had become a jittery place in which to live and work.

Michael started the proceedings, without his normal enthusiasm for the task. 'What about Mrs Dunning, from Hampstead?' he asked.

'Ah, yes,' Kara said, mulling things over. 'She was keen on the John Hibbit still life. Thinking back, it was all to do with the cost of the redecoration of her dining room,' Kara remembered. 'With her, I would think the price was the stumbling block. I'll chase it up. She's definitely worth a try.'

'Hmm,' Michael pondered, jotting some figures down on a pad, 'give her a call. Go in at £9,500, that's just over ten per cent discount. Tell her she can have the painting on approval for a few days.' He hesitated. 'What about the commission at the new hotel on Connaught Street?'

'Delayed, I'm afraid. Apparently there are structural problems and they will not commit to us until they know the wall space available, which now could be smaller than they first envisaged.'

Michael shrugged. 'OK, it will come good – eventually. In the meantime, contact Mr Pointing in Jersey and ask when he is coming over next. Could he be tempted with the new Nicky Jennings? What do you think?'

'A strong possibility; I think he will buy, as he's an avid collector. How about we crate it over to him on approval for a few days?'

'Always a good ploy,' he laughed. 'It'll be too much trouble to return it: much easier to just stick it on the wall.'

They discussed other options which could prove beneficial to the financial welfare of the gallery, but the market was tough, and they had to respond with equal toughness. Leasing artwork was considered, but Michael wasn't keen as the margins were low. Next on the agenda were various issues regarding the spring exhibition in May, called "City Heat."

'Oh, that reminds me,' Kara announced, 'there are three of Marcus Heath's work in the stockroom, ready for collection by the photographer. Just in case you were wondering what they were doing there.'

'He's keen,' Michael reflected. 'A bit early to say the least.'

'I think he panicked! Marcus thought you might change your mind.'

'I'm tempted.'

Kara shared his laughter. 'You can be such an ogre; I can't see why anyone wants to deal with you.'

He shrugged his shoulders in puzzlement. 'Or work for me for that matter. I must have something going for me.'

'Hmm, you think so?' she teased, a mocking frown creasing her forehead.

*

Later that day, Kara poked her head around the door to Michael's office, still carrying a frown. This time it was for real.

'Well,' she asked, with a tone of bewilderment, 'what does a girl have to do around here to get information?'

Michael looked up, bemused.

'It's like getting blood out of a stone,' she added, grinning now.

'Perhaps you could enlighten me a little?'

She sighed, 'Men! Always so secretive.'

Michael fiddled with his pencil, staring blankly.

'Ah, keeping me in suspense, so typical.' She stamped her foot playfully, advancing further into the office. 'How long was it going to be before I got to know?'

'Got to *know*?' Michael was teasing her now.

'Yes, damn it: the meeting with the so-called mistress of the manor. How did you get on with Lauren O'Neill? What was she like?'

'Ah, yes, well – I'm not sure that I can breach client confidentiality.' He somehow managed to maintain a serious face.

'Bullshit.'

'I'm not sure I can relate to that term. Has it got anything to do with a cup of coffee?'

'OK, its bribery and corruption time,' she countered, folding her arms, 'I'll make the coffee. First you spill the beans. Something big, you said on the phone. I'm dying to hear.'

'Just what is it with women and gossip?' he asked. 'Actually, Kara,' he said seriously 'I'm not entirely sure *how* I got on with Lauren. She turned out to be a strange and disturbing lady.'

'Just your sort then,' Kara quipped.

He chose to ignore Kara's jibe, even though it was close to the truth.'The appraisals she wants me to do could prove to be a major logistical nightmare.' His throat stuck on this last word.

'And the Patrick Porters, were they as good as you'd hoped?'

'To be perfectly frank with you, Kara, I didn't get to see those. It was all a bit of a disappointment.' His voice trailed off.

'Oh,' she muttered. 'You seemed so full of it when we spoke on the phone.'

'I got carried away with the excitement and intrigue. In reality, when I got there I soon discovered a tangled mess of, well, people's lives smashed and stolen. Too much for me to take in, really. I ended up being a reluctant counsellor, and a poor one at that. Next time I'll just stick to being a humble art dealer. I've got enough problems of my own.'

*

Within an hour, Kara returned, this time with a face like thunder. 'Michael, how *exactly* was it left between you and Lauren?'

He looked vague. 'There's been nothing...It was Thursday when we last had contact. I'm still hopeful of viewing the Porters, but I don't feel compelled to phone her. It's like opening a can of worms.'

He stared at her vacantly, waiting for a barrage of questions, but instead she stared back at him with a look of agitation.

'You haven't made contact with her *at all*?' she asked.

'No. Perhaps I should write a courtesy letter, explaining our company position. Keep it simple.'

Kara raised her eyebrows. 'Michael, I think you should come and see something. Now.'

'Have we finally had word from her?'

Kara turned on her heels and walked briskly from his office.

'Perhaps you should check out your emails,' she called from afar.

Intrigued, he rose from his desk and wearily followed her, knowing he was not quite on the same wavelength at this point. Kara could be so infuriating at times. Just what was she referring to? It was his policy to leave all the internet stuff to his secretary; it was basically too much trouble for him.

He soon found trouble. On the computer screen, he read:

WHERE ARE YOU? I NEED TO SEE YOU. WHERE ARE YOU? I NEED TO SEE YOU. WHERE ARE YOU? I NEED TO SEE YOU.

Kara clicked through a never-ending list of recurring emails.

'This is one sick chick,' she said.

'Is every one the same?' Michael asked with a nervous edge to his voice.

'Every damn one,' Kara responded, looking back at him. 'There are literally hundreds of them, and look at the time lapse between each message. Every fifteen minutes. This took her bloody hours, Michael,' she said gravely.

*

Searching for reasons which would make some kind of sense to what was happening made his blood run cold. What he did know was this: Lauren was possessive and needy and calculating. What he did not know was this: how far was he prepared to go with his fascination for this woman? Admittedly, he felt he was losing control with his business; and his relationship with Adele was disintegrating to the point of collapse. He felt diminished and unworthy and rudderless. Perhaps Lauren represented another world in which to escape. Certainly, this now appeared as an unwanted intrusion and yet...yet... he had a compulsion to be propelled head first into this alternative universe of the weird and the wonderful. Thinking about it, though, made him realise it wasn't an unwanted intrusion. *Christ. He welcomed it.* It was now becoming a distressing trait in his thought process that he was prepared to search for it and embrace it. What the hell was going on?

Everything he knew and understood and valued in his life was suddenly in question. But, strangely, it bothered him little. A small madness had infiltrated his orderly mind and had become an insidious intruder, gradually overpowering his logical reasoning to illogical fears. In his brain, the dark shadows embraced him perversely. They offered comfort. The further he withdrew into the murkiness, the more he felt protected. Lauren was both the comfort and the protection. He wanted to believe this. She was his salvation, his Holy Grail. It was his fascination with her that held the flaw.

His mind then turned to his other obsession.

Money. It consumed his parallel thoughts. He began to calculate a survival plan which would enable him to rise above the debris of divorce. Adele's financial demands would begin the seeds of gradual destruction, one which his business could not sustain, especially in the current economic climate. He was acutely aware of the damage her actions would cause and it deeply appalled his sense of injustice. The seemingly bad timing of her selfish act also galled him. Callous bitch.

When he considered the various options open to him, each presented a frightening scenario. If he were to hold on to the business then turnover would need to improve significantly in order to fund a substantial loan or provide cash up front to fuel her greed. The advice from his accountants spelled out the caustic truth. Firstly, he owed the Inland Revenue £150,000 for the current fiscal year. The impending tax inspection would incur approximately £9,000 in expenses and untold claw backs, and the rent on the property in Cork Street would rise from £130,000 to £155,000 next year. In addition, business rates were set to soar in the city. At the existing level of projected turnover loss, the gallery would be contemplating a drop in profits of £200,000. Then there was the tiny matter of a possible one million pound divorce settlement and as yet unconfirmed yearly maintenance figure (£100,000 had been mentioned), plus the loss of the investment in the Spanish villa. He would be left with the Chelsea apartment (heavily mortgaged) and the country house, which he had inherited from his parents. Something mighty substantial would have to be sacrificed.

His main concern was the business. If turnover continued to dive in such alarming fashion then how would he be able to sustain the restructuring of the finances, which would inevitably require loan funding of a large scale? This could be achieved, but the equity in his assets would in turn be savagely reduced, thus making the foundations on which everything was built particularly vulnerable.

And then he turned his attention to the sale of the Porter originals. Twelve of them! That prospect certainly whetted his appetite. Lauren had offered him the opportunity to market them, and if he hesitated, then undoubtedly another art dealer would step in quickly. These paintings would be highly desirable and realise big value profits, possibly as much as £750,000. He was aware of his first obligation, which was to the business. Therefore, it would be financial suicide to ignore such an opportunity, tantamount to gross negligence in his own professional integrity if he allowed this chance to pass him by. He was first in the queue, ahead of the pack. That was how he always played the game: being the predator.

He checked for Lauren's contact number. After three aborted attempts, drawing breath and steeling himself, his fingers nervously punched in the telephone number that took him on a path to the unknown: a journey of discovery, a destination without boundaries. The warnings, however, were there. *Sick Chick*, Kara had said earlier. It made him wonder, and then something else crept into his brain: be careful what you wish for.

*

If Kara had been concerned at the odd antics displayed by her boss, she was downright spooked by his initial reaction to the emails. He was too damn calm for her liking, almost undisturbed by the obsessive nature of Lauren O'Neill. What hold did she have on him? What really happened at the house? It was this same concern that justified her decision to listen in on the private telephone conversation between them. Fortunately, Michael seemed to be oblivious to her concealment just beyond the open door of his office. It was a risk she took but a risk worth taking.

This is what she heard:

'Hi, it's Michael, the good Samaritan. How's the head? Uh-uh. I felt awful leaving you the other afternoon. No. No. It was no problem. I thought it best to leave well alone for a few days, but, well, to be perfectly frank with you, Lauren, the emails were rather alarming.' A long pause ensured. 'OK, you don't have to feel like that. No. No, of course I will help you.' Another but much longer pause, followed by a sigh from Michael. 'Lauren, nobody is abandoning you. No, I will not be like all the others...' He took a deep breath, changing the telephone from one ear to the other. He listened patiently. 'Lauren, hear me out. Calm down, please calm down. Right now you are experiencing a very traumatic upheaval in your life and you're not *expected* to behave in a rational manner. Believe me, I know exactly what you are going through - listen, let's meet for a drink and I'll do the talking this time, OK? Come up to town and we'll go out for a meal, what do you think? Great. Great. Catch the train. Do you know the Monsoon restaurant off Monmouth Street, Covent Garden? It's just opened to good reviews. Let's meet tomorrow night, say, eight thirty? Good. No. No. You can stay at my place, are you OK with that?' He paused. 'Fine, Lauren, I look forward to it. Take care.'

Kara heard him replace the receiver. Even from her hidden position she detected his nervous excitement at the prospect of meeting up with her. With any luck, he had sufficient health insurance to cover all eventualities, she thought. Then she quietly slipped away.

*

Kara had agreed to meet Marcus directly after work at a wine bar just a few hundred yards from the gallery, one which she was familiar with. This made her feel more comfortable, rather than enter alone and order a drink in a strange place. Marcus was late. She drank her chilled Pinot and made idle chat with the barman, whom she knew as Jack, an Australian from Perth. Feeling relaxed, they swapped banter and insults as only two people could who came from their respective mother countries. The more insulting the joke, the less offence was taken. That was the way it was between the Brits and the Aussies.

She checked her watch again and sighed. Then the door opened and in breezed the boy.

'Hi, sorry I'm late.' Marcus said, plonking himself beside her on a stool. Catching the barman's eye, he shouted, 'bottle of Becks, mate!'

Kara stared at him, disdain in her eyes.

'How's it going?' he asked, oblivious to her annoyance. He overfilled the space between them wearing a huge grey duffle coat and scarf and a cheeky grin. Kara shifted backwards on her stool, feeling overpowered.

'A good way to impress me,' Kara remarked, glancing at her watch and then deflecting her gaze toward Jack. 'A girl can get easily distracted if kept waiting. Is this your idea of playing hard to get?'

The grin on Marcus's face widened. He grabbed his bottle of Becks and swallowed hard at the ice cold beer.

She could tell he wasn't going to apologise.

'My creative juices were operating big time, I just had to go with the flow,' he said. 'The painting's great, even if I say so myself. Besides, can't have you putting round the rumours that I'm chasing you. I have a reputation to uphold.'

'Reputation?' Kara asked, raising her eyebrows.

'Yup. Being seen to be punctual implies that I have nothing better to do with my day, as if I'm just hanging around waiting…'

'For a date?' she interrupted, punching his arm playfully.

'Well, kinda. Is this an official date?'

'Far too soon, Marcus,' she said. 'I'm distinctly unimpressed with your attitude and now the timekeeping leaves a lot to be desired. It's rubbish. Not looking good, is it?'

'Hmm, I was rather hoping you would give me the benefit of the doubt and put it down to the eccentricities of my artistic temperament.'

'Well,' she amused herself, 'how about we beg to disagree and in the meantime let's put our *so-called* relationship on hold, calling timeout while you undertake a strict period of probation, set by me. Deal?'

'Hell,' he shrugged, 'you're going to be one hard nut to crack.'

They moved to another bar and then on to an Italian restaurant, Mario's, where they shared seafood pasta and a bottle of Chianti. His treat. She was warming towards him.

'Do you know of an artist called Julius Gray?' Kara asked, forking her pasta.

'Nope. Should I?'

Kara pondered. 'No. But I *feel* I should. And yet...'

'Do I need to fear him?'

She was startled. '*Pardon*?'

'For your affections. I need to know the enemy.'

'Don't be silly. You have nothing to worry about on that score.' She laughed generously. 'Apparently, he has disappeared abroad with his mistress after dumping the wife. I'm intrigued, that's all. He is a prolific painter and I've never *actually* heard of him. Neither has Michael.'

'Ah, the *other* man in your life,' Marcus joked, gulping his wine and giving her the hard stare over the lip of his glass.

'You can be so immature,' she replied in a dismissive tone.

He grinned, arrogantly. 'Touched on a raw nerve, have I?'

Kara took a deep breath. 'Marcus, let's establish the ground rules, OK?' She bristled with her words, forcing him to sit back from the table in a defensive mode. 'First,' she said, 'you have done all the chasing and I regard your juvenile banter as mildly amusing and, at best, a somewhat happy diversion from the daily grind of what we all laughingly call '*life*'. Second, if you persist in this line of interrogation every time the name of my boss is mentioned I'll have no choice but to sabotage your forthcoming exhibition.'

The penny dropped. She rejoiced in wiping the grin from his smug face.

'I have the power, believe me.' She produced one of her superior smiles. Then she added, 'And third, just because you have the arrogance to think you will succeed in getting me into bed, I should remind you that juvenile, spotty, coarse and vulgar youths do not – *do not* – get me wet between the legs in the same way as a mature, thoughtful, handsome and debonair art dealer would, with the minimum of effort. Does that give you any idea of how far off the mark you are, or do you need further examples of discouragement?'

'Ouch! I suppose I should leave right now?'

'Possibly…'

'So,' he said, 'do I take it that all my courageous efforts are in vain?'

'Yep.'

'Am I as stupid as I look right now?'

'As stupid as you look.'

'So,' he said, pondering once again. 'On a scale of one to ten, where do I rate?'

'In terms of *what*?' she enquired, mystified.

'Well, how shall I put it,' Marcus said, weighing up his chances, 'in terms of getting to shag your brains out. Sorry about the crudity.. I would hate to offend your sensitivity.'

'No offence taken.' She thought for a moment, bringing her finger to her lips. 'Hmm, two out of ten, max. Sorry. I hate to further humiliate the humiliated.'

'Feel free. It's a kind of control you feel you need to exercise for fear of being put down. You get the rejection in first. It's quite endearing, actually.'

Kara suddenly saw Marcus in a new light, impressed by his progressive insight. For the first time, she felt embarrassed. 'Wow,' she said. 'Am I that transparent?'

'Completely see-through,' he replied.

There was silence and awkwardness.

'I suppose,' she countered, 'I should revaluate your rating to…four out of ten.' Her eyes dropped to her folded arms. The body language was crystal clear.

'Only four?'

Kara lifted her eyes to meet his. 'You should be honoured with that score.'

'I am, believe me. I'm frantically searching for other pearls of wisdom.'

Kara reached out and took his hands in hers, smiling warmly. 'Stop searching, Marcus. Start with the simple things. We'll handle the complications later.'

Marcus returned the embrace of hands and squeezed reassuringly, although more for his comfort than hers. 'Show me how?' he asked endearingly.

She stretched forward across the table, closing her eyes in anticipation.

'Kiss me for starters,' she demanded.

*

'Michael?'

He listened to the familiar voice and his heart sank. He found a chair and took a mouthful of whisky to help clear his parched throat. He was sure she heard his audible sigh.

'Adele.' He swapped the telephone from one ear to the other and remained silent.

'We haven't spoken for sometime,' she said. 'How are you?'

'Fine.'

'I've deliberately kept away from the gallery. I'm sure you appreciate the space...especially after the last couple of weeks. I need to come in to bring the company books up to date. Would you prefer if I worked from home?'

He thought for a moment, his mind elsewhere. 'Whatever suits you, really.'

'Michael, I don't wish to create a scene or bad atmosphere, but it would be preferable to come in. The VAT figures need to be compiled and all the information I need is in the gallery. How about I come in on Monday?'

'Monday it is.'

'Will Kara be in? I need her to help me, if that's all right.'

'She will.'

There was an awkward pause, illustrated in his mind as a ten foot high brick wall separating them. All that was required was the barbed wire to be added on the top.

'Michael, we don't have to be like this.'

'It's what you want, isn't it?'

'No. It doesn't have to be like this.' Her voice softened.

'You asked for a divorce, Adele. I'm not familiar with the rules. How should it be?'

'There are no rules, Michael. We all stumble through things like this.'

He shuddered. 'Really? What about your ludicrous financial demands? No stumbling there, I notice.'

'We can talk. We can still talk.'

'Adele, we have talked, but I still do not know why you want a divorce. You have never really explained yourself.'

'I have,' she replied indignantly. 'But you choose not to listen. Is that my fault?'

'I listen but I do *not* understand. I confess ignorance.'

It was Adele's turn to sigh. 'I feel smothered and I need to find my own identity again. I know you have difficulty comprehending this notion but we've become wrapped up in the business to the degree that we are now more like business partners and that is not enough for me, Michael. There has to be something else, surely?'

'Something else? Or *someone else*?' he asked guardedly.

'Michael, this doesn't have to connect to someone else. It can just be for me.'

'Is there someone else? I need to know. If there is no one then what you are doing is madness...We're throwing too much away. Can't you see that?'

He could hear her draw breath.

'There, there *could* be someone,' she eventually said, almost in a whisper.

He could sense the resignation in her voice.

'I'll see you on Monday,' he said, aware that his reply was cold and remote.

Quietly, he replaced the handset. He then downed the remains of the whisky and threw the glass against a wall, smashing it into thousands of tiny fragments.

*

The next day was a bit of a blur for Michael. He nursed a terrible hangover and cursed under his breath just thinking about Adele. He was convinced that either this unpleasant situation with her, or drinking too much whisky would instigate his downfall. Probably both, he thought. He suddenly felt old and fragile. On top of that, just as he wished for quiet and an uneventful day, he noticed Kara was euphoric, floating on dreams and generally irritating everyone. The end of the working day couldn't come quickly enough for him.

*

At closing time, Kara breathlessly skipped her way home in eager anticipation of a further night with adorable Marcus. He surprised her because he was so unpredictable, one moment infantile and selfish, the next sensitive and caring. He was confident and outlandish, something she initially misunderstood as laddish and arrogant. For her, it was a delight to discover a man within a boy: the best of both worlds.

*

Michael, on the other hand, was slow to close the gallery. His thoughts centred on the conversation with Adele ("there could be someone") and his forthcoming dinner date with Lauren. He decided that he was not in the right frame of mind to speculate on his wife's lover or find the enthusiasm to counsel Lauren if she burdened him with her troubles. Instead, he consoled himself with Lauren's stunning beauty, and the prospect of adventure: the best of both worlds. His mood lightened.

*

He showered at home, towelled down, but chose to remain unshaven, preferring the fashionable light stubble look. Satisfied, he then dressed in a black Armani suit, with open-neck white shirt. He wore Dior aftershave, casual black loafers and, to finish off, selected a neat antique Cartier watch, silver with black leather strap, which he had inherited from his father. Staring at his image in the mirror, he complimented himself on looking stylish and powerful. He felt good. He ruffled his silver hair, switched off the light and walked out into the darkness of the night.

He took a cab into Covent Garden. He arrived early and so paid off the driver to walk the last couple of blocks. The weather was cold and sharp. Adjusting the collar of his brown cashmere coat tightly around his neck, he soon mingled with the other people on the pavement until he became another anonymous figure in the crowd. This was how he liked it. Ambling through Neal's Yard, he inhaled the aromatic smells of the coffee houses and enjoyed the faint intrusion to his ears of different music filtering out from the bars and shops. He turned into Monmouth Street and quickly found himself outside the Monsoon restaurant. He checked his watch: five to eight.

*

Marcus texted Kara: meet me at eight outside the Curzon Street cinema.

He wanted to catch a new movie. It was a French art house film called 'Chanson de Roland.' He didn't ask if it appealed to her. They grabbed the customary popcorn and Pepsi, took their seats and settled down like any other impassioned couple. As the lights dimmed, he felt Kara take his hand. A warm glow of comfort enveloped him. Then he spoilt it. Leaning over, he whispered in her ear, 'In case you were wondering, the film is called The Song of Roland.'

Kara dug her fingernails into his skin. 'Really?' she said.

'Ouch,' he yelled, before adding more quietly, 'and in case you were wondering still further, it's about a knight in shining armour.'

'Thank you for telling me, Marcus.' She wanted to kill him.

*

The eatery was fashionable Asian fusion, with lots of chrome, glass and polished wooden floors, impersonal and slick. Michael made his way to the long bar and ordered a bottle of Alexandre Bonnet Rose, eventually finding a tall table with stools. The overhead starlight fibre optic lighting changed colour every few seconds: it was that kind of place. Monsoon was a new eatery and overcrowded with achingly hip young people and cool staff determined to be mechanically detached and ultra efficiently slow. Michael felt uncomfortable – and ancient.

Relief was at hand. He saw her first through the crowd, luminous, statuesque, delicious and...*his*. The noisy throng parted as she   approached his table, smiling invitingly, her eyes ablaze and her long red hair shimmering under the lights. He stood from his chair and impulsively kissed her gently on the mouth, gesturing for her to sit.

'You look fabulous, Lauren.'

She wore a long black sable coat and high heels and silver drop earrings with diamonds. He smelt her skin and imagined the contours of her smooth body. He placed a flute of sparkling bubbles in front of her.

'Champagne: how lovely!'

Lauren allowed the waiter to remove her coat, revealing her lithesome figure in a hugging sequined black dress, slashed at the front to show her breasts, half covered. Michael inhaled deeply and hesitated for a moment, caught off balance by the intoxicating vision of this incredible creature before him. He was aware that all eyes in the room were on her.

'Are you OK?' she asked mischievously. 'Is it too hot in here for you?'

It *was* getting too damn hot, he admitted silently to himself.

*

After the movie had ended, Kara and Marcus retreated to an old fashioned pub across the street, where they sat perched on high uncomfortable stools at the main bar. He saw her displeasure.

The atmosphere was brash and heated and smoky.

'Not your scene,' Marcus said his voice shouting above the din.

'Why do you think that?' Kara asked, unsmiling.

He ordered a Bud for himself and a gin and tonic for her. 'I had you down as a wine bar girl, to be honest.'

'Never be presumptuous, Marcus. I'm a chameleon, always adapting to my surroundings. I'm a born survivor.'

Marcus shrugged. 'Survival, eh? Is that how you view your life?'

'*Far* too heavy,' Kara said. 'Let's just say I prefer to blend in.'

They swallowed their drinks quickly and decided to reorder, against her better judgement. This time she paid, making her gin and tonic a double.

'So – not unlike the fate of the leading lady in the film?' Marcus said, venturing boldly. 'She chose survival over the challenge.'

Kara shifted in her chair. 'I wasn't looking for similarities.'

He persisted. 'Well, the way I see it, the character only revalued her priorities when she found the reason to open her mind to other possibilities. Then he saved her.'

'The knight in shining armour theory?'

'Exactly. She discovered herself through him.'

Kara screwed her face up. 'And found true happiness and everlasting love?'

'Something like that.'

'Hmm, a little too clichéd for me, I'm afraid.'

'But *that* was the message,' Marcus preached, taking up the argument. 'I found it magical, that two people could find each other and truly connect.'

Kara smirked, sank the last remains from her glass and stood to go. 'Well, if you want my opinion, I found it pretentious tosh.'

Before he had a chance to react, Kara pulled him closer and kissed him hard on the mouth.

'Let's go to bed,' she shouted above the din, catching the startled attention of those closest in earshot. 'That's what you really want. Be honest.'

*

'Would you care for another pot of coffee, sir?'

Michael gazed up at the waiter, somewhat surprised. The restaurant was virtually empty. He looked at his wristwatch: Midnight. Christ.

'We are fine, thank you. Can we have the bill instead, please?' He turned to Lauren, and grinned. 'Amazing,' he remarked, 'The evening has simply flown by.'

Michael had the perfect night of fun and laughter, fine wine and good food. For the first time Michael began to see Lauren flourish and relax and unwind from the problems that had clearly beset her. They talked freely and found ironic humour in their mutual experiences of respective marriage breakdowns. Certainly for him, he gained an inner strength from relating to their shared stories, some painful, some hilarious. Michael fell in love with Lauren this night, without telling her.

Lauren stretched out her arm and took his hand. 'I've had a truly wonderful evening. Thank you, Michael.' She held his eye. 'I hope it doesn't have to end at midnight?'

'There's a club just around the corner,' he volunteered.

'You look absolutely shattered, Michael. We can skip the dancing. Why don't we go back to your place... if I'm still invited to stay?'

Michael took her hand and slowly kissed it. 'I noticed you've come without an overnight bag. I wasn't sure I should be so presumptuous.'

Lauren retrieved her slim handbag from the floor and tapped the side. 'I travel light. I only need a toothbrush and change of clean Janet Regers. Shall we go?'

*

Kara let herself go with an intensity never felt before. Her lovemaking with Marcus was frenzied and heated and unrelenting. Entangled flesh and bone tingled and shimmered. She was intoxicated with the scent of sex. It engulfed them, allowing each to explore the other's body with a passion to which only new lovers can aspire. They rushed, pushed, spread and penetrated, licked and pulled, bit and caressed, searching for pain and pleasure until they were both completely sated. They eventually lay on damp rumpled sheets, breathing fast and falling heavily into that strange suspended time lapse of exhaustion and ecstasy, of heightened senses and a futile gesture of defiance: of taking and being taken. A glorious surrender.

Falling blissfully still further, Kara became aware of his arousal, his reawakened power, and within moments she felt his strength as he turned her over, lifted her forcibly from behind and entered her, thrusting himself into her time and time again, as if minutes became hours, and yet he sustained his motion of her, machinelike, until her pleasure became cruelty, her body a simple tool to his, and her mind a whirlpool of sensual slavery. She could take no more and she cried out. But still he took her, harder and faster.

Long into the night, just as the first light of the morning filtered into the bedroom, he whispered in her ear, 'I bet that's something your *precious* boss couldn't do.'

She in turn pushed his face away and deliberately positioned her back to him. She hated his triumphant boast.

'Fuck off, Marcus,' she said, drifting back to sleep.

CHAPTER FOUR

Michael made love to Lauren again in the morning, less urgent this time; and he found a tender embrace – *a certain touch* – which he had not experienced for many years. She caressed and soothed his body and he in turn yearned for *this time* to be captured and held just for him, so that he could retreat into her protection whenever the need was there. Lauren offered a warm shelter in which to hide away from the cold hostility that invaded his world.

During the night they had remained awake, holding each other in silence, staring into each other's eyes, he slowly mapping the curves of her delicious body with his tongue, she hungrily kissing his every taut limb. He discovered with delight that they *fitted*.

Later, in the kitchen of his apartment, Michael heated fresh croissants which they ate greedily, washed down with chilled, freshly squeezed orange juice. He sat huddled side by side with her at the breakfast table in the glass conservatory. Below them, sleek grey-hulled yachts bobbed in the icy cold Thames. Then, much to their surprise, giant snowflakes began to fall in a swirling mass from the leaden sky. They watched with a childlike innocence, as if time somehow held them magically suspended in this precious moment.

As minutes passed by, the view from the window disappeared behind a blanket of white, leaving their own ghostly reflection staring back at them.

'Lauren, can I be personal?' he said, nervously searching her eyes for a sign of disapproval. He was reluctant to spoil the moment but it had to be said, 'I've asked before, I ask again: do you want Julius back?'

She was silent for a long time. 'I can't forgive him, ever. I have Irish blood in me and my temperament won't allow me to humiliate myself any further. *He doesn't deserve me.* For a long time I wished to harm him. And *her* as well.' Lauren's body stiffened. 'Is that bad?'

'I can understand it,' he said eventually. 'Adele and I shared many wonderful moments. Then, before you know it, it all goes terribly wrong, and you end up searching for the answers and find there aren't any. And then you feel a failure. When you find out that betrayal is the instigator, it is very difficult to come to terms with it. The truth is, however, that betrayal is often the symptom, and we must all share the responsibility. If people were happy, they wouldn't have the need to look elsewhere. We fail despite ourselves. Betrayal is a harsh lesson and we find it difficult to forgive. It is natural to want revenge. Whenever we find ourselves discarded, we want to lash out. It is a very powerful urge. *Is it bad*? Yes, but I want to *hurt* Adele. The rage I feel scares me.'

He watched as Lauren rose from the table. She disappeared from view and suddenly hugged him from behind, kissing the back of his neck.

'In answer to your question,' she said, 'I do *not* want Julius back. Not now that I have you. He has chosen someone else, a whore, to be exact. Rage? Yes, I too have a rage. But right now I feel only contempt. It boils up whenever I think of them together. For me, Julius is dead. From the moment he abandoned me, he will always be dead.'

*

It was long into the afternoon when Michael decided to drive Lauren home to Laburnum Farm, after the TV weather forecast warned of heavy snow overnight. The sky was an amazing violent red and yellow and the air icily sharp. With this in mind it was a sensible precaution, one borne out not of gallantry but necessity.

This evening, he wanted to be alone, to think long and hard as to where the entanglement with Lauren was leading. On the one hand, he was falling in love with – no – he *was* in love with this beautiful and intoxicating creature. On the other hand, he was fearful of her bewitching nature. She was overpowering him.

Come tomorrow, he would pursue another matter, and to do this, to be clear and alert, would mean no distraction beforehand. Hence, his immediate desire to separate himself from Lauren. During the time he was alone in her husband's studio something had bothered him that he could not put a finger on. It nagged him like a bad toothache.

Now, driving the two of them in his BMW along the Embankment, past the Chelsea barracks, he began to see a picture gradually unfold. Like a lot of people, he did his best thinking in a car. Switching on the CD player, he engaged the whispering husky tone of Sade singing *Lover's Rock*. He glanced over to Lauren and glimpsed her smile as she settled down into her seat, closed her eyes, and drifted off to sleep, lulled by the comfort of the music. He, too, enjoyed the soothing nature of the rhythmic beat, but his mind was active now, racing ahead of himself. The same question kept battering his brain. *What* had he seen in the studio that so puzzled him?

His memory, his recollection of what he thought he saw was insignificant, at best, untrustworthy. And yet this piece of the jigsaw had to be important because it caused him to be unsettled and mindful. Above all, it made him question his own motives as to why he allowed himself to be embroiled in this strange scenario in the first place. If he was being totally honest with himself, it proved a necessary diversion from the problems of the shoddy disintegration of his own marriage. The answer – his fulfilment – lay in the ghosts that surrounded him.

Logic was the key. To begin with, he would have to find Julius Gray: this was paramount to saving his own sanity. If he had a future with Lauren, then this was a dilemma that had to be solved. The unthinkable would be if Julius was dead, even murdered, and Lauren was implicated in his death. He shuddered. Without this end to uncertainty, their relationship would always be impaired. With each passing mile on the road, a degree of doom descended upon him. It suffocated him like a thick woollen blanket. Just *how* would he find this missing man? Tomorrow, somehow, he would begin the quest.

*

Kara arrived at the gallery uncharacteristically early, chirpy and especially pleased with herself. She had left Marcus asleep in her bed, exhausted from the frolics of the night before. The cup of tea she set beside him on the bedside table would soon be cold, but she declined to nudge him from his deep slumber. *Some people just don't have the stamina*, she concluded in amusement, satisfying herself with the delicious thought of his frantic all- night performance.

Tucked in behind her desk, she keyed in the appropriate code on the computer keypad and entered the file marked 'Sale or Return', being those paintings which artists left in good faith on the understanding that a commission would be taken by the gallery in the event of a sale. It was common practice. Kara had devised a system whereupon she would list the paintings, do a print off for the artist and she or Michael or even Ron would sign for them, as a safeguard against possible discrepancies. It was a system that was both simple and effective. Perversely, there lay the evidence that Kara was looking for. Within these print-offs, which nobody really cared about, not least the artists who were often idle and inefficient, was a list of *all* the paintings which entered the gallery, which in turn were either sold, kept, or returned. These were, in the great scheme of things, forgotten lists, always left for good old dependable Kara to update. And this she did, diligently.

It worked like this. If Adele sold a painting deemed "under the counter" she would take great pains to ensure that the painting itself was never produced in the first place. It *needed* to disappear. This was easy on a Sale or Return basis as no invoice had been raised in the first place. Effectively, the painting did not exist, satisfying the artist, the gallery and the delighted buyer, who would gain from a generous discount with his purchase. Everyone was happy, everything fine, except for the small matter of one dutiful secretary and her very tidy lists. All it would take was one vindictive telephone call to the taxman. And Adele would be in the shit.

Unfortunately, so would Michael, so she would have to play this carefully. He and Adele were partners after all, and would be implicated together. Kara poured a second cup of coffee and began the arduous task of compiling sales and identifying the missing stock. Something had to surface, eventually. If Kara could rake in enough evidence against Adele, then this in turn could be a significant weapon for Michael. The intended phone call to the taxman was only a threat: a bluff. Just the allegation of possible fraud would suggest Adele's rapid withdrawal from her already ludicrous demands from Michael, thus allowing him to salvage what he could in the divorce proceedings. Scandal was one thing. Impending criminal charges were entirely different. A fair exchange, Kara concluded smugly. She was confident that Adele would back off with this possibility hanging over her head.

'I could do with a cup of that coffee,' Michael bellowed as he entered the front entrance to the gallery.

Kara jumped in her seat and spilled her coffee down her blouse.

'Aaagh!' This was the second time someone had bloody crept up on her. She thought back to Marcus and his similar antics the other day.

'Are you OK?' Michael grabbed a tissue from the desk and handed it to her. 'This is a bit early for you to be in, isn't it?'

Kara regained her composure, mopping the stains with her makeshift towel. 'Couldn't sleep last night,' she muttered. 'Water pipe broke in the street, damn roadwork drilling at six o'clock this morning right outside the flat. No peace for the wicked, so I thought I'd make up for a couple of late appearances recently.'

Speedily, she switched the file on the screen to an alternative client database to hide what she was doing.

He looked over her shoulder, seemingly unconcerned. 'Fine, I'm impressed. What are you doing?'

'Er, searching for Mr Applegate's phone number. I thought I'd follow up his inquiry.'

'What inquiry?'

She was flustered now. Thinking fast, she said, 'He needs a restoration quote for a Dyef painting that apparently has developed hairline cracking on the surface of the canvas. It's worsened over the years, and he is concerned about his investment. The canvas may need relining.'

'Hmm, what a pain. It will have to be an insurance claim.' Michael shrugged. 'Always more trouble than it's worth. Still, get him to drop it over. We'll take a look and get an estimate from the workshop.'

Off the hook now, Kara said, 'You're in early as well.'

Michael drank the cold remnants from her coffee cup.

'Hmm, yes...couldn't damn sleep.'

Kara was aware that he seemed distracted and a little dishevelled. Even more of a surprise, she was shocked to hear him steal her lines.

'I was interrupted by workmen outside the apartment: must have been a burst water pipe. No chance of a lie in.'

She noticed he recovered his composure and returned to more pressing matters. 'Actually, I need you to find some information for me. Fancy a big fry-up breakfast across the street?'

Kara had a ferocious appetite after a night of sex. She was pleased that her little ploy on the computer had not been detected. She grabbed her handbag.

'You tempt me with all the best offers,' she smiled.

*

Poppy's Diner was always busy, mostly with construction workers, taxi

drivers and local retail staff from the department stores and shops along Piccadilly. The language was usually strong at this time of the morning, but Michael ignored the banter from the other tables and tucked heartily into the full English breakfast, with added buttered toast on the side. He declined the black pudding. He noticed she scoffed everything.

'Big appetite,' he remarked, staring at Kara's plate.

'Big girl,' she replied, attacking her food with determination.

'Hardly. There's nothing to you.' He studied her carefully. 'Am I working you too hard?'

Kara looked up, dabbing her mouth with a paper napkin.

'Overworking me, underpaying me, never a day off, the list is endless. Dedication usually has its rewards, but I can't see them.'

'Really? A little bird tells me that a certain artist, who shall remain nameless of course, is providing all the incentives that you want.'

'Who told you that?' Kara snapped, lifting her fork in mock attack. 'Tell me!'

'Oh, a thoroughly shameless acquaintance of ours.'

'Ronald! I'll kill him!'

Michael laughed. 'Nothing gets past Ronald, you should know that. Gossip is what spurs him on. Talking of shameless folk: How is young Marcus?'

Kara eyed him suspiciously. 'Fine, he's fine. Actually, Marcus is more than that, he's wonderful.' She beamed. 'And he is certainly not shameless, not like one woman in particular I could mention.'

Michael took up the hook. 'Speaking of Adele, we are honoured with her actual presence on Monday. She's coming in to complete the dreaded VAT quarterly returns.'

'Oh.'

'Is there a problem?'

'I was rather hoping for the day off, giving me an extended weekend break.'

He frowned. 'Sorry, not possible.' Michael saw the disappointment wash across her features. 'Tell you what,' he ventured, leaning forward, 'help me on this one and the following week take the Monday and Tuesday off and travel up to Scotland. It'll do you good to get away for several days; my treat. Take Marcus.'

'Scotland? Did you say Scotland?'

'Yes, well, Glasgow to be precise.'

She frowned. 'Glasgow? In the freezing winter? Are you insane?'

'It'll be marvellous,' he said enthusiastically. 'It will be a chance for you both to escape from London and really get to know each other.'

'Hang on,' Kara said, her eyes narrowing. 'Get to know each other, or, get to know about *someone* else? I can hazard a guess...'

She knew him pretty well, he was amused to note. 'Well, whilst up there, you could do me a little favour, as you *are* in the vicinity,' he said.

'Damn, what a crappy underhand ploy.' The other diners in the café were suddenly deafened into silence, but Kara was in full flow. 'I cannot believe what I am hearing. You expect Marcus and me to travel up to Scotland, on the pretext of a romantic break for two, probably catch shitty pneumonia, no doubt stay in a grotty all-expenses paid bed and breakfast...'

'Er, two-star luxury hotel,' he interrupted, none too convincingly.

Kara was livid. 'And, the cheek of it, no doubt you would like us to enquire into the whereabouts – the disappearance of a certain Julius Gray?'

Michael looked around cagily, keeping his voice down. 'Never actually crossed my mind,' he murmured. 'Still, now you come to mention it.'

Kara stood up urgently, clattering the crockery on the table as she did so. All eyes turned in her direction.

'My God, I'm so pissed with you,' she shouted, discarding her dirty napkin into his lap. 'How can you think of such a low-down thing? Talk about manipulation. What do you take me for, someone who can so easily be bought?' She moved indignantly and with great purpose to the exit door, all eyes in the café following her every movement. Turning once more in his direction, she announced with theatrical aplomb,

'Make it a four-star hotel, with Jacuzzi, and you're on.'

'Now that's what I call fucking style,' a cockney voice shouted from the rear of the café.

*

Finding Julius Gray and discovering why his relationship with Lauren had catastrophically collapsed was a necessary diversion, Michael deduced. It would enable him to make sense of his own crazy liaison with Lauren, one that had veered between the quite spectacular and somewhere way beyond.

Attempting to cope with so many "bad situations" in his somewhat troubled life, Michael struggled to find a plausible reason as to why *she* was so important to his sanity. Certainly, in the strange balance of things, she was a destabilising influence at a crucial time in his life, a time when an anchor was what he should be searching for. At odds with himself, he craved her, like a gambler searching for the next bet. He reminded himself of the intense passion of their lovemaking. It was addictive. He was also aware of the potential damage she could cause, yet the thrill of the chase always overpowered the need for order and sensibility. A sort of chaos prevailed.

Taking each piece of the puzzle, and beginning the process of fitting them together, enabled Michael to see sense in his own delicate world. Looking back over his marriage, his emotional and sexual connection to Adele was, at best, a fumbling in the dark, and at worst, a protracted business arrangement. They had reached a natural end to their union. With Lauren, however, the relationship had propelled itself into another dimension, sucking him into a vortex of no escape. She possessed him, just as she had once owned her errant husband.

And what had become of Julius? He was forced to ask himself this question yet again.

Michael needed to know, not just for his own peace of mind, but also to gauge the strength of his ongoing connection with Lauren. On a more practical level he needed to authenticate all the paintings belonging to Julius and substantiate ownership of the Patrick Porter originals. This was imperative before he could sell them on. Legally, he needed permission to do this. It begged the question: who did they legally belong to?

After returning to the gallery, he sat alone in his office and turned over the many events which muddled his mind. There were certain things he knew. Julius had vanished, leaving his studio intact. Question: was his current work of no concern to him? Equally baffling, why had Lauren left the paintings untouched and gathering dust? She had made it clear that he was not returning to her house. It made sense, therefore, that he would surely request that all his valuable belongings, especially his paintings, should be sent to a forwarding address. Question: he also had to ask himself why she had not purged the house of all Julius's possessions? It would be natural for her to rid herself of such painful memories. But Michael was learning fast that there was little indeed that was natural in Lauren's house.

There were some things he recognised in the studio which did not make sense: for instance, the dried paint on Julius's discarded palette was rock solid, as were countless tubes of paint where the screw tops had been left off. Michael also counted several expensive brushes which had been carelessly left unwashed when a bottle of white spirit was available to use. These were basic tasks that a professional artist would do without thinking. So, what was the obvious conclusion? Julius had gone, for sure, but in a damned hurry. All that remained was a shrine of sorts. And there was *something* else.

At first, he had overlooked it. But it festered in his mind. Something else wasn't quite right, but until now he had failed to identify it. In the abandoned studio was a pile of exhibition brochures and supporting newspaper articles. Julius was a minor celebrity in the art world. He had gained decent critical acclaim from art critics and the public alike, especially in Scotland. The Oberon Gallery in Glasgow accorded him a one-man show every two years, beginning as far back as 1986: ten good years. And there was the problem.

Searching his memory, Michael was perplexed as to how all the publicity cuttings, stacked neatly in date order, suddenly and inexplicably stopped in the year 1996. Nothing, it seemed, shone a light on his career since then. It must have been at this point that he and Lauren had separated. Whatever happened, the parting was terrible and permanent. Michael had heard *her* side of the story. Now he would pursue Julius's version of the events; if it were indeed possible. And what of the mysterious girl who came between them? She would have to be found, and unearthing vital evidence to this end was paramount to the true picture emerging. Gradually, he was asking the right questions. Now he needed the answers.

So many tantalising clues! There were certain things Michael feared beyond all else: confined spaces, drowning, the dark, wasps and…the irrational abhorrence of faces hidden behind Venetian masks. It was this that dwelt most heavily on his troubled mind. Whichever way he turned, confusion reigned, but, piece by piece, it was the misshapen images from the Italian lagoon that began to haunt him. They lured him, and yet he had almost missed their significance. Like a lightning bolt from the sky, Michael was convinced in a flash that it was here, in Venice, where he would find them both. The lovers: Julius and the girl named Antonia. Just putting their names together made his heart thump in his chest.

It was during his investigation of Julius's studio that he had discovered two paintings that were markedly different from all of the others. These were personal oil studies in a more representational manner, entitled 'Lunch with Antonia' and 'Antonia's Lagoon'. They had been tucked behind a pile of old dusty frames. Lauren had apparently failed to find them. Michael was now convinced they had been deliberately hidden from her. In each canvas, Antonia was depicted as she was: a ravishing beauty, with sleek black hair tumbling down across her slender shoulders. She was young, perhaps only eighteen, with a full glossy mouth and dark eyes. Julius had captured her as a true masterpiece: *His* lover. Disturbingly, Michael was now aware that he had seen her before…displayed in his gallery window.

A bigger picture was beginning to emerge as to the tangled lives of these people. One thing was transparent, however. In order to discover the fate of the artist and his lover, the truth had to be found somewhere amongst the chaos of the abandoned studio. This would be his starting point. Against his better judgment, he decided to accept Lauren's proposal to value the contents of Laburnum Farm.

Coupled with this decision, his avid imagination transported him back to a distant idyll, reached across land and sea. *La Serenissima.* The magic of Venice: a place of sunlight and shadows. A beguiling jewel of shifting islands and tidal waters, of echoing passageways, crumbling stonework and sun-reflected canals. A world apart, inhabited over the centuries by those in search of these very shadows in which to hide. Michael was convinced that it was here, among the labyrinth of lagoons, where he would find Julius and Antonia. He was faced with a dilemma: just how would he find this information out? The answer came quickly. A simple ploy was all that was required.

In need of fresh air, Michael ambled along the streets of his neighbourhood, taking time to think things through. He bought a newspaper, ordered coffee at Carlo's, and eventually found himself in Duke Street; staring idly at Asian artefacts in a gallery window opposite the St. James Hotel. He enjoyed this walk, often stopping to chat with his contemporaries, but on this day he kept his own counsel, withdrawing into his troubled thoughts and the extra protection of his heavy brown overcoat. The snow flurries had arrived again.

Eventually, he took shelter in a doorway and dialled on his mobile. The ploy was in operation. His head pounded.

'Lauren? Hi.'

'You were right about the weather,' she responded. 'Where are you?'

'In Mayfair, near the gallery. Actually, I'm walking in this blizzard.'

'Are you mad? I can't see to the bottom of the garden. There must be two inches of snow on the ground.'

Michael retreated still further into the porch and peered up to the grey slate sky. 'It won't settle, never does in London. I was thinking…'

'Always a dangerous move,' she interjected, catching his mood.

'Listen. I've decided to help you with the valuation of paintings in Julius's studio. I can combine this with the marketing of the Patrick Porters at the same time.'

He caught the elation in her voice. 'Michael, this is wonderful news. You've lifted a huge burden from my shoulders. When can we start?'

'Soon, very soon. First, I need a break. *We* desperately need a break. How do you feel about coming away with me?'

'Sounds divine. When?'

'Oh,' he said, thinking. Then, more triumphantly, he shouted, 'Next week! Tomorrow! How about right this minute?'

'Right now?' she laughed. 'This very minute? Do I have time to get my toothbrush?'

Someone pushed past him in the doorway, cursing impatiently under their breath. He moved out into the street and immediately felt the icy flakes fall beneath his collar and down his neck. 'Well, next week would be perfect for me.'

'Problem, I'm afraid.'

'Oh?'

Lauren hesitated. 'I meant to tell you. I'm going away by myself for a few days.'

'I see.' He knew that his tone betrayed him.

'Just a weekend.'

He detected a shuddering full stop in the conversation. Eventually, he said, 'Where are you going?'

She remained silent for a few seconds longer. 'Ireland. I'm going home to see my sister in Limerick. Maggie needs me over there.'

'This weekend?'

'Yes. I'm flying to Shannon on Friday night.'

'When will you be back?'

'Sunday night. Look, I know you are disappointed, but it doesn't have to change our plans.'

'No, no, of course not. It's just that I was hoping to view the Patrick Porters at some stage. This weekend would have been the ideal opportunity.' He tried to mask his growing dissatisfaction. 'Still, we can arrange something another time.'

'Michael, what's the problem here?'

'No problem. I was just planning your weekend without even asking you.' Then he tried the jealousy card. 'I'll just have to console myself in the Blue Bar tonight, with my secretary.'

'Not a good idea, on both accounts,' she said, her voice hardened. Then she softened. 'Look, I have to go to see Maggie, OK? When I return you can whisk me off to anywhere you fancy.'

'I've chosen, actually.'

'I like a man who makes decisions, although your previous one was not so good. Where are we going?' Her voice wavered with excitement.

His mouth suddenly went dry, and he felt his heart start to leap with more intensity. 'Italy. I thought Venice.'

He waited for what appeared an eternity. 'Lauren, are you still there?'

Eventually, she found an answer. 'Yes, Michael. I'm still here. I cannot possibly go to Venice, is that understood? It is simply not appropriate.'

'Not *appropriate*?'

'I'll call you when I get home,' she replied. Her tone was cold and transparently agitated.

With that the line went silent.

Michael switched off his mobile, and jammed his hands in his pockets. He shook his head, momentarily taken aback by the manner in which she had abruptly ended their conversation. Was it really so great a surprise though? He quickened his pace in the direction of the gallery. Her response was *exactly* what he had anticipated. It told him everything he had long suspected.

CHAPTER FIVE

Later that afternoon Michael had a meeting with his solicitor which lasted an hour.

The matrimonial complications were spelt out to him in no uncertain terms. His wife, Adele, had instructed her side to reach for the sky and demand whatever she felt she was entitled to, without regard to his considerable achievements and damned hard work in building their wealth. He believed this was an expertise that had created their empire from scratch, and her abject failure to acknowledge his true value in what they had accomplished over the years was hard for him to accept. But that was the reality of divorce. Grab what you could, and damn the consequences.

His solicitor was blunt and to the point. 'As it stands, Michael, I'm afraid Adele is out to ruin you. She has filed for divorce.'

'On what grounds..?'

'Irreconcilable differences. In other words, the gradual breakdown of your marriage, I'm afraid.'

'Is that it?'

'Hardly a small matter, as far as the courts are concerned. Do you want to contest it?'

Michael stared back across the wide mahogany desk with its clutter of files and saw a neat bespectacled man by the name of Mr Plumb, whom he had known for over twenty years. He was completely bald but still insisted in dragging a few wisps of hair across the top of his shiny head. It was almost comical but Michael didn't feel like laughing.

Instead, his thoughts were heavy. He retorted, 'Damn right, I do wish to contest it, vigorously.'

Mr Plumb puffed out his chest. 'Do you have sufficient grounds of your own?'

'I believe so. I want to counter-file for divorce.'

The solicitor leaned forward, narrowing his eyes. 'Citing?'

Michael remembered Adele's snide inference regarding '*someone else*'. He almost spat the word out. 'Adultery.'

Later that same afternoon, Michael had a discussion with his accountants on the telephone, finding out his position with regard to the break-up of the partnership and the effect of Capital Gains Tax on their joint homes and the business assets. It was a horrendous picture, too big to grasp at this late hour, and he longed for a large gin and tonic. It had been an eventful day, one of many surprises. But the impending financial disasters which awaited him from the conflict with Adele somehow diminished beside the magnitude of the journey that now confronted him with Lauren.

He decided to act swiftly and decisively. Even though he knew it was imperative to sort out their financial differences, Adele would have to wait. The mechanics of divorce was a slow and laborious process. It couldn't be rushed. It was the equivalent of attempting to turn an oil tanker at sea. It took forever. He wouldn't normally allow himself to be distracted from business (Adele had often complained about him always putting the gallery first. "This obsession", she called it). But hell, let her stew, he concluded rather rashly, with little regard to Mr Plumb's words: deal or no deal.

For now though, Michael had elected to search and examine the studio of Julius Gray. He was sure that vital clues would surface from here. After that a trip to Venice (*Not appropriate, Lauren had said*) which he hoped would enable him to make contact with Julius, thus allaying his worst fears: if Julius was alive, then, and only then, could he and Lauren begin a healthy relationship built on a solid foundation of trust. In his opinion, they currently collided like two exhausted prize-fighters hanging desperately on to each other in order to survive a contest, winner taking all. For Michael, at least, this was not the way forward. He was already feeling battered, and virtually defeated.

There was something else which nagged at him too, but it wouldn't surface, however hard he tried to visualise it. Only one option was clear to him: visit Laburnum Farm whilst Lauren was in Ireland. He wanted to survey the territory on which he would be forced to navigate the thin channels which separated the truth from the lies.

From behind his desk, he leaned forward and punched the intercom button which connected to the gallery.

'Kara. Would you get me the phone number for Agnes Olivetti? She is curator at the Gallery Academia Dorsoduro in Venice.' He checked his watch: 'Almost closing time. Fancy joining me for a celebratory drink?'

'What are we celebrating?'

He raised his eyebrows. 'Good fortune, perhaps. Maybe bankruptcy. The vanity of alter-egos. Take your pick. My accountant tells me I face possible ruin. My solicitor tells me I'm between a rock and a hard place. Given the circumstances, I intend to drown my sorrows in a bottle of fine champagne.'

Kara drew breath. 'Hold on, hold on a minute! I start the day with a fry- up and finish up with a glass of bubbly. I have to guard my reputation here. People will begin a whispering campaign if they keep seeing us together. You know: no smoke without fire.' He could hear her giggling quietly to herself.

'Your reputation is safe with me, Kara.' Michael decided to lighten the mood, 'Although I have had my fantasies.'

He could hear her muffled snort.

'Besides, it would never work,' he continued. 'Although Marcus and you are perfectly suited, I would hate to damage his fragile ego if he knew you would always compare us. There would simply be no contest.'

'Hah, in your dreams!'

'A fair assessment.' He felt somewhat chastised but had enjoyed the banter nonetheless. He didn't want to overstep the boundary between them and changed the subject. 'Listen, Kara, meet me in the Blue Bar in fifteen minutes and bring the file on the works of Patrick Porter, including all the colour images of his paintings we've sold over the years. I think I've found out who Antonia is.'

'Antonia? Who is Antonia?'

Michael delayed his answer for a few seconds. 'The mistress of Julius Gray. I'll explain it all in good time. In particular, bring me all you have on the work entitled 'A' on green silk.'

'I remember. If I recall correctly, we sold it in December last year.'

'I'm not sure how I know this,' he said, his voice rising in pitch, 'but the girl featured in that painting is called Antonia. And before you ask, no, I'm not going crazy. I have more than a hunch about this.'

*

The bar was hectic and noisy and hip. Jay-Z pounded from the sound system. *Everyone* in London, it appeared, wanted a drink. Michael consumed the last mouthful of his iced gin and tonic, the second since meeting up with Kara in the club.

'Another?' he suggested. He knew he was on a self-destruct high, despite his anger toward Lauren, which was twofold: first, her brusque reaction to a trip to Venice, which he had anticipated, and second, her unannounced departure to Ireland, without considering him. For the first time, he sensed her life independent from his, and it bothered him. On the one hand, he hardly knew her; on the other he wanted to possess her. *All of her.* It signalled another notch up on his growing anger.

He realised his involvement in their relationship was all-consuming and he was jealous that she had reached an ordinary decision without his knowledge. It was certainly not unreasonable for her to undertake such a basic decision, but he found it a kind of betrayal. Frankly, he was pissed off.

The third round of drinks appeared on the table as if by magic.

'Fed up waiting,' Kara announced, returning from the bar. 'You do that a lot just recently, ranting on and on and then drifting off.'

'Do I?'

'Yes. It's called pre-occupation, *or*, in your case terminal obsession.'

'Christ. Sorry, Kara. Kick me next time.'

'I did, actually. And you owe me sixteen pounds for the drinks. I got the last round as well.' While drinking, Kara texted Marcus to say she was going to be late home. That would keep him on his toes.

Michael fumbled in his pocket, found a twenty pound note, gave it to her, and then returned to the matter in hand. 'Did you bring the file?'

She smiled forgivingly. 'I have the file. Who is this girl called Antonia?'

Michael took the folder and emptied the contents on the table, searching for a particular image. 'Here it is, here it is.' He pointed to a photo of *'A' on green silk'*. 'We sold this painting, and the title appeared genuine, written on the reverse of the canvas. At the time, the lady who originally sold us the work insisted the 'A' stood for Athena. She said that she and her late husband had acquired the painting from Christies. It was they who had apparently given her this information, so we have no reason to doubt the story. In fact, we know from several paintings over the years that Athena featured in many canvases. She was obviously a favourite model of the artist, rather like Sir William Russell Flint and his muse, Cecilia Green.'

'So?' Kara nudged him with her foot.

'Well,' he continued, ignoring her little dig. 'The information was wrong, or, the name Athena was made up simply as a marketing tool. Who really knows? Whatever her name may or may not have been, up to now we do not actually have her true identity. Usually, an artist would employ a professional model, or use a girlfriend. She may have been a penniless student. But, I have seen her before, just recently, painted by a different artist. Namely Julius Gray. Her actual name is Antonia.'

Kara shifted uneasily in her chair. 'How do you know it is the same girl?'

'I don't, not at this stage. But I am convinced it is. The similarity is uncanny, almost impossible to ignore. I also know that *'A' on green silk* was painted in Venice; I recall seeing the location handwritten as an inscription on the reverse of the canvas. It was at a house on San Marco. Now, this is where it gets intriguing. When I visited the studio of Julius Gray, I inadvertently discovered two paintings of the *same* girl, both painted in Venice. Coincidence? No chance. I stake my reputation on this.'

'Where is this leading, Michael?'

He tried to remain patient with her, knowing that this theory of his was bizarre, but not impossible. He somehow had to show that this girl modelled for both Patrick Porter and Julius Gray. It wasn't going to be easy.

'Well?' Kara said.

He could see that he had her full attention and knew Kara was now fascinated by the weird scenario unravelling slowly before her.

He took time out to finish his drink. 'I believe there is a strong   connection between the disappearance of Julius and this mysterious girl. He referred to her as Antonia, and these two paintings were intimate studies of love and shared moments. The paintings were hidden, and not for the attention of anyone else, particularly Lauren. I believe that Antonia and he were lovers, and that they escaped together, possibly to Venice. I am even more convinced because when I asked Lauren to accompany me there, on the pretext of a holiday, her response was decidedly icy. Why would that be?'

'Beats me,' Kara replied. 'Unless, as you say, Lauren is aware that they are in fact living there, and it is too painful to bear.'

Michael looked long and hard at Kara. 'Exactly. Or…'

She shrugged her shoulders. 'Or?'

'Call me paranoid. But Lauren has a past to hide, one she cannot exorcise. It torments her. It overshadows everything she does. And get this. She often refers to her husband in the past tense. Suppose Julius is dead?'

Kara held up her hands. 'Hey, hold on a minute, you're in the realms of make believe now. For instance, you'll be relieved to know that a trip to Scotland isn't necessary after all. *Yes, thank you, Kara, for saving me the cost of a luxury weekend in… oh, forget it!*' She smiled. 'Anyway, I checked up on Julius using the internet. The Oberon gallery is closed, owing to the death of the owner. However, other enquiries suggest that Julius was a modestly successful artist in Glasgow, with no huge following. He was a likeable artist who simply stopped exhibiting in the city. Two other galleries lost contact and evidently didn't lose any sleep over it. Artists move on, full stop. I found no sinister cover-up, if that is what you were looking for. Chill out, Michael; you have nothing to go on to substantiate such wild accusations.'

'Well, something isn't right. Think about it. Patrick Porter is dead, Julius Gray is missing. Just suppose...'

Kara shrugged again. 'Perhaps Lauren just wished him dead – it is not uncommon. Many women who feel betrayed simply cut the man from their lives. It's called survival, keeping your sanity, your dignity, whatever. It is easier to think of him as gone, in the past, no longer alive.'

Michael scanned the various brochures and newspaper cuttings on Patrick Porter and downed the last dregs of his drink. He decided on a taxi home and summoned a waiter, requesting the champagne that he had first enticed Kara with earlier in the evening. His car could stay put.

'Just a glass,' Kara said, as the waiter popped the cork. 'What are we celebrating?'

'A toast,' Michael announced, clinking her raised glass, 'to absent friends, absent wives, absent artists... and accidental lovers who don't give a fuck for anyone.' He leaned forward and kissed her hard on the mouth.

Startled, Kara pulled away. He saw the confusion in her eyes. Damn. He had overstepped the mark in their relationship. To his relief, she seemed to sympathise with his embarrassment. Taking his hand, she whispered, 'Marcus cares about me. He looks out for me. But who looks out for you? Be careful, Michael.

Maybe there are things best not tampered with. Lauren is a survivor, whatever you think. Her world is unbalanced, and, frankly, you are tilting the wrong way. Leave it alone. Don't go there.' She squeezed his arm reassuringly. 'Please.'

Melancholy threatened to overwhelm him. 'I'm falling down whichever way I turn. Where else is there to go?'

Kara stood to go, hesitated, and then returned his crestfallen gaze. 'I'll call a taxi for you. Go home, Michael, and sleep off the drink. In the morning, you'll feel a whole lot better.' She dialled into her mobile and booked a cab. Searching her pockets, she retrieved a piece of folded paper and passed him the information he had requested on Agatha Olivetti. She smiled, 'And just for the record, someone is looking out for you.'

She stooped forward and kissed him on the lips, prolonging the sensation. She, too, was tipsy.

As he departed, seriously worse for wear, Kara giggled. It was a fun night, just what she needed. Gathering her handbag, she followed the sign to the ladies room, which was at the end of an infinite descent of steps into the bowels of the club. Her footsteps echoed eerily on the tiled floor.

Once inside, two girls rudely brushed past her, leaving her alone. She took a moment to adjust her lipstick in the basin mirror and put a comb through her hair. The lighting was unforgiving and accentuated the darkening bags under her eyes. She groaned. It was a losing battle, she conceded: the aging process was taking hold, girl. *Best start saving up for the cosmetic surgery and Botox injections*...an inevitable date with destiny, for sure. It made her laugh, this notion, although secretly, she wanted to cry. It was hard being a woman. She felt crushed.

Kara settled into one of the empty cubicles and locked the door. Suddenly, tiredness overtook her. The intoxicating mix of drinks kicked in, making her head spin. The heat made her perspire. From above, the heavy music thumped through the floor and rattled her brain. *Far too old for this,* she rebuked herself. Just then, the rhythmic beat grew louder as the outside door swung open and then closed. She was aware of someone else in the room, but their movement was furtive, as quiet as a church mouse. This spooked her. Then, just as suddenly, the music bashed out and diminished once again. She was alone…or was she?

I need to get back home, to my beautiful bed, she thought.

Kara adjusted her dress, flushed the toilet and exited the cubicle. Turning to face the washbasin, her blood ran icy cold in an instant. She stood transfixed, rooted to the spot. She blinked. How was this possible? She blinked again, making sure the drink wasn't playing tricks on her.

What in Hell's name was this?

Scrawled across the mirror, the very mirror she had used only a few seconds ago was a single most God awful word written in red lipstick:

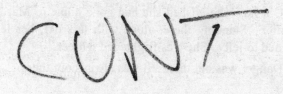

Kara burst into tears. Recovering her wits, she grabbed her handbag and ran frantically for the exit. Her legs wobbled as she climbed the steps. She was breathless; it was if someone had punched all the air from her lungs. Upstairs, she glanced around at the sea of faces, all strangers.

Not all. One of them knew her. One of them was after her.

With her last reserves of strength, Kara searched out the manager and confronted him. Quick words were exchanged. At one point, Kara shoved him in annoyance and then hustled him downstairs, forcing him into the ladies room. The shock of seeing the message on the mirror once again made her gasp and sob uncontrollably.

He, on the other hand, was unaffected. 'Seen it all before,' he said, resigned. 'I have everything going on here, fights, swearing, sex, drugs. Sorry, love, but you get weirdos everywhere, and we're no exception. Probably just some tart who caught you ogling her boyfriend…'

Incensed, Kara spat, 'Don't call me 'love' for a start, and I didn't…' She then put her hand to her mouth, recalling the kiss she shared with Michael.

'Like I said…' The manager muttered, clearly bored.

Kara stared at the offending scrawled word. It was a vile word, written by a vile person. And it was unmistakably directed at her.

Oh, how she wished she had gone home to Marcus earlier. Standing there, alone with this oaf, her legs turned to jelly. She was frightened witless.

Danger was out there. It was always out there.

Somehow, Michael slept, fitfully, awakening from dreams that seemed   cursed.   Beyond this, his perception of reality was off-kilter, as Kara had forcibly pointed out in the Blue Bar. Every hour, he rose from his bed and padded his apartment, restless, de-energised, his body sweating profusely. The intake of alcohol made him giddy, compounded by the thumping headache which refused to abate.   He checked his watch. It was now 4am.

Retrieving a pencil from a drawer, he hastily scribbled down a list of priorities on a scrap of writing paper.   Taking a few calculated moments to digest what he had written, Michael then listed the items in numerical order of importance. The first task was to revisit Laura's house whilst she was away in Ireland. It seemed a priority, but he couldn't grasp why. What was it that drew him in this direction?

Mercifully, utter exhaustion overcame him at last. The torment ceased and he slept deeply.

*

The next few days passed hurriedly and uneventfully. Michael busied himself with the editorial on his magazine and finalised the lead article to be penned by the Arts Minister. *All The Rage* had now firmly established itself as a leading voice on the London international art scene and had attracted many influential experts who contributed both important and light-hearted pieces to the popular appeal of the readership.

All appeared normal, and for a short respite, Michael found a rejoicing in his work which both shocked and surprised him. His passion for the arts had somewhat diminished recently. He was pleased with the desire to refocus on what he did best. He purposely avoided his wife's demand for an urgent meeting to settle "our differences" and spoke only once to Lauren, on the telephone, keeping his high spirited 'Have a good time' as low key and detached as possible. She was still clearly miffed because of his previous contrary attitude to the trip, and played hard to get. Their conversation was short and sharp. He was just making sure she was still catching the aeroplane. He had a plan.

He checked the flights on the Friday, reaffirming there was no cancellation from Gatwick. All systems go.

The idea was to meet again after her return on the Monday to appraise the sale of the Porter collection. Kara agreed reluctantly to go in on the Saturday, which was normally his day to work.

This gave him the opportunity to drive down to Surrey and try a bit of trespassing.

Something in his brain was compelling him to go there. It was his starting point. On his initial journey to this house he had sensed a foreboding atmosphere; unexplainable, but it had hung heavy and claustrophobic like a lingering dense fog. It was not the house itself, although the rambling array of rooms and dark recesses was enough to suggest unease – no, it was something intangible: a sense of sad abandonment. He reasoned that Lauren was living in a suspended state, unable to move forward, waiting, and as a result she had neglected her home, the large and by now overgrown grounds, and her own spiritual well being. This was a house that dwelt in the past.

The drive down was a simple exercise. He found comfort from being alone in the car. Old Hampton retained much rustic charm. Ambling through, he reminded himself of the promise to visit The Royal Oak. The invitation of a roaring log fire and a local pint was irresistible. If he was honest, though, another agenda kept interrupting his thought process: local gossip. It rarely lied.

On entering the premises, it was disappointing to discover a mock Tudor interior, punctuated by loud music and game machines. Normally, he would have left or retreated to a quiet corner but he deliberately sat on one of the red dralon-covered stools at the long bar. He was alone and soon attracted the attention of the woman cleaning down the oak and brass counter.

'What can I get you, love?'

Michael guessed she was in her early fifties, and possibly one of the owners. If this was the case, it suited his motives perfectly.

He smiled generously. 'A pint of Ruddles and a ploughman's lunch would be great, thank you.'

He watched aimlessly as she returned the smile and punched in his food order on the electronic keypad. Unhurriedly, she poured his beer.

'Haven't seen you here before,' she asked. 'On holiday?'

Michael caught her gaze. 'Local business,' he replied. He wore jeans and boots and an old fashioned Harrington jacket. His attire was appropriate for his next line. 'I'm a landscape gardener. I've come down to quote for a possible job in the village. You'll know the place if you live around here.'

She bought him the drink. 'Local as you can get,' she said, pointing upward. 'Dougie and I have run this place for a dozen years. We live upstairs. I run front of house. Dougie runs the kitchen.'

He held out his hand. 'Terry Button. Gardener. No job too small.'

They shook hands warmly. 'Sheila. All work and no play. That will be eight pounds fifty pence, please.'

He paid, enjoyed his lunch and ordered coffee. Later, he caught her attention again.

'I'm looking for Laburnum Farm. Perhaps you could direct me, Sheila.'

After finishing with another customer, she sauntered over and cleared his plate away. 'Not far,' she announced. 'Carry on through the village, over the bridge, past the church. Look for a red mail box. Got a *big* job on there, if you ask me,' she added glibly.

'Entire garden clearance,' Michael said. He pretended to read from a scrap of paper retrieved from his inside pocket. 'Reline the pond. Reclaim the raised beds. A big job, as you say. The owners are Lauren O'Neill and...Julius Gray.' He paused for effect, 'You know them both, I assume?'

Sheila looked at him long and hard. 'They used to be regulars, up until eight to ten years ago. He's long gone now. That's why the garden has fallen into disrepair. Too much work for her on her own. Besides, she's been ill off and on. All got too much for her, I'd say. The house is the same: far too big for one person to handle. It needs a man's strength to put things right.

And I'm not simply referring to the grounds, if you get my meaning.'

'That's where I come in.' He shrugged. 'Big job, big cost.'

She came closer. 'Should've sold the place long ago,' she whispered, 'living with all those memories. Not good for the soul.'

'Do you ever see her?'

'Never.' She corrected herself. 'Well, occasionally, you get a glimpse of her in that old truck coming past. Lauren's become a bit of a recluse, living in the past.'

'What was he like, this Julius?' Michael asked. Immediately, he regretted his over confidence.

'Why would you need to know that?' she asked cagily.

He shifted uncomfortably on his stool. He drank from his coffee, moistening his dry lips. 'No need to know at all, just being nosey.'

'Landscape gardener, you say. Have you got a business card?'

He was beginning to feel cornered. 'In the car, yes.'

Sheila was too quick for him, interrupting his poor attempts at covering his mistake. 'Mister,' she said, spreading her hands along the bar, moving her face even closer to his, 'we get all sorts of people come in here, some pretending to be something they ain't. That's their business. But usually I can see right through them. Now, as for you...What can I say? I haven't got the handle yet, but looking at your soft hands I'd say you haven't got the handle either. Never touched a spade, I'd guess. In fact, you ask questions just like all the others.'

'Others?'

'The police, insurance assessors, even solicitors. They keep sniffing around here. I'm beginning to feel real uneasy about you. I've told them over and over everything that I know.'

'I'm not the police.'

'Private detective, insurance investigator, news reporter: all the same to me. I tell them all exactly what they want to hear.'

Very slowly, she inched forward so that he could now feel her breath on his perspiring face. 'Nobody just vanishes,' she confided. 'Nobody just vanishes without trace.'

Michael needed no further encouragement to retreat from the pub as quickly as his legs would carry him. It wasn't dignified, but necessary. He had been rumbled.

*

Pushing back the entwined brambles, Michael forced himself over the wooden fence and dropped into an abandoned orchard, somewhere west of the main house. He was surrounded by high laurel, and through a gap he surveyed the scene. Earlier, he had parked the car on the outskirts of the village, quickened his step the quarter mile to the entrance of Laburnum Farm and then did a detour until he discovered a way in, without being detected. He now wore additional thick clothing but still it was sharp and cold, and he could see his breath panting in front of him. He then crept forward cautiously to get a better view.

The house lay dark and quiet. No sign of life. Beyond the orchard lay a disused tennis court, covered in moss.

A dank pond was to his right, the water black and still. The grounds were largely walled and this had clearly, he had to admit, been an impressive garden in its prime, with raised lawns and ornamental magnolia trees. The laurel had not been trimmed for years, and encroached in every direction, outward and upward, cutting out light. Moving cautiously around the perimeter, Michael stopped and searched and took photographs, snapping at will, although unable to really justify his bizarre actions. He searched without meaning.

The confrontation he had earlier with Sheila spooked him. Clearly, he was no Inspector Morse. He made a big mistake and paid for it. It made the task in hand even more hazardous, and after retreating from the pub, he did consider giving up on this part of the plan. But he steeled himself sufficiently not to allow Sheila to intimidate further his already fragile state of mind. Fuck her. She was too clever by half.

And then he saw it. Shrouded in mist, the great tithe barn loomed large and tall like a black monolith, menacing with its great height and straddled girth. It appeared to lean and creak, weighed down by two hundred years of forgotten history. Past glories. The gigantic pitched roof was bowed and heavy, exposed in parts by missing clay tiles. The stone walls, ivy clad, crumbled in sections, held together by huge concrete buttresses. Michael advanced, excited by his discovery.

In the shadow of the gable end, he yanked at the rusty unlocked latch and felt the great oak door slowly yield to his efforts. A yellow light shafted down through the gaps in the roof, illuminating the cavernous interior. It was like the ribbed belly of a whale. Through the shadowy dense gloom, his eyes adjusted slowly, first depicting numerous farm tools and a sit-on lawnmower, old bikes and stored furniture. Further in, he was amused to find the grimy carcass of a racing green Lotus Excel, propped up on brick legs where the wheels had been removed. Clearly, this beautiful machine had seen better days. Like everything surrounding him, the neglect was all too apparent. At the far wall, a huge polythene sheet covered the interior stonework, whereupon a scaffold had been erected directly in front and to the entire height of the ceiling. He coughed and shook off the dust from his shoulders. Without warning, something swooped and skimmed his head. Ducking instinctively, he turned and saw a bat rise into the dark abyss. In a corner, a rat scuttled in the blackness. Strangely, amidst the smell of diesel and grass cuttings there was something else more familiar to him…oil paint and linseed oil. It was overpowering. Retreating to the doorway, he regained his breath. Outside, he readjusted his sight. Across from the barn were the sad remnants of a pond, covered with green algae. It stank. Nearer to the house, through a neglected rose garden, he discovered a well. Alarmingly, he found it had been capped fairly recently with cement. It was a crude attempt, certainly not done by a professional.

Turning back from where he started, his eyes refocused on the length of the barn. The last buttress, furthest from the entrance, was also new, again, not constructed nor accomplished by anyone with building skills. And something else wasn't quite right to his eye, either.

Michael made the ground up quickly, re-entering the barn. He began pacing the interior with his stride, measuring the distance to the far wall, where the polythene hung. Suddenly, from behind him the light source intensified. This made him stop abruptly in his tracks, drawing breath as if it were his last. He slowly turned, aware of another presence. The hair on the back of his neck stood on end.

There, framed in the brightly lit entrance was the silhouette of a woman. Beside her, the dangerous shape of Bruno, pulling on a lead, growled with intent. If this was meant to be intimidating, it did the trick.

The stranger spoke first, in a measured tone of menace.

'I could call the police, but from where I come from, I take care of business myself. The dog can certainly take care of business, too.'

Michael remained silent and still, watching intently as she stepped forward and held the dog firm.

'What business do you have here which entails snooping around private property, mister?'

Hesitant, he gauged the level of hostility toward him. After all, he was an intruder. It begged the question: who was she?

'I'm a friend of Lauren's,' Michael explained, attempting to keep calm. 'She asked me to keep an eye on the place. And you are?'

'A friend of Lauren, you say?' Her Irish lilt made him uneasy.

Who was she, for heaven's sake? Had Sheila tipped off a neighbour? Was it the police? Where had she suddenly sprung from?

He took the initiative. 'My name is Michael Strange. I own an art gallery in London. I'm helping her with a valuation of paintings. She's currently away, visiting her sister in Limerick.'

'That will be Maggie.'

'Yes. Lauren is over there for a few days. Are you a friend of hers?'

The woman approached with aggressive intent, yanking hard on the lead. Bruno snarled, bearing his fangs.

'Michael Strange, you say. Odd business this...I'd say you were trespassing. I don't have time for that kind of conduct.'

He protested as best he could. 'As I explained...'

'I know who you are, you've been mentioned.' The woman circled him, drawing even closer, the dog sensing blood.

'Now listen carefully,' she said. Their eyes locked. 'Lauren may be in Limerick, but she is *certainly* not visiting Maggie, if that was the cock and bull story she gave you. How do I know that?' Unexpectedly, and to his immense relief, the woman held out her hand to shake his. 'Let me introduce myself. I'm Lauren's only sister.'

CHAPTER SIX

The story that Maggie had told Michael was harrowing: she'd explained graphically how their family was torn apart by tragedy and deception. Brought up in poverty, Lauren, like her sister, had forfeited her innocence and, ultimately, her childhood. Maggie and Lauren grew up in an environment so harsh, so cruel, it was any wonder that they survived at all. It was no surprise they bore emotional scars.

Hours later, Michael felt a numbness which engulfed him. In truth, Maggie's confession made him want to cry. Now, in the comfort of his car, he began the unhurried journey to London, back to a world that at the very least he understood. *His* world...this was in spite of the upheavals that now beset him. The retreat from the farm was hard to handle. He got more than he bargained for. Driving back through the village, he had caught sight of Sheila walking towards him, laden with shopping bags. He slowed the car, in order to catch her attention. It did the trick.

Winding down the window, they exchanged guarded conversation.

She was the first to speak. 'Find what you were looking for?'

'Of sorts,' Michael sighed. 'Sometimes you find the unexpected. It's been a day full of surprises. Want a lift with those bags?' 'No. I can do with the walk. It's been a long session in the bar.' Reluctantly, she softened to him, and added, 'Whoever you are, I had no right to be so harsh. People have their own lives to lead, jobs to do. To put the record straight, Lauren and Julius were headstrong, volatile, often drunk, but always fun. We had many a wild party at the pub after closing time. Sometimes they wouldn't leave us until after dawn. Looking back, they were a good match. Now though, when I look at her on her own, I see a mere shell of the woman she once was.'

'When did you first witness the slow disintegration?'

'When did it start going wrong? That would be easy: when *she* came on the scene.'

'She?'

Sheila gathered her bags, began to step away, and then hesitated. 'A real firebrand, that one, I can tell you. She oozed sex appeal and *real* Italian passion. When Antonia came to play, the whole village was talking about it.'

The connection Michael was looking for was finally made; proof that the love triangle of Lauren, Julius and Antonia was a distinct possibility, and not a figment of his imagination. The tiny hairs at the nape of his neck bristled. If Sheila spoke the truth, and he had no reason to disbelieve her, then a big question needed to be answered: how was it also possible for Antonia to have been painted by Patrick Porter? If his gut instinct was proved to be correct – that Antonia was the girl in '*A*' *on green silk* – then presumably she would have modelled for him at some point. How would she know him, too? And therein lay the problem. The artist was long ago dead. Michael pondered this, trying desperately to fathom the missing link which would bind them all together. It beat him. Voice wavering, he refocused on Sheila and asked, 'What happened to her?'

'So many questions! If you *are* a landscape gardener, you're in the wrong profession, love. *What happened to her*? Lust and longing are beautiful bedfellows, don't you think? You draw your own conclusions, Mr Button. Just remind yourself who lies alone with her pathetic memories.'

He watched silently in his rearview mirror as Sheila gathered pace, crossed the road behind him and disappeared in the direction of The Royal Oak. Then he thought of Lauren, alone, and Sheila's last words.

*

By Monday, he had heard nothing from her. Previously, they had arranged the appraisal of the twelve Patrick Porters. This was vital in two respects. One, it needed doing. Two, it got him away from the gallery premises. Adele was due in to conclude the VAT returns with Kara.

He couldn't stand the prospect of any encounter with his wife. His solicitor had warned him that Adele would indeed be spending more time in the business, a ploy to show her inflated worth in support of her claim for a substantial financial settlement. This repulsed him.

Fortunately, he received a text on his mobile: "Meet at 2, L". It was that terse. Nonetheless, it dug him out of a hole.

He phoned Kara from his apartment, explaining his reason for being absent from the gallery. As a postscript, he wished her the very best for the day ahead – a day with Adele.

'Shit,' was her response.

He knew how she felt, but somebody had to do the dirty work.

With that, he showered, dressed, ate. Looking at his watch, he had several hours to kill. This, then, was the opportunity to turn his attention to the earlier encounter at the Farm with Maggie. He thought about how the story unfolded.

According to her, the sisters had been brought up in a family ruled by fear. Their father was a Saturday night drunk and habitual wife beater, subjecting their mother, Delores, to years of sustained physical and mental torture. So much so, that even after he died in a car accident from drink driving, Delores was so damaged that she slipped further from the world she knew, withdrawing into a place of silence. For the past twenty years or more, confined to a wheelchair, she had not uttered one single word. Now she was dying. Alone, she was living her last days in a local care home. Over the intervening years, the two sisters corresponded by letter and telephone, with the occasional visit by Maggie to Laburnum Farm, but during all this time Lauren steadfastly refused to return to Dublin to visit their ailing parent. Surprisingly, that is, until now. Maggie had smiled wryly and explained further.

She had begged Lauren to come home and comfort their mother during these last lingering days. Exasperated by her sister's lack of commitment, Maggie decided to come to England and literally drag Lauren back to Ireland. It was, she felt in utter despair, the only option left open to her before it was too late. In their last conversation, Maggie had lost her temper and spoken in anger, slamming down the telephone in disgust at her sister's unwillingness to see reason. A farce of sorts then took hold. She went on to tell Michael, rather comically, that without further communication, the sisters, stubborn to the last, had crossed paths unwittingly. This meant Maggie was in England, and Lauren was in Ireland. It was a mess, and of their own doing. Even Bruno suffered. He was consigned to the local kennel, but Maggie was having none of it. She retrieved him as soon as she found the house empty. They were now best buddies.

It was an account that Michael found plausible. 'Will she see her mother?' he asked.

'I believe so. A kind of closure,' Maggie reflected. 'Although I doubt she will be recognised. Our mother barely acknowledges me when I visit. If the truth be known, our mother died many, many years ago. Her existence has been pitiful. What she encounters in her subconscious mind does not bear thinking about.'

Maggie went on to illuminate the way in which the family had endured hardship and bereavement, from the early years of poverty, the sudden death of their baby brother, to the brutality of their father, Frank, and then the indignity of the sisters being forcibly separated to different parts of the country. Maggie lived in Galway, with Delores's sister, and Lauren eventually settling in Cork at the farm of a cousin. It was a harsh time for Lauren. With little prospect of a formal education, she was expected to contribute to rural life. Rising at six in the morning, working a full day, she would then have to cook in the evening for a family of nine. More often that not, further chores would follow which would mean no rest until bedtime at midnight. She and Maggie were kept apart, both geographically and emotionally.

Later, Maggie learnt that Lauren had been forced into marriage with the son of a neighbouring farmer. His name was Timothy O'Neill. It proved to be a disaster. He was a bully and drunkard. The marriage, mercifully, was short-lived. He died accidentally under the wheels of a tractor. After that, because she was considered an outsider within their tight little community, Lauren was disowned by both families, and largely shunned by the locals around where she lived. Dispirited, she packed what little possessions and money she had and fled.

Maggie had fared better. She married a local schoolteacher, conceived two children and moved to Limerick. She took responsibility for her invalid mother and nursed her for several years before it became all too much. Delores eventually went into the care of the authorities. A type of normal life resumed for everyone. A certain kind of calmness, anyway, was how Maggie described it. During these difficult years, what became of Lauren was a mystery. Much later, she learnt that her younger sister had moved to England. What happened throughout those forgotten years had never been properly told to her. Maggie had posed the question, but Lauren had steadfastly refused to answer.

Maggie then posed Michael a question. It was direct and took him by surprise. All the details of their conversation came flooding back, and it made him flinch. Now as it did then.

'Are you in love with my sister?' Maggie had asked candidly, with a surprising gentleness in her voice.

Michael was shocked by this. In truth, he was miles away, gripped by her vivid descriptions of the past. It enabled him to conjure up many graphic images from a world so alien from his. He remembered shifting uneasily in his chair. He could recall them both in the kitchen at the farm, drinking tea from large mugs. Maggie was privy to where the house key was kept, hidden in the summerhouse, which gave her access to the property. Lauren insisted, after they had eventually spoken on the telephone, that she make use of the house. Their conversation had been strained. However, Maggie decided to stay the one night before returning home to sort their differences out. After speaking with Lauren, they agreed to meet on the Sunday to visit their mother as one final gesture of togetherness. It was only then, perhaps, they could begin to rediscover a kind of inner peace and tranquillity that each of them deserved.

Maggie repeated the question. 'Are you in love with Lauren?'

Michael was reluctant to expose his true feelings. 'We have become very close.'

'Be careful, Mr Strange.'

'That sounds like a warning.'

Maggie's eyes set firm on him. 'It is, I'm afraid. Lauren is not the woman you think she is. It grieves me to tell you that she is a very complex and dangerous character. My sister has been diagnosed as having multiple-personality disorder. Are you familiar with this condition? Her alter ego – the dominant one – can explode with sheer rage at the least provocation. She can be unforgiving, as you are only too aware. Just look at her utter disdain for Julius, for instance. In her eyes, he is dead, consigned to the past. And yet, she must know that he is out there somewhere. But is he? What is the terrible truth that really exists within her calculating mind? The answer lies in her delusion with people and events, which ultimately shape Lauren's fragile existence. What you see is not what you get.'

'You act as if you are an expert on the subject, Maggie.'

'I know enough.'

Michael caught his breath. 'This is difficult to come to terms with.'

'Try to imagine living with someone with different conflicting personalities. Often a person with this disorder cannot recall what they did when taken over by another "alternative" character trait. It would become an impossible situation for you to handle. This I know for sure: do not cross her. *I beg you.'*

The force of these words had hit him like a blow to the heart.

*

At Churchill Fine Art, the daily routine for Kara came to a grinding halt with a terse phone call from Adele: she was otherwise engaged and wouldn't now be arriving at the gallery until the afternoon. Normally, Kara would brush this off but she was still reeling from the horrible episode in the Blue Bar, and every little problem since then felt magnified. She had somehow steeled herself to their working in tandem and was therefore prepared mentally for an early start. Now she was flummoxed. However, every cloud has a silver lining, she reminded herself assuredly. It meant less time together, less aggravation. Small mercies, then.

Lunchtime approached. Although still jittery, at least this presented her with an excuse to take a proper break in order to buy a gift for her mother's birthday. After checking with him, Ronald was more than happy to hold the fort.

Making her way down Albemarle Street, she jostled past the numerous office workers pouring onto the pavement, each seeking food and fresh impetus themselves. Outside Brown's Hotel, a long line of taxis clogged the road. Thankfully, it was a splendid day of thin sunshine and light breeze. From somewhere, an aroma of strong coffee filled the air. Kara imaginatively flash-framed an image of Marcus in her apartment earlier: naked and dishevelled, wandering the rooms in search of the kitchen for food. Any food! He was like a grizzly bear on heat. Wearing nothing but black socks, he had cut a magnificent and an equally comical sight. And she felt elated by this, in spite of knowing that a stalker was on the prowl, watching her every move. Sod that. Love was in the air.

At the junction with Piccadilly, she crossed over and decided to try Fortnum and Mason for something special for her mum. The store was a bit posh and expensive...but she tried not to think about that. But like all good intentions, reality brought frustration. After trailing several floors, cursing her aching feet, she, too, felt the need for sustenance. Checking the floor plan on the nearest pillar, she discovered that she was luckily on the same level as the restaurant. Heavy prices, she conceded, but what the hell! Indulgence she could accommodate, but hardly afford. Tomorrow, she would starve.

Waiting patiently in the small queue at the restaurant entrance, Kara was blissfully idle with her daydreams. First, she planned highlights in her hair. Next on the wish list were new shoes to relieve the pain she now felt in her aching feet. *Why didn't Carrie from Sex and the City ever get aching feet? Life was so unfair.* What else? A holiday in the sun! Yes, with Marcus: just the two of them on a deserted beach. He would be naked, of course. Her eyes rolled. Now there was a wicked image to make her inwardly laugh. *Not so unfair!* But it was another laughter which jolted her awake from such glorious fantasy. It was a faraway laughter; one that she instantly recognised. Searching the room, scanning a sea of faces, Kara spotted Adele. She was seated discreetly to the side of the restaurant with someone else – a man.

Kara cleared her head as best she could and took a deep breath. As the queue diminished in front of her, she found herself deliberately hiding behind the person in front, for fear of leaving herself exposed to Adele. And she wanted to remain hidden from them. This man with Adele was known to her, socially and professionally, and if their eyes met Kara would die of embarrassment.

John A. Fitzgerald was a distinguished marine painter, in his middle fifties, and a past president of the Royal Marine Society no less. He and Michael Strange were old and dear close friends. Indeed, it was Michael who gave him his first one-man exhibition in London. Over the years, John had won many awards and titles and was popular on the private dinner circuit.

Steadfastly single, he was rakishly good-looking and amusing. Often, if he and Michael attended a high profile event, it was they who would take centre stage and inevitably be photographed for the tabloids. Michael affectionately referred to them as brothers; such was the close bond that existed between them. Business associates, golf buddies, holiday pals. John was even godfather to Michael and Adele's only son. It was an unbreakable friendship.

Therefore, it was at first glance no real surprise to see Adele and John together. Why wouldn't old chums have lunch together? Kara's initial shock slowly turned to indifference. Wild speculation was best left to the daily tabloids. But, in spite of this argument with herself, she still felt uncomfortable, gazing inadvertently in their direction one minute, looking away the next.

However, the natural compulsion to snoop was inevitable, and delicious. Kara became transfixed by them, catching sight of mutual shared pleasure and comfort. It was hypnotic. She again forced herself to look away. It was, she told herself, none of her business.

But then Kara recoiled as she witnessed, out of the corner of her eye, the sight of him leaning forward, holding Adele's hand affectionately, and brazenly kissing her on the mouth in full view of the restaurant.

Kara lost her appetite in an instant.

*

For Michael, talking to Maggie was central to understanding how someone with Lauren's deep-rooted complexity could create such a tangled web of emotional bankruptcy. She had alienated her only sister, her mother, then Julius, Antonia and now, possibly, himself. If in fact Maggie was right in her earlier analysis, then Lauren occupied different character traits, which in turn dictated her irrational actions: diverse actions that she was unaware of or simply refused to acknowledge. Conceivably, even dangerous actions, which forced Michael to question everything he knew or thought he'd known up to this point.

One example chilled him to the bone.

Maggie had said in their previous discussion, 'Did you know that Lauren could paint?'

This comment brought the conversation vividly back to life in his head, as if spoken only seconds ago.

He had replied, 'You mean in artistic terms?'

'Yes. I'm strictly an emulsion girl, but Lauren is actually very good. Strangely, this talent materialises from one of *her* characters. For a long time she shared the studio at the farm with Julius. Unlike him, though, she didn't pursue a commercial career. She chose instead to work on development and personal challenge. Eventually, she decided to paint alone, using one of the spare bedrooms. She became reclusive.'

'Did Julius encourage her to paint?' Michael asked, intrigued.

'I have no idea. What I do know is that she withdrew into herself, isolating herself from the outside world. Often, she painted furiously for days on end, locked in the house somewhere. Not eating. Not communicating. This was one of the many diverse personalities that took over her body and mind. A kind of craziness prevailed.'

Michael took a few seconds to digest this information. It made him question once again his involvement in all this. What was he getting into here? Warning lights flashed in his head. In addition, something far flung began to nag at his subconscious.

'How did you know all this, especially as you say you didn't see each other?'

'I'd been over to England a couple of times. Julius rang me once. He was beside himself with worry. To be honest with you, I think Julius thought Lauren was showing signs of madness. I came over and between us we coaxed her out of her makeshift studio, an upstairs bedroom at the time. She was unrecognisable: gaunt, unwashed, and feverish. In my view, her body was seriously dehydrated as well. Lauren refused to see a doctor and I took it upon myself to nurse her back to health. I also found evidence of self-harm.'

'Drugs?'

'Hard stuff – there were needle marks in her arms. Even worse, she had cut into her own flesh with a knife. There were also scald marks on her body. It was a shocking sight. I've since learnt that this self-harm originates directly from the cruelty that she suffered as a child.'

He started to compile a list. 'Self loathing, a cry for help…'

Maggie dropped her eyes from his. 'A hell of a lot more complex than that,' she said. 'Anyway, I stayed for ten days. It was a very bad time. Although her physical wounds healed, I'm afraid those concealed in her head turned cancerous. For Julius, I think it was the beginning of the end.'

'Were they still in a relationship at that point?'

'Barely,' she conceded. 'They had separate rooms. Perversely, Lauren became abusive towards him. It was becoming impossible. Even I struggled to find a reason to justify her ever-increasing demands. She ceased being my sister for a while, I'm ashamed to admit.'

*

This episode took a more sinister turn, one that he was not properly prepared for. Michael again cast his mind back to when they walked together in the quiet of the garden, the two of them interrupted suddenly by Bruno, who scampered with manic intent around their feet, knocking over several plant pots in the process.

Maggie sensed his recoil at this intrusion. 'Don't be alarmed,' she reassured him, 'he won't hurt you, at least, not whilst you are with me.'

Michael wasn't entirely convinced. Composing himself, and with one eye on Bruno, he asked, 'Where are the paintings she supposedly did?'

Abruptly, Maggie stopped and confronted him, holding firm his arms.

'Listen to me, Michael. Leave this house and never return.' Her voice held a conviction matched by the blazing intensity in her eyes. 'My sister is my own flesh and blood, and she is all I will have left after our mother has departed. Our father is dead. Our baby brother is dead. I am the lucky one. I have a husband and two fine children. Lauren has no one to turn to, except for those who madly invade her head.' Maggie gripped him tighter. 'I will look after Lauren. Not you. *You* must get away. Now, whilst you can, do you understand? It is not safe for you. Julius could not cope. What makes you think you can?'

He stared in silence, locked in her gaze, searching for guidance. He needed proof. 'The paintings..?' he said.

'Come with me,' she said, leading him forcibly by the arm.

Entering the house, Maggie took him on a path that was all too familiar to him. Eventually, they stood on the threshold of Lauren's bedroom, where so recently she had demanded that he make love to her. Pushing back the door, Maggie shouted, 'So you wanted to see Lauren's paintings. Take a good long look.'

Reluctantly, Michael moved forward and encircled the interior of the room, gape-mouthed, as he slowly reacquainted himself with the grotesque images on the walls. 'Jesus Christ, Lauren told me...'

'...that Julius had painted them?' Maggie grabbed him again, forcing him to halt his almost manic swirling movement. 'Look carefully at every one of these pictures, Michael. Each one represents a depiction of violation against the female form, most certainly of Lauren herself. It's easy to see the self-mutilation, self-loathing, and self-destruction. She once accused Julius of holding her prisoner in this house, against her will. Not so. He was the prisoner, I see it now. Her wild accusations were all part of the delusion, but this was the biggest delusion of all. She degraded herself: these canvases were painted by her own hand.'

Michael wiped the sweat from his brow. He was shocked to the core.

Unable to speak, it was left to Maggie to finish what he was thinking.

'The really frightening aspect to all this,' she said, 'is that Lauren, my dear sister, sleeps in here. It has become a shrine of sorts. Listen to my words, Michael. Get out while you can. Whatever demons possess her world will control yours too, if you allow it. And Lauren is a very persuasive person.'

'And a manipulative person?'

'In my opinion, yes: someone or something is compelling her to do things beyond our reasoning. Why else would she *choose* to sleep with these images?'

For once he had no clear answers. Perhaps he never would. Standing at the window, he stared into the garden below, which was shrouded in a thin mist. Suddenly, his attention swung toward Bruno. The dog was acting oddly, chasing shadows and barking at unseen ghosts. But now something else grabbed his attention. Bruno appeared agitated, first pacing back and forth; then scratching furiously at the base of the recently constructed buttress, which supported one side of the giant barn. Watching Bruno's behaviour made him feel extremely perturbed. In his macabre imagination, he could see a corpse being unearthed. Even the smell of rotting flesh invaded his nostrils; such was the strength of the image in his head. Like the contents of this room, it made him shudder. Closing the door quickly behind them, he asked Maggie, 'Is Julius alive…or dead?'

'I don't want to even think of *that* horrible possibility.' Her voice trailed off. Then she led him down the stairs, faraway from the prison they had just occupied.

*

Recalling this incident over and over and reliving all that it entailed made Michael both nauseous and emotionally drained. He was in no doubt that Maggie expressed sincere intentions in her desire to push him away from Lauren. It was big sister's fervent wish for him to distance himself from people and events that, in some part, were not for his meddling. It made perfect sense, except that she was too damned forceful, in his opinion. What he did know and trust in *his* world was by now disturbed, too, and he found an imperfect empathy with Lauren's plight. At the end of the day, she had asked – *pleaded* – for help, and in spite of all the complex characters that supposedly inhabited her body and soul, Michael had fallen in love with the real Lauren O'Neill. She still bewitched him.

He would endeavour to find and repair the missing links in her life and ultimately set her free. In all, he trusted Maggie but only to a degree. A deep suspicion remained. He felt she was not telling the whole truth. She was holding back from him.

Now, driving down to the farm for his two o'clock rendezvous with Lauren, Michael was genuinely frightened. Not in a physical sense, more a gut feeling of foreboding. He felt dazzled and confused. As much as he tried, he failed alarmingly to unscramble his brain. It was on overload. He was all too aware, though, that this pre-arranged meeting could have far-reaching implications for everyone. It was a daunting prospect.

CHAPTER SEVEN

John Fitzgerald and the strikingly attractive woman adorning his arm took the short walk from Fortnum and Mason to the park, further down on Piccadilly, just beyond The Ritz Hotel. The couple strolled in the sunshine, as lovers do.

They chatted intimately, held hands, laughed with carefree abandonment and fed the ducks at the nearby pond with leftover bread from the restaurant table. Mingling anonymously with the crowd on this unseasonably warm afternoon was clearly a joy for two people with a secret.

Kara observed from afar, and saw just what Michael had previously referred to in the pub, when he mentioned absent wives. Obviously, Adele had found a new life. Now she wanted the hidden treasure – her freedom – to go with it as well. Kara was incensed. As far as she was concerned, it was obvious that Adele was prepared to destroy anything or anyone who was getting in the way of obtaining her ultimate goal.

Returning to the gallery, Kara took front-of-house to allow Ronald his lunch break. Her mind was a swirling mass of contradictions. First there was the message on the mirror, and now this shocking liaison in the restaurant: had she really witnessed what her disbelieving eyes could barely conceive? Was it really possible? Had she foolishly misinterpreted what she had seen? Unable to settle, or concentrate properly, she effectively busied herself doing nothing. Replacing a painting in the main showcase window, her heart jumped a beat as she caught sight of Adele approaching the entrance. Thankfully, she was alone.

Dressed in Paul Costello and L.K. Bennett, she personified cool and sophistication. Aloof and unfathomable, she sauntered toward Kara without an apparent care in the world. Kara swallowed hard. '*You bitch*,' she cursed under her breath.

*

As he had anticipated, Lauren's greeting at the farm was cold and businesslike. They kissed, but not passionately. He avoided the obvious subject of her visit to Ireland and his inappropriate proposal to go to Venice. In short, Michael decided he would allow her to broach the subject of either when she had time to thaw. The problem, however, was her authentic portrayal of a gigantic block of ice. Global warming would not succeed in melting her. He felt like the captain of the Titanic. A collision between them was inevitable. It would be funny if it weren't so serious. He had a job to do and any conflict would be counter productive to this aim. Besides, he was angry and also on a short fuse.

Two kegs of dynamite, ready to explode. Not a good recipe for peaceful resolution, he concluded wisely.

Instead, they circled each other, giving no quarter. Even Bruno sniffed the tension and backed off. Give her space, Michael decided, and copied the antics of the bewildered dog. Pals to the last.

Julius's studio was a logistical nightmare. It took Michael two hours to organise some kind of system to enable him to assess finished paintings (those signed), unfinished paintings, watercolours, drawings, preliminary sketches, and cast-offs. Then there were the neatly stacked sketch books, photographs, expensive frames and limited edition prints to sort through and catalogue. In cardboard boxes, he discovered cameras, a laptop, table easels, tubes of paint and hundreds of brushes. Everything, in fact, that you would expect to find. Although he worked methodically and briskly, Michael was not particularly focused on this part of the task. This was solely for the benefit of Lauren. It made him appear thorough and professional. What he really wanted to unveil was information as to the identity of Antonia. Find her, he believed, and he would find Julius.

The afternoon crawled along at a snail's pace.

Lauren was the first to weaken. Eventually, at around four in the afternoon, she brought him tea and cakes on a tray. He knew curiosity had got the better of her. Before then, she had steadfastly kept herself to the other side of the house. He could play this game. Keep patient. Be cool.

'Time for a well earned break?' she asked.

In rolled-up sleeves, Michael surfaced from behind a large carton of unused canvases. Brushing dust from his head and shoulders, he emitted a surprised cough. What an actor!

'It can be thirsty work,' he announced, surveying the organised chaos that he had created.

'Winning?' She poured the tea and offered him a cup.

'Hardly,' he corrected her. 'It could take days. I have to somehow value the stock, those that are current and those that are old, against prices of five years ago and the current market level, whatever that may be. Not easy when I am not familiar with the reputation of the artist. However, I do have price lists from past exhibitions and you will be able to help as well. I'll also contact galleries who have handled painting sales. It's a big job. If you don't mind, I'll probably get my secretary to do a lot of this preliminary investigation.'

Lauren's expression bordered on crestfallen. 'I don't want to put you to so much trouble.'

'I gave you my word,' he reassured her, as he took a sip of tea. 'But I need help. Bringing in Kara will speed things up and allow me to concentrate on the marketing of the Porter collection.'

She agreed. 'Fine by me. Shall I prepare dinner for later?'

He looked at his watch, then at her. 'It depends. I don't want to get back to London too late.'

'Then stay the night, Michael.' He was somewhat taken back by her forthright manner.

'Is that what you really want? We've barely spoken to each other lately.'

She looked at him differently now: longingly. 'Yes, Michael, it's what I want. I've had an exhausting few days, and I've missed you. I'm so sorry for my behaviour. I've been under a lot of stress.'

He approached cautiously, but refrained from touching her.

'We all need comfort,' he said softly.

Shockingly, Lauren spontaneously unbuttoned her blouse and exposed her naked breasts. Her breathing was heavy and seductive. In an instant, she reached out for him.

'I need to be fucked, actually. *Now* would be a good time.'

*

Dawn light eventually filtered into the room, bathing them in a yellow glow. Michael stirred, aware of his immediate discomfort. His limbs ached. He slowly adjusted his eyes. In the window frame, Lauren stood silently still, wrapped in a white silk bedspread. Her flawless skin was bleached from the light, her hair wavy, long and entangled from the heated sex. Seeing her like this took his breath away. She was a thing of utter beauty.

Transfixed, he stared in wonder, reminded instantly of 'La Belle Irlandaise', a painting by Gustave Courbet. It was a portrait of Jo Hiffernan, the beautiful Irish girl. The comparison haunted him, enriched him.

He watched her for several minutes. Then the aching returned, disturbing his concentration.

He discovered his discomfort came from the makeshift bed of cushions, which were by now scattered across the wooden floor, leaving him a hard place to rest on. He winced, and then took in his surroundings.

In the gloom, he made out a huge oak refectory table with ten accompanying heavy chairs. Behind him, against his bare back, a massive red sofa shorn of cushions was pushed against a wall. The great dining room was dark-wood panelled from top to floor, with two gothic chandeliers hanging, like giant spiders, from the beamed ceiling. The clinging cobwebs emphasised the illusion. The silhouetted flower arrangements were neglected, dead and lifeless in elegant cut-glass vases atop the table. The smell from stagnant water hung pungent in the air.

Shifting his weight, Michael sat upright against the sofa. Lauren had not moved, unaware of his silent awakening. Looking round still further, his eyes alighted upon the impressive paintings adorning the walls. He counted twelve in total. Then it hit him.

'My God,' he whispered his eyes wide with excitement. She then turned in his direction, almost with a telepathic anticipation of his reaction. Her smile was triumphant.

The paintings were sumptuous and grand and expansive. Each one depicted a young sexually-charged woman, captured in elegant poses; some half-naked, others draped in beautiful and exotic gowns. The inspirational brushstrokes, free flowing and commanding, were reminiscent of great artists of the past: Rossetti, George Frederic Watts, and Whistler. The glazing technique which the artist had employed gave each canvas an effervescent glow, bringing alive each character's fine portrayal; mystical, visionary and perfect. Here was a connection between the sexual and the divine. The paintings contained the three themes of Symbolism: Death. Sleep. Erotic Impulse. Michael was unsettled, and a little overawed. What he saw was a magnificent obsession: An artist at the height of his powers. He instantly recognised the main sitter in *all* of the portraits. Antonia.

Hung grandly before him, in all their individual glory, was the collective work of the deceased artist, Patrick Porter.

For a fleeting moment, time became suspended as the air was sucked from Michael's lungs. He stood and marvelled at the splendour in silence.

'Well?' Lauren murmured, searching his face for pain or pleasure. She came quietly to stand by his side.

Catching her appreciative gaze, Michael took her hand and slowly examined the exquisite paintings, staring intently at the sheer beauty and poetry contained in each commanding brushstroke.

'Simply breathtaking,' Michael said. He had the eye of an expert. 'A truly great artist and a wonderful collection. How lucky you are.'

'A curse, actually.' She dropped her head to his shoulder. He responded by holding a reassuring arm around her slender waist.

'Why do you say that?'

'They remind me of all things difficult in my life. They bring back memories of hurt and suffering, fighting and...and...simply surviving.'

Michael reminded himself of his conversations with Maggie, but this was not the moment to invade those inner torments.

Instead, he asked, 'How did you come to acquire them?'

'Oh, over a period of time. Julius and I bought one every year to celebrate our wedding anniversary; hard to believe that now. During the good times, he earned a very decent living, and as you know, it is only in recent years that a Porter original has begun to fetch huge money. Some of these cost a fraction of their true value today.'

'Did you know the artist?'

'No. We bought from galleries and auction houses.'

Her answer was too swift for his liking. Convinced that she had lied, he didn't press it, instead choosing another path which would test her nerve. 'The girl in the paintings...she's absolutely stunning. Do you know who she was?'

He'd pushed too far.

She abruptly turned away and walked from the room, ignoring his question. It was not unexpected. She had deceived him about the "decent" living from her husband, which Michael knew was not correct because of his conversation with Kara. Also, she was in denial with regard to the identity of Antonia. More disturbingly, why would she continue to have a constant reminder of her love rival so close to home? Any normal person would put the collection out of sight, rather than parade such blatant reminders. It was as if ...but Michael could not finish his train of thought. It would nag like a bad toothache though.

He followed her into the kitchen, and tried to comfort her by offering a shoulder to cry on.

'Lauren, this needs an answer. You have asked me to sell the paintings. How can I do this if Julius owns them as well? It's called entitlement. I would need his permission.'

She broke free from him and recklessly drank stale red wine from a dirty glass, which she had poured the night before. It must have tasted sour. Looking at him once again, she said emphatically, 'Each one was a gift to me. I own every one of them, Michael. I do not need permission. I can part with them in whichever way I choose. I can burn them if I want.'

Michael pondered her response. 'Have you this entitlement in writing?'

She was cleverly prepared for this line of interrogation.

'Behind each painting is a hand written card from Julius that states they are a gift to me. I have verified this with a solicitor. Therefore, I have rightful ownership.'

'Yes, in that case, it appears so,' he said reluctantly.

Lauren reinforced her point. 'Julius will not contest what is rightfully mine,' she replied. 'Besides, he is not in a position to do so.'

'Is that right?' Uneasy, he nevertheless pressed ahead. 'How fast do you want to act on this?'

'Take them and sell them, quickly. Can you do this for me?'

'Yes, of course I can. Naturally, each will need to be photographed and marketed to the right people. We can produce a brochure, sell on-line or go to auction, whichever route brings the quickest and best return.'

'I want privacy.'

'Agreed. Personally, I would organise a special private viewing. I have the necessary clients for this scale of work, many of whom would prefer to remain anonymous. We do not need a fanfare.' He sounded convincing, and in truth, he was right. However, the real motive for this line of action was to eliminate Adele from the equation. Organised correctly, this was his opportunity – possibly his only opportunity – to conduct a financial killing that would bring him back from the brink of ruin. He needed no further incentive. Success equalled reward: money.

'What is your cut?' asked Lauren.

'Forty per cent of retail plus Vat, and I'll cover all costs.'

'A deal,' Lauren said. She smiled. 'Champagne?'

It amazed him to see her transform from icy cold to red hot in an instant. Clearly, she had her reasons to not court publicity, and she was keeping her cards close to her chest. He was impressed. Here was a woman who knew exactly what she wanted. No messing. It was unnerving.

Michael regained his composure, and thought of the celebration toast. 'Normally, I would say no at this time of the morning, but, what the hell.' He felt the devil in him. This was his chance to beat Adele.

'I'll tell you what, Mr Big Shot, I'll go one better. Seeing as we skipped dinner last night, how about smoked salmon and scrambled eggs as well?'

'Perfect.' He didn't just mean breakfast.

Although Maggie had warned him of the danger, he realised that he needed this woman. It was a compulsion, not only for her dead sexy body, but for the dead sexy profitable paintings as well. He would feast on them both.

While Lauren busied herself in mixing the eggs with butter and milk, Michael uncorked the Pol Roger Vintage and began to analyse the mind-blowing preparation that was required in insuring and then collecting the paintings from the dining room, informing the right clients and putting on a private exhibition at the gallery and keeping all this from the grasp of his estranged wife. It would not be easy. Subterfuge would be required. For a start, he would have to enlist the help of Kara. She could be relied upon in matters of secrecy.

Silently, the cogs began to turn.

*

After breakfast, Michael insisted on carrying on with the task of evaluating the contents of the studio. Lauren seemed relaxed with this, choosing a luxuriant long soak in the bath instead. He in turn showered quickly, made coffee for them both, and attempted a second assault on obtaining what he really came for. At last, he would have the necessary time to be alone; time to concentrate the mind.

In order to regain her confidence, he firstly planted the seeds of a new venture over breakfast. Knowing that Venice was a no-go area, the idea of further seduction and romance meant a necessary rekindling of the eternal flame. Although last night truly shocked him, Michael needed to create an unshakable bond between them, which wasn't entirely dependent on just shagging each others' brains out. There needed to be a core. Originally, he had believed that her initial disdain for him on her return from Ireland would be hard to break down. He needed a strategy. Now, it was almost a superfluous diversion, but he decided to go ahead with it anyway. This, he hoped, would dispel any disloyalty which she may have begun to dwell upon with regard to their relationship. On the table he handed her an envelope containing two airline tickets and a weekend stay at the La Colombe d'Or Hotel in St. Paul de Vence. This time it had the desired effect.

After a long pause, Lauren said, 'Michael, this is just divine.'

'A good choice?'

'A simply wonderful choice,' she responded. 'I adore you.'

The idea, he explained, was to go in June, when the climate was kinder. In truth, the idea was to distract her attention away from his intended purpose of unravelling a puzzle, hidden in the studio. A puzzle, he had to admit rather forlornly, that had either crucial pieces missing or, more worryingly, were hidden from his immediate grasp. Nevertheless, the tickets did the trick twofold. Point one, she was back in the core, and point two, he had control.

Leaving her to bathe in blissful solitude, Michael knew that Lauren was now lost in romantic dreams, far, far away on the famous Cote d'Azur. This gave him the luxury of both seclusion and precious time.

Scrambling through umpteen boxes, turning over piles of notebooks, emptying files, he searched in vain. '*Just one name, damn it,*' he cursed under his breath. The unravelling of the studio was a cause of frustration.

There were hundreds, literally, hundreds of art books, photographic journals, sketchbooks, CDs, accountancy files...it was an impossible task. He cursed again. Think. Think. Where would it be, this evidence he so craved?

Frantically searching still further, he was now becoming dispirited. Lauren would soon become restless from her joyous dreams and join him. He was running out of time.

Where? Where? Then he saw it.

A parcel tube was propped in the corner, wrapped in fancy gold paper, now torn and tattered. A red ribbon was attached. This was unmistakably a girl's touch. The thin tube was initially hidden behind a stack of unused canvases, and somehow he had dislodged them. Now the tube was visible. Lauren would not know of its existence. From the evidence of the dust that had accumulated over the years, Michael was sure that Lauren had never taken it upon herself to search this studio. She had been too angry with Julius. If he had disappeared, intentionally or not, it was clear that all the rage, all the pent-up rage in their volatile relationship, was contained in this one space. She had never forgiven him for his sins. As a result, this room was left to rot.

Seizing the tube, Michael carefully withdrew the contents. It appeared to be a drawing, encased in protective acid free paper. Nervously, he unrolled the sheath, revealing a delicate pencil and chalk sketch of a man. It was a head and shoulder study of Julius. In the left hand corner was the inscription 'To Julius.' By now his palms began to perspire. Scanning across the image, his heart pounded relentlessly. In the bottom right hand corner was a signature.

Antonia Forlani. He almost stopped breathing.

Distracted by a noise, Michael suddenly became aware of footsteps on the stairs. Desperately, he rolled up the drawing, reinserted it back into the tube and jammed it once again behind the canvases. Wiping the perspiration from his brow, he barely had time to think before Lauren glided in. He said the first thing that entered his head.

'Feel better?' he asked, closing a random file which he had snatched within easy arm's reach. He hoped the panic wouldn't show on his face.

'*Much* better.' She smiled contentedly. 'All done?'

He pretended to stretch wearily. 'For today, at least,' he said. 'I've made good progress. I'll get Kara to do the final listing. Then we'll assess the value.'

'What's your initial opinion?'

Michael felt hot under the collar. He needed air. 'Hard to say,' he replied. 'At auction, there's money here, that's for sure.' Then he added, 'But nowhere in the league of the Patrick Porter collection.'

'What do you think the Porter collection is worth?'

By now, he simply wanted to retreat from the studio. The atmosphere was becoming oppressive, and he was in panic mode. 'Can I have a glass of water?' It was more of a command.

She led him back to the kitchen. Thankfully, the garden doors were open, allowing him fresh oxygen. He gulped down three glasses of iced water.

'Are you all right?' Lauren asked, slightly amused.

'I blame last night,' he said, shaking his head in mock surrender.

'Too much for an old man?' she asked. 'Perhaps you should make a confession right now – are you having trouble keeping up with me?' Her laughter was infectious.

Grabbing his car keys and jacket, he turned toward the door. She looked surprised by his sudden departure, but didn't make a protest.

'Till the next time,' Michael said by way of an explanation. He smiled broadly, concealing an inner feeling of rising excitement and expectation. *He had found the name.* His nerve ends tingled.

Two things he wanted to say. 'Yes, I definitely have trouble keeping up with you.' Then, at the car, he added rather coolly with no apparent connection, 'One point five million sterling, to share.'

'Pardon?' Lauren said, kissing him goodbye. She seemed bemused.

Igniting the engine, he unwound the car window and looked at her.

'You can do a lot of things with one million pounds. Start a new life. Leave the past behind. That's a conservative estimate of the Porter collection, I reckon.'

Pulling urgently forward on the gravel drive, he shouted over the screech of the car tyres, 'You could make a killing with that kind of money.'

Then he was away in a cloud of dust.

CHAPTER EIGHT

The night drive home gave him a chance to recover his senses and allow for a welcome degree of relief from the lunacy that surrounded him. Why was everything so damned complicated? After he had left Lauren's house, he elected to stay out of London, choosing instead to steer the car through the country lanes of Hampshire, back into Surrey, out to Sussex, beyond the historic town of Arundel, and eventually follow the road signs leading back to the big city. Hours passed. Alone, he felt anonymous and untouchable. He craved this sanctuary. For the first time, he found a kind of inner strength and fortitude which had eluded him recently. Insanity was a lonely business. And he didn't want to remain alone. Refuelling at a garage, he bought a newspaper, a tasteless cardboard covered sandwich and cold fizzy drink. The A3 at Hindhead stretched out before him. Before leaving the forecourt, he dialled Kara at her home.

'Hi, it's Michael.'

'Where are you?' Kara sounded somewhat sleepy.

'Driving back to London,' he answered. 'How was your day with Adele?'

'Best description in a single word? Grotesque.'

'Listen,' Michael said, 'I'll be in the gallery early tomorrow. Will you meet me at nine?'

She yawned. 'No probs.'

'I have a hell of a lot to tell you.'

Kara drew the remnants of a cold cup of tea to her lips. It was ghastly, just like the many images that flashed through her brain from the preceding bad days: The message on the mirror, Adele kissing John.

'I have a hell of a lot to tell you too,' she replied, but he had long gone from the other end of the line. Tomorrow was going to be a long day. In truth though, she had decided to conceal the episode in the ladies room from him; it was simply still too raw and humiliating for her to share at this stage. Besides, it was he who was on the precipice, and he needed no further burden to carry at this stage either, especially with what she was about to reveal concerning his devious wife and best friend.

*

That next morning, Michael entered the gallery in a jaunty mood, almost with a swagger. On the doormat was a solitary letter, which he grabbed. Ronald had the day off. It was just him and Kara. He switched on the lights, the desktop computer, opened the electronic window shutters and filled the kettle. He discarded the envelope in his hand and waited for his trusted aide. She came in at nine sharp.

Over coffee, he relayed the events of the previous day at the farm, omitting the raunchy interlude, and explained the significance of the discovery of Antonia's surname. In his opinion, it was a vital piece of the jigsaw. He told of the fabulous collection contained in the dining room and the not insignificant wealth that could be obtained from their collective sale. More importantly, he requested her complete secrecy on the matter.

After hearing himself speak for what seemed an eternity, he sensed something was wrong. 'Kara, what is the matter? It's not like you to be so withdrawn.'

She drew breath. Pouring a second coffee, she paced the gallery floor before returning to where he sat. 'Michael, there is no easy way to tell you this, so I'll come straight out with it. I've seen Adele with another man.'

'*Another man*?' Although he had raised this possibility with Adele in the past, the idea still shocked him. 'As in…'

Kara looked at him directly. 'As in *the* other man, damn it. The boyfriend. Her lover. Whatever!'

Michael tried to collect his muddled thoughts. *Another man*. He had suspected for many months her involvement with someone else. He had even notified his solicitor of this possibility, but still…

'Another thing,' Kara volunteered. She bit her lip. 'It's someone you know, someone you know very, very well.'

Michael slumped back into his chair, raising his eyes to the ceiling. 'Johnny,' he said, with an air of resignation.

Kara crouched beside him. 'I'm so sorry.'

'Not as much as he will be,' Michael announced flatly.

All morning they immersed themselves in the routine business of the day; everyday details which needed to be finalised. On top of that, Michael explained to Kara the procedure for arranging a security firm to collect the Patrick Porters. It was decided that Kara would remain in charge of listing and researching them, valuing each and checking the authenticity of provenance. Michael still had his suspicions as to rightful ownership. This led him to his next task.

He closed his office door and sat behind his desk. Reaching for the telephone, he dialled the number contained on the scribbled note from Kara. He heard the international tone and waited for the distant reply.

'Buon giorno. Galleria Accademia Dorsoduro. Agnes Olivetti.'

'Buon giorno. How sweet is your voice.'

'Ah, is that you, Michael? It is so lovely to hear from you.'

'It's been too long, Agnes. How are Adriano and the boys?'

'Very well, very well.'

'And business..?' The line crackled, making it difficult to listen.

'Sorry? Ah, business...business is always hard, but we cope. How are you managing in London?'

It was great to reminisce. He and Agnes went back too many years to remember. They had first met as fine art students at St. Martins. She eventually joined the European antiquities division at Sotheby's, working in the capital and then New York. For the past ten years, she and her husband had run their own gallery and restoration workshop in Venice. It was always like old times when they spoke, even though they had not made contact in perhaps eighteen months.

Old friends, treasured friends, it didn't truly matter that time and space separated them.

He took up her theme of conversation. 'Very similar circumstances, Agnes. We live in an entirely different world after 9/11. The bombings here in London have made us all feel, well, unsafe and insecure. But, like you, we cope.'

'How…how is Adele?'

It was the line of enquiry he was dreading.

'Listen, Agnes, the line is bad. Adele is fine. Can you do something for me?'

'Anything, Michael.'

He shifted the phone to the other ear. 'I'm trying to track someone down whom I believe lives in or around Venice.'

'An artist?'

'Possibly. Her name is Antonia Forlani. That is all I know.'

Agnes was quiet, as if weighing up the possibilities. 'That is enough for now, Michael. I have people who can help. Adriano's brother works in the local police force. If she is here, we will find her.'

Michael was elated. 'Bravo. It is urgent. If you have any kind of success, ring me on my mobile. Do you still have the number?'

'Of course.'

'Agnes, I cannot thank you enough. Ciao.'

'Thank me later with flowers. Ciao.'

Michael replaced the telephone, and reflected: another gearshift, moving forward.

*

Beyond anything else, he was beginning to hate John Fitzgerald. A close friendship lasting over three decades, they were confidantes, business associates, playboys, gamblers, winners and losers, Christ, they considered themselves eternal blood brothers. They shared everything. *Everything*. Even the same woman, it now seemed.

It stuck in his throat. Trust and betrayal, such close enemies. Oh, how he now remembered the "little" things which added up to a trail of deceit and dishonour. Searching his memory, it was always these little things that spelt denial: the mutual laughter that only John and Adele shared; the awkward touches that went unnoticed; the sugar coated concern they had for each other. It went on. The exclusion of others, most notably of himself and John's long suffering wife, Suzanne. The secret phone calls. Looking back, how many of those were there? Countless conversations, he guessed. Then there were the furtive meetings; too many to even speculate. On one occasion, he recalled seeing hidden sidelong glances between them. Was it his imagination playing tricks? No. It was all there. Now, thinking about it, he was sure that Suzanne knew. It was only he who failed to recognise the blatant signs at the time. He so wanted to trust her. Blind fucking optimism always got in the way.

He slammed the tabletop with his fist. '*Bloody fool! What a bloody fool I am!*' He spat out the words with venom. Contemptible rage boiled in his skull.

No longer would he be the bloody fool. If John and Adele wished to flaunt themselves in the public gaze, unapologetic and shameless, then he too could conduct himself accordingly. So far, he had respected Adele's viewpoint, agreed in principle to her demands, and wished for a harmony of sorts to reflect a relationship of many years standing. Then there was their son, Toby. He lived and worked in New York. So far, they had managed to keep the lid on the situation and deflect the problem of their marriage from him. But now he would need protecting. The shit was about to hit the fan.

In the main gallery, Michael found Kara busy on the laptop, bringing the address labels up-to-date. It was a laborious task, but a vital one. The street outside was empty. She looked up. 'You OK?'

Agitated, he rearranged the vase of freshly cut white lilies, but in his haste only ended up staining his striped shirt in the process. His mind was elsewhere. He could no longer avoid it. With a heavy heart, he asked, 'Tell me exactly what you saw.'

He listened impatiently whilst Kara relayed her lunch break sortie and the manner of her initial sighting of Adele with John. He knew she was being ultra careful with her description of the after dinner amble in the park. It hurt. Accordingly, he could see on her face that it was hard work hiding the truth. She was a poor liar, and it showed.

'What was she like with you during the afternoon in the gallery?' he asked.

'Businesslike. Somewhat aloof. She practically hijacked my office, insisted on working alone, making herself look important and necessary. The *cow*.' Bringing her hand to her mouth, Kara said, 'I'm so sorry, I shouldn't have said that.'

'Forget it,' Michael said, 'I was thinking the same.'

'What are you going to do?'

'Murder them.' He said the words without the trace of a smile.

Kara stood and stretched. 'Shall we have a cup of tea first?'

*

The afternoon went surprisingly quickly. At one point they were overrun with a coach load of tourists from Belgium. Always a dead loss, Michael concluded dismissively, more often than not holidaymakers looking for prints of Big Ben. Kara, on the other hand, was master of this situation and kept everyone moving…towards the exit. Michael retreated from the fray and involved himself with an old acquaintance from a nearby restaurant, a keen collector who had popped in unannounced. After a little haggling, they agreed on a price for a small watercolour of Hampstead Heath by Miles Birket Foster: a mere £12,000. It made the afternoon go even quicker.

'Still got the old magic touch,' he announced triumphantly.

'I would have sold him two.' Kara said with a sly smile.

*

Later, Kara took a private telephone call from Marcus. Michael heard her giggling as she retreated to a corner of the gallery. Other calls came in from the framing workshop, the printers, a client wishing to sell a painting because he had fallen on hard times and the countless obligatory cold calls from mobile phone companies and electricity salesmen. On top of that, the downstairs toilet developed a leak. Again.

Michael buried himself in paperwork. It was dull and repetitive but necessary. At 4pm, Kara asked casually, 'Have you got the VAT figures that Adele was working on?'

Michael shifted the workload on his desk, frowned, and looked around him. 'Try the filing cabinet.'

'She usually leaves them on my desk so that I can verify the amounts, but I can't find them.' Kara checked the filing cabinet, to no avail. 'How odd.'

'They'll turn up.'

'Will you be speaking to her?' Kara asked. 'It's just that if she was working on them, then maybe she took them home to finish off.'

'If I truly must.'

'It's fairly important, Michael. The VAT deadline is only a fortnight away. The last thing you need is a penalty fine.'

'OK, I'll contact her, in the next century.'

Kara ignored the joke and appeared preoccupied. 'Hmm, it's not like her,' she said, with a shake of the head.

*

The day appeared to end on a high. Just before closing, a well known actor from a long running television series came into the premises. Kara instantly recognised him and kept her own counsel, believing that a discreet charm offensive was a suitable reaction to someone who probably expected to be fussed over. More often than not, many famous clients preferred this modest approach. Over the number of years working at the gallery, Kara had met movie stars, politicians, even royalty. Never had she personally encountered what the tabloids would describe as "outrageous behaviour" from a celebrity, which was, she knew, chiefly designed and manipulated to attract the attention of the national press.

But then never had she encountered the likes of Paris Hilton, who was at this very moment standing across the street, modelling the latest fashion creation for the TV cameras, and surrounded by an entourage of pampering, silly people. Kara found it quite spellbinding.

'Vulgar,' said the actor, observing the action from the window.

'Another world.' Kara sighed.

'Would you like my autograph?' the actor asked, shamelessly.

It turned out the actor was in fact passing time before meeting a publicist at Brown's Hotel. He regaled Kara with stories of his adventures as an A-List celebrity; named the starlets he had taken advantage of, and listed the terrible insecurities of his profession. She in turn nodded sympathetically, counting the lines on his surgically enhanced features.

When he finally departed, he insisted on giving her his mobile phone number.

'Be sure to ring now,' he said, kissing her fondly on both cheeks, adding, 'You have an impeccable disposition, my girl. You could go far in theatre.'

Watching intently as he sauntered across the road, Kara was then surprised to see him greet ('Hello, Darling!') the model with an infectious huge hug and an array of over the top air kisses. Old friends. Old foes. Old luvvies. Acting to the last. Kara howled with laughter.

*

Coming out to see what all the commotion was about, Michael gathered up the envelope which he had found on the doorstep in the morning.

'Am I missing all the fun?' he asked, moving to the window. A crowd had gathered on the street to watch the photo shoot. Michael did a double take. 'Is *that* Paris Hilton?'

'Never heard of her,' Kara said, sarcastically.

Removing the contents from the envelope, Michael too was somewhat caught up in the circus. It was truly entertaining. Unfolding the letter, his eyes glanced down. He was silent as he read the contents.

'*Jesus Christ*,' he murmured, ashen-faced.

'What is it?' Kara asked, following his gaze down to his outstretched hand.

He passed her the unfolded piece of paper. 'What the hell do you make of this?' he asked.

On what appeared to be a photocopy of an old newspaper clipping, Kara read:

Dublin Evening Herald, 1978

NORTH STRAND DEATH. FAMILY MEMBER HELD.

At 8 o'clock this morning local emergency services rushed to a disturbance at a house on Clonmore Terrace, after being alerted by neighbours who heard the sound of screaming. The property, as yet to be identified by the Gardai as part of their ongoing enquires, has been sealed off as an investigation begins. It is understood that a body of a man has been discovered. A senior Gardai spokesman has issued a statement announcing that a possible murder inquiry is now under way.

The identity of the victim has also been withheld until a forensics team can confirm the exact nature of the cause of the fatality. A press conference has been set at 10am tomorrow morning.

What can be substantiated though is that a member of the immediate family has been detained in custody for further questioning. A source for the local Gardai has revealed that they are not seeking anyone else in connection with this incident.

Reporting piece by Frank Magee.

Kara's eyes were now firmly fixed upon the typed message on the bottom of the newspaper cutting, which read:

YOU ARE IN GRAVE DANGER

'Oh, Michael, what is this? I don't understand.'

He watched her shake her head and saw a tear form in the corner of her eye. Like him, he knew she was undoubtedly trying to digest the contents of the cutting, and make sense of it. A kind of rushing fear suddenly engulfed him.

She handed the cutting back to Michael, who re-read the details and then checked the envelope. It simply stated his name in capital type.

'Christ,' he said again.

'Should we call the police?' Kara asked.

'I need to think,' Michael said, and aimed himself toward a private cabinet in his office. He retrieved two glasses and a bottle of scotch. Pouring generously, he handed one to Kara. 'Here, get this down you.' They swallowed hard and fast.

Michael paced the gallery. 'This envelope was delivered by hand, earlier this morning. I collected it off the doormat. There is no address or postmark. *Someone* wants me to know *something*...something that I am not actually aware of. Or am I? Whoever was responsible for this is also warning me.' Michael finished the contents of his glass and poured another. Kara declined. He was dismayed by the cryptic message. 'I need to think...'

'What does a possible murder story from 1978 have to do with you, Michael? It's scary.'

Michael pondered this very question. A thousand thoughts re-entered his brain, swirling crazily and without meaning. He recalled his conversations with Maggie and the connection she made with her family life in Dublin. Could this be the thread? Surely not, but it was a plausible explanation.

'We do absolutely nothing,' he said.

Kara jumped, startled. '*What*?'

'This isn't actually an implied threat, Kara. It is a warning. We do not know what it means at this stage. So we wait.'

She downed her scotch and now impatiently insisted on a refill. Michael replenished both their glasses.

'*Wait*? Wait for what?' Kara asked.

'Whoever was responsible for this,' he said, waving the piece of paper in the air, 'is local to us. They have to be. That's why they felt the need to put it directly into our letterbox. They now know for sure that we have read it. We don't understand the implications. Therefore, we wait.'

Her eyes widened, and he knew for sure that Kara had taken the point.

'We wait for the next instalment,' she said.

'Exactly,' Michael said, without a care thanks to drinking three whiskies in as many minutes. It was the kind of situation that called for it. But he knew deep down that his response was all false bravado. 'And it will come, you can be sure of that,' he added.

Much to his dismay, the bottle of whisky was empty. More crucially, he sensed that his reserves of courage were going the same way, too,

CHAPTER NINE

Later that evening, in the solitude of his home, Michael thought of everything and nothing, such was the confusion that cluttered his overworked brain. This bewilderment seemed to compress his skull and cause a pain like a deadly arrow shooting between his eyes. Extraordinary images from the past few days flashed before him with frightening speed. From somewhere, the first conversation he ever had with Lauren sprang into his mind. He thought of Kara, and the fear she tried to suppress on witnessing the mysterious press cutting. Then there was Adele and *him*...enough! *Enough!* His head throbbed and his mouth felt like dry parchment.

He showered and wrapped himself in a white towelling dressing gown. Retreating to his bedroom, he took two aspirin and prayed for a decent night's sleep, freeing him, momentarily at least, from the dark entanglements which were shaping and manipulating his life.

He had to ask the question: who was doing the manipulation?

This was what he knew.

Lauren was seeking to rid herself of the past by means of masterminding a new beginning, which was a perfectly reasonable thing to do, in his view. But in this dark, muddled past were many demons that brought conflict into her rational thinking. *They* dictated to her, controlled her and owned her. It was clearly evident that the two people closest to her, Maggie and Julius, could not offer release from this inescapable torment. Now Lauren was using him – the respectable art dealer – as the bargaining tool, the prop, on which to lean. The point was, though, just how far was he prepared to go to save her?

If Julius was a victim, it was becoming apparent, according to Maggie, that he, too, could be dragged down a similar path.

And what of this woman called Maggie? The sister who appeared from absolutely nowhere and yet knew of everything and everyone, himself included. Her description of Lauren's childhood was both deeply affecting and plausible. He had no reason to doubt her story. And yet she troubled him. For all her nobility, Maggie was an unknown quantity, a person capable of placing the blame for Lauren's behaviour squarely upon Lauren's own shoulders. Maggie was a damaging force. Not to be messed with. On the one hand, he should steer clear of her. On the other, he would probably need her help. However misguided it could prove to be.

Julius and Antonia were intrinsically connected, he was sure of it. They were linked, body and soul. Finding Julius was the key, *if* he was alive. So far, there was not a shred of evidence that he was. Inexplicably, the image of Bruno scratching at the base of the renewed buttress made him shiver with the sudden recollection. What secrets did the soil hold? He imagined bones and flesh decaying in the ground. In spite of this, he had to believe that the artist was alive. The alternative was too shocking to grasp. But it played relentlessly on his mind all the same.

The telephone rang downstairs. He hurried to get it but was unsuccessful. Instead, the answerphone kicked in. He listened to the message:

'Michael, this is Adele. Sorry to ring at this hour. I'm going into the gallery tomorrow to do the VAT returns. I should arrive just after eleven, but I'm at the dentist first, so I could be later. I know we have issues to resolve and I know that you might want to avoid me, so this is a little warning if you want to stay away. I know you hate confrontations. If there is a problem, let me know. Bye.'

He replaced the handset and pondered. He was niggled. Once again, she was setting the agenda, always calling the tune. His imagination ran wild. Was she now retiring to the bedroom with John? Graphic images tortured his mind. He could barely contain his anger which was directed squarely at them both. But just as this simmered and boiled over, another thought crept in to his head and then slipped away again.

He cursed. What really bothered him so deeply as to override the stark possibility of them making love?

Just then, he was interrupted by the ringtone on his mobile. Racing upstairs, carelessly knocking over the glass of water on his bedside table, he just caught the signal.

'Hello, is that you, Adele?'

'Michael, I hope it is not too late to call. This is Agnes.'

Agnes. Agnes! He had clean forgotten about her, but was greatly comforted to hear her voice. 'Never, never too late for you, Agnes. Have you some information for me?'

The line crackled with interference, which made him concentrate even on the silence before the first sentence.

'Michael,' Agnes shouted above the din, 'I thought you should know, even at this late hour. Tomorrow I'm away on a business trip to Turin, which would make it difficult to talk.'

'Yes, yes. I understand.' He was desperate for news.

'It's about the girl,' she said, pausing to cough lightly, 'we have found her.'

*

He did not sleep. Instead, using the Internet, he booked a seat to Venice from Gatwick on the 9am flight. Hurriedly, he packed an overnight bag, booked a taxi for 5.30am and rested as best he could. The sheer excitement of making contact with Antonia overrode all other emotions. Through her, he would learn the truth of what happened to Julius, and dare he hope, shed light on his whereabouts. If he was alive and living anonymously in Venice, then, even in his wildest dreams, could there be the possibility of a meeting? It was worth a shot. A bloody long shot, he had to admit. But he never wavered in his belief that somehow going to Venice was the key to unlocking the mystery of the vanishing artist.

He would meet Antonia face to face, and seek the answers. To do that, he would have to do all the running. If he was clever, she would talk. If he was dumb, she too would disappear and remain untouchable. The door would stay firmly locked. Therefore, the softly softly approach was paramount. Although he felt his visit was necessary, the rush to get there was a little rash and chaotic, and he had to slow down. The last thing he needed was to transfer his anxiety to Antonia, and ruin everything. Exhausted, yet contented, he finally closed his eyes in the knowledge that the truth would finally emerge. He had to believe it.

At four, his alarm rang. He showered again, hastily consumed black coffee and burnt toast, and dressed in a smart navy blue light woollen suit by Georges Rech. An open-necked white shirt, brown leather shoes and belt conveyed just the right impression – elegant and relaxed – he guessed.

The taxi was prompt, the journey straightforward. At Gatwick, he had time for a proper breakfast, whereupon he phoned Kara. He explained the events of the night before and the action he was now embarking upon.

'Be careful, Michael. I don't like what's happening,' she said.

'Everything will be fine. I'll be away for just a couple of days.'

'What if you don't find Julius?'

'What if I do?' The conversation hung heavy in the air, creating a void between them.

He knew she wasn't convinced.

Eventually, she argued, 'Michael, I don't understand why Adele is coming in again. Normally, she would finish the returns in an afternoon. Now you tell me she needs more time.'

'Watch her like a hawk,' he instructed, reminding himself of the telephone message from Adele earlier. Something didn't add up.

Then the penny dropped for him, and, he suspected, for Kara as well.

'Bloody hell, Kara,' Michael yelled. 'You told me that she commandeered your office. Did you work together at any time after she arrived that afternoon?'

'No. I explained how territorial she was. I was made to feel unwelcome in my own space.'

'And the VAT files were nowhere to be seen.'

It was Kara's turn to interrupt. 'Oh, my God, Michael, are you thinking what I'm thinking?'

Michael suddenly saw a new perspective that made his stomach churn. 'She never did the returns,' he figured. 'That's why we couldn't find them.'

'So,' Kara said. 'In that case, what the hell did she find to do all afternoon?'

The question remained unanswered as flight number BA1267 was called over the intercom.

*

Banking steeply above the clouds, the Airbus 2000 levelled out for a routine flight which landed safely at Marco Polo airport at just after 11.45am. Security was tight, but eventually Michael just managed to catch the crowded Alilagura water taxi before it throttled back from the jetty. The white spray from the churning water tracked their journey across the lagoon to a distant magical city, a city built on an archipelago of 118 islets, the buildings of which stood precariously upon millions of sunken larch poles. Venice.

This fantastic city never failed to enthral him. The great mass of decaying gothic buildings, squashed and squeezed, burnt and faded by the blazing sunshine, was testament to mankind's ingenuity. Fighting a constant battle against the forces of nature, the old lady of grandeur was sinking slowly, whilst the relentless tides ensured the waters would continue to rise. And submerge her treasures to the murky deep.

It surely was the most romantic, yet doomed place on earth. The Bridge of Sighs would be the final epitaph.

Arriving at the Hotel Danieli, a former Doges' residence, Michael settled into his opulent room overlooking the Piazza and started to retrace the conversation he had with Agnes.

*

All that morning, Kara continued to build up resentment at the impending arrival of Adele. She fumed. Being effectively sidelined from her own office was one thing, having Adele camp down again on her territory was another. What was going on?

Ronald was in today and his constant chirpiness was grating on her

fast-receding patience with the world. Even Marcus got it when he phoned to arrange a date for the evening. 'Don't bother me just at this moment, Marcus. I'm having a bad day.' He didn't deserve it, but someone had to pay.

The newspaper article directed at her boss bothered her. It was eerie and intrusive. Who was out there watching them? On entering the gallery earlier, she was nervous of discovering yet another envelope. There was none, much to her relief. She was spooked by everything, including Ronald's vulgar pink tie.

Whatever she did, or tried to accomplish, was a total disaster. She was clumsy and loud and fidgety. In short, she was looking for a fight. Ronald must have read the signs and kept a wide berth. Wise man, she reckoned. Marcus didn't have the same intuition, she reminded herself, forcing a smile.

What was most galling was the bloody deceit of *that* woman. Why did Adele pretend to occupy her time with the sod awful VAT returns, for Christ sake?

Bloody Jesus Christ! It hit her like a sledgehammer.

The files.

Kara's blood ran cold. She and Michael had guessed right: Adele never intended to do the VAT returns... all she wanted was access to Kara's computer. That's why she insisted on privacy. She was withdrawing detail from the files that could incriminate her. Kara hurried to her desk and worked fast.

Over the past couple of weeks she had systematically built up a name base containing the sensitive information that showed Adele's involvement in cash sales. In turn, this would enable Kara to prove tax evasion, and thus be able to be used as evidence in order to get Adele to back down in all her ludicrous demands on Michael. If she could achieve this, the business could be saved. Michael could be saved! If there was one thing she was convinced of, it was that Adele would back down from any kind of scandal. It was a persuasive weapon.

Shit! Just as she had feared, scrolling quickly down her file bank, all the appropriate 'names' had been wiped clean. Adele had gone to war and won.

It had now become a dirty business. And Adele had come to the table better prepared than most.

Ronald interrupted her thoughts. 'Marcus is on the line again…'

'Tell Marcus to piss off,' Kara barked.

*

Antonia Forlani was twenty-eight years of age, Venetian by birth, born to an architect and his wife, a beautician. Both parents were still alive and living in the city. Antonia was a part-time legal secretary, working on the edge of the San Marco district, on the Calle della Bissa. She lived with her parents, near the Rialto Bridge. Home was a small cramped third- floor apartment. According to Agnes, through her contact, Antonia was saving her monthly income to help find a place of her own.

There was another thing. She had a four year old child, a girl named Manuella.

She lived with her parents and Manuella. And that was that.

At first, Michael was disappointed. There was no mention of a husband or boyfriend. The search for Julius looked flat. But he still had her to pursue. Surely one would lead to the other.

Agnes had been very thorough. She furnished Michael with Antonia's exact route to work, her hours of employment, and more importantly, her daily ritual of stopping off for wine and simple tapas each afternoon at the Cantina Do Spade. She did this every day at four o'clock, without fail.

Agnes, too, expressed disappointment. She was away for three days and their paths would sadly not cross. Another time, they agreed. Ciao.

*

Kara drew breath, her brain exploding from the fix she was in. Momentarily defeated, she wallowed in self-pity. It was clear that Adele had suspected a possible backlash from loyal staff and anticipated any eventuality that could weaken her position. Adele was clever and very, very smart. Working closely together in the past, Michael's wife would be only too aware of how tidy and methodical Kara could be. This had proved to be her downfall, and Adele moved in for the kill.

All that was left was a damage limitation exercise. Sod this. There was no time for feeling sorry. Working with renewed frenzy, Kara transferred the remaining files and introduced a new password. It was a start. But she knew only too painfully that it was a case of locking the stable door after the horse had bolted. She felt sick in the stomach.

'Ronald,' she said, finding him in the stockroom. 'Do you mind if I go home early? I've got a splitting headache.'

'Not at all, I can easily cope.'

'You're a star.' She managed a thin smile. 'Adele is coming in again. Explain my absence.' She turned, and then added, 'Tell her my office is locked. If she wants privacy, she can always use the downstairs loo.

Oh, I almost forgot. There's a leak in the cistern, but she'll know all about that sort of thing.'

Ronald kindly escorted her to the main entrance. 'Take good care of yourself. Get plenty of rest.'

She smiled once again. 'I'd better speak to Marcus, assuming he's still prepared to speak to me.'

'That would be an excellent idea. He's a fine young man, much misunderstood.'

Kara kissed Ronald affectionately. 'You're right, on both accounts. Marcus is wonderful and I don't deserve him. I'll see him tonight and then get plenty of rest.'

Ronald sighed, 'Marcus...and rest? I doubt that will be the case.'

*

At precisely 4pm, a young woman of breathtaking beauty walked along the narrow alleyway, across a small bridge and settled on one of the chairs outside a bar beside the sun-drenched canal. On the table she placed a magazine and her knapsack, and soon entered into idle chitchat with the clearly besotted elderly waiter who stood beside her. They spoke with friendly familiarity. After a while, the waiter returned with a chilled glass of white wine, accompanied by a plate of warm entrees.

Michael waited patiently, opposite the bar, watching her silently from the shadows. He too had bought a magazine and, biding his time, slowly ambled toward the Cantina Do Spade, choosing a table outside, in the sunshine, next to a girl in a white linen floral dress.

Soon, they were joined by others, mainly tourists, meeting for drinks. It was an idyllic scene, a crowded bar surrounded by pink encrusted buildings, faded green shutters, freshly washed sheets crisscrossing on wire between the narrow buildings, and a shimmering light that sparkled and danced on the canal water.

Michael ordered a glass of fine house champagne and gelato al forna. He knew it would do the job of catching her attention. When the waiter returned with his order, the girl at the next table raised her eyebrows.

'I like your style,' she said admiringly. Her startling green eyes flashed in the sunlight. Although she had heard his voice when ordering, she asked politely, 'Are you English?'

Michael raised his glass in courteous acknowledgement.

'Beautiful day, beautiful view,' he said appreciatively, catching her attention still further with his disarming remark.

She smiled and remained silent, though she seemed to be amused by the banter.

Michael was the first to speak again.

'I believe the notorious Casanova used to visit this establishment.'

She closed her magazine. 'He did,' she concurred, 'not only that, there is a secret door inside the building from where he would plan his escape, if the situation demanded it. I suspect he used it many times.'

He devoured his dessert and laughed at her last comment.

'Are you a student of history?' he asked.

'I was born in Venice, and so I'm well versed in the great traditions of the city.'

'A truly wonderful heritage,' he agreed. 'Think of the great poets, musicians and artists who made this their home or place of rest. Byron, Wagner, Proust. The list is endless.'

'You're well informed. Are you here on business?'

'Yes.'

'And how long are you staying for?'

'Two days. Perhaps three...it depends upon what distracts me.'

The girl stood, caught his mischievous remark, and shook his hand warmly. 'Have a delightful few days. It was very nice to meet you.'

Michael also stood. 'My pleasure.'

He remained hawkeyed as she slowly disappeared over the bridge and out of sight. A strong feeling of elation erupted in him. Bull's eye: the first contact with Antonia. It went exactly as he had hoped. The next day he would return at 4pm to this exact spot.

*

Kara was shattered. The anonymous document addressed to Michael continued to unsettle her deeply. It simply wouldn't evaporate from her thoughts. It crushed her spirit. On the flip side, he seemed unperturbed. Now he was in Venice, pursuing a mad notion of finding someone who could, in fact, be anywhere in the entire world. What was her boss playing at? It was beginning to drive her crazy, trying to work out his motives.

This brought her neatly to another madman, Marcus; and their helter-skelter relationship that somehow survived in spite of itself. He was an absolute adorable lunatic. She couldn't wait to see him. Luckily, the headache was slowly diminishing and he was on his way over to her flat.

Dealing with men was so bloody hard. Coming off the phone from a conversation with Michael, in which he badly explained his odd logic in visiting Venice, she was at the point of exhaustion. How on earth was she going to explain to him the bizarre action of Adele stealing files? It smacked of James Bond. At every turn, a seemingly calculated set of unexplainable circumstances was conspiring against her, and what she perceived as normal life. She longed for normality. What was going on?

Thankfully, Marcus, *adorable Marcus*, was in forgiving mood. Men did have their uses, she concluded. He came over and cooked a comforting meal and listened to her tale of woe. He had the patience of a saint. Kara considered the two men in her life. One soothed her; the other drove her to distraction. Thinking about it, she didn't know which description fitted which man, such was her confusion.

When she and Marcus eventually went to bed, Ronald's earlier assumption was proved wrong. She collapsed into an instant deep sleep. All night: her dreams undisturbed by her boyfriend.

*

Much earlier, Michael had finished his champagne and followed Antonia at a discreet distance. She walked briskly through the back alleys, stopping once to buy long-stemmed magenta flowers from a florist. Over the Rialto Bridge, she made her way along the Salizzada S Giovanni Crisostomo until she came to a halt in front of an undistinguished weathered wooden door, next to a wine merchant's shop. He watched as she vanished inside. On entering a few moments later, he could just make out the sound of a child's laughter from somewhere high above the spiral staircase. He then retreated quietly.

Within minutes, he walked to a small unpretentious trattoria by way of a bridge over the narrow canal, and ordered a light snack and a glass of local red wine. From here, he had a vantage point virtually opposite to the apartment where Antonia lived. He had phoned Kara earlier, and his recollection of their rather stilted chat was not good. He consoled himself with a refill of wine. He began to worry that she was not coping. More wine was required, that would do the job of quelling his anxiety. Eventually, he grew fatigued. It was nearly ten o'clock. There had been no comings-and-goings from the building opposite. He was deadbeat. In the morning, he would rise early and return.

*

Breakfast heralded the dawn. He felt refreshed and invigorated, especially sitting atop the Danieli Hotel on the grand rooftop terrace overlooking the majestic sweep of the lagoon far below. A thin haze descended, bathing the city and its colourful inhabitants in a rich golden glow. Shielding his eyes from the glare, he marvelled at the imposing dome of St. George, opposite his perfect panoramic viewpoint. Below, the first gondolas of the day set forth on the shimmering water.

According to Agnes, the girl known as Antonia left her home each morning at 8.15am for the short stroll to a pier and then the water ride on the Vaporetto. Sure enough, on his return to the apartment building, he watched as she came into view accompanied by a young child and elderly woman. They all hugged and blew kisses, until, reluctantly, the younger woman broke free from the embrace and made her way down the cobbled street.

Michael followed.

*

When Kara awoke, Marcus was gone. This was unusual considering his normal lazy morning ritual of sleeping in until lunchtime. No note either. Not even a whisper of undying love. She would catch him later. Boy, was he in trouble.

Feeling so much better, she bathed quickly, dressed, and ate a bowl of mixed fruit, washed down by iced water. She was ready for the day. So much so, she took a taxi to work, arriving before the ever punctual Ronald. One thing she was sure of, nobody was going to mess with her today.

Then her heart sank. On entering the gallery, her eyes affixed upon a brown padded envelope on the floor. It was addressed to Michael Strange. There was no trace of a postmark.

Michael listened with increasing anxiety to the hysterical and incoherent rant.

'Kara, calm down, calm down,' he pleaded.

She was having none of it. 'Michael, you – we – are being harassed! Stalked, for God's sake! Aren't you frightened?'

'Yes, of course I am.' He tried to picture her, sobbing on the other end of the phone. 'Listen to me. What does the envelope contain?'

'You want me to open it?'

'Yes, now.'

'Are you *sure*?'

'Do it, Kara.'

He waited for what seemed an eternity. 'Well?'

'It's a DVD.'

'Okay, okay. At least it's not a bomb.' Instantly, he regretted the flippant comment.

'Michael…Jesus, that's *not* funny!'

'Right.' He tried to keep control of the situation. 'Open the gallery as normal. When Ronald comes in, go to my office, close the door and watch the DVD. Then ring me back.'

He didn't give her chance to protest. He clicked his mobile phone off.

*

Kara didn't normally bite her fingernails. Nor did she drink scotch so early in the morning. Fuck it. Alone in his office, she did what she was instructed to do, except for the additional support of the alcohol. Slowly, she inserted the DVD into the TV box, pressed play, sat back and felt physically sick in the stomach. The grainy images came into focus.

The screen showed a media reporting shoot for RTE Television. The text headline read: DUBLIN, 6 O'CLOCK NEWS. OUTSIDE ON THE STEPS OF THE HIGH COURT: MONDAY 23rd FEBRUARY, 1979. VERDICT ANNOUNCED.

The immediate picture was of two women on the steps, surrounded by a bank of cameramen, all jostling for position. Camera bulbs flashed. One of the women, on the left, held a microphone. She was talking directly to the TV screen.

'This is reporter Ann O'Brien speaking to Head Teacher, Brenda Connor, who attended the last day of this explosive criminal trial case. Miss Connor (turning towards her), I believe you knew all the members of the family involved. What can you tell us about this final outcome?'

Above the din, the other woman replied loudly:

'I am deeply shocked by the revelations and fresh evidence which came out during the long trial. Frankly, my colleagues and I are outraged. It is a dreadful indictment that we, as a society, are so unaware of what really goes on behind closed doors. My heart goes out to anyone who is subjected to habitual physical abuse. It amounts to torture in your own home. We are all victims in cases like this.

People, particularly young and vulnerable teenagers, should be protected.'

'A guilty verdict. Are you surprised?'

'Yes. Yes I am. I'm appalled, quite frankly.'

'I believe you in fact taught the assailant.'

'Yes.'

'Were there any signs of violence that you became suspicious of, given the fearful testimonies described over the past few days? Any comment?'

The woman took a deep breath. 'She was a model pupil, diligent, caring and hard working. I taught her for three years and knew her family very well. Well, not well enough. At no time did I or my colleagues suspect anything. It has all come as a great shock to everyone. I really need to go now.'

'One final question. Do you have any compassion for the killer given the tragic circumstances that surrounded this case?'

'Absolutely. Many lives have been shattered. But this was a young girl, just twelve years of age, driven to murder in the most harrowing of situations. How would any of us react if we were put in the same position in which she found herself? I believe most strongly that she is the real victim.'

'Thank you.' Further jostling, and questions being thrown from off screen. 'This is Ann O'Brien, reporting on the steps of the courthouse, where today a verdict of guilty was pronounced, to the shocked gasps of a packed gallery.'

The screen then went blank.

Staring at the TV for what seemed like a matter of hours, Kara eventually shook herself into action and phoned Michael on his mobile. She replayed the soundtrack for him to hear.

'Did you understand it?' she asked. 'It's not the best quality.'

'Loud and clear,' he answered. 'Is there no reference to a name for the killer, or did I miss something?'

'Michael, I have a gut feeling here. This tape has been doctored. There are gaps in the dialogue.'

Michael finished her thought, '...Meaning that the name of the killer has been deliberately edited out.'

'That's how I see it.'

Michael thought hard. 'Put the DVD in the safe with the newspaper cutting. Don't let anyone in my office under any circumstances. Only you and I know of their existence.'

Kara cut him short. 'Wrong, actually.'

'I've got your thread, but I have a plan for our reluctant go-between. Have you noticed the CCTV camera opposite the gallery which suddenly sprung up several months ago?'

'Yeah, to monitor the traffic, right?'

'Yes. It swivels. Now, we know that the packages have been arriving before opening. If we could arrange for the camera to somehow act on our behalf, and do a little spying...'

'I'm on to it.' Kara said. She was pissed off with herself for being so spooked. She was tougher than that. Enough was enough.

'Good girl,' Michael said encouragingly. 'In the meantime, act normally. Go about your business as if nothing has happened.'

'Easy for you to say, being over there.'

'Stay calm. I will be back tomorrow.' Michael sincerely hoped she would follow this instruction.

*

For several hours, and with no particular place to go Michael meandered along the canal paths, zigzagging between the sunlit waterways and pretty squares, but without absorbing the unique beauty that surrounded him. Instead, he retreated into a world of eerie shadows and shapes that clawed at his subconscious. At one point, he halted by a metal railing and peered over into the black watery depths below. He craved silence and solitude, but there was to be none. Above his head, a seagull shrieked and swooped, forcing him to take evasive action. From somewhere, a forgotten child cried for attention from an open balcony window. In another direction, soft guitar music reached his ears, but offered little soothing comfort.

All faded into the background as he closed his mind to the sights and sounds of this wondrous place: a place of poetry and people.

What mattered now was the inner silence which allowed him to think. This in turn brought him to an inescapable truth: that a murder in 1978 had somehow forged a link with the people of the present day. People he knew. This thought now consumed his every move. The usual suspects. Lauren. Julius. Maggie. Antonia. He almost laughed. This was a dance with a four-headed devil. Just what was the secret they all shared?

CHAPTER TEN

At 4pm, Michael reacquainted himself with the girl from the Cantina Do Spade. She was pleasantly surprised to find him sitting at the same table as the day before. This time, he confidently beckoned for her to join him and share a bottle of vino, which he had presumptuously ordered before her arrival. She was delighted to do so.

They chatted light-heartedly, caught in the splendour of the early evening sun casting mysterious shapes across the dappled sunny buildings. For him, especially, it was enchanting being opposite this stunning woman, resplendent in a strapless powder blue dress and white sandals. Her honey-coloured skin shone with the vitality of youth. He imagined that she simply enjoyed the unexpected entertainment, an interlude of fun and gaiety. And attention was always a welcome distraction, after all. Although he had some serious questions to ask her, patience was the key. Once on the hook, he had to reel her in very gently.

*

Antonia allowed the Englishman to take centre stage, laughing at the right moment, teasing him when it was appropriate, even consoling him whenever he recounted stories which were self-effacing. She liked him, drawn to his natural charm and warmth of personality. In different circumstances, she could so easily fall for his good manners and strong jaw line.

The boyish twinkle in his eye was most certainly appealing.

In different circumstances. She almost felt cruel in the easy manner in which she controlled him: A crossover of bare-toned slender legs, a sideways glance. A finger to her lips, even. He fell into her hidden charms without a murmur of protest. It was that simple. Her power was overwhelming, if she chose to engage it. She would decline, of course. The rewards of the deception were too great to jeopardise.

'*You* are laughing at me,' Michael announced playfully. He had been talking non-stop, caught in the light of her eyes. It had been good entertainment, she had to admit. She giggled. Then she stopped.

It was time for a reality check, mister gallery owner. Sipping white wine, she said casually, 'We have not swapped names.'

His reaction was mock horror. 'Goodness. I'm so sorry. What is your name?'

She dropped her gaze from his. 'Antonia.'

He took her hand and gallantly kissed the back of it.

'How delightful,' he said. 'My name is…'

She raised her hand to halt him in his tracks. ' … Michael,' she interrupted. 'Your name is Michael Strange.'

His jaw stiffened. Eyes that had been so attentive were now vacant pools of confusion. 'But, *how did you know*?' he began in protest, but she spoke over him again.

'I have been expecting you.'

*

Later, Michael found himself in her apartment. He never quite expected this situation. They were alone. Antonia explained that she had talked earlier with her parents and organised for them to take Manuella to a nearby children's party, giving them an empty home in which to talk in private and without interruption.

'I have brought you here to see how I live, Michael. To show there is no pretence. My daughter and I live in a one-bed attic room, with small sofa, television and little cooker stove. This allows us our own space if we wish for it. Most days though, we eat in here with my parents. It is not ideal, but reality.'

This time, Antonia was different; she stood before him, arms folded, defiant.

'I'm curious,' Michael said. 'Who told you to expect me?'

'That does not concern you, Michael. What does concern you is the respect I deserve and the privacy I now require. My only concern is the welfare of those I love.'

'Does that include Julius?'

Antonia remained tight-lipped and began pacing the living room floor.

'I can tell you only so much,' she said eventually. 'After that, you must leave and not return. Agreed?'

He had little choice in the matter. 'Agreed.'

'I need to protect my family,' she continued, her deep set eyes moistening. 'I need to live a normal life.'

Overcome by a mixture of wine and sheer tiredness, he empathised immediately with her. It was the very least she could expect from him.

For the next two hours, he listened quietly to Antonia's confession. She explained that her initial introduction to Julius was as a professional model for one of the life classes, which he held at Laburnum Farm, often in the great tithe barn in the garden. Students would come from all over the county, and beyond. They had been special days, a heady mix of serious work and serious play. After a time, she had developed an emotional and spiritual connection to both Julius and Lauren, often staying over for the weekend. Eventually, she was invited to live at the farm permanently. It was a perfect arrangement. Antonia had found a home.

Being so young and carefree, crazy parties and booze was a big thing in their life. The parties could last up to three days. On many occasions, over fifty people would camp down, spaced out on a heady cocktail of drink and drugs and music. These were wild, wild times, she emphasised, as if in preparation to help tell what was coming next. Michael listened. An incredulous look spread over his face. His misspent youth was never like this. Clearly embarrassed by her past, she reluctantly went on with further lurid details…Was he ready for them?

Lauren and Julius were more than family to her. They were everything. During these parties, it was not uncommon for things to get out of hand. Free love, and all that. Sex was available, and Antonia was a free spirit. On one such occasion, she found herself drunk and in bed with Lauren.

'It was a fabulous and intense relationship,' Antonia said. 'I loved her, and she loved me. We were lovers for six months. But I was growing up, confused, and my feelings for Julius grew. It's just something that happens.'

She looked flattened, sad.

'Take your time,' he said softly.

'Of course, this couldn't go on. I was sleeping with them both, for Christ-sake! One night, Lauren discovered Julius and me together, and she went berserk. Jealousy and tension came between us. I felt like a puppet tossed from one to the other. I became suicidal...Do you understand what I went through, Michael?'

He nodded his head gently, but his reply was a lie. 'I do.'

'There was no way out, each one of them wanted to possess me. Own me. For Lauren in particular, I had become an obsession. I was trapped.'

'But, you loved Julius, am I correct?'

'Yes, more than life itself. We planned our escape. By this time, Lauren was threatening us.'

'Harming you?'

'Julius, especially,' she emphasised. 'Once, she attacked him with a hammer. On another occasion, she used a knife. Luckily, he always managed to defend himself and disarm her. It became too intense for me. I was terrified. One day, I escaped. Julius promised to follow me, but somehow he stayed. She appeared to have a hold over him. He was almost like a prisoner, held captive by unseen chains. It was bizarre.'

'What did you do? Where did you go?'

'At first, I found refuge in Scotland, staying at a house near Loch Lomond, which belonged to Julius's brother. I was safe there. I waited for everything to calm down. I waited for Julius.'

'Did he come?'

'Yes, eventually.' She smiled. 'It was a big surprise. They were glorious, happy days: just the two of us. We planned a new life, away from her. That's when we decided to hide our identities. Julius had always wanted to write, and I wanted a child. We planned to run away to Venice. I knew people, had contacts. If we could disappear without trace, Lauren could not find us and hurt us.'

'And that is what you did?'

'Yes. I became pregnant very quickly, but I lost the baby.'

'Manuella...is this little girl your lovechild with Julius?'

'Yes, our prayers were finally answered.'

'What happened to him? Why isn't he here with you?'

Antonia sobbed from the heart. Michael brought her water from the tiny kitchen whilst she somehow composed herself.

'I'm sorry. This is so difficult. Julius had to return to confront Lauren. I begged him not to go. But there were things that had to be resolved, he told me. It concerned money. There were big issues that I never understood. I didn't care for any of that. I just wanted Julius.'

'And he never came back?'

'No.'

'Why didn't you call the police?'

'Before he left for England, he made me promise that if anything happened to him, I was not to call the police. He said the past would be raked up and he wanted to protect me.'

The silence between them was like death itself.

*

As the story unfolded still further, Michael learnt about the suffocating fear which Antonia lived under. From afar, she searched for the whereabouts of Julius through friends and family. But to no avail. In the end, she even suspected that his family wished for her to stop meddling. In her paranoid state of mind, she found herself questioning her own sanity, the betrayal of all those she trusted and the overriding sinister shadow of Lauren O'Neill. With a daughter to fight for, Antonia abandoned her search and stayed in her homeland to escape the forces beyond her control.

Michael was not entirely convinced by her story. On each turn of a stone, every person in the equation had a plausible reason for his or her individual path of action. If Julius had met an untimely death, then a police operation would surely have uncovered it. If Julius were alive, why would he deliberately choose not to see his daughter? If he were indeed alive and well and living anonymously, he would surely wish to do so in the bosom of his beloved family. Was Antonia telling the whole truth? Was this all a charade, an attempt to show him he was searching in the wrong place? It was a compelling act, if that is what it was. How could he tell? Should he trust this girl called Antonia?

He tried another avenue of enquiry, in order to make some common sense stick convincingly. His aspirations were not high, but he pushed forward cautiously in the hope of breaking new ground.

'Antonia, I feel we've met before.'

She raised her eyebrows. 'I don't think so!'

'Are you familiar with the work of Patrick Porter?'

'I am, actually. Julius and Lauren began collecting the odd piece when they had a bit of money to spare.'

'I'm puzzled,' Michael said. 'The collection is now considerable, and worth a substantial investment value. For instance, I once sold an original for £55,000. It was called *'A' on green silk*, and featured a beautiful girl not unlike you, in fact. The resemblance was uncanny.'

'Meaning?'

Michael held back from mentioning the entire twelve paintings at the farm, which also featured this same girl. This would undoubtedly spook her and give the game away if she knew that he was armed with so much incriminating evidence. He didn't want to overcook things, not at this stage anyway. As a child, his mother taught him that in cooking the best way to extract vital juices from the raw ingredients was to slow boil and then simmer. This process he adapted from the kitchen to the art of interrogation.

'Well, did you ever model for him?'

Her eyes flickered. 'No, Michael. I can't think why you would think that. It is purely coincidental that I remind you of this girl.'

'Yes,' he replied. The tension in the air could have been cut with a knife. Michael had his answer. She had lied to him again, but what would her reason be to deny it so emphatically? During Antonia's earlier conversation, there was a message of sorts hidden in the reference to Lauren and her being "lovers." Shocked though he was by this revelation, this suddenly became important to him, but he was damned if he knew why. Like a dog with a bone, he wouldn't let it go. For the time being though, he chose to ease off: to simmer gently.

'You have my story, Mr Strange. Will you now leave me in peace?'

Michael stood to go. 'I'm flying home first thing in the morning,' he said by way of reply, giving her the reassurance that she sought. In spite of the trust being broken, he decided to believe her story, for the moment at least. Besides, as a mother she was entitled to wish for a world without fear and harm. Above all, she was free to find happiness and fulfilment, on her own or with another. It was not his right to judge. This girl, this room, this life, was real.

Or so he thought. Then something caught his eye.

'Do you paint?' he asked casually, embracing her fondly before his departure.

'Like Julius? No.' She pulled away from him. Facing her, he stared intently into her eyes. Eventually, she said, 'I can draw competently, but actual painting is a different discipline. My daughter could do a better job! No, music is my talent. I occasionally play the viola.'

'Your father then?'

'No, none of us has that rare talent. My father writes poetry, my mother, well, she acts as a childminder for Manuella now. She used to be a beautician. Why do you ask?'

'Simply conversation.' He shrugged. He casually picked up a threadbare rag doll from the sofa and held it, smiling to himself.

'Signor Cielo,' Antonia said, explaining, 'That's Mr Heaven.'

'Isn't it supposed to be a little girl?'

She smiled and gently took it from him, 'Yes, but we haven't the heart to correct Manuella as yet.'

Michael moved toward the door. 'Good luck, Antonia. I sincerely hope you find what you are looking for.'

'I will.' They kissed a final farewell.

*

Down on the street, Michael breathed in the early night air. It had been suffocating in the apartment. Whilst talking with Antonia, his eyes had inadvertently wandered along the wooden shelves fixed between the two window encasements in the sitting room. They contained an array of musty books, some pottery, a pretty spiked-leafed plant, candles, a silver framed family photograph of her mother cuddling Manuella... and, strangely, a bottle of Liquin.

Recalling this last item had made him catch his breath. Liquin was a substance used for improving the flow and transparency of oil paint. It was a medium used only by artists, usually professional artists.

He couldn't help but think he had been duped. Once more.

*

He ate badly. He slept fitfully. Venice was for lovers, not middle-aged men on a mission of redemption. What was he thinking, being here? What was he trying to accomplish? Alone, he was deficient of energy and good thoughts. He now felt as low as he could possibly go. Ghosts of the past were one thing. Those who inhabited the future were entirely different. These were by their very nature unpredictable. And hostile.

Sleep was overtaking him. Engulfed by blackness, he remembered Antonia's words, '*I have been expecting you.*'

I have been expecting you. The words sent a shiver racing through his veins. Had he been duped on a far greater scale than he could ever have imagined? What did these words mean? Only one person knew of his every movement, the only person that he confided in, in all matters: his secretary, Kara.

What the hell was he to make of all this?

CHAPTER ELEVEN

He was so incensed with Adele that, on his return from Italy, Michael drove straight to their country house in Bedfordshire to confront her. He was sick and tired of the lies that manifested themselves straight from her mouth, and it needed sorting. She was destroying everything in her path: their marriage; their business; their very existence. These were matters central to his life. If John Fitzgerald was worth all that sacrifice, then she needed to hear it straight, how it really was. No holds barred. In Michael's opinion, Adele could find a deep hole and crawl into it, never to return. Such was his contempt for her he didn't announce his arrival with a courtesy call beforehand. Instead, he banged on the front door with a heavy fist.

Opening the door, Adele's eyes widened, startled to find Michael standing there. He felt a rage contort his features, and she saw it.

'Michael. What has happened? Why are you here?' She stood back, holding a protective hand to her chest.

'Expecting John, were you?' Michael spat the words, pushing himself past her and into the hallway. His eyes darted in all directions, searching for tangible evidence of another man's presence: a pair of shoes next to the sofa, a jacket thrown over the back of a chair. He knew she would be too clever for that. He shot the question anyway, 'Perhaps he's here already?'

'No he isn't! Have you been drinking?' She sounded frightened.

'Possibly. Have you been having botox?'

'If you are going to just insult me, I think you should go right away…now!'

'Adele, just shut up. Just bloody well shut up. What's going on between you and that bastard, John?'

'This is not the time to discuss –'

'This is *still* my damn house.'

'I'm well aware of it.'

He turned on her, moving closer. 'Tell me, dammit! What is going on between the two of you?'

'I don't know, if you want the truth, Michael. What do you want me to say?'

'Are you in love with him?'

Adele sniggered. 'What is love? Of course I'm very fond of him, he pays me attention, he cares for me, he treats me like a woman.'

'Well, if it isn't love, then what the fuck are you playing at, destroying both our lives and our future together? What about Toby? Have you thought about him? Are you going to tell him his precious mother is an unfaithful slut, or shall I?'

Her eyes widened further. 'Michael, he already knows!'

'*Whaaaat*?' Michael reeled back and clattered into the imposing oak sideboard, dislodging a row of porcelain plates displayed on the shelves.

Adele tried to calm him.

'Christ, Michael, everybody knows. When did you last speak to Toby? You live your life down a blind alley. Because you're so fucking busy, you never just look around to see what anyone else is doing.' Adele attempted to straighten the plates. 'I am unhappy, Michael. Can't you see that?'

'And *he* makes you happy?'

'Yes. Yes. Yes. More to the point, it was you who stopped me from being happy in our relationship. It's not rocket science. He came along and filled the void, but I don't expect you to grasp what I'm trying to tell you. Listen to my words.'

'It's that straightforward, eh?'

'It's never that simple. Just reality…it happens.'

'How has Toby taken it?'

'You really want to know, Michael? The truth, that is? He saw it coming years ago. Why do you think he moved to New York? It was to get as far away from the tension in our marriage. He wanted to make his own way in life, rather than be forced to work alongside us.'

'Jesus.'

'You have been running away from everyone and everything for years, Michael, including those closest to you. Toby hated what he saw in us.'

He felt lost. 'When did you stop loving me?'

'I have *never* stopped loving you.' Adele tried to reach out, but he took evasive action, turning his back on her, and thumped the wall with both fists.

'Why are you so angry with everyone?' she asked.

'Because…' But then words failed him.

'Michael, I am not stupid. Over the past years of our marriage, I know there've been other women in your life. Not serious, but enough to threaten what we had. Now the tables are turned.'

Momentarily lost for words, he was taken aback by Adele's confidence. It took a few seconds to catch his breath, before he muttered, 'What can you possibly see in him?'

'More than you think. He's the man you used to be. In the end, a wife gets fed up playing second fiddle and I want to feel special once again. Emotionally, you can't do that for me any more. You're no longer there, consumed instead with business matters, which never seem to go away. I guess I'm exhausted with it all. Michael, I know it's hard.'

He laughed aloud. 'Hard? Are you aware of just how close we are to bankruptcy?'

'Of course, I do the bloody books, remember? It isn't that bad.'

He went on the attack, ignoring her last comment. 'When you asked for a divorce, Adele, did it not occur to you that your very actions would be tantamount to pulling me apart limb from limb?'

'That's an exaggeration. You get to keep the galleries, the apartment, the income...'

'What income! By the time you take your half share of the profits, this house, the place in Marbella, what do you think the value of the company will be, after I'm remortgaged up to the hilt? The Shoreditch gallery is failing and business in the West End is crap. It's too damned easy for you to take the fucking money and run, leaving me with the broken pieces to put back together again. You'll bleed the business dry with your ridiculous demands. Whatever I'm left with will not be sustainable and I will not be able to survive. Happy with that?'

'You will *always* fall on your feet, Michael.'

'Is that so?' He paced the hallway. 'Then I have a proposal for you, one that should appeal to your sense of justice and fair play. Listen carefully. You get to keep the fucking business and I will take the money. We are business partners, if you remember. Fifty-fifty it says on the tin. If you are so confident of the gallery succeeding, then you put your name to it, and I'll lie in the sun. But you'll soon come running.'

Adele's brave demeanour crumpled like a crashed car. 'Are you serious?'

'Absolutely. Do you have a problem with that?'

'I need to consult with my solicitor. You know we can't discuss these matters.'

He knew she had been caught on the hop.

'You discuss everything you need to with your solicitor. But you know what, Adele? At the end of the day, you haven't got the bloody balls for it. You talk a good story, but behind the scenes, there isn't the courage, expertise or gumption to do anything about it.'

'Get out...*now*!'

Michael was in full steam. 'You're pathetic, Adele. I know your game, your little plan. Don't think that I'm not watching over your shoulder, because I know every dirty trick you're trying to pull, including tampering with the computer files. Just remember, if I go down, you go down. You need this business to survive, just as I need it to. You say you're my equal, so here is your golden opportunity to prove you can do the job. The prospect of success is almost beyond a joke. You'd be finished within a year.'

'Please, please go.'

He put his face close to hers, and spat the words, 'A real pleasure. Think on what I've said. You always lived in my shadow, Adele. And do you know why? I'll enlighten you, because at the end of the day, you had nowhere else to go to and hide behind. You had nothing to offer anyone. Not then. Not now. Being with me just fed your ego. Beyond that, you are of no consequence.'

Adele fumed. 'I'll see you in court. I'll get what I'm entitled to, you'll see. The law's on my side.'

Michael turned on his heels and made for his car. 'You'll get what you are entitled to; I'll make sure of that. Take my challenge, I just dare you. I'll take the botox.'

*

Kara had made excellent progress with the Traffic Division of the Greater London Council. A very nice and accommodating young man listened to her tale of woe on the telephone, which was, in essence, a complete cock and bull story from beginning to end. She almost fluttered her eyelids as she spoke.

She needed to fabricate a story which he had to have empathy with, or else her ploy would soon fall down. Her plan involved deception, which meant she would never go to heaven and meet Brad Pitt. Oh, well, putting that aside…she carefully explained to this guy that over the past month there had been a spate of attempted break-ins at the gallery. More a case of mindless vandalism, she added, but it scared her, being the only girl on the premises etc, etc. On four occasions now, she emphasised to him, one of the small glass panels in the entrance had been smashed. Therefore, every time she organised a glazier to repair the damage, lo and behold a few days later, the glass was broken again. She sighed helplessly, telling him the police were useless, undermanned, and far too busy to consider her plight. In addition, the cost of repair was down to the gallery, owing to the excess on the insurance policy. In other words, there was no one to help, no one to care...no one to assist a damsel in distress...*unless*. Then she waited, breathlessly...

Minutes ticked by. Eventually, he came back to her, and gallantly agreed that something could be done. His superiors had given the nod. He went on to state that it was not normal practice to use council property in this way, but it was possible, in exceptional circumstances, to use the camera sparingly, within a certain time frame. He would need to speak to the local police, for final approval. His suggestion was for the camera to be swivelled onto the gallery entrance each day for five days between the hours of 6am and 9am. It was the best he could offer at such short notice.

Bingo. Kara stressed just what a knight in shining armour he was. She gushed a little bit further, just to make sure he wouldn't think of letting her down, then made her excuses ('so much glass to sweep up!') to terminate the conversation before she was found out as a fraudster, and sent to the Tower. His name was Kevin, she discovered. Hmm, there was a certain ring to it: Kevin and Kara. God, she was good at this deception lark. She even teased him to believe in the delusion that he could order the windscreen vinyl nameplate for his racy Ford Fiesta, now that they had become an item. Dream on, Kevin. Oh, how she hated herself for such cruelty. Needs must.

Kevin promised to get back to her within two hours, and bless him, he did. From tomorrow morning, he explained, they had action stations. More seriously, Kara felt reassured that she was able to contribute towards discovering who was behind the mystery envelopes found on the doorstep. She felt threatened and intimidated, even though they had not been personally addressed to her. Kevin slipped from her mind.

Somebody was playing a strange game. Although effectively outside the loop, Kara increasingly felt a danger in the air, and, more scarily, an unseen hand drawing her closer in. This, frankly, terrified her. In order to understand it, she would need to learn how to fight. And fast.

And where was Michael when you needed him? What was going on? This little separation, with him gallivanting abroad, was making her feel vulnerable. He was acting impulsively, and irrationally, in her opinion. All was wrong in the world ever since he had first made contact with Lauren and her unique madness; it was as if he too had been possessed with some kind of sickness. And that was the nearest to the truth that she could find. It *was* madness. Lauren had somehow infiltrated his mind and infected it. Christ. What kind of a person could do this?

More worryingly, Michael had spoken to Kara with regard to the forthcoming inventory of the Patrick Porters. He wanted *her* to do it. He wanted *her* to travel down to Laburnum Farm. *On her own!* Was he truly thinking straight, or was he showing serious signs of psychosis? Much more alarmingly, she had stupidly agreed to this request.

She needed aspirin. She needed an arm to comfort her. She *needed* words of tenderness. Above all, she needed a knife.

*

When Kara eventually saw Michael, she was mortified. She almost mistook him for a tramp when he came into the gallery.

'Michael, you look absolutely terrible. Where have you been?'

'Fighting it out with a rottweiller, and I think I probably lost.' He was unkempt and unshaven, and couldn't recall what exactly had happened after his confrontation with Adele. He *thought* he had slept in the car overnight.

'You can't possibly meet people in the mess you're in. I've never seen you in such a state. For your own good, go home. I can manage the gallery.'

Michael tried to ignore the disgust on Kara's face. 'I need to examine the DVD. I'll hide in my office. Have we had any other communication with our mysterious postman?'

'No, thankfully.' Kara sighed heavily with relief. She told Michael of her success with the repositioning of the CCTV camera, indicating it would be in operation by tomorrow. This thrilled him. But he could hardly keep awake.

Kara made the decision. 'Right, this is the deal. Go home. Get some sleep. For God's sake, take a shower and get a clean shirt on. I'll call round at eight o'clock. I'm taking you to Tom Aikens, my treat. This will give us a chance to go through everything. By then, you'll have a clear head.'

'Kara, you're a star!'

'You don't deserve me.'

*

When he finally got back to his apartment, he watched the DVD which he'd retrieved from his office. He could make little sense to it; he was too exhausted, in truth, to try. He fell asleep fully clothed on the sofa and slept solidly for six hours.

In his dream, he was adrift, floating on clouds. He had no knowledge of his whereabouts, nor possession of a compass to bring him home. He was high above, looking down. Surrounding him were faces he did not recognise: strange faces, seamless, without expression. The further he looked, the more faces materialised. It was a sea of faces, stretching as far as the horizon.

He could not speak; nor reach out and touch. All he had was his sight. Below him, he saw a planet. Through the thin vapour, he observed that it was planet Earth from which he came. It was startlingly beautiful, a vastness of vivid blues and purples, interspersed with twinkling lights. It was an oasis of calm and tranquillity. What really surprised him was his ability to fly! He could go anywhere, in seconds. In any other sense, this would bring unbridled joy. The capability to travel unhindered, all in the blink of an eye. Like Superman. But he was troubled.

Where was this ethereal place he occupied? It was not of this world. Nor were the other million faces that floated around him. Try as he might, he could not shake them, push them or wake them. Yet their bulging eyes remained steadfastly open. These were lost souls.

Michael awoke with a jolt. He was sweating profusely. His initial vision of blissful peace transformed into a scenario of nightmarish images he wanted to forget, in an instant. It was a bad, bad dream. These were the dead people, Guardians of the living. Still shaking, he asked himself if this was a foretaste of death and the afterlife.

He took refuge under a blisteringly hot shower. The fierceness from the jets of water pummelled his aching limbs. It felt good, but he couldn't rid himself of the dream. It was like a premonition.

He checked the clock. Hurriedly towelling down, shaving, dressing, he was punctual to the second as the front doorbell rang. He punched the intercom button marked 'key' and moments later Kara entered the hallway of his apartment. He caught sight of her in the ambient lighting. She was stunning in a short black sequined dress, high heels and simple pearls around her neck. Her hair was drawn up, clasped at the back with a silver slide.

'Wow,' Michael said, admiring her from top to toe. 'Marcus would be jealous.'

'Marcus wouldn't know a good thing even if it bit him on the arse,' she replied, perfecting her red glossy lipstick in the mirror. 'But to be honest, I told him that. I also told him I'm with you.'

'Was that wise?'

'Absolutely, it'll keep him on his toes. He's in my bad books as it is.'

Michael felt less confident. 'How did he take it?'

'He's spitting blood, if you must know. I rather like all this attention.'

Michael grabbed a jacket, kissed her on the cheek and switched off the lights. He took Kara's arm and escorted her to the elevator, adding appreciatively, 'This is a rare treat. Dinner with the best looking girl in town, and you're picking up the tab. I rather like all this attention as well.'

*

Marcus was seriously pissed off. At first, he paced Kara's tiny flat until the floorboards began to creak, then went to the nearest corner pub and downed three pints. What was she playing at? Why did she persist in trying to make him jealous? He felt foolish and unwanted, especially after all the support he had given her. What special occasion was so damned important to warrant going out, looking like she did, with her boss to a swanky restaurant? And bloody Tom Aikens as well! Eventually, gaining courage from two large Jack Daniels and Coke, curiosity got the better of him. Now, standing in the shadows of the building opposite the celebrated restaurant, he watched with mounting frustration as they sat, in full view, at a candlelit table for two. Just bloody perfect!

*

The meal was splendid, the bill less so. Kara gulped at the total, but before she had time to settle the account, Michael whisked it away from her fragile grip and paid by his own credit card.

'Michael, I *said*...'

He raised his hands. 'Better to take me to Poppies Diner next week, that way you won't ask for a raise on your salary.'

'I can pay!' she protested.

'You have, by accompanying me here tonight. It was just what I needed. It's been a very difficult few days.'

Over coffee and brandies, they once again analysed all that had happened over this period. It was a lot to digest. Several things emerged to which there was no immediate answer. One was the identity of the mysterious carrier. Also, Michael had been worried by Kara's behaviour lately. He was deeply troubled that whenever his movements or actions came into question, the only person privy to these was...her. What was she doing? What was her motive if she was revealing information against his will? Trust was of a paramount issue here. Therefore, he reasoned, should he now conceal certain things from her in the future? Was she in fact misguided or manipulated or just feeling the need to overprotect him; or was Kara actually part of something far bigger? Up to now, her allegiance was beyond reproach. But only she *knew* of his trip to Venice. How did Antonia find out? Who tipped her off? It needed answering. And fast. For the moment, however, he wouldn't let this line of enquiry spoil the evening. It could wait for another day.

*

She interrupted his thoughts. 'Michael, I'm bothered by this inventory of the Porter collection you've asked me to do.'

'Oh, why is that?'

Kara hesitated, trying to mask her embarrassment at sounding like a thorough wimp. 'It means me going into the lunatic farm.'

'The inventory needs doing, Kara. Lauren is expecting you.'

Kara bristled with his comment. Lauren, Lauren, Lauren! He was so bloody compliant. Well, fuck Lauren, but she held back from saying it aloud. Her response was feeble. 'When?'

'Early next week, if that's all right. I need digital photos, sizes, and titles. Secure transportation and extra insurance will need organising.' He picked up on her reluctance. He tried to be tough. 'You are the best person for the job, Kara.'

'Why?'

'Because I can trust you, because you are detached from everything. You will work fast and without distraction. I need a professional approach.'

'Why can't you do it?'

'For that very same reason: I will be distracted,' he argued. 'What's the problem here, Kara?'

She fell silent, fully aware that she had never told him of the fear she felt when confronted by the disgusting message in the Blue Bar. It was all too raw. 'To be perfectly honest, this Lauren woman scares me.

I know you are involved with her, but that is your situation to deal with. Not mine. Since she arrived on the scene, all sorts of weird things have happened, and none of them are to my liking. Something, call it paranoia if you like, tells me this is a dangerous business. I just don't like it, OK?'

Michael leaned forward, his eyes narrowing. 'Or her, maybe?'

'Spot on,' she said with a reluctance borne of fear.

*

During a second brandy, when they had been largely silent, he eventually stepped up the rules of engagement. He wanted to find out just where Kara positioned herself. Once again, she was the only person to know of their conversation this evening. *A dangerous business,* she had said only moments earlier. What did she really know? Absurd, but the thought entered his head that it was maybe *she* who was planting the envelopes. Perversely, he was now becoming suspicious of everyone, including his secretary. However, he had to cling to the notion that Kara's motives were genuine. If it was she who sent the envelopes and, indeed, even had contact with Antonia, then surely it had to be for the best intentions? *Surely...*

Michael broke the awkwardness. 'Kara, I need you to do this one thing for me. Please, finish the inventory. If you are worried, take Marcus with you.' Then he added an afterthought. 'You'll be perfectly safe, I promise.' His parched throat almost betrayed him, but he masked it well with the last of the cognac.

*

It was getting colder. Marcus was resilient, if not patient. *How fucking much longer were they going to be?* He sat hunched in the doorway, kicking litter. Twice, a roving police car edged past, looking for tramps and loiterers to move them on. Luckily, he remained undetected. Breathing warmth into the cup of his hands, he sighed with relief as Kara and Michael emerged finally from the restaurant. He watched intently as the couple faced each other closely on the corner of the lamp-lit street. *Kiss her and you'll be dead, pal.*

*

Kara broke her resolve. 'I'll do it, Michael,' she said.

He nodded. 'I'll let Lauren know. And thank you.'

They smiled affectionately and clasped hands. From afar, they could have been mistaken as lovers, embracing under the moonlight. They made a striking couple.

'Thank you for a wonderful evening, Kara.'

She laughed. 'No. I thank you.'

'That Marcus, he is indeed one lucky guy. If you want my advice, hold on to one another, and see it through.'

She continued to laugh. 'We will.' Then she hugged him with all her strength. They clung together from a mutual desperation.

'You know,' he began, and then stopped in order to move her away so he could see into her eyes. Then he said, 'This could be embarrassing, but I'll say it anyway. I only have a son, whom I love dearly. But if I could choose a daughter in this world, it would be you.'

Her eyes misted over. 'Wow, that's the most beautiful sentiment I have ever heard, Michael. I'm deeply touched.'

He kissed her gently on the cheek and, stroking her hair, whispered, 'You once said that you would always look out for me, do you remember? Well, just remember this, wherever you are, whenever you need someone, I will always be there for you, too.'

'Is that a promise?' Kara said.

He saw her vulnerability and recalled her telling him once of her parents' difficult relationship. After they divorced, her distraught father died within two years of the enforced parting. Often, though, her mother would still talk to him to find guidance whenever she had a problem to solve. This, according to Kara, gave comfort and a sense of belonging, and she too spoke to her deceased father whenever she needed help. He was still alive, in her mind. This, her mother had explained, was being truly receptive to the impossible: talking to the dead. *You had to believe.*

'A solemn promise,' he said with a final hug, still troubled by his own dream. What did it signify? It was so vivid, almost suggesting a corridor between those living and those dead. He shivered, as she shivered too. Then, the word *receptive* invaded his head again…from where he did not know.

A taxi came into view and Michael hailed it to take Kara home. He decided to walk his short journey home along the King's Road; it would help to alleviate his overstretched stomach. The joys of middle age crossed his mind as he helped Kara into the cab.

'Goodnight,' she said, and leaned forward from her seat and kissed him again. Then he closed the door. As the tail-lights disappeared from view, Michael crossed the road and made his way down the empty pavement. It was past midnight, but he was in no hurry to arrive at his vacant and lonely apartment.

*

Marcus was in no mood for niceties. It galled him to witness this act of tenderness. Shocked and confused, it hurt him that he could not provide the kind of love that she so obviously desired. He felt isolated. He so wanted to help them, damn it, but this "thing" was now getting in the way. Big time. He headed for the bright lights of a nightclub, one which would keep him in cold comfort as he drowned his sorrows and got blind stinking drunk. He was good at that.

*

In the shadows of an alleyway, a match flared in the gloom as Lauren lit up a cigarette. She stepped out onto the pavement. Her face was partially hidden by the upturned collar of her long black raincoat, and the trilby hat stylishly tilted to one side of her head. But, under the glare of an overhead lamp she was suddenly exposed: The white skin, red lipstick. She was now also recognisable. But Michael and that damned girl were long gone. She searched the street with her intense gaze. It was deserted. The agitated young man was long gone as well. The restaurant lights dimmed. Outwardly, she appeared to be unperturbed and in control. However, under the cool calm surface, a burning rage simmered behind those unfeeling dead eyes. She had witnessed everything just moments earlier, and felt utterly diminished by their mutual show of public affection, which repelled her. As she moved into the road, Lauren inhaled deeply and recalled the image of the two of them kissing. It was the ultimate betrayal. Two could play this game, she decided.

Across the road, she saw a vagrant come into view, moving in her direction. She guessed this was his place to settle down for the night.

He cursed aloud, seeing her there. Lauren held ground, finishing the cigarette. A stray cat darted between them and disappeared just as quickly, sensing the fear in the air.

Lauren stubbed the cigarette on the tarmac and finally moved away. She caught sight of the tramp returning to his territory. Just then, she realised that her white silk scarf, which had been loosely draped around her neck, had slipped to the ground in the alleyway. No matter. He could have it and use it as barter for a swig of cheap whisky. Now it was his possession. Just like Michael was her ultimate possession.

CHAPTER TWELVE

'What the hell do we actually know about Patrick Porter?'

Ronald had remained impassive up to this point, allowing his boss to let off just enough steam. Then he responded, 'Are you actually asking *me*?'

Michael sat at the outer desk in the main gallery, searching through the backdated brochures which he had accumulated on the deceased artist.

This time he swore. Looking up over the rim of his glasses, he remarked, 'Just thinking aloud, Ronald.'

'Odd,' his assistant observed. 'Some artists have an aura attached to them. This is often built on a somewhat flimsy reputation. It's called hype. In the case of Patrick Porter, it was the manner of his death that was intriguing and puzzling. Like John Stonehouse…one day he's here, the next he's gone. Or is he? Apparently, just like in the case of the disgraced politician, his discarded clothes were also left on a beach, near Flamborough Head. Suicide or another bloody fiasco? A cryptic suicide note suggested that a troubled life left the artist with no alternative but a rather horrible death by drowning at sea. The body was never recovered, presumed dead.'

'When was that?' Michael asked.

'1996, he was only thirty.'

'Hmm, and he had such an impressive career for someone so young,' Michael said, turning a page. 'It mentions here that he was born in 1966, near Bunratty Castle, County Clare.' This prompted him to mutter, 'The year Lauren was born.' Ronald didn't appear to have heard. Michael's moving finger underlined the continuing text. 'He was the only son of a dock worker. No formal education. No formal art training. Completely self- taught. Over the years, Ronald, how many of his originals have we handled, do you think?'

'Three, possibly four,' Ronald guessed, with a shrug of the shoulders.

'From what source?'

Ronald pondered. 'Usually private sales, the odd auction, but I can look them up.'

Michael had deliberately withheld the impending sale of Lauren's collection from his colleague. Ronald adored gossip, and could never be entrusted to keep information from Adele. Kara was already working on a secret list of potential clients who would be interested in acquiring a painting from this prized collection. It was imperative that those contacted thoroughly understood the need for no publicity. It was to be a secret sale. In fact, Kara's job was made easier as many clients insisted on this. It was called money-laundering.

In three weeks time, Ronald would be in New Zealand on vacation for nearly a month. This was the time to conduct the sale. Already, Michael had earmarked the basement gallery for the display, away from prying eyes. The next trick would be to keep Adele at a safe distance, away from the fun and games. Fortunately, this exhibition space was concealed behind locked doors. A faultless plan was taking shape.

In the meantime, Michael himself was informing clients directly, organising a closet viewing. Exclusivity was always the key to success. In a separate negotiation, he and Lauren had already agreed on a sixty/forty split, hers being the greater amount. Of course, he would have to charge VAT on top, which would come out of the overall total, minus cash sales of course. If the sale was entirely successful, Michael confidently predicted a gross turnover figure of around £1.6 million, netting him £640,000, give or take a fiver. He jotted these figures down and smiled. It made impressive reading. On a good day, with eager buyers on tow, it could be even better.

Keep all this from the grasping reach of his estranged wife, and he could settle his tax bill and other outstanding amounts and allow himself a considerable cushion when the divorce settlement kicked in. Twelve paintings. Twelve golden geese. Already, over seventeen clients had responded. There was a fantastic chance that these figures could increase in value with greedy demand. The stakes were high, incredibly high.

'Ronald,' Michael said, after savouring the thought of this considerable pot of gold, 'find me as much information you can on the artist, will you? In particular, have you noticed that in all of these brochures there isn't one recorded photograph of the artist himself? Somewhat baffling, don't you think? Try and dig me one out.'

Ronald stifled a yawn. 'I'll be on to it straight away.'

*

Later, Michael caught sight of Kara. She appeared a little preoccupied and tetchy. He dismissed this as probably a symptom of PMT. That morning, and much to his relief, there was no package awaiting him, and therefore the air was more relaxed. Things were at long last going at a smooth pace, without hindrance.

The dream still bothered him though. It kept flashing into his head. He related it to how death might be: the afterlife? *A portal to those still living, a means of communication?* He banished such a far-fetched notion from his mind, but it wouldn't go away entirely.

Neither would his thoughts of Lauren. She had not replied to his phone calls or emails. He was anxious to bring her up to speed on the forthcoming sale and fix a time for Kara's proposed visit to the farm. Then there was the small matter of removing the paintings by Securicor, and keeping them under lock and key until the sale. She would be delighted with the progress, he was sure. Things were moving lightning fast.

In his office, he went over the DVD time and time again, and re-read the newspaper report. He had a friend, Terence Miles, who worked for News International at Wapping. Michael phoned and asked him to search out the case of the 1978 fatality in Dublin. Perhaps then he would be clearer as to the connection of all these untied fragments that needed piecing together. At the back of his mind, a picture began to form. But the images were still too murky to decipher.

And what about Maggie? They had agreed to keep in touch, whenever he felt the need. Because he was involved in such a volatile relationship with Lauren, Maggie had given him an emergency number in which to reach her. In this way, she could offer some kind of support, even from afar. It was a case of when and not if, she had stressed. In the meantime, Maggie had returned to her family in Limerick and waited for the next crisis to loom.

The door to his office suddenly burst open. Kara stood there, ashen-faced and clearly agitated.

'Christ!' he said, 'What's the matter?'

Kara bit her lip. 'It's Marcus. He didn't come home last night. He's been staying over for a few days and I'm worried. I left a message on his mobile. Apparently, the police had retrieved the phone from a gutter and called me as the last number dialled.'

'The police…what's happened, Kara?'

'He was found about an hour ago down behind the embankment near Blackfriars. Apparently, he was unconscious and bleeding. He'd fallen. He's been admitted to hospital to have his stomach pumped. From what I gather, Marcus had been on an all-night drinking binge, finishing up with the meth drinkers under the bridge.'

'Do you know which hospital he's been taken to?'

'The one just down from Whitechapel.'

'The Royal London.' Michael rushed to her side and hugged her. 'Go to him,' he said.

Kara burst into a flood of tears.

'I'll take you,' he said. Without stopping to turn off the DVD, they rushed from the gallery in a wild panic. Ronald remained in the middle of the gallery, gape-mouthed, seemingly puzzled by their antics. Michael had caught sight of him. He had no time to give an explanation.

*

At the hospital Michael and Kara were informed at reception that Marcus was out of immediate danger. Her relief was overwhelming, so much so that her entire body reacted in an uncontrollable shake. She let Michael sit her down, wrapped in a heavy blanket provided by a nurse. In the meantime, a doctor explained the patient was being detained overnight as a precaution and would be released the next day. It was a close call.

Kara gathered his shirt and jeans, which were caked in dry vomit and blood, and arranged to return the next morning with fresh clothes, for when he came home. She was determined to look after him. He could stay at her place for as long as he liked. As soon as he felt better, Kara concluded, they had some serious talking to do. Whatever problems he had, she vowed to help him recover from them. In the meantime, she sat by his bed and stroked his hand. He was oblivious to her concern, with eyes firmly shut and a breathing tube shoved down his throat.

*

Michael did all he could and eventually left them to it. He headed back to the gallery, greatly relieved that Marcus would be fine. Kara would look after him, he was sure. On his return, he was annoyed that he had failed to switch off the television. Had Ronald been witness to the DVD? He sighed heavily, and placed it back into the safe. A very strong black coffee followed. He then told Ronald what had happened. The rest of the day was a blur.

At home that evening, Michael settled into a malaise of either rubbish channel hopping on the TV, or an even poorer attempt at the crossword solutions in the newspaper. Such glamour, such panache. Add to this an even worse mix of takeaway Chinese and overindulgent drinking in whisky and wine and anyone would get the picture: sad lonely living. For once, though, it was sheer bliss. There was something to be said for living selfishly on your own, he thought.

Sprawled on the sofa, half cut, he rekindled the happy memories of his night out with Kara...*his daughter!* God, it made him smile and cringe all in the same movement: had he *really* said that to her? With so much falling down all around them, he meant every single word, even though he still needed to nullify his suspicion of her involvement with Antonia. He didn't want to believe it. When this was all over, he would make sure that she and Marcus would find a safe and loving world in which to live. It was a promise from him to them.

When this was all over...The words stuck hard in his throat. The 10 o'clock news on the TV announced the usual flurry of obnoxious headlines featuring gang youth warfare, child pornography, abuse in an old people's home and corruption in the city. It finished with a postscript of news just breaking: a spate of racial fighting between rival mobs in Leeds city centre. Bad news was the order of the day.

When this was all over. What else had he spurted out, '...a safe and loving world in which to live?' Crap. It would never be all over. Blackness descended. The whisky glass fell from his grasp and tumbled to the floor. The gold liquid spread quickly and stained the carpet. With his eyelids folding over, Michael thought only of anger and spite and frustration: a rage of sorts.

*

At breakfast next morning, he had no appetite for food. Instead, he drank milk. On the doorstep was a pile of letters. He recognised them all: official correspondence from solicitors, accountants, the tax office, circulars. He scooped them all up and rammed them with the others into the bin in the hallway. By now, it was overflowing.

He returned to the kitchen and rang Lauren. No answer. He rang Kara: the answerphone kicked in. He rang Adele. Answerphone again.

'Bitch!' he cursed. It was going to be that kind of day. Again.

He took the car into town and instantly regretted it. Gridlock. He pondered the choice of either turning around or ploughing on, but everywhere was congested. It was a bad, bad day. Ahead, he could see flashing blue lights. Heavy rain hit the windscreen. From the rear, a car horn beeped impatiently. A motorcyclist weaved past at speed, dislodging his wing mirror. *Jesus.* The fury burning within him was bubbling to the surface like molten lava, ready to explode.

His car phone bleeped.

He engaged loudspeaker and said, 'Hello, Michael Strange.' He kept his eye on the slow moving traffic. He edged forward, bumper to bumper.

'Michael, this is John.'

His stomach knotted. 'We have nothing to say to each other, so fuck off.' He imagined John standing next to Adele, comforting her.

'Michael, hear me out. We need to talk.'

'We need something, and it probably involves the use of my fist.'

'I know you're angry, but there is no need for the abuse thrown at Adele. Your comment on the answerphone upset her.'

'Christ, John, you've got a bloody cheek. I'll upset Adele just as much as I want to. What has to be resolved is between us, do you understand?'

'She is vulnerable, Michael.'

'Tough.'

'I'm warning you, Michael. I thought you would show a degree of compassion…'

'Compassion? You can shove any notion of compassion straight up your arse, John. I suggest that you and Adele slink off to your little hole and bury yourselves deep enough for the rest of us to avoid the stench. Is that abusive enough for you? Now fuck off.'

He pressed the button to disconnect them. In the same moment, he pressed down hard on the car horn. He was getting even hotter under the collar. Fuck them all.

He arrived at Cork Street fifty minutes late. Ronald had the day off; Kara was excused for obvious reasons. He hated being late. It always put him in a bad mood. He resigned himself to another bollocking day in the gallery. In spite of two aspirin, he couldn't shift the monumental headache blasting across his brain.

At lunchtime, Kara rang in. It was good news. Marcus had been discharged and they were home at last, where he was confined to bed. She was exhausted and still tearful, but enormously grateful for his safety. Kara also explained they had deliberately avoided the reasons for his lapse into a drunken stupor. Things were still too delicate and that could wait for another day. Michael almost laughed. A drunken stupor was often a great state to be in.

He consoled himself with a ham and salad sandwich. It was dull. The day unfolded in just the same manner. Nearer closing time, a bohemian type came in and tried to introduce her work to the gallery. The metal installation was ghastly. It was the wrong day to call, but she wasn't to know that. Michael gave her short shrift. She departed rapidly, muttering some kind of obscenities under her breath. Try the local tip, he had suggested helpfully. He hated himself, but what the hell.

Another visitor, someone he instantly recognised, shoved past the irate artist as their paths crossed on the doorstep.

'Blimey,' Terence Miles said, raising his eyebrows. 'Do you treat all the girls the same way, Michael?'

'Only when I'm mad, and she made me seriously mad.'

They shook hands warmly. Michael checked his watch.

'Fancy a pint?' he asked.

After closing, they retreated to the Duke of Westminster pub on the corner adjacent to the gallery. Although the main bar was crowded, they found a private booth at the rear in which to talk.

'Cheers,' Terence said, raising his glass of Guinness.

'Have you got anything for me?' Michael asked, skipping any kind of pleasantries.

'Plenty,' Terence replied. The old fox downed his black amber and smacked his lips. He moved to the bar and reordered identical drinks, plonking another gin and tonic in front of his companion. This had all the hallmarks of a very long night, Michael thought. He had known Terence since schooldays. He was a damned good news reporter, the right guy to have on your side. Hard as nails, he could handle anything, although last year had been a harrowing time for him. Terence lost his wife to cancer, and just three months ago he had been subjected to a beating from local youths after he had exposed a story of drug trafficking on an estate in East Ham. He still carried the scars on his face. Michael wondered what scars he had concealed in his heart.

'Everything all right, Terry?' Michael asked.

Terry gave a world-weary shrug. 'Could be better, I suppose. I'm still having physiotherapy on the shoulder, the wire in the jaw is out, but now I have to have corrective surgery on my teeth. On top of that barrel of laughs, I have persistent headaches and dizziness, which could mean the loss of my driving licence. Bravo. Life is just dandy. How is it for you, you idle rich tosser?'

They enjoyed the moment, laughing at the obvious disparity in their lifestyles, although Michael was quick to correct him on one thing which rankled. 'Right on two counts. Leave the rich bit out.'

'Ah, the old divorce swansong, eh?'

'Not good.'

'Never is, unless your name's Donald Trump.' Terry shrugged again. 'To be honest, I couldn't stand her, Michael. She always looked down on people, particularly those like me.' He scanned the bar; then moved closer, whispering, 'I'll arrange a timely demise if you want. I know some boys out at East Ham.'

'That's sick, Terry. Besides, you could have been killed that night.'

Terry leaned back and savoured the remains in his glass, smacking his lips. 'Sometimes, I rather wish I had been.'

Michael reflected on the long battle that Terry had with his wife's illness and understood a little of the pain his friend had gone through. They always say that death and divorce have the same impact, but Michael wasn't prepared to argue the point. Given the circumstances, Terry was in a far darker place.

'Just believe it will get better...' It was all that he could offer. It wasn't much. 'I'll get the next round in.'

They discussed football, a favourite subject. It was another hour and two more rounds before they exhausted the argument of the fight for supremacy between Chelsea and Arsenal. The banter was good, and just what Terry needed, Michael realised with a rush of pleasure. In fact, it was what they both needed. It replenished them.

Now it was down to business.

'This story,' the reporter said, in a more sober tone, 'does it have a connection to you?'

'Possibly,' Michael said. 'At this stage, I would prefer to hear what you have to say. Only then can I make a judgement. I may need you to dig up more information.'

Terry nodded, and took a notepad from his pocket. 'On the face of it, it's a straightforward case that wouldn't be out of place in an episode of Eastenders. It transpired that one member of the family, a young daughter, killed her father in retaliation for persistent abuse. He was a drunkard. It turns out that he – the father – subjected all of the family to this routine violence. It stands to reason then that he was more often than not pissed on a regular basis. The girl battered him to death using a poker. She was only twelve years of age, a minor. Against overwhelming evidence to the contrary, she was found guilty of manslaughter owing to the severity of the attack. It was not deemed self-defence. The case attracted huge national coverage at the time. The girl was detained in a psychiatric secure ward for minors, her sentence and appeal reassessed by specialist doctors during her time in prison. When she was finally released, she obtained a new identity, and slipped into obscurity.'

'What was her name?'

'Laura.'

'You say "all the family." What were their individual names?'

Terence Miles flicked a couple of pages. He put on glasses and read slowly, focusing his eyes. 'The parents were Frank and Delores. The other daughter was Margaret.'

'Maggie,' Michael said, stunned. This was the very same Maggie that had told him a pack of lies when they first met. What had she claimed? Their father was killed in a drink driving accident. Was everything that came out of her mouth a lie? He feared so.

Terence raised his eyebrows. 'Do you know her?'

'Just maybe…tell me their surname.'

'Hang on.' He turned a page. 'Porter.'

The word slammed into Michael's chest as if he'd been kicked by a mule. He could hardly breathe, the sudden shock necessitating him to gulp down a full glass of gin and tonic. He removed his tie and felt the sticky sweat on his brow.

'Jesus Christ, are you all right, mate?' Terry asked.

'I'm fine,' Michael replied, feeling not at all fine. His head was pounding. The noise and heat from the crowded room closed in and began to suffocate him. His reasoning had gone. Dizziness started to overcome him, so much so that he hardly registered Terry's last remark.

'Oh,' his friend added, scrolling down the next page of his notepad, 'It seems they also had a baby brother, aged three, who died under suspicious circumstances. His name was Patrick.'

Patrick. The stale air and intake of alcohol overtook Michael for the last time. He slid under the table, gasping for breath, grasping for something tangible to hold on to. Above all, he wanted to grasp onto something that he could positively believe in. The dividing line between the whole truth and damn lies was a barely visible thread.

CHAPTER THIRTEEN

It took three men to lift him from the flagstone floor. It was a hard place to land. He was drenched in spilled beer from the upturned table. Between them, the group of men helped him to an outside bench at the front of the pub, where he remained slumped and dazed. Inhaling fresh air, he slowly recovered his composure, if not his dignity.

'What the hell happened?' he asked, drinking slowly from the glass of water that Terry had brought from the bar. The crowd dispersed.

'You passed out, mate, simple as that. No food, too much drink.'

'Christ, I feel rough.'

Terry knelt beside him, touching his shoulder to offer reassurance. 'Stay calm and breathe deeply, Michael. I've called a cab. Lucky you didn't bang your head. I always thought you had thick skin.'

Michael gulped the cold air and tried to unwind. The conversation with Terry had knocked the wind from his sails. Could it really be true? If so, then Maggie had deliberately lied to him, on all counts. Was the past so evil that she felt it necessary to protect him from it? *Was that it*? Or was there something else, an altogether more sinister background – a cover up, that he was only now stumbling upon?

'Terry, that last part…' He tried to clear his head. 'Were you right in saying that the young child died aged three and his name was Patrick? Are you absolutely sure about that?'

'Yeah, it was well documented in the Press at the time. He died from injuries consistent with a fall. The mother said he fell down the stairs, unsupervised. A tragic accident, supposedly. However, in light of the history of violence within the family, the circumstances were regarded as highly suspicious. But no charges were brought, as no criminal evidence could be used against the parents.'

'Can you find out the name of the senior police officer who conducted the investigation into the murder on Clonmore Terrace?'

Terry stood, and peered down the road. 'For sure.'

The headlamps from the taxi loomed into view, blinding them momentarily. Rain began to hit the pavement. Terry helped Michael into the rear of the vehicle.

'Are you going to be OK?' the reporter asked with concern.

'Perfectly,' Michael said. 'Ring me, Terry.'

The taxi pulled out into the ribbon of traffic and headed toward the embankment. Michael turned and glanced back at his friend standing on the pavement, watching his tail lights. The rain drilled down now, hammering on the roof of the cab. Michael couldn't decide which was worse, the noise from above or the noise in his head. Both were relentless.

*

Michael dragged himself in at eleven, still feeling the effects of the fainting episode in the pub. This had never happened to him before. Perhaps he should phone Age Concern. His humour was turning black.

Over coffee, he found out from Kara the heartening news that Marcus was much better and had resumed painting for the forthcoming exhibition at the gallery. Kara would not dwell on the reasons for her boyfriend's sudden collapse. It was a closed book, so Michael decided to drop the subject as well. It was a private matter. The episode with Terence was a different proposition, and was all consuming. It kept nagging at him like a persistent toothache.

Searching for answers put him in an impossible predicament. Maggie was hiding an unpalatable truth; her sister was living one. No wonder she had problems that appeared insurmountable. Julius, he was sure, was alive and seeking an anonymous existence in Venice. Antonia was protecting him and their child, to the exclusion of all others. As Lauren lived a life of self delusion, which seemed likely, then they were right to find a new life, as far from her as possible. They were entitled to a fresh beginning. It began to dawn on Michael that Lauren was capable of great destruction in all matters of human contact. She simply could not handle alternative patterns of behaviour from anyone else which strayed from her own mad moral high ground. This displayed itself as a form of betrayal directed back at her, and was punished accordingly. In her eyes, she had killed Julius, just as she had killed her father in 1978. If anyone stood the wrong side of her, they were in danger. Mortal danger.

A decision had to be made. In the past, he had given Lauren the benefit of the doubt. He desperately wanted to believe in her, to fall in love with her. However, it had now become an uncontrollable situation, and Michael readily admitted to himself that he was frightened. The goalposts had been moved. It was time to leave the pitch. Quit the game.

His overriding fear was that someone would get hurt. No amount of money would compensate for this. The sale of the Patrick Porter collection was not his salvation; it was his demise. Whichever way he looked at it, the shadow of the Porter family was like a blanket which hung over everyone, blotting out every last lingering light. It was evil, and contagious. It touched the very soul of goodness.

And yet, despite all this, the mystery as to the true identity of Patrick Porter was a cause he could not give up on. Who was this man? This genius who no one really knew or understood? Michael suspected that it had to be Julius who masqueraded as this artist. After all, he too was an accomplished painter, and was more than capable of producing the fine collection at Laburnum Farm. The two portraits of Antonia bore out the quality of his work. Julius had the location, the motivation and the expertise to carry out this audacious ruse. This would also explain how Antonia could be the model to the both of them. The connection was there. It all began to make sense, except for the question of why did Julius need to – *want* to – become someone else, and adopt a nom de plume? In view of the name he chose, it was also clear that he and Lauren were accomplices in whatever they were trying to achieve.

Now they were at each others' throats. Was blackmail the motive for the war between them? Here was the contradiction, and it had to be solved. This was a scenario so bizarre it defied logic. The answer had to be found in the forbidding links between Maggie and Lauren. What were they really hiding? Between them, the sisters had lived through a vivid history of lies and camouflage, self denial and a vindictiveness bordering on obsession and insanity.

In spite of himself, he had to discover the truth: the whole truth. He, too, was deeply flawed. Entwined in the complexities of his own world, he sought an escape from a sharp reality that was simply overwhelming him. He felt strong and resourceful, and yet everything pointed to the exact opposite. For a long time now, he had been acutely aware of his own massive shortcomings in dealing with deeply personal issues. In short, they were swamping him.

He tried to hold it together, but it was becoming an increasingly impossible task. Just as he contemplated the merits of Age Concern again, all hell broke loose.

Kara rushed breathlessly into his office, without knocking. She brandished a piece of paper in her outstretched hand.

'Another calling card,' she announced. He saw the thunder descending on her face. 'An email arrived, just a moment ago,' she said, placing the paper in front of him. 'I've printed it off. Michael, this is really pissing me off, big time. Whoever sent this is aware of the repositioning of the CCTV camera across the road. He or she is now using another route in order to get to us. They used my personal email, Michael. It's as if I'm being targeted in this as well...'

Equally alarmed, Michael saw the panic in her eyes. He could hardly speak, failing for the first time with a gesture of futile words to help calm her. Instead, he looked down and examined the document.

It read:

16ᵗʰ July 1982

Confidential Report

From: Dr. Joseph O'Connor, Psychiatric Unit, Young Offenders Ward, Dublin Prison Hospital, 'C' Section.

To: Eric Stanton, Governor of Prisons, Eire.

In my opinion the patient is undergoing a process of prime case psychotic self delusion. This is based on extensive interviews and examination over the last twelve months. On the one hand, she bears the scars of her past actions and shows deep remorse and understands fully the consequences of those actions. On the other side, I see a gradual diminishing responsibility, borne out of guilt for the suffering it has caused her family, in particular her mother, who is now frail and confined to a wheelchair. The patient clearly acknowledges the reasons for her violent conduct, but refuses to atone for it, as a testament to the plight of her mother.

The patient is currently in solitary confinement, under constant supervision. I strongly believe that she would harm herself if left alone. Strict medication is stabilising her behaviour, which will eventually enable her to gradually engage with the other inmates. In the meantime, my recommendation, at this stage of my findings, is for her to remain here, under guard, and under my direct scrutiny. This will be a long recovery process.

At present, she is considered a clear danger to herself and the public and remains on "high risk" alert.

In the past three months the patient has failed in one suicide attempt and my colleagues and I firmly believe this will not be an isolated incident.

Signed;

J O'Connor

Michael digested the words carefully. Coupled with what he now knew, it brought home the sheer gravity of the whole sad bloody "human cost" picture.

'Who the fucking hell are they referring to, Michael? For God's sake, what do you know in all this? What are you hiding from me?'

For the very first time, Michael turned on Kara and vented his anger. He stood abruptly and thrust the document under her nose.

'What am I hiding? What am I hiding?' he snarled. 'Perhaps you should question your own misguided motives before rounding on me!'

'What are you talking about?' Her eyes blazed.

'I'm talking about your involvement. I'm talking about the simple fact that whatever I do, whatever I say, or wherever I go, it seems that my movements are continually monitored. It concerns me that my trust in you is being eroded. What are *you* hiding from me, Kara?'

She looked startled. 'Are you implying that I am working against you, Michael? Is that what this is all about?'

He pressed on. 'On my visit to Venice, I discovered that Antonia was expecting me. Now, how could that be possible, Kara? Tell me that, if you can. Only one person knew of my plans…'

'Well, clearly someone else does as well.'

They stood head to head, inches apart. Michael gave no quarter, fuming, 'Nobody else knew; that's the point. I phoned you from the airport. I booked my ticket online. I paid cash whenever I could. Even at the hotel I managed to keep my passport in my possession. I even booked in under an assumed name. Everything was done deliberately with the assistance of the Italian police. I have reliable contacts over there which enabled me to travel with a good degree of anonymity.' He stood even closer, glaring at her. 'So tell me, how come Antonia wasn't surprised to see me, uh?'

'Sod you, Michael! Is this all the gratitude I get for watching over your arse? And now you are accusing me of tipping off someone I have never met in my life. What are you thinking? Have you gone absolutely mad?'

'Quite possibly,' he said. 'However, if you analyse it rationally, if it isn't you, Kara, then who have you been confiding in?'

Kara paced the room.

'No one, damn it,' she replied indignantly. 'My commitment to you is rock solid. A promise is a promise. You entrusted me with the secret sale of the Patrick Porters, remember? It was me who organised the CCTV cameras, remember? I was asked, no, instructed, to do the inventory of the paintings at the wacko farm, remember? Michael, get a grip.'

He shook his head, slowly. 'Just do your job, Kara. Trust has to be earned from now on.'

She almost spat in his face. Visibly shaking, she shouted, 'Oh, fuck off, Michael. You'll have my resignation on your desk this afternoon. Don't you see what all this is doing to you? To us? To everyone?' Without waiting for a reply, Kara turned sharply and stormed from the room.

In her wake, he was left shocked by the hostility that reared up so suddenly and unexpectedly. He couldn't work out how the hell that all happened, and with such speed. He was losing his grip.

*

Kara hurried to the downstairs kitchen, slamming doors as she went. She wept uncontrollably and kicked the waste paper bin across the floor.

'Fuck you!' she screamed at the empty room. She felt the mascara running down her cheeks like the black markings on a circus clown. She felt like one. Utterly humiliated, and ridiculed. How could he possibly think like that?

'The bastard!' This time the word came out unintentionally loud. She washed her face in cold water. When she removed the towel from her face, Ronald was standing next to her. It gave her a sudden jolt.

'Jesus, Ronald. Stop creeping around.'

'I was just making sure you were all right.' He raised his eyebrows in a theatrical manner. 'There appears to be a lot of commotion going on, and I was concerned. Can I do anything to help?'

'No, I'll be fine.'

'You don't look fine, if I may be so bold.' He went past her and retrieved the upturned bin. He began filling it with the discarded tissues scattered over the sink.

'Just a misunderstanding, that's all,' Kara said, to reassure him. 'Thanks for coming down to check on me.' She grabbed another tissue and wiped her eyes.

'Well, I've never seen you like this before.'

Kara needed air. And space. 'Well, just be thankful that you don't have to put up with me when I've got PMT, OK? I can be the bitch from hell.' She watched his eyes glaze over. This greatly amused her. It was a sure fire way to make his retreat a hasty one. All men were the same. It was her first chuckle of the day.

*

Michael hated himself for being so brutal. He had hurriedly departed from the gallery just to gather his thoughts. He had been a bully, and his anger was getting the better of him. He walked the streets aimlessly, cooling off.

*

Kara made tea. Ronald gave her a wide berth, she noticed. She was still seriously pissed off by the outburst from her boss, who hadn't returned to the gallery for over an hour. It was so out of character. What was going on in his head? She cupped the drink to her lips, but she was still shaking and managed to spill hot camomile on her blouse. The telephone rang and she answered it. It was the engineer from road traffic security. He was matter of fact, explaining that as the required days had lapsed, the department was no longer able to offer assistance in the apprehension of the vandals who had previously broken windowpanes in the front door. He was powerless to do more. The camera would now revert to its normal duties.

Kara thanked the engineer, but felt guilty for using him in her little game. Some little game. She thought of the camera. Only she and Michael were aware of the trick they had been trying to pull. They had never let Ronald in on the ruse. Then there was the latest intrusion with the email. Why the change of tack? More disturbingly, it was on her personal email. Who had access to this? She counted only a handful of people. The name of the sender had provided no clue either: guardianangel@aol.com. That could be anyone, friend or foe.

Trying the obvious thing she had emailed a simple demand: who are you? No reply was forthcoming. Some guardian angel!

Her scrambled thoughts turned to work colleagues. Such a peculiar arrangement, millions of people around the world cooped up with each other daily. It was universally accepted that workers in an office saw more of their co-workers than their partners at home. Often, as a result, a special bond developed, creating a strange and alternative existence like living in a bubble. Consequently, a thin line between love and hate connected all those people, bringing dependency, intimacy and sometimes, betrayal. Why, then, did this thought bother her so much?

Just then, she caught sight of Ronald standing transfixed by the door. She craned her neck for a better view and followed his gaze. He was staring at the CCTV camera as it swivelled back to its original sightline. After a moment, he scurried off to make himself busy. He had a knack of keeping busy. But nothing got past Ronald; he had the ears of a hare, and the eyes of a hawk. And he had access to her private email. Just supposing, what if Michael was right? Had she given out information without realising it? Thinking back, her colleague had a knack of doing this expertly as well: extracting gossip. Idle chitchat, picking up on a slip of the tongue...call it what you like. And another thing, he never took sides. He was as comfortable with Michael as he was with Adele. He always sat on the fence, as if, should the axe begin to fall, he was ready and waiting to go with the victor.

She studied him closely. Was he the messenger, or the instigator?

Was he the puppet or the puppet master? Was he the guardian angel? Kara shuddered, thought of Michael, and made a plan.

*

It was easy, really. Tomorrow was her day off. Michael was away at the Shoreditch gallery. Ronald would be alone. Before closing, she made a makeshift printed card and hid it in her desk. Michael returned to the gallery, avoiding all eye contact with her. For the moment, this suited her well.

Hours passed. It was Michael who made the initial move. He found Kara in the kitchen, preparing her own Caesar salad.

'Looks good,' he remarked.

She glanced up. 'There's enough for two.'

'That would be great.' He pulled a chair out from beneath the table and perched atop it. He was still uncomfortable and she sensed it. He felt clumsy and intrusive. She remained at the sink, with her back to him, occupying herself with tossing the chicken and cos lettuce in a bowl.

'Do you want croutons with yours?' Kara asked.

'Whatever you do, it will be perfect...unlike my manners.'

She half turned. 'What did you say?'

'I owe you a big apology. I was totally out of order with what I said.'

She turned full circle. 'It was a heat of the moment thing, I know that now.' She wiped her hands on a dishcloth. 'We are both under enormous pressure, and you know what they say about hurting those nearest to you.'

He shook his head. 'It was still unforgivable, Kara. I am so sorry for the accusations that I threw at you. They were unjustified.'

'I'm sorry, too. It's a very bad time. Everything is slowly falling to pieces. I'm freaked because Marcus won't open up as to what is bothering him. These unwanted messages we keep getting are doing my head in. What do they mean? On top of that, I've discovered that Adele has been tampering with my files, even more than we first suspected. I hadn't the heart to tell you, I thought I could be clever and sort it.' Then she looked at him anxiously. 'Michael, I'm scared. I think you should call the police.'

'No. We can handle it.'

Kara finished mixing the salad and served up the plates. She sat opposite him and took his hand. 'That's the whole point, Michael. I don't think we *can* handle it. Just look at us earlier in the day, at each other's throats.'

Michael picked up a fork and fiddled with his food. 'No police. I can deal with Adele. A friend of mine is unravelling the messages. Someone close to us is feeding information as a warning. I now know just what that warning is, but,' and he emphasised the point, 'I think the less you know at this stage the better. I have deliberately kept things from you, Kara.' He lowered his voice. 'Someone knows my every move. That is why I became suspicious of you. Can you see my point?'

'Yes, I can, but I don't like it.'

'What I can tell you is I have evidence that Julius is alive. It's flimsy at this stage, but it's all I've got. Only two people have the motive to send those messages, and that is Antonia and Julius. And it isn't Antonia.'

'Are you suggesting that Julius is here in London?'

'It's a possibility.'

'Why doesn't he make direct contact?'

'Because it suits him to remain invisible,' Michael said. 'I made a pact with Antonia. I agreed to leave her alone. This is their way of repaying that faith, to warn me. I'm on to something, Kara. We are in the process of conducting a multimillion pound sale of paintings. I stand to make a great deal of money, which should save the business. At the moment we're on the brink of financial ruin. But...and it is a big "but", the twelve paintings to be disposed of have a gigantic question mark against them, as to authenticity and rightful ownership. Until I find out the answer to these facts, we carry on as normal.'

'*Normal?*' Kara bit her bottom lip. 'I can't remember what that is!'

She picked at her salad. Michael seemed to have no appetite, either.

'We need to act as if nothing has happened,' he said. 'It's imperative that I am given the time to sort this bloody mess out. I need your undivided support.'

She wasn't convinced. 'How?'

'Carry on with the inventory on Monday. Go to the farm. I've suggested that you take Marcus. Use him. Do what is necessary and then get out. Take the easel and camera and tripod. Do the photography of each image. Look and act smart. Do not get entangled in conversation with Lauren. Just do your job and then get out of there ASAP.'

'Where will you be?'

'Dublin.'

'I've read the anonymously sent messages, Michael, and I can see the connection, but what do you hope to achieve with this trip?'

'The content of the messages relate solely to one family, and the history of that family has a direct bearing on the sudden availability of the Patrick Porter collection. What I hope to uncover is pivotal to the story that is only now, finally, unveiling itself to us.'

Kara screwed her face. 'Does the story have a happy ending?'

Michael pushed his plate aside. 'It is my firm belief that Julius and Antonia want their freedom at any price, but not at Lauren's considerable gain. They can't come forward for fear of jeopardising their future, so they are asking me to scupper her plans.'

'Julius wants his revenge.'

'Exactly, and that includes his pound of flesh.'

They stared long and hard at each other.

Confused, Kara wriggled her nose. 'Why would Julius expect to enlist the help of someone who would have a great deal to lose if everything then went pear-shaped? It doesn't make sense.'

'That's precisely what I need to find out.'

Kara picked up the unfinished salads and scraped them into the bin.

*

Later, Michael took a phone call from his solicitor. It was in connection with his aggressive manner in his recent dealings with his wife.

'Michael, back off,' he instructed. 'I have a letter here from Adele's solicitor. Apparently, you called at the house and threatened her. You are also accused of abusive language to a certain John Fitzgerald. They warn that any repeat behaviour will not be tolerated. If it happens again, she will take out an injunction which will forbid you access to the family home.'

'Hang on a minute, he called me!' He then considered his solicitor's last sentence. 'Can she do that?'

'Yes.'

'Can I take out an injunction that forbids her to leave the house? That way everyone is happy.'

'Michael, this is not helpful.'

'Neither is sabotage. I have evidence that Adele is tampering with company files. Is that not construed as threatening behaviour of a different kind?'

The line went quiet. 'Michael, perhaps you should come and see me. I also have an official offer of settlement.'

'Email it.'

'I would rather we discussed it face to face.'

'That bad, eh?'

'As bad as it can get.'

*

His composure surprised him. Adele was clever, but not that clever. He would test her patience. She could stew on it, whilst he weighed up his options. Then he would give her his considered response. She could have everything if she so desired, including the debt. He would quietly take the money and run. She always maintained that she could make more of a success of the business than him. From a distance, it would be fun to watch her floundering in the sea, without a life jacket, surrounded by sharks.

*

Kara organised his flight to Shannon International airport. He had elected to travel to Limerick first, by hire car, in order to keep a watchful eye on Maggie. Then he would travel northeast to Dublin. His flight time was 7.30am, the next morning, from Gatwick. His return ticket was open.

*

Before departing for the day, he had time to give Kara written directions to Laburnum Farm. She was hardly enthusiastic.

'I'm not entirely sure about this, Michael.'

'Neither am I. But I've been thinking about it. I've been a bit of a bastard recently, and you need cheering up. If this all goes according to plan, I think it is only right that you receive a little bonus.'

'A pay rise?' Her eyes lit up in anticipation.

'Better than that, how about £25,000 in your hand: Have we a deal?'   Bribery and corruption extended to all walks of life, Michael concluded. He *really* needed for her to do this for him. The money was an inducement, a confirmation of her commitment to him. She was vital to him. Now he was offering the bait. He wasn't buying trust, but it was a close second best.

'Are you crazy?' she asked, suppressing a giggle.

'Take it. I'll only offer it once. It also ensures that you won't hand in your resignation which you threatened to do earlier.'

'Done,' she said, somewhat embarrassed.

He then embraced her warmly. Then he was gone.

*

It unsettled her to discover it was near closing time, and Michael was no longer by her side. Now she had to put her plan into practise. Tracking down Ronald to the stockroom, she explained that she would be working late and therefore happy to close up. It was quiet, she suggested, and therefore unnecessary for both of them to see out the last half an hour. Ronald was equally happy to take up her offer to catch an earlier train than usual. After he left, Kara retrieved the card she'd hidden in her desk and sellotaped it to the entrance door, facing out, so the message could be clearly read in the entrance porch, but not from the pavement. Whoever entered first in the morning would have no difficulty finding it. That person would be Ronald.

After closing, Kara went home, exhausted, soon to be richer by £25,000, and just a little apprehensive. She ran through the message she had written. Each word was imprinted on her mind:

MEET ME AT 12.30PM. BRITISH MUSEUM. PRINTS & DRAWING ROOM, NEXT TO THE EPIFANIA CARTOON BY MICHELANGELO. FAIL

TO SHOW UP AND I WILL GO STRAIGHT TO THE
POLICE. I KNOW YOUR GAME.

*

All night, she was restless. She watched television but
couldn't recall one single programme that held her
attention. She sat alone, ate a crap sandwich and drank
half a bottle of chilled white wine. Marcus was painting in
the back room, behind a closed door. Since the episode
with his drinking blackout, he was distant and
uncommunicative. She brooded on this, determined to
confront him if this continued for much longer. She
despised his childish stand-off. Something was seriously
up. Just to confirm it, he even refused his favourite supper,
the cold remains of last night's chicken tikka marsala,
which he usually shoved between the folded stiffened and
stale Nan bread. Simply *glorious,* would be his usual
response to this culinary delight. This time he simply
turned up his nose at the idea. That told her everything.

CHAPTER FOURTEEN

Michael was packed and ready to go within an hour of arriving at his apartment. He travelled light and always prided himself on organising his life in double quick time. He ate sparingly and took the call he was expecting. Terence had unearthed all the vital information he required. He was now armed with names and contact addresses that related to all those connected to the 1978 murder investigation. In particular, the whereabouts of retired senior police officer, Paddy McGuire, who led the murder enquiry, and Dr. Joseph O'Connor, who was instrumental in treating the child named 'Laura' whilst in the prison psychiatric hospital. He, too, was retired, living on the south side of the city of Dublin. More importantly, Terence gave him another unexpected lead. It was a surprise one which he wasn't sure he should pursue at this stage, especially as it could be construed as a morally repugnant move. But he would see how it all went. It was his trump card. He could stoop as low as was necessary.

He pondered his next move. In his hand, he held the card which Maggie had given him with her telephone number. He was reluctant to give his movements away, but felt compelled to make contact. He needed to know where she was. He dialled.

After a long pause, he heard her familiar, daunting, voice.

'Maggie Conlon.'

'It's Michael, Michael Strange from London.'

There was a longer pause. Finally, she said, 'What has Lauren got up to *this* time?'

He was not surprised by her remark. Her telephone number was issued to him only for emergency purposes. He and Maggie were hardly going to be best buddies.

'She's not answering my calls. Is she there with you?'

'No, Michael.'

'Have you spoken with her?'

'Not since we last visited our mother. Do you think there's a problem?'

Michael prolonged his answer. 'I don't know, Maggie. We were together last week and she was in fantastic form. We spent the day at the farm and made some big plans for the future. Lauren was excited. Since then I've heard nothing from her. I wondered...' He drifted into thought, hoping Maggie would interject.

She did. 'It's not unusual for Lauren to simply go off into another world, Michael. I explained very carefully to you the complexities that exist in her mind. Do you not remember this?'

'Yes, but...'

'Am I wasting my breath on you, Michael?' Her voice suddenly altered sharply, expressing annoyance. He sensed that she hesitated, closed a door and was now holding the telephone tightly to her ear. Her tone was guarded. 'Michael, can you still hear me? Listen to what I have to tell you.' She waited once again, and then continued with the lecture, in a whisper this time. 'Lauren is trouble, everything she touches is trouble.

If she is up one day, she will be down the next. It is the nature of the beast. Did you not heed my warning when we last spoke? Jesus Mother Mary, I explained everything to you, in plain old-fashioned English. What exactly didn't you understand?'

It was his opportunity to interrupt. 'You told me everything?'

'Meaning?'

He took his time. 'I was doing a little research, Maggie. It seems you weren't totally honest with me in regard to your family history. It contains a few nasty skeletons in the cupboard, which you omitted to tell me about.'

Maggie's discomfort was palpable. 'Keep away, Mr Strange,' she said. 'Don't go meddling in the affairs of other people.'

'It's a little too late for that, Maggie. Telling me a pack of lies brings the worst out in me.'

Her anger erupted. 'What can you possibly know about my family? Tell me, or God forbid, I'll chase you down and show you precisely what the very worst in me is capable of. And believe me, the consequences of that will bring all the trouble you can handle. Is that something you can relate to, Mr Strange? Keep away from Lauren. Keep away from me. Are you still there, Mr Strange? Jesus, are you even listening to me?'

Michael slammed the telephone down and stood for a moment in the kitchen, taking in the force of her words. He found himself shaking. Even a large scotch on the rocks failed to abate the nervous tension raking every sinew in his body. Tomorrow was going to be a very long day. Raising the whisky bottle to the spotlight above him, he noted the generous level which remained. It was going to be a very long night too.

*

The alarm went off at 6.30am sharp. Kara stirred, then drifted her hand across the bed and found emptiness. The sheets were cold. She couldn't actually remember if Marcus had come to bed: stubborn mule that he was, he had probably slept on the sofa, away from her. She was beginning to resent him for staying at her apartment, rent free, emotionally free and getting sex free. Why did men sulk? She wondered. Although the pair of them had skirted around the reason as to why he had ended up in hospital, things weren't back to normal, which pained her. He was holding back, which stopped them going forward. Too tired to fight it, Kara slipped into the shower, dressed quietly and was out of the apartment in under an hour. Before leaving, she checked the sofa. *He* wasn't there. Shit. Where was he? She couldn't bring herself to even say his arsehole name. *Men!*

This was going to be a big day, with all sorts of possible repercussions. Although nervous, she kept cool and took the tube on the usual route, walked Piccadilly, and arrived outside the gallery, albeit earlier than normal. She installed herself in the café on the opposite side of the road and found a window seat, affording her a perfect view of the gallery entrance. A newspaper obscured her face from the passers-by. Coffee and croissants helped the minutes tick down. Ronald eventually appeared, fumbled for his keys and stepped into the porch. She watched as he hesitated, bent forward and appeared to be reading something that caught his eye. He then entered the darkened gallery, tore at a white card which was attached to the inside of the glass door, looked around sheepishly, and disappeared from view.

Kara finished her coffee refill, paid, and swept out into the street, using her umbrella as a shield. It wasn't raining, but needs must. She then planned her route to the British Museum. She had chosen this location because Ronald had once remarked that he went there as a young boy. His father took him. He was still an avid visitor. Kara also reasoned that in the hushed confines of a museum, it was the least likely place for him to create a 'scene' if things got a little heated between them. She had absolutely no idea how he would react to her message on the door. It would be a civilised affair though, she concluded hopefully.

*

Michael, in the meantime, had travelled without hindrance, changing his plans at the last moment and flying directly to Dublin. Originally, his proposed trip had included a visit to Limerick. However, a confrontation with Maggie in her volatile frame of mind wasn't a sound idea, on reflection. Besides, he did not want her to know his whereabouts. Instead, he arrived at the airport at just after eight-thirty. He took a taxi into the city and arrived at St Stephens Green thirty minutes later. Standing in the foyer of the Shelbourne Hotel, he booked into his suite at reception, took the stairs up to the second floor and unpacked in his room. It was a glorious day, with the sun streaming in through the windows. He then became aware of how hungry he was. The food on the flight had been abysmal. He headed for the downstairs restaurant without delay, a full English breakfast demanding his immediate attention.

*

Ronald's nerves jangled. The note on the door had thrown him totally off guard. He felt like a complete and utter wreck. Nothing like that had ever happened to him before. The message surely was directed clearly at him, or was it? Several weird incidents in the past few days made him deeply uncomfortable, to the point of paranoia. First, there was the argument between Michael and Kara, which he had overheard. In fact, the whole of London heard that one, he reckoned. Prior to that, he had discovered a DVD playing in Michael's office which he found baffling. Add to this the fact that both his work colleagues were showing distinct signs of hysteria and the overall picture resembled the nightmarish portrayal of Heironymus Bosch's painting depicting the descent into Hell. Not a pretty scenario. What was going on? Ever since Ronald got wind of the breakdown in Michael and Adele's marriage, he was aware of a gradual deterioration in everything that he held dear to his heart. It was saddening.

There was more. For several days he had noticed that the CCTV stationed across the road was actually fixed upon the entrance to the gallery. This spooked him. How was that possible? And yesterday, just as suddenly, the camera returned to its original position, monitoring the flow of traffic, as was the intended purpose. Amusingly, he had heard of people talking of Big Brother, but to him these were idle mutterings of conspiracy theories by lunatics. Utter bunkum. Not any more. Here was the evidence. It made him decidedly uneasy.

And now there was this sinister new development. He was at a loss as to what to do. The deadline of twelve-thirty was fast approaching, and the morning ticked by at an alarming speed. Whoever was behind the note on the door clearly meant business. It just had to be Michael, his boss: the fact that he was absent from the gallery pointed strongly to this. But then, he reasoned that this was not his style. Michael was the sort to simply confront him in the gallery, face to face. Why then the British Museum? It was as if by being forced to be present at the meeting was also by his very action a sign of complicity. But what else could he do? The alternative was police involvement, and that would be an intrusion too far. He was too old for all this nonsense.

*

Michael's first meeting was at 11am, in the coffee lounge on the ground floor of the hotel. The French windows were open, with several couples seated at tables on the sunlit terrace, shaded by parasols. A couple of businessmen toyed on their laptops. Searching around the unfamiliar faces, Michael found his intended target seated alone in a quiet leafy corner. He was a small man conservatively dressed in grey flannel suit. Unremarkable in every other way, he perched like a bird on the edge of his chair, his beady eyes scanning those around him. Even though he was in his late seventies, he was alert and watchful. He had clearly seen Michael before Michael had spotted him.

As Michael approached, the man stood politely and extended a hand. Taking it, Michael introduced himself using his real name. Terence had obligingly organised the meeting, setting up the "interview" in which Michael would masquerade as a bona fide news reporter. He had been well briefed beforehand.

'I'm Paddy McGuire, pleased to meet you.'

'Can I get you a Guinness, Paddy?'

'That would be a very fine thing, Michael.'

They sat and faced each other. A waiter took an order for duplicate drinks and departed.

'Have you been to our fair city before, Michael?'

'Yes, particularly during the troubles north of the border. Although Belfast was my normal port of call, I had reason to visit Dublin on many an occasion. My wife also has family connections in Cork, so it is a landscape I know, with great affection I may add.'

'I've lived here all my life. Seventy-nine years in total, thirty-six of those in service. My wife and I celebrate our golden wedding anniversary next month. We'll spend a few quiet days in Galway to celebrate, I reckon.'

The waiter brought the drinks.

Michael raised his glass. 'Congratulations, that's a hard act to follow.'

'Are you not married yourself, Michael?'

'Separated.'

'My son lives in London. He is also going through a rather painful divorce. It is difficult to give advice. Angela – that's my wife – and I, well, we count our blessings every day.' He shifted in his seat, pulling back from the glare of the sun. 'I've seen and encountered many unpalatable things over the years, Michael, some of which still haunt me to this day. Marriage though, it's what has kept me going. Without it, I would have been burnt out years ago.' He shrugged wearily. 'Different times now, though. It seems even a blessed union has a shelf life.'

Michael remained silent, allowing Paddy centre stage.

'My son asks me what the secret of a happy marriage is. That's a big question. He should ask his dear mother, not me.' A twinkle sparked in his eye as he explained, '*Now* she would answer that we were only married for five minutes, not half a century! How come? Let me enlighten you. During all my years in the force, I only got to see her perhaps three times; such is the workload of a policeman!' He chuckled. 'I was never around to get under her feet. That's the recipe for an everlasting marriage, she would tell you.'

For the second time, Paddy's austere features broke into a generous smile. He was an endearing man, Michael decided. He liked him a great deal.

Paddy continued. 'Your colleague, Terry, said you were writing an article on minors who commit murder, and the effect it has on their lives after they are released from prison. There have been many high profile instances of this, most notably the recent Bulger case in England springs to mind. What happens to the fate of the killers, is that your drift?'

Michael took up the thread. 'A convicted criminal gets a new identity, a new beginning, but can the past really be erased? Is there genuine remorse on their part? Can the history of violence resurface? Why does society protect those who by their very actions are a threat to that same society? I want to explore how the victim has become a secondary issue, or concern, in crimes of violence. Equally, how does a convicted killer, even with the cloak of anonymity, merge into so-called ordinary life without behaving like a misfit?'

'And just how can I be of assistance, Michael?'

'Many years ago you were involved in one such case.'

'Ah, the Porter murder enquiry. Terry mentioned it. It's all on record.'

'Indeed.' Michael wanted to appear to be world-weary on this, avoiding any emotion on the subject, for fear of betraying his real motives. Keep it flat, Terry advised him. 'But you were there, from the beginning. This is a classic case for my article. Taken as a broad sweep, a young girl – a minor – kills her father. But what other choice did she have? Subjected to a daily life of habitual abuse, she lashed out after being cornered with no means of escape. She retaliated. *That* was her escape. But years later, how does society successfully integrate her so that she can lead a normal life, and put the past behind her? My question is: why do we owe her that privilege? I would like to understand your perspective on it, as you were on the frontline so to speak.'

Paddy McGuire consumed the last remains of his Guinness. He indicated to the waiter to bring more drinks. He lit a cigarette, and watched the smoke unfurl away from him.

'Do you smoke, Michael?' He gestured with the packet of Marlboroughs.

Michael raised a hand. 'No.'

'Good man. They'll be the death of me, Angela says. But death reaches us all in the end. I've seen every kind, mind you. Death is always a shock, no matter how many times you witness it.' He continued to inhale with pleasure, saying nothing more as a waitress brought the drinks. He thanked her, remaining on guard until she departed. 'It has always been said that policemen get hardened to violent crime over the years,' Paddy continued. 'Not so, if you consider the macabre roll call which we deal in: suicide, rape, murder, drug abuse, torture. Every case uniquely occupies a little corner of the brain. You convince yourself that you've seen it all. Nothing can further shock you. Eventually, the brain is full, then overflowing with inhuman debris. What is the final result to the immune system? Breakdown. Burn out. Of course we are affected. I still recall every minute detail of every case I've worked on.'

'A hazard of the job,' Michael observed.

Paddy shook his head slowly, 'More a damnation of the soul, if you want the honest truth.'

They drank quietly for a few moments. Paddy lit another cigarette as the sun moved off the terrace.

'Laura Porter. Was she a victim?' Michael prompted.

'For sure,' Paddy replied. 'The whole family were. The father was a beast, well known in the area for his brutality. As with a lot of families, Saturday night was a ritual of drunkenness and violence. Laura and her sister were sitting targets as they reached their early teens. Maggie, the eldest, eventually left home. This isolation left Laura in a very precarious position, at the mercy of this low-life. She was defenceless, or so we thought. On one such day, after hours of physical and mental torture at the hands of her father, she reached for a poker from the fireplace and battered him to death. He was unrecognisable from the attack. The first two or three blows would have killed him, but it was the ferocious assault on the victim which ultimately turned against her in the courtroom. A plea of self-defence became a prima face case of manslaughter.'

'What happened to her?'

'Laura was twelve at the time of the conviction. She was hospitalised for the next four years in a secure unit where she underwent a strict monitoring process to determine her state of mind. She was diagnosed as suffering from multiple personality disorder. Later, she was transferred to a psychiatric prison to serve her remaining sentence. Eventually, she was released under the protection of the law and gained a new identity. She now lives in Britain.'

'Did you keep in touch with the family?'

'I did for a long time. This is a small community. Delores, the mother, was a sick woman. She is now in a nursing home. The sister, who I've lost contact with, lives in Limerick, I believe.'

'There was a baby brother, I understand?'

'That would be Patrick. He died aged three or four, if I recall correctly. It was a very long time ago. The findings from the official enquiry indicated accidental death. He fell backwards from the top of the stairs and sustained multiple internal injuries. To this day I am of the opinion that the father was responsible, but nothing could prove his guilt. No one was spared his bullying. Even the family dog was kicked to death.'

'The police enquiry into the father's death became headline news, both here and in England. Why did Laura need specialised medical help?'

'Firstly, she was a minor in the eyes of the law and secondly, because she perceived herself as the victim, there were serious concerns for her health, which was deteriorating rapidly. In hospital, she attempted suicide on several occasions. The magnitude of what happened had virtually destroyed her. You could ask: why was she on trial in the first place? According to Laura, she acted in self-defence. If she had not protected herself that day, she was convinced that he would have killed her. After being raped and then beaten, she snapped, having been taken to the limits of human endurance. It was not then surprising that Laura would need sensitive psychiatric help. She was a broken child after all, Michael.'

'As the senior police officer on the case, did you concur with all the legal findings which led to a guilty verdict?'

'I deal with solid evidence, Michael. It was a straightforward investigation. I had a victim, a motive, and a confession from the killer. Rarely has anything been so open and shut in all the years of serving the force.'

'Was the father dead when you arrived?'

'Yes.'

Where was Laura found after the attack?'

'Being comforted by her sister,' Paddy replied, as if it had all happened only yesterday. 'We found them huddled together in an upstairs bedroom.'

'Where was their mother?'

'Delores had been away for the day. She returned several hours later, to a scene of utter carnage. It was she who identified the body after it had been taken down to the morgue to be cleaned up. It was bludgeoned beyond all recognition.'

'Who found the body?'

'The sister. Laura was discovered wandering the garden at the rear, in deep shock. There is a gate at the back, where Maggie gained access. Laura had earlier telephoned her with the news of what had happened. She pleaded with her to come home. On finding her sister, Maggie investigated the house and discovered the body. She then contacted the police.'

'And that was that.'

'Indeed.'

Michael pondered his next move, acutely aware of not overstepping the mark. Already, he felt his line of enquiry was close to the wind. He decided to push it further anyway. 'Ideally, I would like to look at the files. Is that possible?'

Paddy shifted uneasily in his seat. His eyes narrowed. 'Enough for today, Michael,' he said. 'I am tired. The files cannot be scrutinised, I'm afraid. Besides, I have told you everything.'

They stood and shook hands.

'You certainly have, Paddy. I'm very grateful. One last question though: Given the terrible circumstances of her past, did Laura eventually discover a kind of life worth pursuing?'

Paddy and Michael walked in silence to the front of the hotel. They shook hands once more.

'I always wished for her to find a kind of peace, if that was possible,' Paddy said, adding, 'But I believe the past was so shocking that it would always shape her future.'

Michael knew the truth of the statement. He asked, 'A curse then?'

The retired detective summed it up. 'We all live with our own inner demons, Michael. In her case, the curse is magnified a million times. Draw your own conclusions.'

Michael watched in silence as Paddy McGuire hailed a taxi and vanished from sight. One from the old guard, thought Michael. The trashy modern world today was so far removed from his perception of good old fashioned morality. Michael had a great deal of admiration for such tenacity against all the odds.

*

Ronald closed the gallery at midday and dashed by taxi to the British Museum on Great Russell Street. He was angry at this unwanted intrusion into his life and angrier still with Michael for playing this game, if indeed it was him. But he had no choice but to play it. It was a case of proving a point and removing an unnecessary stain from his good character. He was determined to clear this matter up once and for all.

On entering the building, one that he knew well, he quickly crossed the Queen Elizabeth II Great Court and took the west stairs which led to the Mesopotamia Room, via the glass bridge. His head pounded. Scanning the faces of those visible to him, he saw no one he recognised. Unable to relax, he then searched each darkened aisle, ending with the same disappointment. The tall glass display cabinets, containing ornate gold caskets, loomed either side of him. Where was Michael? Turning full circle, he retraced his steps and quickened his pace, to no avail. At the restaurant, he peered over the balcony and searched the atrium below. No sign of anyone he vaguely knew. He checked his watch. Two minutes to go. He was beginning to feel rather foolish, avoiding the inevitable confrontation.

Ronald took a deep breath, turned and moved swiftly through the Egyptian Room to the stairs which led up to the Prints & Drawing gallery. Just then, to his right, he caught sight of someone familiar leaving the Ladies bathroom. Ronald's heart skipped a beat. It was Kara. Their eyes met. Startled, he stood transfixed like a rabbit in the headlights of a car. She was fast approaching and he didn't know what to do.

If that wasn't enough to contend with, something else now held his absolute attention. This is weird, he thought. Who was that standing directly behind Kara? Surely, it couldn't be? Why on earth were they both here? Sudden panic gripped him. What the hell was going on? No matter! It was time to leave. Without a second thought, he turned abruptly and scampered to the north stairs exit and descended as fast as his legs would carry him.

*

Kara came out of the ladies' room and immediately caught sight of Ronald. Her stomach was tied in knots but she was determined to keep aloof and resolute. This confrontation had to be done, she reminded herself forcibly. In spite of their long friendship, she was not going to be the fall guy in this, and accordingly Ronald's admission of complicity would clear her name in Michael's eyes. Ronald had been wise to show up, now he would have to be gallant with his confession. Their eyes met. She was in control and felt strong. With each advancing step, she kept her gaze firmly fixed on his. Just as quickly, however, she detected a peculiar change in his demeanour. He wavered slightly, and diverted his attention to a space beyond her right shoulder. Even more disturbingly, he suddenly took flight, running down the stairs as if the building was on fire. It made her stop dead in her tracks. What on earth was going on? Before she had a chance to recover her composure, she almost jumped out of her skin as a firm hand grabbed at her shoulder from behind.

An unexpected yet familiar voice whispered close to her ear, 'I think you have found what you are looking for.'

Kara's heart pounded. How was this feasible?'

Turning slowly, she could hardly gather the strength to utter the one word that stuck obstinately in her throat. She was momentarily speechless. It was only in seeing him in the flesh, just inches away from her face, which brought home the impact of his voice.

Her own response, when it came, was faint and without resolve. 'Marcus,' she whispered incredulously.

CHAPTER FIFTEEN

It was too much to take. However, Kara recovered her wits sufficiently to shout, 'What the hell are you doing here, you scared the fucking life…'

Marcus calmly raised his finger to his lips, reminding her of where she was. Strangers turned in her direction, their ears pricked.

Kara fell silent, looked around apologetically and then kicked Marcus in the left shin with all her might. He grimaced and grabbed her shoulder for support, cursing her name under his breath. He took her by the arm, forcing her to retreat backwards into an unoccupied corridor, away from prying eyes.

This time, she grabbed him. 'You've got a helluva lot of explaining to do. You've just pissed on my plan. Why are you here, Marcus?'

Perspiration formed on his brow. It was his turn to look confused.

'What am I doing here? Is this some kind of a joke? Where is Michael?'

'He's in Dublin.'

Marcus looked rapidly in either direction, as if mindful of being overheard. He used the back of his hand to wipe his forehead. 'Jesus, Kara, if that's the case…was it *you* who left the note on the door to the gallery?'

'Yes, numbskull!' she said angrily. 'And you've just frightened off my only contact!'

'Ronald? Is that who…' Then he stopped.

Kara stared in disbelief. *'What?'*

'Is that who you really thought was sending the anonymous messages?'

Kara eyed him contemptuously. 'Yes, of course, who else do you...?' She halted in mid-sentence as she hurriedly tried to unscramble her brain. Something was amiss. Then the circuitry connected. 'My God, what are you *really* doing here, Marcus?'

He shook his head and diverted his eyes to study the polished marble floor beneath his feet, rather like a child caught out in some naughty misdemeanour. He seemed agitated. 'Kara,' he said calmly, raising his eyes and cradling her face in his outstretched hands, 'Ronald is not your contact.' He searched her face for reassurance. 'I am.'

Her jaw dropped. 'Marcus, you are scaring me now. What are you saying?'

Marcus sighed, and then, to her astonishment, kissed her hard on the mouth. He removed an envelope from his jacket pocket and handed it to her.

'Give this to Michael,' he instructed. 'Make sure he gets it, OK?' Fumbling into another pocket, he found a crumpled handkerchief to wipe away her tears. 'Listen, Kara, and listen carefully. It was me who delivered the first two envelopes. This is the third. I called at the gallery early this morning and saw the note on the door. I decided to come clean, suspecting Michael knew of my involvement. I made the mistake of using your personal email, which blew my cover. Or so I thought. Previously, it was easy to deliver the envelopes until I spotted that the CCTV camera had been repositioned to catch me out, so I panicked and used another method to make contact. I should have waited and thought it through before being so rash, but I needed to make fresh contact.'

Kara took his hands and held them tightly. 'I don't get it, Marcus. Why are you involved in all this?'

'I'm just the go-between, Kara. This goes back over many years. At school, my best mate had an elder brother who was an aspiring artist. This bit you can guess. His name was Julius. Ring a bell? Because of our shared interest, he and I have always kept in touch. One year, I spent time at his studio, which was in a huge house down in the country...'

She interrupted him, 'Laburnum Farm?'

'Yeah, that was the place – an obscene pile, the boy made good, uh? There was a girl staying there as well. Her name was Antonia. I knew something was going on between them. There was a bad feeling in the house. Anyway, Julius asked me to get her away to Scotland. He knew I was broke and paid me decent money to assist him. The deal was for me to look after her until he could come at a later date.'

'Did you meet Lauren?'

'No. She was away at the time, in Ireland I think. That was his big chance to plan their escape. It was obvious to me that he and Antonia were serious about each other. He begged me to help. I wasn't sure if I should, but he was a mate. And besides, I needed the money.'

'What happened to them?'

Marcus flinched. 'The star-crossed lovers? I did as he asked, but Julius didn't show in the end. After a month, on Antonia's insistence, I left Scotland and returned to the farm to find out what was happening. There was no sign of Julius. I met a woman called

Maggie. She insisted that he had gone away, for good. There was no discussion, nor an opportunity to investigate his disappearance. She left me in no doubt that I was not to return, ever. Antonia was distraught. We managed another three weeks in hiding but we never heard from Julius. Eventually, the money ran out. Antonia contacted her family in Italy and she returned home. I never heard from either of them again until several months ago. Antonia got in touch. I've since learnt that they have a child. I never knew that they had got back together. She simply instructed me to pass on the envelopes to Michael. I don't even know what they contain.'

Kara stared blankly. 'I need to speak to Michael. Why didn't you tell me this before? Is that the real reason why we are together? I feel a complete idiot, Marcus.'

'We're together because I'm crazy about you! I was asked to be a messenger, that's all. Meeting up with you was totally unexpected.'

'But you knew of Michael's search for Julius. We discussed it, don't you remember?'

'Of course. It was difficult.'

'*Difficult*?' She dropped his hands abruptly. '*Difficult*? Is that how you see it?'

'I was helping out. I had a loyalty to Antonia, not to Michael.'

'What of your loyalty to me, Marcus?'

He searched for her hands but she twisted them away, folding her arms instead.

He tried desperately to defend himself. 'Kara, I don't know where I stand with you!' He appeared angry and bewildered. He struggled to find the words. 'One day you're cold with me, the next red hot,' he said feebly. 'I am torn. An old friend asked for help. I thought, naively, that I was helping you *all*.'

'You actually spied on me, Marcus.'

'I did *what*?'

'It was you who forewarned Antonia of Michael's visit to Venice.'

'Wait a minute!' His consternation was cut short abruptly by a plump, red-faced attendant, who asked them to curtail their conversation. In short, they were being ordered to leave. They vacated in silence.

Outside, they sat on the broad concrete steps in front of the building. The incessant drone from the passing traffic, coupled with the noise from the school party milling around, made conversation hard. Marcus lifted himself up from the steps and paced back and forth, deep in thought. 'I was *never* a spy, Kara!' he shouted. 'You gave me all the information freely. Can't you remember?'

'How did I manage that, clever arse?' she asked indignantly.

'You confided in me most nights, whenever you sat beside me on the sofa,' he said. 'Eventually, you would always lie down with your head in my lap. I stroked your hair. We drank a bottle of wine. You talked. I listened. All those times, you simply unburdened yourself, seemingly without realising the information you were passing over.'

'Christ. And they say men never listen.'

Marcus returned to where she sat, propped against one of the huge stone columns, and huddled next to her. 'Kara, you didn't betray Michael. You were simply confronting your fears and I was the proverbial sounding board. I used that same information in order to protect Antonia from Lauren. I owed her.'

'And me? Do you owe me?'

'Big time,' he admitted. 'When I went on that bender, I thought I had lost you for good. I couldn't see a way back. But you saved me. You were there for me. I just wanted to do this last one thing for Antonia.'

'What about Julius? Is he alive?'

'Yes. But for now, he remains in hiding. Antonia had no choice but to withhold the truth from Michael. Is that OK with you?'

'Michael needs to know.'

Marcus shook his head vigorously. 'Not yet, Kara. Julius is warning Michael through the contents of these envelopes. He is warning Michael as to the danger Lauren poses to his very existence, especially if his whereabouts is revealed. None of this would have been necessary if she had not decided to sell the Patrick Porters. They are worth a great deal of money, half of which is rightfully his, as is the farm. They had a deal. All he wanted was the paintings. She could keep the house. But Lauren is greedy, and intends to keep everything for herself. Michael shouldn't have got involved, but he, too, is driven by greed. Julius will not let this go. She can have the house, but not the paintings. They are too precious to him, especially as they all feature Antonia. He feels that she has controlled him for long enough, and isn't playing fair. Now is the time to get even. Julius can't come forward with a long line of incriminating evidence against her because, under British law, she is a protected person. He will not be afforded the same privilege. Therefore, he must remain hidden, in order to protect himself and his family. This is the woman that swore to harm them all. To expose Lauren for what she is, Julius is using Michael to discover the truth, and reveal her true colours. And only then can Julius come out of obscurity, claim what is rightfully his, and live a proper life with his family without fear.' He hugged her tightly.

'How much danger is Michael in?' Kara asked.

He frowned. 'A helluva lot, I would say.'

'I reckon I've had a run-in with that sick chick. She's been stalking me, but I can't prove it. How dangerous is Lauren to me?'

'Fucking scarily.'

'What do we do next?'

'Open the envelope.'

Kara retrieved it from her back pocket. She ripped open the flap and extracted what appeared to be a grainy black and white photograph. It was of an old decaying building. 'What is *this*?' she asked. In truth, she felt utterly exhausted.

Marcus raised his eyebrows. 'It's a tithe barn. I know it well. It's part of Laburnum Farm.'

'Then I'll also get to know it well.'

'What do you mean?'

Kara studied the photograph. It was a dark and haunting building. 'I am going to the farm tomorrow. I have an appointment with Lauren. Michael has asked me to do an inventory of the paintings at the house.'

'Jesus, are you kidding, especially after what I've just told you?'

'It's my job, Marcus. It has to be done and, despite everything, I want to meet this woman face to face. Besides, I'm going to make some serious money on this.'

'This is not a good idea, Kara. You need to talk with Michael before making that kind of decision.'

'I already have. Decision made. But I have a correction to make to my earlier statement. You say you owe me big time?'

'You bet.'

She saw the implication of her comment begin to dawn on him.

'Now wait just a minute...' he said.

Kara stood and held out her hand to stop him in his tracks. 'It isn't "I" that is going to Laburnum Farm, Marcus. I'm afraid it's a "We".'

*

'Did you know that there are three Nobel Prize winners for Literature from this great city of Dublin, Mr Strange? Can you name them?'

Michael deliberated, not wishing to show unnecessary arrogance. Then he answered, 'W.B. Yeats, Samuel Beckett and, I believe, George Bernard Shaw.'

'Impressive,' Dr Joseph O'Connor remarked. The two men stood on the immaculate lawns of Trinity College. They walked side by side, the older man with the aid of a walking stick. He had a shock of white hair, and stooped slightly. He was dressed impeccably in a cream linen suit, polished shoes, blue shirt and striped tie. A figure of sheer elegance, thought Michael admiringly.

'And do you know what priceless treasure is housed right here where we stand?' the doctor asked, with a youthful sparkle in his eye.

'The Book of Kells,' Michael replied immediately.

'Excellent, excellent!' The doctor laughed heartily. 'Finally, whose resting place is at St. Patrick's Cathedral, where he was Dean from 1713 to 1745?'

Michael pondered the question, delaying his answer just long enough for his inquisitor to start to feel superior. 'Jonathan Swift.'

'My word, Mr Strange, you do know your history! I am humbled.'

'Beginner's luck!'

'Hardly,' the doctor retorted warmly, 'you underestimate yourself. I like a man who commands respect. I'm sorry for the little test, but I cannot resist. I'm pleased you humoured an old man.'

'My pleasure,' Michael replied. 'I also am most grateful that you tolerate me with your expert knowledge in the field of medicine, which is something I could not remotely hope to achieve.'

'We do what we can, Mr Strange. At my age, knowledge is a dangerous thing. On the one part – yes, I am considered an expert in my field; on another level – take my grandchildren, for example – I am but an imbecile! A nice one though, but considered ancient and beyond my sell-by-date. It puts things into perspective.'

'Indeed it does.' Michael checked his watch. 'Will you join me for lunch?'

'Are you paying?'

Michael enjoyed the blunt approach. 'It will be my pleasure.'

'Then, yes, I accept your kind invitation.'

'Not so imbecilic,' Michael observed wryly.

*

They sat at a window table in The Oliver St. John Gogarty restaurant on Fleet Street. They ordered Irish stew and dumplings, accompanied by a bottle of sparkling mineral water. Michael was still suffering from the protracted Guinness count he had accumulated rather rashly with Paddy McGuire earlier.

'What is your book called, Mr Strange?'

'Myth and Modern Man.' Michael knew he was treading on decidedly dodgy territory with his own myth of authorship.

'And where do I come in to it, if at all?'

He pressed on, hoping to sound convincing. 'One section is dedicated to Multiple Personality Disorder. I have it on good faith that you are an expert in this specialised field. I would like you to spell out the myth of the old and the modern truth as we understand it today. There have, I believe, been great advances in this "hidden" world that we, as a nation, have ignored or been too frightened to confront. Is this correct?'

'Hmm,' Dr Joseph O'Connor shifted in his seat, finding comfort of sorts. He took a gulp of water. 'You have to remember that I have not practised for over fifteen years. But I do write the occasional paper, and I keep up on new developments. MPD is now referred to more logically as DID, that is, Dissociate Identity Disorder, a condition in which a person has more than one distinct personality.'

'So it is true that one person can in fact have several alter personalities?'

'Indeed. It is known that in females, there are up to nineteen alter identities; less so in men. However, thirty, forty, more, even, is not impossible; although very rare, I should add.'

Michael was fascinated. 'Can you describe, in simple terms, what DID actually is?'

'Yes. It is a disorder of "hidden-ness". It is a survival tactic, a creative attempt to protect oneself from the trauma of life. If, for instance, you have experienced a catastrophic event, which has traumatised your thinking process, then the simple act of compartmentalising or separating this event is in itself a way of hiding it. We can invent alter personality traits which allow us to forget the pain or suffering we would otherwise feel. In other words, a wall is invented. We would dissociate in order to survive.'

'Is this not amnesia?'

'Partly.' The doctor was interrupted as a waiter brought their food, which they consumed heartily. Eventually, he continued, 'Amnesia is a barrier, an escape. For those who suffer the most, anything that does the job of hiding the root of the trauma is considered a necessary diversion. Hence, "walling" off trauma is a main function of those with multiple personality disorder.'

'Do all of us not compartmentalise our problems?'

'Absolutely, but "walling" off is a massively different process.'

'Where does it begin, at the point of trauma?'

'Not necessarily. It certainly begins in childhood, and normally with those cases of extreme child abuse. It does not happen in adulthood. Only in childhood is the flexibility and vulnerability there for a "host" personality to manifest itself. Later, many personality changes can be invented. But it can only begin within the traumatised child.'

'Is an "alter" considered, therefore, a friend?'

'Yes. They rescue and protect. The strategy displaces the suffering on to another identity. If you can dissociate the pain, you can effectively bury it. It is that simple.'

'Can the identity disturbance become too controlling...even dangerous?'

'In extreme cases, yes.'

Michael decided to push hard. 'Can you give me an actual case as an example of this?'

The psychiatrist finished his food with gusto, using the bread from a side plate to mop up the remains of the gravy. Michael refilled his glass with water.

'Would you like a glass of wine?' Michael asked.

'A glass of port with coffee would be just perfect. I have to be careful with my diet.'

Michael carried on with his meal, which he had started to neglect; such was his enthusiasm for the subject under discussion. 'An example?' he repeated.

'Unfortunately, that is not possible, with regard to patient/doctor confidentiality, which of course you will be aware of.'

Undeterred, he asked, 'Can we look at it in a purely academic sense then? Can someone with multiple personality disorder be controlled in fact by a dangerous "host"? Is that possible?'

'Yes, that is possible.'

'Have you witnessed, or treated, such a case?'

The doctor frowned. He shifted his weight. 'I have,' he said reluctantly. His eyes narrowed.

Michael pressed. 'Forgive the comparison, but is there such a condition made infamous by Dr Jekyll and Mr Hyde?'

'Yes.'

'And have you witnessed it for real?'

There was a long pause. 'Yes,' he confirmed.

'Are there such people with this condition living freely in our society which you would consider dangerous to themselves, or a threat to others?'

'Where is this leading, Mr Strange?'

'I am trying to establish if people do exist who have a self-destructive behaviour to their personality, which in turn could be deemed dangerous if that "alter" state is threatened in any way. Is this possible?'

'The "host" personality can have control. If it becomes confused, threatened or uncertain, even frightened, then hostility can surface. Many of those that suffer this disorder come from a harrowing background of drug abuse, self-mutilation, panic attacks, and depression. In this environment, under certain conditions, a DID patient would feel ashamed, hear voices, undergo seizures and show suicidal tendencies. Taking this further, a person undergoing these extreme anxiety attacks could have a catastrophic identity disturbance.'

'In other words, an angry sufferer with embittered internal persecution complex could, in theory, blame others for their suffering. And in turn become hostile?'

'It is possible.'

'So the answer is "yes".'

The reply was clear. 'Yes.'

Once again, the conversation was halted as coffee and port was served. They took time out to savour the fine vintage. Michael then resumed.

'Is it also possible for adults, who have developed multiple personalities in childhood, to continue introducing more "alters" during adulthood?'

'Of course it is possible.'

'Are they aware of this?'

'In a few cases, yes, but over eighty per cent of adults do not have a clue that they are in fact "multiple".'

'What triggers a new "multiple"?'

'As I have explained, it manifests itself in childhood, as a result of severe physical, sexual or emotional conflict. In adulthood, the answers are not so clear. For instance, the different personalities do not have to be visible. Also, each personality can have a different name, a different past and self image. Each "alter" has its own independent traits – even different gender.'

Bang. Michael at last began to see what had eluded him during the past three months, as he had tried desperately to draw a clearly defined picture of Lauren O'Neill. Up to this point, he had failed abjectly. Now it was beginning to make sense. However, what he saw was a nightmarish vision that terrified him.

Michael had one last question. 'Tell me, sir, in your experience have you ever encountered this very prognosis? I'm referring most notably to a woman who was under your supervision in the late seventies?'

It was one question too far.

Dr Joseph O'Connor rose abruptly from his chair. He discarded his napkin and reached for his walking stick. 'Mr Strange, it has been a pleasure. Thank you for lunch and best of luck with your book. Our conversation is now at an end. Good day.'

Michael stood awkwardly and offered his hand. It was refused. 'Sir, I sincerely hope that I didn't offend you. I obviously have. The woman I refer to is Laura Porter, but of course, you already know this. Today, she lives her life under the new name of Lauren O'Neill. I believe that she is in grave danger not only to herself but to others who have direct contact with her.' He extracted a business card from his jacket pocket. He pressed it down into the doctor's own lapel pocket before giving him a chance to object. 'Lauren is *many* people, as you are fully aware. But one such identity asserts itself above all others. It controls with aggression. This "host" personality brings intense fear, and loathing. It first brings self-injury, depression, possible seizures but – and I emphasis this – it always ends up by striking out, with vicious intent, against those who betray her. If you have anything to say to me, please call me. I beg you. It could save lives.'

'*Who* are you, Mr Strange?'

'A saviour, if it were possible.'

'I spent my entire professional life in the prison service with exactly the same morality as you, that is, just hoping to save someone – *anyone* – from the broken body they occupied, and the broken mind that they were forever trapped in.'

'And did you succeed?'

The doctor sighed heavily. 'I wish I could say "yes". Now, if you'll forgive me, I'm rather tired. Good luck, whoever you are. I hope you find salvation. But it is a very long shot. I never did, I'm ashamed to admit. Have a pleasant flight home.'

With that, he turned and walked slowly away. For the second time in the day Michael felt isolated, with fear as his only ally. But the more his mind became entrenched with this notion, the more he became nervous of what he had to confront. It was close now, this fear. He could smell it.

*

Kara took the rest of the afternoon off, avoiding Ronald at all costs. She felt an utter fraud, and would somehow have to make it up to him with a grovelling apology, and whatever else it would take to help mend matters. In the meantime, she prepared for the forthcoming trip to the witch's coven the next day. She and Marcus agreed to go in his car, an old Suzuki jeep, which would accommodate the large easel better than in her battered red mini. She loaded a digital camera, tripod and specialised lighting equipment. As Marcus was not known to Lauren, it would be easy to explain his role as technical support. They agreed beforehand to do the job in a disciplined two-hour turnaround, and then get the hell out of there. For her, having Marcus as a companion was incredibly reassuring. Without him, she knew that she would be utterly terrified.

She tried several times to telephone Michael on his mobile, but on each occasion there was either no signal or he had switched off. This unnerved her. After packing the vehicle, Kara selected the clothes she would wear. Normally, it would be smart casual, businesslike. Not this time. She chose army combat trousers, a plain cream crew jumper and a padded waistcoat. This made her almost laugh out loud, but she felt obscurely that she should prepare for the very worst. Only she didn't know what this could entail. Her imagination was beginning to run riot and cloud her judgement. *Still, what could possibly go wrong?*

Marcus had gone out to buy canvases, leaving her alone in the apartment. Normally, this wouldn't present a problem, but every slight sound, or movement, spooked her. It was as if she was being watched. Even the sound of next door's cat scratching in the communal hallway forced her to check the doors and windows and lock herself in. She felt like a prisoner in her own home. Time crept by. In the meantime, she found herself padding back and forth across the floor, drinking endless cups of coffee, checking the time, waiting anxiously for Marcus. It made her sick with apprehension.

There was one thing she could do. Swiftly, she moved into the kitchen and extracted a thin bladed fish knife from the drawer and ran her finger down the sharpened edge. Just the thing. Without further ado, she went back to the bedroom, wrapped the knife carefully in a handkerchief and inserted it into one of the long pockets on the army trousers she had picked to wear.

Lying next to her neatly folded clothes atop the bed was the photograph of the old barn. Looking closely at it again somehow gave her the creeps. It was such a place of desolation and abandonment. It looked as if unseen eyes lay hidden and watchful: a place of lost souls. What was the message that was contained here? What was Antonia telling them? It made her shudder. The walls closed in on her. She felt sick. Where was bloody Marcus?

She could hear laboured breathing. Twisting furiously, she found herself alone. It was then that she realised it was the sound of her own exertions. She wiped her forehead. It was wet. She extended her hands for inspection. They were shaking. Her stomach churned. Holding on to the bedpost for support, the room was fast becoming a whirling mass of indeterminable objects. How could that be so? She felt faint. She felt like she was about to freak out. Where the bloody hell are you, Marcus?

The photograph in her hand fell to the floor, face down. Kara bent down and retrieved it, but dizziness overcame her. She sat on the bed and examined the faint inscription on the reverse of the black and white image. It was barely visible to her eye, handwritten in pencil, but she read: Patrick Porter R.I.P.

What the hell was this? Kara didn't care anymore; such was the pain in her head. She was just thankful to lie back on the bed, closing her eyes to the increasing mayhem which invaded her world.

CHAPTER SIXTEEN

Early the next morning, before his lunchtime flight, Michael packed hurriedly and settled his bill at the Shelbourne Hotel. This gave him the opportunity for an appointment with a very special person. He was going to meet the one woman who could effectively be of the greatest significance in his journey to Dublin. He had endeavoured to avoid this moment but it was now inevitable. What he had gained from Paddy McGuire and then the doctor was of huge importance, but the door was still only half open, he felt.

This person he hoped to meet had no idea of his existence or his intentions, nor, he imagined, had she any real recollection of past events that had been so responsible in misshapening her life. To all intents and purposes, Delores Porter was but a barely breathing corpse, a pathetic shell of a woman. Worse still, she had not spoken for over twenty years. It was a long shot, but Michael needed to find a way to communicate with her.

Bridge Nursing Home was situated on the south side of the City. Michael took a taxi and arrived at 8.45 am. Once again, he was indebted to Terry who had provided the vital information to help track her down. He had also laid the groundwork to enable him to gain access to her. This time, he was masquerading as a solicitor working on forgotten papers that just needed verifying. His story didn't need to be convincing, just plausible enough to get through the front door.

The care home was an imposing red brick three-storey gothic building, surrounded by massive oak trees bordering either end, like bookends. Overgrown shrubbery partially hid the imposing façade. The tarmac drive was cracked and badly worn. It was a place of neglect for the forgotten people. Inside, it was grossly overheated and sadly threadbare, with nurses coming and going, carrying trays of tea and biscuits, and elderly patients, sitting forlornly, dotted around the cavernous rooms, waiting to die. The sound of several television sets boomed across the hallway. Michael hated the sight and smell of these places. It made him feel nauseous.

'Can I help you?' From behind a heavy desk, a matronly figure in starched white uniform peered closely at him from behind rimless glasses. She was as cumbersome as the desk.

He approached her in confident manner. 'Michael Strange, from Strange and Churchill, solicitors,' he announced. 'You will have been expecting me.'

The woman scrutinised him from head to toe, examining his immaculate navy wool suit, sky blue shirt, navy tie and highly polished black shoes. The shoes were a must: they would gain entry to anywhere on the planet on gleam alone. Satisfied, she searched down a typewritten list on her overcrowded tabletop, frowning intently as she went. 'Here you are. A man telephoned to make an appointment at two-thirty in the afternoon.' She frowned again. 'You are rather early, don't you think?'

Michael knew Terry had made the appointment on the day he left England. It was a mistake not to have kept in contact. They had made an error. 'Unfortunately, my plans have changed. I am expected in court this afternoon. I have a flight to catch, and I needed to rearrange my timetable.' He raised his eyebrows, lowered his briefcase to the floor and surrendered his arms to her mercy. 'Quite clearly, you should have been informed. I apologise. Does this present a problem?'

The woman puffed out an almighty huff. She opened a large book from a shelf and inspected the contents. Again, she ran a finger down a list. Michael caught sight of her badge. Miss Brogan.

'I have a taxi waiting for me,' he said firmly, adding, 'What I have to accomplish will only take a few minutes. I would appreciate your cooperation, Miss Brogan.'

She looked up, and straightened her back. She was as wide as she was tall. And she wasn't tall.

Michael glanced at his watch for additional impact.

The formidable Miss Brogan relented. 'Very well, Mr Strange. You have fifteen minutes only. I must warn you that you must not upset her in any way, is that understood? She can easily get into a distressed state of mind, and she must remain calm at all times.'

Michael gave the reply she wanted to hear. 'Understood.'

She wasn't quite won over. 'I will be keeping a very close eye on you, Mr Strange.'

'Indeed.'

'Wait here. I'll make her comfortable and explain who you are.'

With that, Miss Brogan disappeared down the long corridor to his left. Waiting patiently, he made way for a mobile bed being ferried past by two male nurses. A fragile old lady barely glanced in his direction. The smell of urine invaded his nostrils.

Several minutes elapsed, making him restless.

'Come,' Miss Brogan barked, waving at him to follow in her path. At the end of the hallway, Michael stepped into a grand glass orangery. It had seen better days, but it was impressive nonetheless.

'Fifteen minutes,' came the instruction.

Michael silently crossed the black and white tiled floor and recognised the woman who had passed him in the bed. She occupied a place by the entrance to the garden and was bathed in light from the vast windows. The back of the bed had been raised, allowing for Delores to be propped up using extra pillows behind her shoulders.

Michael pulled a chair across and sat beside her. He had to act quickly. From his briefcase, he pulled out a photograph of Lauren and himself taken several weeks ago. It was in the garden at the farm. They were smiling together. He had to make immediate impact with Delores, and this he hoped would be the start.

'Hello, Delores. My name is Michael. Do you recognise the pretty girl in the picture?'

He held it up in front of her seemingly vacant gaze. Her eyes did not flicker. 'It is your daughter, Lauren…' Shit. He quickly corrected himself. 'Laura.' He disguised his mistake by adding, 'The good looking fellow is me. We are friends. Good friends.' Thankfully, he seemed to get away with his stupidity. Although her daughter had undergone a change of identity, it was inconceivable that *any* mother would relate to another name than the one that she herself had chosen.

Delores remained impassive. It was a bad start.

'I know that she came to see you recently, with Maggie. That must have been a wonderful surprise. Laura told me all about it. I've been to Dublin on business and I promised your daughter that I would call in and say "hello". It is a real pleasure.'

He took her hands in his and gently caressed them. They were gnarled and cold and bony. He suddenly felt awful, attempting to deceive her with his false tales. Just what did he think he was playing at? He reached into his case once more. 'These are for you.' He placed a gift-wrapped box of soft jellies on her lap, and then, rather more secretively, a tiny bottle of brandy, which he slyly slid under her bed sheet. 'I know this is naughty,' he glanced around in a bold gesture of defiance, 'but what the hell...'

For the first time, he registered an inkling of response; just the slightest movement of her mouth. It was a smile. And slowly, he traced it to her eyes.

'You can hear me, can't you, Delores?' His heart beat faster. Just then, they were interrupted by Miss Brogan, who marched over to the bed. She silently wiped around Delores's mouth and chin with a sterilised cloth, finishing with a cold stare in his direction. 'Ten minutes.'

He waited until they were alone again. Michael needed *something*.

In desperation, he tried another tactic, more underhand. 'Laura, your daughter,' he whispered. 'She and I are to marry. Does this make you happy? Did she tell you about us when she visited recently?' He cradled her hands once more. 'We can arrange for the ceremony in Dublin, if you like. Then you can attend, if you feel well enough. What do you think?'

He felt a reflex from her hands, a gradual tightening. She really was aware of everything he was telling her. It was a big breakthrough.

'Squeeze my hand if it pleases you. That is, our marriage.'

Delores did not respond.

'Would you be unhappy with this?'

He felt a tightening.

'Are you not happy for Laura, Delores?'

Tighter.

'Do you not approve of what she is doing?'

Tighter still.

'I know it is difficult for you, but can we somehow talk about this?'

No response.

A commanding voice roared from behind him. 'Five minutes, Mr Strange.'

Michael leaned closer to her. In the strong light, her skin was pure white and translucent. Her hair was sparse and wiry, revealing a fragile scalp. Blue veins protruded on her bony arms.

'Delores,' he said softly, 'I would like to help your daughter. She is seriously ill. I believe that she urgently needs medical supervision. If you cannot talk, squeeze my hand again if you agree with what I am saying.'

He felt her grip on his hand.

'Is she a danger to herself?'

She responded again.

'To others?'

A firmer tightening.

'Delores, I will only get one chance to say this. I need you to trust me. I know the family history. I am aware of the tragic circumstances that have befallen you all. But I need to know what happened to Patrick, your son. I know this is distressing for you, but it is pivotal in understanding where the first trauma manifested itself with Laura, because in my opinion it obviously deeply affected her. It shaped her later life, far more than when she killed her father.' Michael watched for signs of distress but Delores remained unreceptive. 'According to the police, Patrick died as a result of an accident. But there were doubts cast. Do you believe it was an accident?'

No response.

He tried again. 'Was his death the result of harmful activity?'

Engaged pressure.

'Was your husband responsible?'

Static.

'I have to ask this. Were you implicated?'

No response. He was aware of her breathing becoming erratic. Her skin was sticky. His questioning was causing stress.

From afar, he heard Miss Brogan yell, 'Time for you to go, Mr Strange.'

He heard her footsteps approaching. Fast.

'Delores,' he pleaded, 'however painful this must be for you: tell me now, because I know you want to unburden yourself. Was Laura responsible for the death of your son?'

'That will be all,' Miss Brogan demanded, her immense shadow looming over them both. She cleaned Delores's mouth and chin again, and wiped her brow. 'No more talking.' She then turned and admonished him. 'Delores is clearly exhausted, Mr Strange.'

Michael clung to her hands just waiting for a sign – *any sign* – but to no avail. She was too feeble to respond. Her eyes were closing.

Miss Brogan persisted, 'Mr Strange; that will be all, now I must ask you to leave.' She raised her formidable eyebrows. 'Immediately.'

Michael stood and fastened his briefcase. He was beaten by his own impatience. He hated himself. Loosening his tie, he turned for the exit.

'Goodbye, Delores,' he said, adding, 'I hope you find a peace that you deserve. I will do everything in my power to protect Laura from the demons that possess her. You have my word.'

In the hallway, he became agitated and despondent. He had subjected an old lady to a painful reminder of a brutal past. *But she had wanted to communicate with him. She was not hiding from the past. She was confronting it.* The fact remained that with his final question Delores had chosen deliberately not to respond. Christ. He retraced his steps and found Miss Brogan barring his way. Behind her, Delores was being wheeled off in the other direction.

'Is there a problem?' Miss Brogan asked. 'Or did I not make myself absolutely clear.'

Michael protested. 'I need to ask just one last question…'

'Time is up, Mr Strange. You have caused enough anguish for my patient.'

'Delores!' he shouted.

'Mr Strange, I must warn you...'

'Delores!'

Miss Brogan snapped her fingers and suddenly a uniformed male nurse grabbed him by the arms. He struggled to get free, mindful of her final order: 'Have this man escorted from the premises. Now!'

He had but one slim chance. Above the din and chaos, he screamed, 'It was Maggie, wasn't it?'

But he knew it was a futile request. She could not tell him. Speech was truly beyond her, her voice sealed by a suffering beyond the comprehension of others. She existed in a tomb of remorse.

Just then, a peculiar crack invaded the mayhem. Momentarily, everyone hesitated, almost in slow motion. It gave Michael time to direct his gaze to where the sound had come from. Then he saw it. Rolling toward him, across the highly polished floor, was the miniature bottle of brandy that he had hidden under her bed sheets. Delores had managed to secure it in her hands and then, with great fortitude, released it to fall to the ground. He was convinced it was her way of catching his attention.

It was her only possible way to communicate. He had to believe it. Delores was a determined old lady. She had made her last defiant signal. It was a call to witness.

*

Outside, Michael brushed off his escort, dusted himself down and gulped clean air. His taxi driver had nodded off. He checked his watch. It was time to make the airport, get home, and coordinate with Kara and Lauren. He had deliberately switched off his mobile during his short stay at the care home. He didn't want interruptions. Now the bloody battery was almost dead. It was vital to make sure that his plans were proceeding as normal, and that Kara knew exactly what she was doing. *God, the very thought turned his stomach. Did she know what she was doing? Had he gone too far with this?* With regard to Lauren, he was confident that she was not aware of his journey to Dublin. What concerned him now was whether Miss Brogan would contact one of the two sisters and spill the beans of his visit to their mother. He had made one mistake, now an even bigger mistake, causing a ruckus in the nursing home. It brought unwarranted attention.

Maggie scared him. She had already warned him not to mess in family affairs. He had now. Big time. He now knew a family secret that had been kept silent for over thirty years. If it could be seriously believed, that is. Maggie was the elder sister, and held a firm stranglehold over both her sister and her ailing mother. Secrets are best kept *secret*. Maggie, he felt, would go to any lengths to protect her own guilt. What wasn't known, of course, was how much of this did Lauren have knowledge of?

Michael found a payphone in the street, just a hundred yards from his stationary taxi. He dialled Maggie's number. No response. Just where was she? It bothered him. He dialled Lauren's number. It was disconnected. He tried Kara. No connection. It was past ten o'clock. By now, Kara should be on her way to the farm. Shit. He had to reach her, to warn her of the danger she was in. It was only now that he could see this clearly. It was inconceivable that she should be left alone with Lauren, and that's precisely what he had stupidly organised. He hoped that she had the sense to take Marcus. What had he been thinking, putting Kara right into the lion's den?

He roused the driver from his slumber. 'To the airport! Fast!'

*

Ronald was not happy. After the weird episode with Kara yesterday, he had decided to contact his boss and make an official complaint about her. He considered the whole affair a direct attack on his integrity. He would also now consider his position in the business; such was his humiliation at being challenged by a mere secretary. It was the last straw. He came into the gallery this morning as a sense of duty to Michael. That was all. Where Kara was, he could not care less. What worried him, though, was not being able to contact Michael by phone. What was going on?

As instructed, he had spent considerable time over the past couple of days digging up information on the artist, Patrick Porter. But that was the trouble. He had spent time and energy *not* finding out information. There simply wasn't any. Not of any great substance, anyway.

He considered the facts. Like a lot of artists, whether local or international, information is usually forthcoming from sketchy biographical records, either through the artist themselves, the artist's agent, the internet, the auction houses or official art publications, such as Who's Who in Art. Of course, many artists introduce themselves to the galleries with a personal appearance, or present their work on CD. However, in the vast number of cases, the gallery and artist never meet. The actual identity or description is taken on face value, without cross checking the credentials. It was the way it was, unless the gallery had direct contact with the artist, as was the situation with Marcus Heath.

Ronald was aware of many, many artists who had found great success with Churchill Fine Art. Michael had discovered their early talent, represented them, or promoted them to the wider buying public. But here was the rub. The artist, in many cases, was never personally known to the gallery, very rarely to the public. Why? Because there were thousands and thousands of successful artists from all over the world, who either employed agents or simply crated up their work and posted it straight to the gallery concerned. It was impossible to have a relationship with all but a handful. In reality, the bottom line was supply and demand. The artist himself – unlike his name – was often inconsequential to a commercial gallery. He or she was just the vehicle to a potential sale. It was the actual painting that was the essential asset, a tangible tool to turn a profit.

The work of Patrick Porter was one such case. Internationally renowned, but who had actually met the artist? Certainly not Michael, nor Ronald. The two most noticeable things about Patrick Porter were his sublime artistic abilities and his untimely, mysterious disappearance: the perfect ingredients to create intrigue and romance to promote keen sales. If the quality of a canvas was of the highest calibre, and reflected in a high price tag to match, then the profit was the guiding force in the mercenary art world. It was a multi-billion dollar franchise. Art was now the hotly traded commodity of the super rich. As far as Ronald was concerned, it didn't require much analysis that in order to publicise the "next best thing", a group of shrewd art dealers would willingly join forces to reinforce this line of thinking. He chuckled to himself. There were several prominent public figures that did this to brilliant effect. In a nutshell, these people created a manufactured market overnight by simply lending their names and reputations to these unknown artists, underpinning the perceived success of the next "big thing" by sustainable investment. First, the speculation and then the manipulation. As a result of the publicity and hysteria, the wheels would begin to turn, with lucrative returns coming in. The monster was born.

Ronald understood this. He had been in the business a long time. There was always somebody ready to create an opportunity to dispose someone else of his or her money. It was called salesmanship, and all you needed was product and chance. It was the way of the world.

Patrick Porter was a product. The rest was immaterial. It did not surprise Ronald that he had very little to report to Michael. One thing he did have though - a poor monochrome photograph of the artist, taken from an exhibition brochure for a one-man show in Miami, Florida, in 1991. He looked gay, Ronald observed, with a smirk.

*

Kara and Marcus got out of London early and travelled mostly in silence, down the A3 toward the little village of Old Hampton, where Laburnum Farm was located. Marcus knew the way and drove at a steady pace. He was nervous. The memory of the farm and the bad vibes he had encountered were not something he wished to relive. However, he was with Kara and this made him feel reassured. Although he was dead set against the reasoning behind the trip, he was immensely proud of her professionalism and guts. On the flip side, Michael was, in his opinion, a fucking arse for allowing her to enter the lion's den. He would make his opinion known at a later date.

*

Kara sat quietly beside Marcus. She fiddled distractedly with a camera, trying to occupy her muddled brain with thoughts other than dealing with Lauren O'Neill. Their meeting would not be a joyous occasion, she was certain of that. She had decided that if she encountered any kind of hostility or lack of cooperation, then she would down tools, so to speak, and retreat in a manner as dignified as was possible. Michael had his viewpoint. So did she. In her view, this woman was a complete and utter "off her head nutter". It didn't need further qualifying.

'Are you going to be all right?' Marcus asked, glancing her way.

'Yes,' she lied. 'It's going to be a blast.'

*

At the airport check-in, Michael was suddenly aware of someone standing close to his left, and staring at him. He was unnerved, expecting a security check. Glimpsing from the corner of his eye, he was somewhat startled to find Joseph O'Connor just two feet away from him.

'I'm glad I found you before your flight, Mr Strange.'

They shook hands warmly, in stark contrast to their icy farewell at the restaurant.

'This is a surprise, Dr O'Connor.'

'Please, it's Joe. Call me Joe.'

'Michael, then. What can I do for you, Joe?'

'I slept rather badly last night, thinking of what you had to say to me. I spent the entire early hours of the morning reacquainting myself with the Laura Porter case.'

'Oh?'

'Reading her case notes, I discovered many things about her that I had forgotten. I am disturbed by the way in which she was manipulated at the time of the crime. It made me feel uneasy.'

'Manipulated?'

'Yes, by the police, her family and the press. Laura was deeply traumatised when I first met her. She was suicidal, in fact. It took six years of constant therapy and hypnosis to restore her to a young woman who could at last begin the adjustment to the normal world. She had many complex and dark personalities, all of which vied separately to take control of her identity. It was a huge task to re-establish a level of sanity to her existence.'

'What are you trying to tell me, Joe?'

'That you are a kind and sincere man, and I underestimated your intentions. This is highly irregular, but I would like you to have this.'

The doctor handed over a thick brown folder. 'I believe you will find everything you are looking for is in there.'

Stunned, Michael took the folder eagerly, holding it tightly to his chest.

'I am an old man, Michael. The past is the past. We can only look to the future. Holding back these files is like holding back the future.'

'Thank you, Joe. I am indebted to you.'

Joe chuckled. 'It is I who am indebted to you. However, just remember, Michael, if I have to be accountable for that file, I will crumble easily under interrogation. I will say you stole it from me and I fought defiantly to the bitter end to keep it from your grasp!'

Giving Joe O'Connor a parting hug, Michael moved on to the departure lounge and finally boarded his aircraft at just after midday. He was flying home. On his lap, he tapped the precious folder nervously before opening it. Slowly, with great apprehension, he began to read the story of the life of a young girl named Laura Porter. It proved to be a turbulent journey. Like the thunderous weather outside the aircraft, he had no choice but to endure it. There was no going back on this one.

*

Marcus and Kara arrived at the entrance to Laburnum Farm one hour ahead of schedule. The temperate climate had changed dramatically, with a strong weather front of cold gusting wind sweeping in from the south. The sky turned slate grey. It matched Kara's mood.

'Wait,' she suddenly announced. Marcus braked on the gravel drive, out of sight from the house.

She took out her mobile and dialled Michael once more. No response. 'He must be on a flight. Sod it.' Her mood darkened still further.

'What now?' Marcus demanded tetchily.

Kara took a deep breath. 'Onward, my fine soldier.'

With the farm coming into view, it was as bad as Kara had imagined: dismal, windswept, inhospitable. To the right of the house, a great structure in black loomed like a menacing dragon, crouched and ever watchful. It gave her the creeps. All around, the overgrown foliage and skeletal trees seemed to suffocate all light and air from the immediate vicinity. Everything clung together, like spider webbing, under a thick blanket of drizzle and swirling mist.

'Christ,' Kara said, catching her breath.

As if by some unexplainable trickery, an encircling mass of crows exploded from an adjoining field and descended upon them as they alighted from their vehicle. The noise was tumultuous, filling their ears with a high-pitched screeching sound. The sky was liquid black.

Marcus ducked and dived and lost sight of Kara. Then, mercifully, the shrill abated. Within seconds, the hundreds of birds had departed, as if by order of a hidden command. Marcus whistled in mock relief and caught sight of Kara, cowering down beside the car in search of protection from the frenzy above. It was like a scene from a Hitchcock movie. Now, mercifully, it was over. *Shit*, thought Marcus.

In vain, he tried to lighten a bad situation. 'Times change,' he grinned, unconvincingly. 'When I was last here, we threw a crazy non-stop alcohol fuelled party which lasted for three days.'

Kara lifted her head and stared at him, incredulously. 'Who with... The fucking Munsters?'

CHAPTER SEVENTEEN

Michael was enraged. During the flight, he hastily read and re-read numerous official files, transcripts, hypnosis analysis, profile charts, drug reports, professional diagnosis and Home Office recommendations. It was a heavy load to digest. It turned his stomach queasy, although he couldn't decide which was responsible for the discomfort he felt: the gruelling paperwork or the dramatic air pockets the aircraft encountered on its return to Gatwick. On board, all the passengers suffered from the turbulence. Not Michael, however. He had other more pressing matters to contend with right now, and somehow fought off the nausea which threatened to creep up on him.

Reading still further, what greatly surprised him was Laura's/Lauren's capacity, under the supervision of Dr Joseph O'Connor, to confront her heinous deeds, and somehow embrace a form of recovery. This kind doctor very slowly reintroduced the building blocks. Ultimately, this gave her the opportunity and the will to survive. During their time together, he and his team educated her, restored her self-esteem and introduced a return to a kind of normality; one which she could depend upon, in spite of the enormous conflict which still infiltrated her troubled mind.

Without his unstinting support, moral guidance and professional integrity, Laura would not have survived her time in prison. It was testament to him that she pulled through, intact but scarred. This was the truth of the matter. Her father was a savage brute, who had terrorised the entire family. Without a shadow of doubt, Laura was the victim. Her childhood had been removed from her, systematically and remorselessly, until she could no longer tolerate further punishment from his hands. She had snapped, and in an instant, become the aggressor, killing the man who was her father in name alone. It not only changed her life forever, but also that of those dearest to her as well: her mother and sister.

What also further surprised him was Laura's love of art, which she developed whilst in the hospital jail. She completed an Open University degree course, obtaining top honours. She read avidly, becoming an expert on the life and works of the Dutch masters, notably Vermeer. She learnt their skill in glazing techniques and became an accomplished artist. Michael thought suddenly of the grotesque portraits which now adorned her bedroom walls, so different from what she was truly capable of.

His deliberations were interrupted by the "Please fasten your safety belt" sign illuminated above his head. He closed the bulky file on his lap and fastened the fold-back tray securely to the seat in front. Closing his eyes, Michael thought of Maggie. He felt that she was a far more dangerous proposition than Lauren. He recalled the episode of the discarded bottle at the care home. What if Delores had truly sent him a signal? Could he really believe that Maggie was responsible for her tiny brother's death? Was this possible? Why would she do such a thing? Was it an accident or an act of malice? Was Maggie capable of uncontrolled rage? If so, did she have a secret history of violence?

More important, was this a violence that had gone on, unabated and unchecked? Michael had felt it firsthand, both at the farm and on the telephone. Was this a rage too frightening to be challenged? She was not to be messed with, and her frequent warnings to him could no longer be ignored. Michael winced as his gut tightened.

He was deeply perturbed. Searching back through his conversation with both Paddy and Joe, something nagged at him. What had he missed? The unthinkable...maybe? Looking out through the tiny window, green and brown patchwork fields came into focus as the aircraft descended over the Surrey countryside, breaking through the last of the groundcover cloud. If only his mind could clear as easily.

What if?

He reopened the folder, and sifted through the ream of paperwork. Running his finger down each page, he found a recurring theme within several of the files: a confession of simplicity. As Paddy had explained, it was as clear a case as was possible – a suspect, a motive, a confession.

And there lay the problem.

Michael had seen reference to the missing link on several occasions during his study, but the significance of what it implied had evaded him and everyone else at the time of the crime. Going back to 1978 Laura was, undoubtedly, a tragic figure and her confession was as clear as you could wish for, especially if you were from the prosecution team. Guilty, as charged. No one looked further, not even the defence, who reluctantly recognised the futility of the situation and went for a plea bargain of manslaughter, on the grounds of diminished responsibility. Speaking imploringly on behalf of their client, they got what they wished for: Job done.

The problem was in her testimony. On every reference point, Laura, although heavily traumatised, always insisted, and repeated, that she had killed her father with two heavy blows to the head, using a poker from the fireplace. Michael found this point unerringly consistent. He checked and rechecked to make sure this was correct. The hypnosis reports also confirmed this version of events, which meant that she never, ever wavered in her confession.

But what if?

To all intent and purposes, Laura had killed her father. She had struck him, and violently. But was the intention to kill him, or simply to render him incapable of further harm to her? In a moment of panic and fear, she had struck out in self-defence. Laura was a tiny fragile girl. He was a giant of a man. What happened then in those mad, insane moments when she instinctively knew her life was in mortal danger?

Michael knew the answer. She panicked, *and got lucky.*

It was as basic as that. The killing was not planned. How could it be? It wasn't possible for him to be overpowered in such a manner and to be bludgeoned to death by a weakling of a girl who was in fear of her life.

Bludgeoned to death? These words stuck in his throat. Paddy had told him earlier: "He (the father) was unrecognisable. He was bludgeoned beyond all recognition."

Jesus Christ. What had he stumbled on?

The aircraft suddenly lurched, dipped and bounced on the runway, screeching to a halt to the collective sigh from the passengers. It was a bad landing, provoking a ripple of ironic applause. Michael ignored the commotion, closed the file, and felt the impending cold sweat of realisation engulf him. He could hardly comprehend what he now knew to be the unpalatable truth.

Little Laura was guilty, for sure; guilty of striking her assailant, twice.

Frank Porter wasn't dead. He was dying.

But who was the last person to witness this carnage? Who was the person whom Laura called when she needed help? Who was it in fact who had the opportunity to finish off Frank as he lay dying, and defenceless, on the floor?

'Are you all right, sir?' the stewardess asked, shaking his shoulder. 'Do you need assistance?'

Michael glanced up, disconnecting from his trance-like state. He cleared his throat. 'God help us all,' he murmured finally.

The girl in the uniform appeared startled. 'Pardon me, sir?'

Slowly, Michael composed himself, gathered his things, and made his way to the far exit of the aircraft. He stumbled slightly, preoccupied by the realisation that a serious miscarriage of justice had occurred all those years ago. A terrible dread surfaced in his head.

Laura. Laura. He couldn't erase the image of this young girl – a vulnerable child – serving a prison sentence for a crime she did not actually commit. If his theory proved to be true, she would also serve a life sentence of another kind. The doctor was right. Laura was truly cursed, trapped in a complex web of conflicting "worlds" from which there was no escape.

This knowledge brought great sorrow. It was a sad conclusion knowing that if Maggie chose to serve her own selfish interests, her younger sibling would go to her grave never able to resolve her own   inner turmoil. Incensed, he vowed to restore this imbalance of justice. Maggie's whole life was a lie, he had now discovered. She had betrayed her one and only sister. Blood was not thicker than water.

*

Outside, on the tarmac, it was cold and blustery and wet. Michael buttoned his raincoat, switched on his mobile phone and followed the queue to the arrivals desk, then through passport control. His BMW was in the underground car park. He tried to contact Kara but the signal was poor on his flip top, and the battery useless. He plugged it into the recharger socket, but still no signal appeared. He drove steadily, deep in thought. Beyond Gatwick, he headed for Reigate, through Dorking, around Guildford and onto to the A3. He had a decision to make: either turn left, toward the farm or right, up to London and home. He dialled the gallery, and got through to a familiar voice at last.

'Ronald, everything OK?'

'Just bearable.'

'Have you seen or spoken to Kara?

'Briefly.'

'I'm worried about her. I can't get her on the phone. Do you know if she made her appointment with Lauren O'Neill?'

'When was that?'

His impatience grew thin. 'Today,' he snapped.

'I'll check the diary.' After what seemed an eternity, Ronald replied, 'The entry is there, and she isn't in the gallery. I suppose that makes the answer "yes" then.'

'When did you last see her?'

'Yesterday lunchtime; she was with Marcus.'

'Marcus? Did they appear to be OK together? I've been concerned about the two of them.'

'Difficult to tell,' Ronald said. 'I've been rather concerned about a lot of things myself recently. Certainly, those two have issues to sort out, Kara in particular. Then there's the lack of business which is worrying. You, of course, have your own problems. Then there is the matter of trust. I feel neglected. To be honest, Michael, I need to review my position in the company.'

'It will have to wait.' Michael was tetchy and hardly in the mood for this kind of conversation. Ronald's problems were way down the line of priorities at this moment. 'Listen. Did you get the information I asked for on Patrick Porter?'

Ronald sighed wearily. 'Of a sort,' he said grudgingly. 'Not much to report. But I do have a photograph.'

'*Really*? Can you send it to my mobile?

'Will do.'

Michael clicked off, found a lay-by and pondered his next move. It was all too damn quiet. Instinctively, he dialled Maggie's number in Ireland. No answer. Then he tried Lauren's house line. No answer. This didn't add up, especially as Kara was supposed to be at the house. Then a text message came through. It was sure to be Ronald.

But it wasn't. It was a message that was both short and shocking:

THE CUNT WILL DIE

Michael gasped, and felt the tiny hairs lift on the back of his neck. He checked the dial number and found it blocked. But the crude inference was crystal clear. Kara was in a perilous position. Her life was being threatened. The message *had* to come from Lauren's mobile. Fear leapt into his every pumping vein.

He checked his watch. He calculated that he could make the farm in under twenty-five minutes. He redialled Ronald.

'Churchill Fine…'

'Ronald. It's Michael. Listen very carefully. I'm going to the farm; I'll be there shortly. If you do not hear from me within the next two hours, I want you to call the police. It will be an emergency situation. Is that understood?'

'Yes, but what's going on?'

'No time to explain, Ronald. Just do it. Two hours. Then get the police to Laburnum Farm.'

Clicking off, his heart was pounding, his mind racing way beyond him. He could hardly grip the steering wheel. From somewhere, courage returned. Without a second thought, he selected "drive" on the automatic gearshift, floored the accelerator and weaved recklessly in front of the traffic coming up from behind. A blast of car horns fractured the air. Michael didn't glance in his rearview mirror. He didn't need to. He could taste the dust in his throat from the cloud thrown up by his tyres.

*

Kara wasn't happy that she had lost communication with Michael. It was bloody inconsiderate of him, she decided. It made her anxious. Still, she consoled herself that Marcus was with her. It made a difference. After the episode with the Hitchcock crows, it was a case of getting on with the job and getting away. Fast.

Lauren met them at the main entrance, and Kara was surprised by the way they were greeted with both charm and graciousness. Not what she had expected at all. Somehow, in her head Kara had built up a compelling picture of the character Glenn Close portrayed in *Fatal Attraction*. As in the movie though, appearances can be deceptive. For now, she would reserve judgment. Oh, sod it; Lauren was still a complete *bitch*. Case closed.

She introduced Marcus as her assistant, and Lauren was equally warm and welcoming with him, too. From somewhere in the house, a dog barked and growled. For the next twenty minutes, she and Marcus unloaded the jeep and methodically set up the equipment in the huge dining room, where Lauren had directed them.

Looking at the array of fine paintings, Kara was impressed and a little daunted. It was a magnificent collection, and left her and Marcus breathless in admiration. Kara was thankful for Marcus's presence for other reasons. Several of the paintings were large and heavily framed. It would require a man's strength to lift them individually from the walls in order to be photographed on the easel. Michael had not taken this into account, when he had first asked her to do the inventory alone. It was an oversight, luckily now rectified by the genius of his secretary: engaging Marcus to do the donkey work.

Marcus cursed under his breath, gradually lifting the first painting from above the mantelpiece.

Lauren largely left them to it. She was distant in manner, but dignified and helpful. Again, Kara was surprised by this, expecting this woman to be overbearing and ever watchful. Yet everything about Lauren was beginning to grate on her nerves. Kara could not help but notice just how beautiful and serene she was. She seemed to glide in and out of the room, silently, her skin china white and her long hair flowing magnificently behind her. Flame red. She was like a ghostly apparition. In artistic terms, Lauren resembled a Pre-Raphaelite beauty. Kara observed that this did not go unnoticed on Marcus. How shallow, Kara thought, concluding that Lauren was most definitely an irritating one hundred per cent supernova *cow*. She fixed a smile.

'Phew,' Marcus said, admiringly, as Lauren drifted effortlessly in and out of the room.

'Down, boy,' Kara told him.

They worked steadily and diligently. It was a bigger task than she had first anticipated. Each painting had to be removed from its place, repositioned on the easel, tilted and then lit with the makeshift lighting that Kara had set up. It was vital that no "flashback" was evident for the reproduction of the brochure images. Each piece then had to be measured, catalogued with the correct title and any possible provenance and finally, numerically listed. On top of that, each painting then had to be put back and secured in its rightful place in the dining room. Transportation would come later. It was tiring and thirsty work.

Lauren eventually brought refreshments. Earl Grey tea in china cups. Kara was appreciative, Marcus less so. She knew he preferred drinks in cans.

'How are you progressing?' Lauren asked.

'Perfectly well,' Kara answered. 'Beautiful collection, I must say.'

'Thank you.'

'It must be hard to part with them,' Marcus chipped in, adjusting a lens on his camera.

Lauren turned her attention to him for the first time. Her eyes were like diamonds, her lips wet and inviting. She ran her hand through her luxuriant red curls. Her antique braided white dress gaped at the front, revealing a hint of cleavage. This woman stretched like a cat, effortless and feline, her pert breasts just visible under the thin delicate fabric. Marcus was captivated, in an instant.

'It will be hard, but not impossible,' she replied. 'Circumstances change. I must sell them.' Lauren took a long moment to look him up and down, from head to toe. She was brazen; flaunting her sexuality which she knew was having an intoxicating effect on the poor boy.

Kara was furious. Cunning bitch, she screamed, silently.

'Did you say your name was Marcus?' Lauren asked, enticing him still further.

'Yes…'

'Are you an artist, Marcus? You look like one, if I may say so.'

'Yeah, I'm kinda finding my feet.'

'And what style do you paint in?'

'Mainly abstract, with a figurative twist.'

Kara interrupted, feeling left out. 'He's very, very good, actually.'

'Indeed,' Lauren mused, raising an eyebrow. 'It seems you have an ardent fan, Marcus. You're a very lucky boy.'

Marcus hovered, caught awkwardly between the two women, acting self-consciously and feeling stupid. He dropped the lens cover. 'Well, Kara and I need to press on,' he muttered.

But Lauren stopped him with a raised hand. 'Come with me, I'd like to show you something.'

Kara protested. 'We really need to finish.'

Lauren turned on her. 'Can't you manage on your own, just for a little while?'

Kara hesitated, flashing her gaze back and forth between Marcus and Lauren. 'Well, I suppose…'

'Good, then that's settled.' Lauren instantly took Marcus by the arm, and led him from the room.

Kara was gobsmacked. Anger boiled within her. 'You dumb, docile drip,' she said, forcing the words through clenched teeth.

Standing alone, isolated and feeling a touch vulnerable, she couldn't decide if the words were directed at herself, Marcus, or Lauren.

*

Michael drove insanely fast, taking the car and his concentration to the limits of endurance. Every second counted. On the Guildford bypass, he reached 120 mph. It was on this very road in 1959 – he was suddenly reminded – that Mike Hawthorn, the racing driver, had been killed in his Jaguar. What he was doing was madness. But still he raced on, red lining over Box Hill, down past Old Compton, relentlessly gathering speed whenever he could, his mind working overtime. He just had to get to Kara.

His phone bleeped. Out of the corner of his eye, he could see it was the phototext from Ronald. No matter now. Each second that passed was like a time bomb ticking, each minute a lifetime wait. Overtaking a slow moving car, he shouted, 'Get out of the fucking way!'

Jesus fucking hell! The road was blocked. Michael reacted with lightning speed, slamming on the brakes, his car veering violently before coming to a rapid standstill, leaving a strong smell of burning rubber in the air. Directly in front of him, a farmer was demonstrating his anger by waving his stick at him as he also attempted to manoeuvre his flock of sheep across the road. The screeching from Michael's tyres unnerved the sheep and they began to scatter. 'Arsehole!' the farmer was shouting furiously in his direction.

Michael was trapped. He tried to reverse, but was now boxed in by the traffic pulling up behind. *Jesus fucking hell!*

Another farmer approached, tapping on his window. 'Are you trying to get us all killed, mate? What's your problem?'

'It's an emergency, I need to get moving!'

'Yeah, yeah…'

Michael ignored him, and tried to keep calm. He estimated that the clearance of the sheep from the road would take several more minutes; vital seconds that he could not afford to lose. This was all of his making.

He retrieved his phone, which had flung forward into the foot well. To begin with, he checked the phototext. It was poor quality, but it was his first sighting of Patrick Porter. His heart jumped. Looking closely, the portrait had more than a passing resemblance to images he had seen of Julius Gray: only much younger, of course. If Michael was pushed for an explanation, at this stage he would have to guess that Julius was "made up" in disguise for this image. What other explanation could there possibly be? He was by now totally convinced that they were one and the same. Although their individual style of painting was worlds apart, Julius was versatile and clever enough…*what was going on?* His mind raced.

He dialled Kara. *Jesus fucking hell,* just answer the bloody thing!

*

Kara endeavoured to carry on as best she could minus Marcus. Distracted, she struggled to concentrate. Without him, she elected to photograph the smaller paintings, those she could lift from the wall herself. In a huff, she began doubting her ability to do the job. Stretching precariously on a small stepladder, she slipped and almost dropped a painting, recovering her balance just in time. Christ, concentrate girl! Her mind was in complete turmoil. Where the hell was Marcus? She checked her watch: he had been gone for over thirty minutes. Intense jealously exploded in her head. This woman was a manipulative cow, flaunting her body...making eye contact with Marcus... taking him away as if she owned him...bitch! Bloody, bloody bitch. She needed air.

Outside, she inhaled the freshness from the surrounding fields that had eluded her in the stifling heat and stale air of the enclosed dining room. It was becoming too damn claustrophobic. She opened the jeep door and searched for a water bottle in the side pocket. Unscrewing the cap, she emptied the cool welcoming contents down her throat in huge gulps. On the seat, she found her mobile phone, which had obviously fallen out of her pocket earlier. She scanned the missed calls. Michael had called, several times. Thank God, she prayed, with great relief. She decided to ring him right then.

Her thoughts were rudely interrupted.

'Kara.' It was Lauren, calling from the main entrance. By her side, a huge dog pulled aggressively on a lead, snarling in her direction. 'Are you...all right?'

'Yes, I'm fine.' It was hardly the case, but Kara humoured her. In truth, the sight of the dog terrified her. Keep calm. 'Just getting some fresh air,' she said.

'Have you finished your task?'

Kara hid the phone in her trouser pocket and discarded the empty bottle on the vehicle seat. She decided to ring Michael later, in private. She answered, 'No.' She felt dejected by her inability to contact Michael. Then she returned to earth, and faced Lauren full on. 'Three more paintings to do, but they are too heavy for me to handle. I need Marcus.'

'Then come inside.'

Kara trudged back with a reluctant step. Inside, Lauren held the baying dog close to her side, and slammed the door tight behind them. Then she bolted it. Kara instantly froze. Something was hideously wrong. Marcus was nowhere to be seen.

*

Marcus screamed with the pain, and felt blood trickling from his swollen knees and bruised left cheek. The last thing he remembered was that awful helpless feeling of falling into space, and then landing with a sickening hard thump against a concrete floor. He could taste blood in his mouth. Scrambling in the pitch dark, he reached out with his clawing hands to somehow fathom out where he was, discovering fuck all except dirt on the floor, and a sound of dripping water above him. In the dank and eerie darkness, shapes slowly began to emerge. He sat and rested against a wall, desperately trying to clear his head.

From a corner – *somewhere* – his ears pricked up to the scurrying of tiny feet. Rats, his worst nightmare! The very thought of them – how many? – made him instantly coil his legs to his chest and heighten his sense of panic. *Think. Think. Think.* Clearing his head, he guessed he was in some kind of underground basement, perhaps a cellar. He recalled asking Lauren for the bathroom. On opening the door, she pushed him fiercely from behind, his whole weight careering down the steps, tumbling helplessly, unable to find a safe footing. Now he was alone and trapped. More worryingly, he had left his mobile phone in the dining room, beside his car keys. He had been ensnared by Lauren, and foolishly fell for her trick. He was terrified of two things in life: rats and the dark. It simply couldn't get much worse. A far greater fear suddenly crept up upon him though. Kara. She too was alone and isolated, in the company of a mad woman. Without his phone, Marcus could not see any possible way to help her. Damn, it was he who needed rescuing.

*

'Where is Marcus?' Kara asked nervously, her eyes fixed permanently on the menacing dog.

'In the barn,' Lauren said.

'I need to see him.'

'All in good time.'

'*Now* would be a good time.'

'Bruno!' Lauren shouted, as the dog, fangs bared, yanked on the short lead, pulling her forward. Kara retreated further into the hallway, realising how futile this action was if she thought it took her out of harm's way. She was trapped.

Her voice quivered. 'What do you want, Lauren?'

'Everything that Michael can't give me.'

'Michael? *Michael?*'

'I saw you with him.' Lauren's eyes blazed with an intensity of hate. Her face contorted with an inner fury. Her voice was changing, deeper and vitriolic, almost as if a character transformation was taking place...

Who on earth is this woman? Kara thought, petrified. What the hell am I to do? Do I try to reason with her or make a dash for it?

Instinctively, she turned on her heels and ran for her life, clattering furniture and ornaments as she wildly tried to put distance between them. Behind her, she heard the shrill laughter of Lauren echoing in every direction. Kara became dizzy with fright, not knowing where to run – everywhere appeared to be a maze of rooms and corridors, darkened recesses and false exits. Twisting to confront her worst fears, she nearly leapt out of her skin at the terrible sight of Bruno fast on her heels.

*

'Come on, come on! For chrissakes, answer the phone, Kara.'

The sheep were gathered at last and penned in the opposite field. Michael saw his opportunity, floored the accelerator and sped past. In his rear view mirror, he caught sight of the irate farmer screaming at the top of his voice. Michael guessed the likely words of the man's frustration: Bloody city hooligan! Or worse. This would be close to the mark though.

Michael estimated he was less than fifteen minutes to his destination.

*

Kara frantically dodged through an open door, finding herself back in the dining room. Breathless, she slammed the door shut, wedging a chair against it to fix it in place. This gave her a few seconds respite. Oh, God, where are you, Marcus?

Her phoned bleeped, startling her. She fumbled, dropping it. Keeping her nerve, she managed to retrieve it from under the table with the sweating palm of one hand. *Breathe*, girl. This was her last chance of rescue. She clicked on and blurted, 'Will someone help me...please!'

*

Christ, she finally answered!

Hearing the desperation in her plea, Michael shouted, 'Kara, I've been trying to reach you.'

'Michael! Michael! Thank God you can hear me.'

'Where are you? What's happening?'

'I'm at the farm, Michael. Lauren's got Marcus, and now she is after me...I'm really scared Michael. Where are you?'

'Very close, Kara. Now listen, stay focused. Don't do anything silly. I'll be with you in a matter of minutes.'

Kara wasn't listening any more. Suddenly, fierce kicking from the other side of the door forced it to jerk and heave, dislodging the chair and propelling it in her direction. Kara ducked, kept her wits and pushed her entire weight against the broken door, as the sound of splintering wood reached her ears. The pit of her stomach twisted.

Above the din, Michael yelled in her ear, 'What's that noise, Kara? Tell me!'

Kara's strength gave way. She could no longer hold on. From afar, as her phone slipped to the floor again, she could hear Michael's distant screaming: 'Kara, get out of there. Get the fucking hell out of there!'

But her inner resolve failed dismally. Instead, dread gripped her. With such fear looming, paralysis took hold, closing down all resistance in her body. As the door smashed open and broke from the hinges, she sat huddled, childlike, in the middle of the room, rocking back and forth, eyes clamped shut. Tears rolled uncontrollably down her cheeks. Barely able to look up, she forced one corner of her eye open and glimpsed Bruno lurch into the room, teeth exposed and foaming at the mouth. Behind him came a sight of sheer terror. She could hardly whimper, let alone scream. No sound would come.

Not one – but *two* women – stood over her, brandishing an array of long-bladed knives and a machete. Lauren gripped Kara's hair, yanking her head back, whilst the other, not known to her, pressed cold sharp steel to her throat.

Bizarrely, she remained calm, and accepted the bleak realisation of death. She was too weak to resist, even when she felt the pressure of the blade increase on her skin, and sensed a trickle of blood descend her neck. From somewhere deep within, she experienced a last power surge of defiance. 'Marcus. Marcus,' she could hear herself repeat over and over. Then she succumbed to the inevitable, as the blade began to penetrate beneath her soft flesh.

CHAPTER EIGHTEEN

Michael drove at breakneck speed, approaching the last bend in the road with reckless intent. He swerved violently, dislodging the red pillar box at the entrance to Laburnum Farm, scattering the pieces across the road. The car spun, hitting the gatepost with a resounding thud; indenting the rear side panel and wiping out the lights. The boot lid sprung open. He didn't care; such was his fear as to what was happening to Kara. In front of the house, he found an unoccupied jeep parked up, with the driver's door flung wide open.

He braked sharply, spewing gravel and choking dust in all directions. Switching off the ignition, he scanned the immediate vicinity for signs of life. No one was visible. He climbed out from behind the steering wheel. It was as silent as a church cemetery, weirdly so. Where was everybody? The house was in darkness. To his right, the barn stood still and quiet.

'Kara!' he shouted.

His first instinct was to rattle the front door to the house. It was locked. Moving rapidly to the rear, he suddenly realised he was defenceless. Searching around, he picked up a piece of discarded lead piping. The door to the kitchen was ajar. He had little time to be frightened and entered fearlessly. Again, he found no evidence of *anyone*. He expected to see signs of a struggle. He listened intently. Silence. From a worktop drawer, he further armed himself with a pair of scissors.

Stealthily moving into the hallway, he knew the approximate layout of the ground floor area. The lounge was clear, so too was the second sitting room. Beyond that was Julius's studio. It was clear. Retracing his footsteps, he glanced over the breakfast room, checked the small glass conservatory, and the secondary hall. His heart pounded. Broken crockery was strewn across the carpet. He then came to the dining room, which also displayed evidence of a huge disturbance of some kind.

The door was open, hanging unsteadily on its hinges. Michael crept in and held a tight grip on the metal bar. A chair had been tipped over. In the darkening gloom of the impending evening, he could make out the easel and lighting equipment that he assumed Kara had taken from the gallery. A painting had fallen, face down. Paperwork, with Kara's handwriting on it, was scattered across the table and floor. Something else caught his eye. Under the window bay, Kara's mobile phone lay discarded. Everything was in disarray. Clearly, this was where he had last spoken to Kara. The situation alarmed him. What had Lauren done to her? What was she really capable of? The text he received was vile and threatening in the extreme. Was Lauren really a cold-hearted killer?

Beside the upturned chair, a crimson stain glistened on the carpet, still wet. Someone had been hurt at this spot, and badly.

*

Marcus took stock of his precarious situation. *Think, man.* He reached into his pocket and found his cigarette lighter. He flicked it on, and in the gloom he discovered he was in a disused wine cellar. Climbing back up the narrow concrete steps, he found his exit barred by a heavy door, locked from the outside. He shouted and banged, but knew it was a futile gesture. On returning to the basement, he searched for some kind of strong lever, in order to prise open the door. There was none to be found, just a stack of redundant heavy wine racks and empty broken bottles. This room had not been employed for many, many years. Like him, it had been left to rot.

He was very much alone, with no way out. Given the circumstances, he was in deep shit. His left shoulder ached. His hands bled from the fall. And he had rats for company. *Just great.*

Grimly pondering his predicament, he watched, by the only source of light he had, a line of rodents come and go in the far corner, almost in regimental fashion. Where had they come from? Marcus moved across, mindful of the scurrying, and peered through the latticework of the furthest wine rack. He could feel a draught on his face. With all his strength, he pulled at the wooden construction until it rocked back and forth and finally, came crashing down at his feet. Dust and glass showered the area. He coughed and hastily protected his nose and mouth with a handkerchief.

When the thick dust settled, Marcus almost wept with joy. Concealed behind the wine rack was a tunnel. It was low and narrow, but on closer inspection, appeared to be *just* passable. If this means of escape was good enough for his four-legged friends…

…Bollocks. This was his only possible route to freedom. He had no idea where it would lead, or how long the passageway would be. His worst nightmare had come true. The sweat poured from him. All that remained was his aversion to the rats.

Reluctantly, he lay face down on his stomach in readiness. With a flickering light as his only companion, Marcus drew breath, cursed aloud, gritted his teeth, and began to crawl into the abyss. Almost at once, the tiny scratching of feet reached his ears. In the gloom, he saw them coming.

*

Michael searched the upstairs bedrooms and bathrooms. He found no further signs of struggle. In one bedroom, he discovered two large suitcases, containing women's clothing. He had a horrible feeling about this. Inside a holdall, there was a huge wad of cash and two passports. On examining them, his heart sank. One belonged to Maggie. Now he had two unstable women to contend with, as if one wasn't enough.

The house was empty, he concluded, or Kara and Marcus were prisoners elsewhere. He had to cling on to the notion that Kara was still alive, and was by now forcibly removed to a new location. And where was Marcus? He was a strong lad, more than capable of defending himself. He had simply vanished. Everyone had simply vanished.

Descending the creaking stairs, he chanced upon a partially hidden door, located in a secondary hallway. It was heavily padlocked. 'Kara, Marcus!' he yelled, banging on the door. He waited. Only to be met with more silence.

Michael closed his eyes. His breathing was laboured and erratic, the palms of his hands moist with sweat. He could hardly grip the iron bar he carried. Maggie and Lauren: what a combination. The vision this implanted into his brain was too dreadful, too ghastly, to contemplate. But he had to face it. He needed to gather his last remaining dregs of courage. For Kara's sake.

With or without Marcus, his battle against the sisters would now begin. Striding purposefully from the house, Michael headed straight for the barn.

*

Marcus could feel the rush of cold air on his face, and discerned a glimmer of light ahead of him. It was just a pinprick, but his spirits soared. He had been tunnelling on his belly for about forty to fifty feet. The shaft was ancient, but well constructed, and remained relatively dry. He moved faster now, his optimism gaining the same momentum as the light expanded. It was still a tight squeeze, and three times he had to halt progress and remain motionless as the rats crawled over him, nibbling and sniffing as they went about their journey. Twice, he puked violently. The stench was unbearable, but somehow he pressed on. With each mighty push, he covered the remaining ground until he reached an opening, of sorts. Clawing with his fingers, he encountered a makeshift tarpaulin in his way, ripped and partially eaten by the rodents. Beyond this, a heavy wooden chest barred his exit. *Dear God*...using his uninjured right shoulder, he levered himself forward and, with one almighty effort, asserted his last remaining ounce of strength. Mercifully, the furniture inched forward, allowing him just enough space to drag himself through. The utter relief of perceived freedom was palpable. The sheer strain of squeezing into a black hole to nothingness had been unbearable. He could so easily have wept; instead, he involuntarily urinated in his pants. But he didn't care. He was alive.

*

Michael manoeuvred himself to the rear of the barn, taking shelter behind one of the gigantic buttresses, which hid him sufficiently until he planned his next move. In truth, he felt woefully exposed: inadequately armed, and outnumbered, especially so if Bruno was still on the scene. He fumbled for his phone. Shit, it was in the car! He swore aloud this time. Hopelessly unprepared, he had no firm plan on which to rescue Kara. He was a sitting duck. They – Maggie and Lauren – had the upper hand.

*

Marcus blinked once, then twice. His eyes cleared and very slowly, he lifted himself to his feet. His trousers were sodden and uncomfortable, but there wasn't a whole lot he could do about it. In the half-light, he adjusted his vision and surveyed his new location. He stood in a narrow chamber, the walls of which were heavy stone. High above him, the exposed thick-timbered ceiling gave a clue to his whereabouts. He was in the gable end of the tithe barn, but the wall to his left was, on closer inspection, fake. It was obvious, even to a layman, that a later interior construction made of a studded wooden façade had been added and extended along the entire width of the building. There were no windows, except for two small glass roof lights. Marcus searched for a means to illuminate the room, marking his territory with his outstretched hands, feeling for a wall switch, or socket. He was aware of shapes and clutter, and endeavoured to keep his clumsy movements to a minimum, for fear of attracting attention and inadvertently hurting himself. It was a difficult terrain to manoeuvre around. Just then, he made physical contact with an object he was familiar with. It was a standing lamp. Tracing the lead, he reached the wall and found the switch.

In an instant, the room burst alive with fierce light, stinging his eyes with the stark brightness. It was one of those big arc lights, used on movie sets, and was positioned in the middle of the floor. Looking around, Marcus gasped, and immediately became aware of the significance of what he had stumbled upon.

'Wow,' he said, under his breath. He was standing in the middle of a secret room: An artist's studio. Next to the lamp, a huge unfinished canvas dominated the space, affixed to a beautiful ornate easel. Marcus recognised the style of the work. Looking further, he unearthed several other paintings, some propped against furniture, others framed and positioned on the walls, some hidden behind dust sheets. 'Wow,' he repeated, shaking his head in wonderment, almost afraid of allowing himself the satisfaction of what he had discovered. There could be no mistake though. All the paintings were the work of Patrick Porter. This was his workplace, his hidden studio. Marcus stared in astonishment. If Patrick was dead, as reported, then here was a shrine, untouched and unseen, a forgotten time capsule. It had at last been uncovered.

At first, he was too nervous to examine anything. He just stood in awe for a full minute. Eventually, his breathing settled.

What really shook him to the core, though, was his discovery during a secondary search of numerous drawers and cabinets. He found detailed accounts of 'sales' going back over a twenty year period. The financial rewards were highly lucrative. The figures ran into thousands of pounds. Big, big business, Marcus thought admiringly, trying to get his head around the money mountain recorded in the ledgers. It blew him away.

But nothing prepared him for the series of photographs he found, portraying the artist at work, and standing at the very easel Marcus had first encountered. The pictures recorded each stage of a painting, from the preliminary charcoal drawing, to the initial oil washes and through to the final glazed masterstrokes. Without doubt, this was the work of a real genius. Bizarrely, he also discovered it was – *good God* – the work of a woman, dressed in male attire. *What the...*

Here was the indisputable proof as to the identity of Patrick Porter.

Marcus could hardly believe his eyes. In each image, the person identified applying the paint was unmistakable: the artist's name was Lauren O'Neill.

Shocked, Marcus tried to make sense of the sheer magnitude and grand scale of this deception. It was something he found almost impossible to take in. What the hell was he to do now?

His answer came soon enough. From afar, his concentration was jolted by an array of voices: pleading voices, desperate voices. Voices raised in anger. My God, Kara's voice! Placing his ear to the makeshift wall, Marcus instantly recognised the seriousness of Kara's predicament, just yards away from where he stood. She was being threatened. He knew exactly what he had to do. And fast.

*

Michael had never imagined that his judgement, like his abrupt lack of courage, would become questionable as well. By crucially delaying his next move, he quickly realised he had allowed Maggie to gain the initiative. Whilst he hesitated, she declared her intent and, without warning, was on to him with alarming speed. She sprang from nowhere, leaving him defenceless. Looming menacingly over him, she brandished a gleaming black double-barrelled shotgun aimed directly into his face.

'I gave you fair warning not to meddle into our affairs, Mr Strange. It appears that you are as stubborn as you are stupid.'

He found little to argue with.

'Now get up, and no funny business,' she warned, adding, 'I know how to use this thing, and I never miss from one yard.'

Michael rose unsteadily to his feet.

'Drop the weapon,' he heard her say, prodding him in the side with the gun. 'I ought to finish you right here, but little missy is hollering and squealing like a lame dog, so you can have your last goodbye, and then I'll end it for the both of you. Kind of poetic, don't you think?'

'Kind of sick,' he answered, tossing the lead piping to the ground. This sudden movement gave him the split second he needed. With her eyes diverted, Michael jerked his arm and deflected the shotgun. With his other hand, he withdrew the scissors from his pocket and, in one swift action, plunged the twin blades upward into her thigh, as hard as he could. It was enough. Maggie's eyes popped, her face a contortion of shock and horror. She yelled and fell backward, firing off one barrel of the gun, which exploded in his ear and momentarily shattered his concentration. The cartridge propelled harmlessly over the roof of the barn. Michael reacted instinctively, his heart pounding, and in the next movement he furiously yanked the gun from the stricken woman. She gripped her leg, with the scissors still embedded in her flesh, cursing his name and writhing in agony. He didn't care if she bled to death.

He fumbled into her jacket pocket, pulling out a handful of cartridges. He reloaded his newly acquired weapon. In his haste, the rest of the cartridges fell to the ground. Dashing forward, he reached the double- fronted doors, which were open by a few feet, allowing him just enough space to squeeze through. Crouching down, he ran forward, frantically searching for cover in the deepening gloom of the building. He had been here before, so, zigzagging smartly, he made himself the smallest target possible in case of counter attack. Lord knows what he would find in this hell hole. Ducking behind the rear wing of the abandoned Lotus, he cautiously raised his head to get a better viewpoint. Fuck.

Barely fifteen feet away from him, Lauren commanded the arena, legs planted wide. By her side, a snarling Bruno pulled on the lead which she grasped tightly. The blade of a long knife flashed in her other hand. Even more alarmingly, Kara was slumped kneeling at Lauren's feet, with the blade at her throat. Michael knew in an instant that she was hurt. Blood smeared her blouse, and caked her tousled hair.

Michael stood tall, and raised the shotgun in defiance.

'Let her go, Lauren,' he ordered. 'Nobody needs to die. We can stop all of this right here and now.'

'Where is Maggie?' Lauren countered, her eyes staring with confusion.

Michael shook his head. 'You're on your own, I'm afraid. Big sister is otherwise engaged.'

'What have you done to her? I heard a shot.'

'Figure it out all by yourself.' He edged forward carefully, before halting in his tracks, as Lauren grabbed Kara by the hair and brandished the knife with hostile intent.

'Don't come any closer, Michael. I won't hesitate to kill her, the bitch.'

He stepped back one pace, lowering the gun barrel so that it pointed in the direction of the dog. He could tell that Lauren was physically weakening, and that Bruno's brute strength was winning the battle to pull free from her grasp. Michael had perhaps two minutes grace.

'Lauren, listen to me. Kara is innocent in all of this. Christ, she's like a daughter to me. Let her go. Take me instead.' He was desperately praying to find answers that would bring a halt to this madness. 'Why do you want to harm her?'

Lauren spat the words, 'Because she is just like the rest. I know what's going on.'

'What's going on, Lauren? You need to explain.'

Lauren curled her lip. 'I saw the both of you with my own eyes!'

'Where?'

'At the Blue Bar; and then outside that fancy restaurant, embracing and then kissing each other, I felt sick to the stomach seeing you so close.'

'Jesus Christ!' Michael's mind charged back and forth, trying to picture the scene of him and Kara in the street. *Oh, God.* 'You were there, watching us?'

Her eyes widened with anger. 'First Julius betrayed me, and now you! Why do you all want to take advantage and then cruelly abandon me? What have I done to deserve this? Fools, all of you! No matter, it's payback time.'

'Lauren, Lauren, you were mistaken,' he pleaded.

'Mistaken? Do you take me for a complete idiot?'

'Listen to me, Lauren. You're unwell, and exhausted. Take a moment to hear me out. Please, I beg of you.' Michael felt time slipping by too quickly. Kara was fading fast, and must have lost considerable blood. 'I know of your past, and the anxiety you suffer. You're not aware of your true self. Come back to me, Lauren. I have not betrayed you. Drop the knife, please. Then we can get the expert medical help you require. I will not desert you, I promise.'

'What is a *promise*? Such empty words, such a futile gesture…far too late, I'm afraid.'

'No, Lauren. This is a genuine opportunity, so take it. Get help, and rebuild your life…with me!' Right now he spewed out *anything* which entered his head. 'Put your trust in me. Get away from those, like Maggie, who have always suppressed the past in case you found out the truth.'

'Maggie? Maggie? What truth?'

He had to be brutal, it was his last chance: 'The truth concerning your father's murder, Lauren.'

'My father?'

Michael sighed deeply, and lowered the gun still further, stepping as safely as possible in her direction. *Slowly, slowly.* Bruno was so close he could feel the heat of his foul breath touching his skin. But it was vital that he expressed no apprehension, no backing down, of his own at this stage. He *had* to gain her trust.

'Christ, Lauren. I'm so sorry. The truth has been hidden away for so many years; you really need to be strong for me. Can you live with the truth?' He could almost reach out and rescue Kara in one swoop, but he hesitated. One false move and a bloodbath could ensue.

Lauren looked bewildered. What worried Michael was her ability to be as aggressive as a bully. She could turn in an instant. He was treading on very dangerous ground. Right now, he had no idea which "personality" was controlling her. He had to go with his gut instinct.

'Tell me the fucking truth,' she demanded, 'or so help me…'

Michael realised that she was in bitter conflict with her demons, those extreme alter personalities that shaped her volatile character. She was literally on a knife edge. So was Kara.

'Lauren, you were not responsible for your father's killing. Yes, you hit him. Yes, you meant to hurt him. But it was your sister who actually did the deed. When she was alone with him, she discovered he was still breathing. This made her pick up the poker and finally smash him to death. She finished the job you started. This she did with vengeance in mind, for all the years of torture that he inflicted on both of you. He was *still* alive after you attacked him.'

'No! No!' Lauren's voice reached a pitiful crescendo.

Michael held out a comforting hand for her to take. 'Don't you get it, Lauren? Listen to my words. I repeat: your father was *still* alive when you called Maggie for help. It was she who murdered him, but it was you who paid the ultimate sacrifice. And for *what*?'

From behind him, a voice boomed, 'Liar!!'

Michael turned abruptly and saw the hobbling bulk of Maggie stagger into the interior of the barn. In her hand, she carried the bloodied scissors that he had embedded in her leg just moments before.

Maggie seethed. 'What has he been telling you? It's all lies. He's just trying to poison your brain against me.'

Lauren stayed silent, alternating her glare between the two of them, as if unsure of whom to believe. Big sister had the upper hand, Michael felt.

He spoke hurriedly. 'Ask her, Lauren. Ask her why she found it necessary for you to go to prison for a crime you didn't actually commit.'

'He's lying,' Maggie snarled. 'He's just trying to get the girl released. Kill her, as you should have killed Antonia.'

Michael thought desperately. His position was considerably weakened, flanked on both sides by two unstable and violent women, and a dog hell-bent on sinking its teeth into anything that moved. He had to get them to squabble and doubt each other in order to draw attention away from Kara. Then he would make his move.

'If I'm the liar,' he said, staring directly into Lauren's eyes 'then how come your dear sister was also instrumental in the death of your brother, Patrick.' He was at the last chance saloon.

'Whaaat?' Lauren screamed.

'Do not believe him. Can't you see what he is doing to us?' Maggie countered.

Michael became aware that Maggie had gained ground, stealthily closing in on him. He tried again, punching below the belt. 'You don't necessarily need to believe me, Lauren. I only learnt the truth from someone who you can truly rely on. Your mother.'

Maggie laughed hysterically. 'This man is evil, a monster. Release the dog, and that will be the end of it. We can still get away.'

'No! Leave him alone!' Kara's voice suddenly pierced the air. She stumbled to her feet, despite Lauren's struggle to control her. She spat blood. 'He's trying to help you.'

'The cunt…slit her throat!' Maggie yelled. 'Now! Do it now! Listen to your sister, before it is too late.'

'Listen to your mother,' Michael retaliated. 'Listen to your conscience. Above all, listen to your *heart*. You're not a killer, Lauren. I implore you, don't become one now.'

For the first time, Michael detected a whiff of victory.

'Did you kill our father? Did you kill Patrick?' Lauren asked, her voice trembling. Her eyes appeared cemented to those of Maggie, who visibly began to wilt from the cross-examination. Then she recovered.

'I finished him off; he was already half-dead,' she said. Did you *want* him to survive, and live to rape you *again*? Is that what you wanted?' Maggie stood like a stone statue. 'It was a pleasure to see him dead. I'd waited years to get retribution for what happened to our brother.'

'I…I thought he died in an accident,' Lauren said pitifully.

'You were too young to remember. Before he ever got his filthy hands on you, I'd been at his mercy for years. That fatal day, you had gone to church with Mother, leaving me to look after Patrick. I knew what was coming. Father returned home drunk, and had me cornered at the top of the stairs. I was petrified and screaming for help, with him ripping at my underclothes.' Maggie began to shake uncontrollably. 'It should not have happened…I had no idea that, bless him, Patrick had climbed the stairs to see what was happening…he witnessed things he should never have seen…but as I fought for my life, our father shoved me angrily onto Patrick. I reached out in desperation, but…it was too late. He fell. I've had to live every day of my life with the knowledge that I was responsible for his death. Every day, Holy Mother of God. Not a single day has passed without me praying for his soul. When I had my chance for vengeance, I struck a blow for every one of our brother's precious lost years.'

Lauren shook her head in despair. Finally, she spoke with measured words, trying to come to terms with the confession.

'I truly hated him, despised him; but look at the consequences of that fateful day. My mother has spent her entire life without speaking, and I have spent my entire life imprisoned, either in jail or in the confines of my fucking head. What was your punishment, Maggie?'

'You have to understand, I did it for *you*, I did it to protect us all from a suffering far worse than if he had survived. I had a family, Lauren, a husband and two children, I couldn't possibly leave them…it was unthinkable. You were alone, damn it. As far as anyone cared, you *had* struck the fateful blows. He was a dead man, taking his last lingering breath. I just made sure the job was done.'

Michael took the narrow opportunity afforded him. 'Lauren, give me the knife, it's all over.'

'Marcus!' Kara screamed.

At the far end of the barn, behind where Lauren swayed, still clutching at Bruno and Kara, Marcus appeared silhouetted in an open doorway, at the top of three concrete steps. He had removed the tarpaulin. Now defiant, he stood holding an unidentifiable object in his outstretched hand, above his head.

This turn of events threw Michael's plans into disarray. It reminded him tantalisingly of the confusion he had experienced on his last visit to the barn. At the time, he was sure that the interior of the building was foreshortened. He was in the process of measuring it out when Maggie first introduced herself. And he now realised, behind the tarpaulin that stretched from the full height to the full width of the interior, was a secret room hidden from view. His notion was proved correct. Now he had to contend with the boy, and his madcap solution, assuming there was one.

'In case you are all wondering,' Marcus said, matter-of-factly, 'this bottle in my hand contains a rag soaked in white spirits. And this,' he added, equally flat in tone, 'is a cigarette lighter.' He flicked with his finger and a flash of light flared in the semi-darkness. 'It goes without saying, that when one meets the other, nasty things start to happen.'

Maggie was the first to react. 'Burn in hell, be my guest, just don't expect us to join you.'

Michael responded by taking a firm grip on the trigger of the shotgun. 'Marcus, be careful!' he shouted. 'This place would burn to the ground with just one careless spark. It's all it would take.'

Panicking, Lauren reinforced her grasp upon Kara, swinging her fully round to face Marcus.

'Step down,' Lauren said.

Marcus gasped, seeing the facial injuries to his girlfriend. He had to hold firm and find a way to help her escape. 'A trade-off is in order, I believe. Let Kara go and the paintings in the studio will survive.'

'*What* paintings?' Michael asked.

'A simple enough solution, Lauren,' Marcus said, ignoring Michael. He had to keep focused. 'What do you reckon? Have we a deal?'

'Step down!' she repeated.

'No go. This isn't negotiable.'

She implored him. 'Don't destroy a lifetime's work, in honour of my beloved brother. Don't destroy his memory.'

'Just how much is that worth then? Just imagine, a lifetime's work gone in a puff of smoke, burnt to cinders.'

As if to highlight his threat, he brought the naked flame closer to the rag that was exposed at the neck of the bottle. 'It just takes a connection, Lauren, as I found out with the discovery that Patrick Porter and you...are one and the same person.'

Michael couldn't speak, his brain amassing a thousand conflicting visions in one almighty revelation. All he knew, and wanted to believe in, was a deceit built upon a foundation of lies from the two sisters: a deception beyond reason. Here was a woman, whom he thought he loved, who sheltered behind the mask of others, to the extent of being convinced that her own true-self was, in fact, worthless. *A true curse.* Only through the identity of others could Lauren ultimately function. The trauma she experienced as a child was so painful, so destructive, that all she endured throughout her life was a shell-like existence. No more, no less, *except* until she transformed into her alter ego. Into the special "world" she inhabited as an inspirational character, one which she truly found a heart and soul with: her long lost brother.

The paintings of Patrick Porter were a magnificent testimony to his forgotten and wasted life, re-enacted through his sister, a woman who could not, would not, forget him.

Michael now truly understood the disorder in her mind, and the significance of the deception. It literally encompassed all those who entered into her "alternative" existence. Most notable was Julius, who Michael now believed, against his earlier misjudgement, was probably caught up in this obsession with the resurrection of Patrick Porter. He posed for the official portrait of the artist which Ronald sent to him. Fuelled by excessive drink and drugs (as Antonia had testified) Julius – as a young and impressionable man – was besotted by Lauren and her overpowering nature. And who wouldn't be?

His motive back then was money and lifestyle. Whilst he struggled with a decent career and income, she, through their deception, brought in massive hordes of cash. Caught in her web, he simply went along for the ride in the beginning. It was glamorous and intoxicating. It was only now, in later life, that he saw and understood the error of his ways. Julius had found salvation in his new family. With the passage of time, and away from this hellhole Michael swore he would endeavour to return Lauren to a semblance of normality, and help her find salvation too. He owed her that much, provided he was given the chance. It was becoming a very slim chance. This was a critically dangerous stand-off.

Terry had provided much more than mere information on the Porter family: in fact, he presented all the clues that ultimately would bring about their downfall. If only Michael had been more astute, instead of charging right in. *Little things...* Michael recalled his reaction to the data on Patrick Porter: born 1966, near Bunratty Castle. He now knew this to be the actual birth date and place of Lauren's own origins. Again, Patrick 'died' in 1996, the year Julius and Antonia ran away. Lauren was so traumatised by them deserting her that she never painted again, and faked Patrick's death. For her, it was the end of everything she held dear.

In the following ten years she sustained a living by reluctantly selling one of her cherished "babies". That's why, he guessed, she still displayed the twelve paintings of Antonia at the farm, instead of storing them away. They were too precious to part with, this testament to her dead brother and Antonia, a former lover. Yes, Antonia and she were once passionate lovers...perhaps the love never quite died for Lauren. Michael remembered all too clearly his last conversation with Antonia. When he asked if she had ever modelled for Patrick Porter, her answer was an emphatic "No". She had told the truth, in a manner of speaking: Because in her eyes she had posed for Lauren. Everything else she had told him was a lie, in the hope it would throw him off the trail. Michael had a sudden flashback, visualising once again her evocative pose for '*A*' *on green silk*. He now knew the sheer lust Antonia conveyed in that painting was undoubtedly directed toward her lover during those days…Lauren, the artist. Although she was in a love triangle, her devotion to Julius came later. Then the problems came.

Like at this very moment. But the history of these people could not be ignored. It shaped their destiny. Only today, of course, the artist was broke and needed to sell up everything she owned. Julius too was desperate for money to support his family. He came calling, exerting pressure on Lauren, seeking a divorce, which she would never agree to, and threatening to expose her sham. The very idea that Lauren could cash in substantially to his exclusion was unpalatable to him. He knew the game she was playing, and decided to wreck it at all costs. In order to seek retribution undetected, for fear of reprisals, he used an obvious outlet: Michael Strange, a man on the edge. A man who could be manipulated by greed. A greed which, he knew, would always overcome any deep reluctance Michael had to walk away and dump Lauren. It was never going to happen. They were *all* desperate people. However, Julius had the ultimate control over Michael, knowing the fascination he had for this beguiling woman. He too was imprisoned.

During this few moments of respite, Michael not only understood past lives and present treachery, he was now confronted with a huge dilemma, right here in the barn. He also understood his own weakening hold on making sure there was an escape route for Kara and Marcus. For the rest of them it mattered little.

Michael stared in disbelief, knowing the awful consequences, as Marcus suddenly brought his hands together. Oh, God.

Maggie reacted first. Sensing Michael had briefly relaxed, she seized the chance to lunge at him with the scissors. She caught him cleanly, stabbing him in the right shoulder.

Michael endured the full impact of the thrust, which knocked him clean off his feet. As he fell, his last clear recollection was pulling the trigger of the shotgun. The massive bang imploded into his ears, catching everybody off guard. The shell smashed into an overhead beam, propelling razor sharp splinters in every direction. In the confusion, Michael cracked his head as he landed heavily on the hard floor. Scarcely conscious, he involuntarily fired off the second barrel, this time directing the deadly shot across the floor. All hell broke loose.

*

In a split second, Lauren responded by lifting the blade of her knife to Kara's throat. In the same instance she lost control of Bruno, who pulled clear of his master and charged headlong at the figure on the steps.Immediately, the snarling dog was hit by a hail of gunshot, cutting him down in full flight. Losing concentration, Lauren watched aghast as her beloved dog was ripped apart in front of her eyes. As a result, she loosened her grip on her captive, allowing Kara the precious moment to fight back at long last.

*

Kara took her chance. Seeing the dog unleash itself in a frenzy, she had the presence of mind to fumble for the thin-bladed knife she had stuffed in her trouser pocket. In one swift movement, as the dog fell from the gunshot, she withdrew the knife and forcibly stuck it behind her blindly, piercing flesh and bone in her assailant's body.

*

Marcus watched in abject terror. From a position of control, suddenly complete mayhem erupted in front of him. Foolishly, he had lit the fuse in the bottle to show Lauren that he was the boss. Bad move. He watched Maggie lunged forward, bringing down Michael. Lauren threatened Kara with the knife, and the raging dog broke free and without warning leapt in his direction. In the ensuing melee, he panicked, tossing the flaming bottle into the studio behind him. Jars of white spirit ignited. He just had time to see the dog collapse at his feet, and Kara stagger away from Lauren, when a massive explosion and fireball erupted, flinging him sideways and down the stairs. Red hot flames and billowing acrid smoke quickly engulfed them all, reducing visibility to a few feet. In seconds, the intolerable heat began to melt everything in its rolling path. The ancient barn was becoming a tomb for them all.

Marcus felt himself being pulled to his feet by Kara. Dazed, he was aware of blood pouring from a gash on his face.

'We've got to get out, Marcus,' she shouted, choking back deadly fumes. 'Help me find Michael, before it's too late.'

Marcus cleared his head, and heard the tumultuous roar of the fire. All around, thick black suffocating smoke whirled about them, cutting off their air supply. He knew they had but seconds to survive. The flames were intense, and rapidly began to encircle them. Grabbing Kara by the hand, he pulled her forward and, with every last drop of his strength, ran with her toward the great door for their one chance of freedom. Their mad dash seemed to take an eternity. As they made daylight, he could hear the thudding sound of great ancient timbers falling from the ceiling, and the crackling of firewood. It was impossible for him to imagine anyone else getting out alive from the blaze.

Kara, bloodied and exhausted, screamed hysterically with fear: 'What about Michael? We can't just leave him!'

Marcus swivelled, and saw the flames leaping fifteen feet into the air. 'Run for the house!' he demanded. 'Call the fire service. I'll try one last time.'

She was reluctant to leave him, clinging to his arm.

'Go, for fuck's sake!' he shouted, forcing her away from him. 'Every second counts…'

Shielding his face from the inferno, Marcus stared in disbelief. It was hopeless, he knew. Going back in was an act of suicide.

*

Moments earlier, before the torch exploded, Michael had stirred, and felt a searing pain in his shoulder.

Worse still, Maggie had reached over, and was attempting to strangle him. She had the strength of a lion. Her rage was an awesome spectacle, and he had no way in which to fight back. She punched and clawed at him, throwing her weight upon him, rendering him defenceless. Her objective was to kill him, and she was succeeding. Fast.

For Michael, it was over. Through swollen eyes, he saw the end coming. Only the grace of God could save him. Then it happened. From somewhere, an explosion ripped through the building and knocked Maggie off balance, giving him an unexpected opportunity to fight her off. He whacked her clean on the nose, leaving her dazed. Michael raised himself just enough to find the shotgun by his side and, in one single movement, swung the butt so that it crashed into her spine, sending her sprawling across the earth. Surprisingly, this wasn't enough to render her unconscious. She groaned, and then set on him again. To his left, however, he was aware of something else, something far more terrifying than the madness of this woman...a huge roaring ball of spitting fire, a firestorm! And it was coming his way.

With all his might, he tried one more time to dislodge Maggie. She was now on top of him, clubbing him with her fists. The punches were relentless. Thankfully, though, just as they began, they stopped. Michael miraculously felt the weight of her lift from him again. Opening his eyes, he saw that Lauren had grabbed Maggie from behind and they were now entangled, fighting each other. With the thick smoke descending, and the flames licking as high as the great ceiling, Michael could barely trace their hazy outline, as the two fought with ferocious intent. Dragging his battered body toward the exit, Michael made one last desperate attempt to escape, but as he agonisingly inched forward, his route was blocked by falling white hot debris. The truth dawned on him. God had dealt him his last card. He was slowly choking to death, his skin aglow; his shredded clothing melting into flesh.

From high above, a heavy timber beam plummeted to the floor, showering sparks and red hot splinters like confetti. It was his dying moment, and in that moment, he saw someone go down, vanishing forever beneath the fallen structure, a stricken figure trapped and ablaze, screaming until silent. The remaining shadowy figure, which he did not recognise in the deepening fog of acrid smoke, turned, hesitated and fled to safety.

Michael could hear the distant wail of a police siren.

He could sense the last breath of air exhale from his crushed body.

From somewhere, he felt strong hands miraculously reach out and grab him. He was finally being torn from the grip of the raging fire.

'Lauren, Lauren...' he heard himself inwardly lament. And in the last fading remnant of light, he wondered if it was *she* who had fallen, and found her final resting place: A place of peace, and everlasting beauty. Her demons had been vanquished.

Then the blackness descended on him.

CHAPTER NINETEEN

'Is *he* going to make it?' Kara screamed. Her skin and clothes were caked black with soot. She *willed* the surgeon to give her the answer she craved.

All around her, it was chaos.

Just moments earlier, the calm of the hospital was shattered as medics rushed to the A & E entrance, ready for action as the ambulance carrying Michael screeched to a halt outside on the tarmac. He was quickly removed on a stretcher and rushed into intensive care. Kara watched in horror. She knew in her heart that he was close to death.

She and Marcus had arrived seconds before him in a police car, their wounds less severe than his. He was on a life support machine.

Marcus, breathless, stood beside her in the corridor. He saw her reddened eyes, ablaze with an intensity of utter confusion and defiance. He cradled her as they faced the white-coated doctor, who looked grave, his face the colour of his coat.

'Are you an immediate relative?' he asked.

Kara lied, desperate for news. 'I'm his daughter.'

Marcus shifted on his feet and looked to the floor.

'Very well,' the doctor responded, 'your father is in a critical condition, and you should be prepared—'

Kara's legs buckled. 'Oh, God, please don't let him die!'

He emphasised again. 'You should be prepared, young lady. We are doing everything in our power to help him but his internal injuries are severe. We are dealing with smoke inhalation, burns to his lungs and external skin damage.' The doctor gripped her shoulder, offering futile comfort and hope. She could read his face. His eyes betrayed him. Kara knew it was hopeless.

Marcus grabbed a chair and sat her down. A nurse brought a glass of water. Kara gulped, removing the horrible taste of smoke in her throat. Just what was Michael going through? She was lucky, escaping the worst of the flames. Somehow, drifting between such terrifying images, her brain failed to register the conversation between Marcus and the doctor, although the words "cardiac arrest" and "the next few hours are vital" cut through the air like a knife into her heart. It was bad, very bad. All she saw was blackness and despair. *Live, damn you!*

Kara fainted. The nurse caught her fall. After that, everything went into a haze of organised commotion. On recovering, she was helped to a side ward to have her wounds cleaned up and stitched. Kara didn't care about herself, but now, as nurses attended to her needs, she realised just how close all of them had come to certain death. She trembled, delayed shock taking hold. For the first time since escaping the fire, she examined herself: her clothes were saturated in blood. Her own blood. The pain kicked in. Nausea overwhelmed her. Tears flowed.

*

In the next cubicle, Marcus sat on the bed as a female doctor dealt with his hands, which were badly burned. Although in severe pain, he was only concerned for Kara. How the hell would she react if Michael didn't make it? According to the first doctor he spoke to, the prognosis wasn't a good indicator for survival. Shit.

He heard voices in the corridor. Marcus was informed that detectives had arrived and were awaiting the opportunity to interview him and Kara to find out what had happened at the farm. *Jesus.* He thought of the utter carnage. He was sure someone had died in the barn, but who was it? Caught up in the confusion, it was impossible to know who had escaped. His only priority at the time was saving Michael. Now, things were complicated. Had the farm become the scene of a murder investigation? Was he a suspect? His blood ran cold. They were all implicated. A feeling of panic and helplessness rushed over him. How could this be happening? Feeling trapped, he had this sudden sense of foreboding that for all of them the problems were only just beginning. But they were alive! And together! Nothing, he reasoned, could jeopardise this, surely?

From somewhere close, a loud electronic bleeping shattered his scrambled thoughts. All hell broke loose as the intrusive sound pushed the medical staff into a frenzied response. He watched as the corridor and beyond filled with people.

'Tell me this isn't happening?' Marcus heard Kara plead above the din.

Marcus looked at his doctor, who said, wide-eyed, 'Emergency, wait here.' Then she was gone. Marcus shifted to the corridor and was amazed to find it suddenly empty. Then his eyes stared at the adjoining room to his, the very one where Michael had been taken to. Christ. Everyone seemed to be crushed in there.

There was so much shouting and activity. Marcus was scared. Kara joined him, and held on to his arm as if her life depended upon it.

'What's happening?' she pleaded. 'Tell me, please.'

The last words he heard came from the very doctor who had greeted their arrival at the A & E. What was he saying? What was he fucking saying?

The words slammed home.

'We're losing him, team. We're losing him . . .'

*

Drifting, I search endlessly. But I do not find. It is a ritual without end.

Where am I? I have no voice. No feelings. Only the hunger.

I am called to witness, allowing me to create a vision, but I am powerless to act. Some of those living are receptive to my presence; others close their mind to imagination. Those I cannot help. Around me a vast sea of dead faces is each cursed in the same manner. Is this eternal conflict? I don't know. But it is a damned infliction.

'Stand back, everyone!'

Thud.

I see continents. I see countries. Places I recognise. One such place is there before me now. It is a place of love and sorrow. I remember it well. Although I'm not supposed to have feelings, or attachment, I cannot observe without a certain dread entering my head.

This is a beautiful location. I see water and buildings. I'm getting closer now, and familiar objects strike me: little boats, narrow canals, sunlit squares. People are scurrying about their business, unaware.

One such building is a five-storey apartment block. It's in an affluent area. On the top floor, a family live in harmony. I hear the laughter of a child. It is a good home, at least for now. The man is occupied at his desk, dictating a letter on his laptop. A dog sits by his feet. In the kitchen, a woman prepares lunch, helped by the little girl. There is much gaiety. From somewhere, a classical recital soothes and embraces the well-being of each of them, uplifting their spirits. Happiness flourishes here.

'Stand back, everyone!'
Thud.

The telephone rings. The young child answers, and shouts for her mother. She in turn wipes her hands and goes to the hallway to take the message.

I am called to witness. But I want none of it. The woman lifts the telephone to her ear and listens. She hears a voice. It is Irish. Although distant and faltering, the message is quite clear nonetheless.

'Once again, everyone! Let's get it right this time.'
Thud.

The mother is at first polite and patient. Then her complexion turns to white.

I shout. Then I scream. But I am not heard.

Antonia, I am so sorry.

As for the other woman on the telephone? She is known to me.

Bleep. Bleep. Bleep.

'Okay, everyone. We have a signal! He's coming back to us…'

*

Adele Strange burst into the ward corridor, her expression a sudden mask of terror as she was confronted by a frightful sight of blackened faces and the smell of burnt flesh. John Fitzgerald followed her in. He kept his distance and hovered sheepishly, avoiding eye contact with anyone who looked his way.

'I got your message,' Adele said, bewildered.

Kara and Marcus clung together despite the discomfort of their burns.

'Christ,' Adele murmured, but she didn't have it in her heart to reach out and offer some kind of comfort. Deeply shocked, she asked instead, 'What's happening? Where's Michael?'

Kara sobbed, and nodded in the direction of the melee.

Marcus took up from what she was thinking, and pointed further down the corridor. 'Mr Strange is in that room, there seems to be a major problem.

He shook his head. We don't think he's going to make it –'

Adele drew breath and swayed unsteadily on her feet. She composed herself and moved forward, jostling with the doctors, shouting, 'Please let me through, please let me through, I'm his wife…What's happening?'

Then she disappeared into the chaos.

*

It was only later that Kara realised that three long hours had elapsed, but she couldn't recount one minute, such was her fear and utter exhaustion. It was all a blur. Now though, reality kicked in. She sat alone in an office, weak and numb, suspended somewhere between agony and ecstasy. Opposite from where she sat, a man in heavy glasses looked at her, indignation etched across his face. He spoke in an official tone.

'Young lady, I am only too aware of the harrowing experience you have gone through. However, as the senior surgeon at this hospital, I must make my position quite clear. You lied to one of my colleagues pretending to be the patient's daughter. Under normal circumstances, I wouldn't tolerate this.   However, after discussing it with his wife, I'm prepared to let it go. Certainly, Mrs Strange is in forgiving mood and asks of me to bring you up to date with her husband's condition.'

Kara raised her shoulders and lifted her eyes to his.

'The patient remains on the critical list,' he said. 'However, he survived the trauma of a failed heart stoppage. It was difficult to revive him and only the expert intervention of Dr Seaman prevented his death. I hasten to stress, however –'

Kara wiped a tear from her cheek and blew her nose, interrupting his chain of conversation. She drew breath.

'– that the condition of the patient gives great concern to us. He continues to live, despite himself.'

'Can I see him?'

'No. Only immediate family can see him. His wife and son are beside his bedside as we speak.'

'Will he die?'

'It's a possibility, although we are doing everything in our power to prevent this happening. He has a 60/40 chance of survival, at best. He has severe smoke inhalation which could have lasting damage to his lungs. His eyes too are damaged by toxic fumes. In addition, he suffered third degree burns on his face, hands and chest. Presently, he is attached to a respirator and heart and lung monitor. He is under 24-hour supervision by the pulmonary specialist. We will see.'

'Thank you for telling me,' Kara said. She felt utterly redundant, waiting and praying for some good to come out of all this crap.

The man stood and extended a hand. 'My name is Dr Yuri Oksana. Call me if you need anything.'

'Are you Russian?'

'I was born in England, but my parents are originally from Yalta, on the Black Sea, which is now the Ukraine. Now young lady, take my advice and concentrate on getting better yourself. You are a very lucky lady to have survived the fire.'

Kara raised herself from her chair and winced from her bandaged wounds. Feeling crushed, she took his hand gently and said, 'He will live, you know.'

'I believe you,' he replied.

*

Kara was able to go home, whilst Marcus was admitted to the burns unit for a week to undergo further treatment. Michael was a long-term patient.

After speaking with Adele a few days later, Kara learnt that Ronald was taking responsibility for the gallery short-term, with Adele covering for him between visits to the hospital. Toby, as she knew, had flown over from America to be beside his father as he slowly recovered from his near death experience. Kara felt pushed aside, but, in truth, she was in no fit state to go to work.

She took ten days off. She had decided to resign from the gallery at the earliest opportunity. Now, standing alone in her apartment, she was in reflective mood. The scars and bruising on her face were still angry red, as raw and tender as the mood inside her head. She was a mess. Around her neck, a surgical bandage protected her damaged throat. Her body still ached. She would never, she reasoned, come to terms with what had happened.

A flicker of hatred shone in her eyes. Adele was milking the current situation for all its worth, portraying herself as the dutiful and caring wife and business big shot as well. As if she was some kind of Superwoman.   Hardly.   God, how she despised this woman! When their paths had crossed at the hospital again, Adele at last introduced her to Toby.   Just looking at him took her breath away. The likeness to Michael was uncanny. He was the exact replica of his father.   In the fullness of time, she thought, she would sit down with Toby and tell him Michael's story. It needed to be told, as far as she was concerned. This   would   redress   Adele's   distorted   and despicable version.

Later, Kara forced herself to go to the gallery in order to help Ronald. Just an hour's work, she told herself.   However, things between them were still strained. This bothered her. Ronald saw the troubled frown on her brow and flitted timidly around her, unsure of how the ground shifted between them. She was the first to speak candidly.

'I'm so sorry. Ronald,' Kara whispered, before he had a chance to talk. 'I doubted you, and I was wrong.'

He smiled. 'All is forgiven.'

'What will you do now?' she asked, fully aware of the rumours flying about concerning the fate of the gallery.

Ronald picked up on her anxiety. 'It's true, I'm afraid. Adele wants to take control. Ironic, don't you think? Who knows if Michael will ever make a full recovery?'

'Will…will you stay on?'

Ronald diverted his gaze. 'Adele has asked me to,' he replied. 'There's a great deal to sort out. Eventually, Toby will leave America for good and run the business. He has money to invest. What else can I do at my age?'

Kara reached out. 'I understand, Ronald.'

They grasped hands and held tight, lingering in silent reflection.

'What will you do now?' he asked finally.

'I will offer my resignation, which *naturally* Adele will accept. I haven't any wish to return, the memories would be just far too painful.' Kara held back the tears. 'I need a break, to get away from everything. Besides, this art lark is far too dangerous for a country girl like me.'

Ronald laughed; glad that the awkward situation which had existed between them was now resolved. It was fine, she knew, and this gave mutual comfort. After a cup of coffee, she helped him with the paperwork over the next hour, just to occupy time. Then tiredness overtook her.

'Keep in touch, dear.' Ronald said.

'How sweet, of course I will.' As she left the gallery, Kara couldn't help but think of him as one of the last dinosaurs to roam the Earth.

*

Two days later, Kara received a visit to her apartment which brought further apprehension.

'Kara Scott?'

She stared out from behind the half-opened door. It was the police.

'That's me,' she replied.

'Detective Ian Smart, CID, London West End Division.' He pointed a badge in her direction. 'May I come in? I think you know why I am here.'

Kara opened the door and led him into the kitchen.

'How are you feeling?' he asked.

'Not good.'

'I've been assigned to the investigation into the death of a woman at Laburnum Farm. As you are a witness, I have numerous questions that need answering. Do you feel ready to assist me?'

'I'll try, detective.' Kara put the kettle on. 'Will there be an enquiry?'

'Full scale,' the detective replied. 'A major fire, a dead body, a missing suspect, possible fraud, the list is endless. It's Ian, by the way.'

Despite the heat of the apartment, Kara was feeling cold and fatigued.

'I'll help in any way I can, Ian. Right now I'm feeling pretty shitty…'

In truth, she was panicking, unsure of how to respond to his line of questioning. She knew that anything she said could implicate Marcus. After all, it was *he* who started the fire. They needed to get their stories straight.

'I understand,' he sympathised. 'I've spoken to Marcus. Perhaps you can both come down to Headquarters, and I can take a joint statement to help clear matters up.'

This was the first she knew of this. What had Marcus said?

'How is the investigation progressing?' Kara asked, keeping her voice as low key as possible.

'Slowly. We still need to interview Michael Strange urgently, but at the present time he is not well enough to cooperate. Then there is the huge forensic investigation, hampered by the ferocity of the fire. But we are getting there. I can see this is causing you distress. I should have phoned.'

'Yes,' Kara said. She was feeling shot-through.

They shook hands.

'Sorry about the tea. Another time?' she said.

'Yes. I'll phone and make an appointment. There's plenty to discuss.'

As he prepared to go, Kara said, 'Michael is a good man, you know. I will not have a bad word said against him, in spite of what you might hear to the contrary.'

He nodded. 'We just need to get to the truth. This is a major crime investigation, Kara, and at present you and Marcus are vital witnesses. We are, as you know, conducting a nationwide search for a missing person, whose identity is not clear at this stage. A bit tricky, that one.'

'Have you any idea as to which sister perished in the fire?'

He shook his head in bafflement. 'It is impossible to identify the body as yet, even with DNA technology. The fire was so intense, she emulsified, burnt beyond recognition. Even dental records are inconclusive. Perhaps we'll never know until we find the missing sister.'

'My God,' Kara gasped. The image of either Maggie or Lauren on the loose filled her with dread.

'Are you all right, Kara?'

'I just need to rest, if you don't mind.'

He handed her a printed card. 'Speak to Marcus and arrange a time for the both of you to come in.'

His next words almost floored her.

'You might consider making sure a solicitor of your choice is present at the interview.'

Then he was gone.

*

'Penny for your thoughts?'

Kara and Marcus walked in the hospital grounds. It was sunny and warm, and it was his suggestion to get out from his bedroom and enjoy the fresh air.

'I'm worried,' she said finally. 'Adele is keeping me away from Michael. It's as if she is punishing me. I need to see him.'

She was so relieved to see Marcus on the mend. However, she couldn't help but smile at the way he looked in a silly long black coat and sunglasses to hide his swollen eyes. His right arm was in a sling and he wore a large facial bandage across his cheek. His lips were still split and bruised. He resembled a prize-fighter, battered but still standing after twelve gruelling rounds of boxing.

'Are you laughing at me?' he said, pretending annoyance.

'I'm laughing with you, drippy dope. Now give me a hug.'

The embrace was awkward and painful.

'Ouch!' he screamed in mock discomfort.

She managed a laugh. 'What a baby, no pain, no gain.' Kara inched forward and snuggled as close as she could bear, without putting pressure on her wounds. It felt divine.

*

Later, Kara ate with Marcus in the canteen. She was quiet.

'What's up?' he asked.

'I think we are in trouble.'

'How so?'

'The police called to see me. They want a statement from us, and I'm scared. I have a hunch that they don't think of us as just witnesses.'

'Meaning?'

'They think we're involved...'

'We are.'

'Marcus, don't be so bloody flippant. A woman died. She died from a fire, a fire that you started. We are all to blame. What if we go to prison?'

Marcus drank from a can of Coke. 'Not you, Kara. We'll think of something. Get your strength back, and don't say anything, especially to the police. Leave it to me, OK?'

Then it hit her. All this rage. It burned like a beacon. It terrified her that she contained so much anger. If it came to it, she would move heaven and hell to protect and restore the good name of Marcus and Michael. In particular, Michael had been the father she never had, a friend and mentor who had forged her and shaped her thinking.

Marcus read her thoughts.

'We will all come through this, Kara.'

'Will we? The only person holding all the aces is Adele. She'll come out of this whiter than white. I won't let it happen. When I worked in the gallery just recently, I downloaded all the files which I still had access to. I have evidence which will incriminate her in unlawful transactions. And I'll use that information in the future if necessary.'

'You could make a lot of trouble for that woman,' he said quietly.

'Which woman would that be?' Kara asked. Her thoughts turned toward two sisters, one of which was out there, and on the run. A curse was how Michael had described Lauren. It could equally apply to Maggie.

Out there, somewhere. It gave her the creeps. Kara would always look over her shoulder, jump at the slightest sound. She would lie awake at night, listening to her own heavy breathing. A curse? The corner of rooms would forever hold shadows, whispers and rage, of another darker kind.

Marcus picked up on her inner demons.

'We need to stick together, Kara.'

*

Two days later, Kara and Marcus made an official statement to the police.

Marcus kept to all the facts, except in the case of how the barn ignited. His story related to how Maggie had fought with him and as a result the fire started accidentally. Kara concurred with this version of events. They weren't concerned if the surviving sister, if found, disputed this version. Kara had managed to relay their story to Michael on one of her rare visits to him. It was now three against one.

Relieved, Marcus bought Kara coffee and brandy in a nearby café. He stared into her eyes.

'That's that,' he said. 'Now we can get on with our lives.'

If it was only that easy, she thought.

*

'I'm lucky to be alive,' Michael said.

Kara kissed him on the cheek, pulled up a chair, and sat by his bed. She almost cried. He looked a hundred years old.

'We all think the same,' she muttered.

'Marcus saved my life. I underestimated him. It took immense courage to come back for me.'

This was the first time that Dr Oksana had allowed her an extended visit to the hospital. Adele had been so protective, but Michael was now off the danger list. His injuries were still extensive and, as the doctor had explained to her, recovery was going to be a very slow process. It would take months, he had warned her.

'I'm going home soon,' Michael announced triumphantly.

'That's wonderful.' She marvelled at his optimism. 'Who is going to look after you?'

'Toby, and a live-in nurse that he's employed.'

'Toby?'

'Incredible, isn't it? We've had an opportunity to do a lot of talking. He's been here virtually every day. We now understand one another, so much so that he is supporting me in the gallery. He's resigned from his job in New York and intends to invest in the business. Seems he made good over there. More than can be said for his old man, eh?'

'What about Adele?' she asked.

'The divorce will go ahead, and she's agreed to leave the business. Money talks. It's best for all concerned. I'll pay her off by remortgaging the main house, which I'll keep. She's taking the Marbella property. For the time being, I'll keep Chelsea. Toby will become my new partner, and his investment will settle the tax demand. This way, he gets to keep both his parents, without the bickering.'

'That's great news, Michael.'

He changed the subject. 'I'm so pleased you've come.'

'Nothing could keep me away. I'll visit you in Chelsea and help as much as I can.'

'Terry has been to see me. He's a good man. I've given him your phone number, and he's someone you can trust. He has valuable information which will help you understand what has been going on.'

'I want to hear it from you, Michael, but not yet.'

'It's complicated.'

She smiled. 'You need to rest for now.'

Michael pulled himself up in the bed, wincing.

'She saved my life too, you know.'

'*Who*?'

'Lauren. It was she who pulled Maggie off me. She died fighting her sister. That's the only reason I escaped. Marcus, of course, got me out but if it wasn't for Lauren I would never have survived. I will find Maggie, believe me. Lauren was misjudged for most of her life because of her sister's wickedness.'

Kara remained silent. Then she said, 'Michael, the body has yet to be identified. We don't know who died and who escaped.'

'I do.'

'How can you be so sure?'

It was his moment to keep quiet. She watched him, her eyes expressing doubt.

'Kara,' he said reluctantly, 'I had a weird dream when the surgeon was bringing me back from death's door. It scared the shit out of me. Do you remember that you once talked about being receptive to people who were no longer with us? Well, I believe in it. Call it an out-of-body experience – whatever – but it was very real to me. I've had the dream before, but this was different.'

He recounted the dream.

Kara's blood ran cold.

'I think Antonia and Julius are still in danger,' Michael said. 'And I think that Maggie is alive and keeping low. Remember, she was injured and needs time to recover. But she has the resources and, mark my words, she'll be back. All of us are in danger, so watch over your shoulder. Be vigilant.'

'What can we do?' she asked.

'Maggie won't surface, not yet while the heat is still on. I reckon she got back into the house, retrieved the passports and escaped. There was a hell of a lot of cash lying around, which she would have taken as well. The police haven't mentioned this, so it stands to reason that they never found it when they searched the house. This was getaway money. I believe that Lauren and Maggie were about to do a runner. When I feel better and able to travel, I'm going to Venice to see Antonia and Julius. So much needs to be explained. Will you come with me?'

'Wow, that's a big ask, Michael.'

'They are good people, Kara. You'll like her. Besides, they can help you by filling in the missing pieces. I've asked Terry to broker a meeting. So much has changed. Julius will now lay claim to the farm and the twelve paintings, which survived the fire. The main house remained intact. As the surviving spouse he will get everything. Provided he can prove it was Lauren who perished in the barn, of course. It's all about legal ownership. A neat twist on things, don't you think? Lauren was manipulative and greedy and paid the ultimate price. Through her arrogance and deceit, she scuppered her devious plans and sealed her own fate. If she had played fair with him, they both could have forged a future of some kind – apart from one another of course - and shared their wealth jointly. But there was the rub. Lauren was insanely jealous and would not forgive a singular act of betrayal, even though he had betrayed himself in order to help her so many years ago. In masquerading as Patrick Porter, he was part of the deception, hiding her secret. Their whole life was built on a lie. Deep down, he resented her for her skills, but she brought in the big money. So he played along. He was talented, but she was *truly* gifted. His only excuse was blind love, shallow attitude, youth and stupidity.'

'And your excuse? How are you going to come to terms with all that has happened?'

'I'm getting there. Blind love or lust can be rectified. However, the shallow actions of a middle-aged twat are not so easy to sort out. That part will need working on.'

Kara bit her lip. 'I lost my bonus,' she joked in a solemn manner.

He caught her mood. 'Lighten up, Kara, and count your blessings. I do, everyday. Come to Venice and meet with them. They can bring a sort of closure, if you like.'

'It's too early for that, Michael, but yes, I'll meet with them.'

'Good.' Michael smiled, and looked into her eyes. 'Enough about everybody else, Kara: what are you going to do now?'

She returned his gaze. For the first time, she saw the future, and decided to take his advice and lighten up. Misery was now a thing of the past. They all lost *something* that fateful day.

Her face lit up. 'I have plans. Watch this space.'

*

THREE MONTHS LATER

'What a fantastic surprise. Come in.'

Michael led Kara into the conservatory of his apartment and poured iced water from a jug on the table.

'Are you alone?' she asked.

'Yes.'

'You look great.' She hugged him.

'One more skin graft operation, then I'm off to the Caribbean,' he joked. 'Coming?'

'Don't tempt me!'

'You look radiant, Kara.' He noticed she wasn't drinking. 'Do you want something else?'

'Something stronger, perhaps?'

'Gin and tonic, wine…'

Kara giggled. 'Champagne?'

'Are we celebrating?'

Kara moved to the window and marvelled at the huge expanse of London, which stretched out as far as she could see to the blue horizon. The cityscape looked magnificent, the light reflecting off the gleaming tall steel and glass structures. For the first time, the sun broke through the low cloud and bathed her in the warmth of the day. She heard the pop of the cork.

'Well?' he said.

She turned to him. *Wait for it.* 'The police are treating the fire as an accident, in view of our collaborating testimonies. Basically, this is the official line and gets us all off the hook. Great news, eh?'

'I heard yesterday. It's huge relief, Kara. We can once again get our normal lives back on track, without this hanging over our heads. Maggie can't remain a fugitive forever. Is that why you've come to see me?'

Kara smiled. *Wait.* 'Sort of,' she teased. 'Do you recall my remark about making plans?'

'Hmm…'

'Well, this is my last alcoholic drink, for a while, anyway.'

'Because..?' Then it clicked, and he smiled too.

She beamed. 'I'm having a baby.'

'Bloody amazing!' He yelled. 'Does Marcus know?'

'Yes. He's jumping up and down with the excitement of becoming a dad. He's driving me crazy! I just thought that you should be the next to know, after all that we have been through. It somehow feels right. Marcus and I want you to be the godfather to our first child.'

'A double celebration.' He raised a glass to her glass. 'This is the best news in the world.' A mischievous glint appeared in his eye. 'Assuming it's going to be a boy, how are you going to tell Marcus that you've chosen Michael as a name?'

'That will have to wait until he comes back to earth, and who knows when that will be!' She laughed. 'Don't you think I have enough on my plate looking after one oversized child already?'

*

The news of Kara's pregnancy and the decision by the police to drop the investigation against them had a huge impact on Michael. It gave him the impetus to awaken the spirit within, which he felt had been lost forever. The dark side lifted, allowing for a renewal of faith in all things good. Within days, he severed his dependence on the daily visits from the nurse, and, like Kara, began to make plans. Revitalised, he ventured out on his own for a short stroll beside the harbour, aided by a walking stick. Slowly, his strength was returning. Little steps, he reminded himself.

During his walk, he rested on a bench and took stock of his situation. Life was returning to how it used to be, but without the aggravation and worry. Toby was now integral to everything, taking on and winning the battle for financial security, which had become a burden to Michael, notably with the taxman who was breathing down his neck. Toby had reached a compromise with the authorities, allowing the gallery to continue to trade without hindrance. His son had certainly proved his worth, stabilising both the business and, incredibly, the bad relationship which previously existed between his mother and father. Straight talking was the order of the day. It was Toby who eventually got the message across to Adele that hard line tactics would sink them all, which would ultimately be counterproductive to her cause. He had to admire his son's logic: in other words, Adele understood which side of her bread was buttered. Michael knew the situation wasn't perfect. Never would be, but a kind of truce was struck between them.

The icing on the cake was Kara's happiness, and the overwhelming joy everyone felt toward the forthcoming birth. Michael had to smile. Marcus was now a different man, extolling the virtues of fatherhood even before experiencing it first hand. That was Marcus! His enthusiasm, as always, was getting the better of him. Kara wouldn't have it any other way. They were made for each other, Michael was delighted to admit.

On his return to the apartment, Michael was overtaken by physical exhaustion. Even a short walk became an endurance test. The London marathon was certainly out of the question at this stage. His humour had not deserted him, thankfully. In time, his speed of recovery would hasten, and then nothing could stop him conquering the world again. For now, a cup of tea would suffice.

The telephone rang. It was Terry. The world tipped over again. 'Thought you should know,' his friend said, without the need for social niceties. 'Delores Porter has passed away. Died yesterday, after a bout of pneumonia. Quite suddenly, but not unexpectedly, owing to her old age and frailty.'

Michael was not entirely shocked, more saddened by the news. It put a damper of his renewed optimism. Then an ugly thought crossed his mind, but before he could speak, Terry beat him to it.'This throws up quite a scenario, don't you think? The funeral takes place in five days. Can you see where this is leading?'

Christ. When it rains, it pours. He knew exactly where this was going.

'The police will be expecting Maggie to suddenly turn up,' he replied, his voice wavering under the weight of the conversation. Out of nowhere, a ferocious headache blasted into his skull.

'Maggie's husband is taking charge of the funeral arrangements,' Terry said. 'He maintains that no contact has been made with his errant wife. That's hard to believe, especially as they have two children. Also, he seems remarkably unaffected by her apparent disappearance. The police aren't buying into his story either.'

'Assuming she's still alive, of course.'

'Of course.' Terry paused. 'But where is the anguish that you would normally expect from a husband in these circumstances?'

'Do you think he's protecting her?'

'Got to be. It's inconceivable that a close knit family would be driven apart without secretly communicating in some way. According to the police, this is the official line they are following. It stands to reason, therefore, that the likelihood of her death seems remote. In all probability, he is shielding her. But this new development changes everything, Michael. If she is lying low then she's making a damn good job of it. There's been the odd sighting by the public, but often by misguided do-gooders. This has led the police down a blind alley on several occasions but no concrete evidence can point to her whereabouts. So it's all conjecture at this stage as to whether she will surface at long last.'

Michael knew better. *She's alive, without a doubt. Fuck.*

He moved to the drinks cabinet, forgoing the tea for a large measure of brandy. He closed his eyes and let the whole picture sink in. When he reopened them, the contents of his glass had miraculously vanished.

'Are you still listening, Michael?'

This time, Michael turned his back on the bottle and discarded the glass in the kitchen sink. Alcohol would simply cloud his judgement, and he wasn't going in that direction again. This time, he needed his wits to be razor sharp, because the war of attrition was about to start. Only this time, the enemy was hidden. Keeping undercover. Approaching the fight, unseen. Playing clever.

Terry spoke again. 'The burial will take place in Ireland. Plain- clothed police officers will travel over and stake out the funeral service, with the help of the local Gardai. This is their chance, in the belief that she'll not be able to keep away.' He fell silent, waiting for a reaction. There was none. 'Michael, are you still there?'

The brain can only take so much. In Michael's case, it began to shut down. Swiftly. He had control, but only just. Moments earlier, he felt able and strong-willed, but courage began to desert him. This was hell revisited, but in his heart he knew this moment would come one day.

'Yes, Terry, I'm still here,' he said finally. Beyond this response, he couldn't fathom his next words. Instead, he gripped the phone and stared into space, imagining the venom contained in this killer called Maggie.

This vision was unnerving beyond belief. His body trembled, the warm sticky sweat seeping into his shirt. Faith was lost in an instant, and that, out of everything, was the hardest thing for Michael to come to terms with.

He remembered his promise to Kara, *when this was all over, there would be a safe and loving world in which to live.*

An empty promise, he now feared.

Coming soon, the next Michael Strange novel,
to be published 2012. Extract:

A CALL TO WITNESS

PROLOGUE
WINTER, MAYFAIR, LONDON, 2006

A million deadly shards of glass lay sprinkled like
jewelled confetti outside the vandalised grand facade
of the gallery. Snow fell gently.

The glazier trod carefully, crunching glass under
foot, as he expertly removed the last of the razor sharp
broken fragments still lodged precariously in the
window frame. It was hazardous and noisy work,
hampered by the slippery pavement as the snow turned
to sleet then to rain. A thin drizzle descended through
the artificial light from the Georgian street lamps.
With the remainder of the splinters cleared away, the
man and his colleague worked methodically and
silently on the boarding-up process. Between them,
they heaved several enormous sheets of heavy
MDF into position, covering up the gaping hole which
had, hours before, been part of the most impressive
shop-front on the street. It was now a repaired
wreck, a sorrowful sight amongst some of London's
finest shops.

The loud retort of the nail gun fractured the air,
repeatedly. Those that lived in the apartments
opposite peeped through curtains to express their
displeasure at the continued disturbance to their sleep.

One or two late night revellers gathered on the pavement, watching the activity as the alarm continued to shrill. The flickering strobe lighting danced off the walls of the wet buildings.

Within the gallery framework of interconnecting rooms, a man, standing alone, looked on at the surrounding chaos, his eyes as dark as the night that engulfed him. For a fleeting moment, he was happy to remain anonymous, alone with his puzzled thoughts. In the choking dust and debris, he saw a parallel scene of his own making: a fading picture of ruin.

He managed to clear his head of such a mundane judgment and dragged his weary limbs to the pavement, a mobile stuck to his ear as he tried to contact his colleagues. The workmen, meanwhile, had thankfully downed tools and one of them busied himself with documentation. The other lit a cigarette, his beer belly protruding flabbily over his trouser belt. The alarm automatically ceased at last, and in the relative calm, the man with the phone took the opportunity to punch in fresh numbers on his keypad. He waited, agitated. Outwardly, he remained calm but his voice wavered and betrayed this facade.

'It's Michael. I'm here now,' he explained. 'No, no. The paintings are fine. No damage, but it's a miracle, I can tell you.' He waited, listening to the response; then added, 'I need you to come in early in the morning to help with the cleaning-up operation.' Pacing back and forth, he listened again; then said, 'thanks.'

With that, he clicked off, pondering the next move. In the light, his silver hair glistened. Rain settled on his jacketed shoulders. Punching the keypad once more, he spoke quickly. 'Toby, it's me. I hope you get this message. Just an update from our earlier conversation...everything is under control. I've just spoken to Ronald. He's coming in early tomorrow to help. The alarm company is on the way now. I'll stay until the premises are secure and the police have done their report. No need for you to come out. Luckily, there is no damage to the artwork. It appears that someone threw a brick at the window, probably some drunken yob ejected from the nightclub down the road. It's happened before.' He yawned, aware that a police car was parking up opposite, and continued: 'The glaziers are here, and should be finished shortly. I'll speak to the insurers first thing tomorrow.' He fell silent again; checked his watch and then said, 'Should be wrapped up by midnight. Hope the concert was good. Perhaps I'll grab a cup of tea but, in the circumstances, a double whisky would be preferable. Anyway, get here when you can in the morning. I'll open as normal. OK. Bye for now.'

Michael clicked off, and suddenly felt the chill of the November night clatter his bones. Retreating once more into the gallery to find warmth, he offered tea to the workers and moved to the kitchen, switching on the interior lights as he went. This incident with the broken window spooked him more than the previous occasions, however seldom they occurred. The shock never diminished. You just have to deal with it, he reminded himself. Usually, it was an empty bottle of beer that did the damage, never a brick. This was a deliberate act of destruction, he sensed, not just an impulsive booze-induced prank. Many years ago, someone even pissed through the letterbox. *This* was more sinister. It implied a personal statement of attack. In his increased anxiety, Michael dropped a mug of tea onto the floor, smashing it. Scolding water splashed his trousers, instantly saturating his legs. He cursed. *Fuck.* He tried again, refilling another cup with trembling hands. *For Christ sake, get a proper grip.*

Out on the street, he encountered the workmen and offered the hot beverage. One of them (the one with the gut), handed him a piece of blackened rock.

'That's what did the damage, Boss. Found it at the back of the window.'

Michael took the offending missile. 'What is it?' he asked.

A policeman approached, reached out and inspected the evidence.

'Flint. Unusual… especially in this neighbourhood,' the officer pondered. 'This is the kind of thing more suited to a country barn, hardly a Mayfair mansion.'

Michael's heart pounded; his mind racing. *What did he just say?*

The officer, peering at a notepad, said mundanely: 'Our station had a call-out from a Michael Strange, a key holder…is that you sir?'

Ashen-faced, Michael stared at him. Preoccupied suddenly by a ghost from the past, he nodded his reply and felt the jagged edges of the piece of flint as he took hold of it again. His world almost somersaulted in that second. *Christ: a barn.* That's what the officer implied. His brain shifted gear, shuddering at the memory – and acrid smell – of flames and burning flesh. He was still haunted by his lucky escape from the fire at Laburnum farm. This incident brought it back so vividly, with the reference to the chunk of flint. Was there a connection between the two? Surely, surely not...he closed his eyes for a moment and thought first of Lauren, and then Maggie; the two psychotic sisters who, not so long ago, had almost destroyed him.

Lauren was dead. Was this the work of her mad sister hell-bent on revenge? It didn't bear thinking about, but the possibility was strong: compelling, in fact. He opened his eyes, felt dizzy and in the same instant nervously scanned the road in either direction. Maggie was a very dangerous fugitive with murder in her heart. She had tried to kill him once before. She would try again given the chance.

'Sir..?' The policeman repeated. 'Are you the key holder?'

Michael caught his breath and thought of the double whisky again. No amount of firewater would calm his unease on this night.

It had to be *her*. She was out there somewhere, watching his every move from the shadows.